Underwater

The Aurora

Chronicles

Underwater

The Aurora

Chronicles

Brittany Bowman

Underwater: The Aurora Chronicles
Published by Arctic Fox Press
751 S. Weir Canyon Rd. #157-746
Anaheim Hills, Ca. 92808

www.ArcticFoxPress.com
www.BrittanyLB.com

© Cover design: Franziska Stern - www.coverdungeon.com - Instagram: @coverdungeonrabbit

ISBN E-book: 979-8-9869338-0-1
ISBN Paperback: 979-8-9869338-1-8
ISBN Hardcover: 979-8-9869338-2-5

Dedication

This book is dedicated to my loving husband, Jason.
Thank you for always believing in me, loving me,
and supporting all my endeavors.
You are and always will be my best friend.

Acknowledgements

There are so many people I want to acknowledge for the creation of this story.

First and foremost, to God. Thank you for giving me the creativity and courage to follow in this path.

To my amazing husband, Jason, thank you for your encouragement and support with this story. All your input, brainstorming, and dreaming of this story has helped make it what it is today. I feel you have your own personal stamp within these pages. Thank you also for always encouraging me to finish this first book. Without your constant persistence, I fear this story would never have seen the light of day.

To my parents, I could never have asked for two better people to call mom and dad. Thank you for always pushing me to follow my dreams and believing in me when I doubted myself.

To Kathy and Ian (the best in-laws ever), I also speak to the same sentiment that I could never have asked for two better people in my life to call family. Thank you so much for your belief in me and encouragement along this journey. It has meant so much to me.

To Lucy, Jill, and Korrin, thank you for being the greatest friends this girl could ask for. Thank you for always taking an interest in my progress and for your feedback when the time came to read it. I love that I can always trust your honest opinions.

To Fran at Cover Dungeon Rabbit, thank you for such an amazing, beautiful cover. Your work speaks volumes and was well worth the wait. I cannot wait to work with you on future covers.

To Jennifer Roachford at Curly Tales Publishing, thank you so much for your keen eye and extremely helpful advice on this manuscript. I know it is a thousand times better because you helped with the finishing touches. I am so happy I found you at such a crucial time in this story's progress and look forward to working with you again in the future!

To my fellow readers, thank you for your support in reading this first novel of mine. It means the world to me you chose to pick up my work and dedicate your time to getting lost within these pages.

Chapter One

Missing Pieces

"Maybe we feel empty because we leave pieces of ourselves in everything we used to love." – R.M. Drake

***

"YAHTZEE!" Garrett yelled.

"Really?" I stared at him, fuming.

He grinned like the Cheshire cat. "What?"

"Do you have to yell so loud?"

"Well, that is how you play Aurora. You yell Yahtzee when you get a Yahtzee." Garrett chuckled, acting fifteen years younger than his age.

"Obviously! Do you have to yell it into my ear?" I half yelled, overdramatizing my finger to my left eardrum.

I rolled my eyes to Ryder smirking, shaking his head. He was used to the sibling bickering.

It's Wednesday. Family Night.

Every week, for the past three years, we kept the tradition going. It was a night I would rather forget. Instead, I was tortured every week with the absent reminder that my parents, and oldest brother Tanner, would no longer be joining us on these family evenings.

Though Garrett and Ryder did their best to keep us together, it has never been the same. The bickering was still present between Garrett and I. Ryder still laughed at our immaturity. But without them, it felt empty.

My best friend Kate was a staunch supporter of these nights as well. She would discretely bounce out of family nights with her boyfriend Chris to give us siblings "quality time".

It can probably go without saying; we all knew why my brothers kept family night going. They were trying to stay close. Their overprotective behavior was unwarranted, however. I haven't had an episode in almost two years.

"Oh, stop being so sensitive," Garrett chided, still grinning. I wanted to say something snarky, but I knew he could keep this up all night. Instead, I huffed and turned away.

Ryder took his turn throwing the dice. Feeling my stare, he gave me another quick smirk.

"Have you—," a pounding at the door cut him off.

"Are you guys expecting someone?" Garrett asked, turning an irritated gaze towards us.

"Nope," Ryder said, popping the P. "You?" he asked, lifting his chin towards me.

"Uh-ugh," I said, shaking my head. The only person I'd expect would be Kate, but she didn't need to knock. That is, unless she forgot her key again.

Garrett stood up, ripping the door open, as a second impatient knock grew louder than the first. His large frame blocked my view, but his tense shoulders told me all I needed to know.

"What do you want?" Garrett sneered.

"I need to speak with Aurora," Tony said, his voice low and

raspy.

Even without seeing him, I could hear the anger simmering beneath his even tone. Over the past few months, I've come to know the subtle nuances of his voice. Despite this, I couldn't stop my heart squeezing in yearning from hearing his voice in so many weeks.

"You want to talk to her, talk—" Garrett barked, stepping to the side. Ryder stood up with me, placing his hand on my shoulder. Was he trying to hold me back or himself?

I gasped at Tony's disheveled appearance as he came into view. It looked like he rolled down a hillside and played in the back of a garbage truck. He was filthy! A stark contrast to the well-groomed, preppy vibe he always went for.

His puffy, red-rimmed eyes fell onto mine as he focused past Garrett, "Alone."

"No. Whatever you have to say can be said here," Ryder said, taking a protective step in front of me. Tony eyed them, measuring his risk. I didn't know what he expected coming here but he wasn't comfortable. He walked into the proverbial lion's den.

I hadn't seen him since our last explosive break up two weeks ago. The man standing before me was a shadow of who he had been. I missed him but I did not miss the past few months with him.

He became jealous and quick to anger. Fighting became our relationship. I wanted to make it work because I had seen in him the man I had come to love. I wanted that sweet natured man back; but everyone else wanted me as far away from him as possible - my brothers especially, overprotective as they are.

"It's alright guys. I'll talk to him. We'll just be at the park." I stepped around Ryder as I grabbed my sweater off the back of the sofa, trying to diffuse the tension. Garrett and Ryder mirrored each other with the same dumbfounded expressions, gawking at me. They could've been twins.

"You can't be serious Aurora. You aren't going anywhere with this douche. He's obviously drunk," Ryder demanded. Garrett stood in front of me, blocking my way to Tony.

"Garrett, move. If I want to talk to him alone, I will. I already told you guys where we are going to be," I said. That method wasn't working with them. "If I'm not back in thirty minutes, then come find me, okay?" I added to appease them. I knew it was a lost cause.

They were none too happy but what could they say? I'm an adult; perfectly capable of making my own choices.

Garrett glowered, "Fifteen. If you're not back in fifteen, we'll be there regardless if you're done talking or not." He glared at me, but the menace was unmistakably meant for Tony.

"Fine. Whatever."

There was nothing I could do. They were exasperating sometimes.

I walked around Garrett the same time he stepped out of my way. I glanced back as Garrett slammed the door. I could see nothing but concern in Ryder's expression and absolute anger in Garrett's.

Garrett tolerated Tony but never took a liking to him. He always called him weasel.

I turned to see Tony paced a few feet ahead of me, beelining it for the park. He didn't slow down. He didn't even turn around. He shoved his hands into his pockets and stalked forward, the glow of the streetlights highlighting the frustration plastered on his face.

Sure, he may be drunk like Ryder had suggested but I wanted - no needed - answers.

Though I broke up with him, he had been M.I.A. from all

our social circles for the past two weeks. And if I'm being honest with myself, I couldn't help the lure of being in his presence once more. I'll admit, our relationship was unhealthy, but after this long without him I found myself not caring about the shit we put ourselves through.

Did that mean I wanted him back? The jury was still out on that one. When we were good, we were great. When we weren't, well, let's just say I didn't want to be anywhere within a ten-mile radius of him. Like I said, our relationship was an unhealthy one.

Lost in thought, I almost ran into him when he came to an abrupt stop. His rigid posture turned from me, though his broad shoulders slouched as if defeated. He leaned against the park bench, hammering his fingers on the tabletop like it were to blame for his problems.

He stilled his hand, ending his abuse on the tables surface before turning towards me.

"Aurora," he paused. "Answer me truthfully. Why did you leave me?" His voice cracked. His brows turned in as he stared at the ground. He braced himself for the answer and it pained me to see him in any amount of anguish.

I stayed silent. What's the best way to answer such a blatant question? Especially with so much pain added to it?

Should I go with the "it's-not-him-it's-me" excuse? Or should I tell him straight out - his behavior scared me to death?

With the way he was acting, I felt like I had done something wrong.

"Aren't you going to answer me?" he asked through tight lips. His hardened eyes rose to meet mine.

"Tony, I don't want to rehash this tonight. We've already had this discussion," I said. I had instant regret coming here.

"Just—tell me—I need to hear it again," he closed his eyes, waiting, as if I were going to land a blow to his face.

Here goes nothing.

"I don't know what you want me to say. We didn't work, okay? We are explosive when we are with each other. We are not good together," I stated what I had said before in so many words.

It was one of the hardest things I had done in years - breaking up with him. Call me a glutton for punishment, but I kept finding myself missing him. I hate ending anything - relationships, projects, you name it. The finality of an ending is what I shy away from.

Over the past two weeks, I've been going through the motions of being okay without him in my life. Now that he stood here, it ripped open the fresh wound all over again. My body yearned for him, to go into the comfort of his arms, but my mind kept me planted firmly where I stood.

"No. It's not okay. I miss you. I'm a fucking mess without you," he said, "I can't eat. I can't sleep. I need you." His passion and his pain were so palpable, I wanted to give into his pleading.

"Don't make this harder than it already is," I croaked, my heart pounding out of my chest.

Truth was, I'm a mess without him too. I was also a mess with him. The pros and cons were weighed, and at the end of all our struggles, I knew we were better apart.

"I'm sorry! For everything I ever said. For even laying a hand on you. I wasn't me that night. Please, you must believe me," he cried out. My heart clenched as he all but fell to his knees for me to take him back.

And I wanted to. I wanted to so bad, but the proof on my cheek had almost faded. The events of that night were all too fresh.

The drunken argument.

The fight in front of my house.

His fist connecting with my cheek.

Garrett opening the door and beating his ass.

Yes - all too fresh.

"I can't," I said, my eyes stinging as I blinked.

"Is there someone else?"

"What? No," I said, shaking my head.

"You don't have to lie to me. I overheard some of the guys in the locker room the other day," he said, the sudden chill in the air having nothing to do with the weather.

"I'm not lying to you. I don't even know what you're talking about?"

"You and Brad hooking up last week ring any bells?" he scrutinized.

The blood drained from my face. "Because I *what?* You cannot be serious?"

"Dead serious," his eyes locked with mine.

My pulse raced at the implications of what he said. Last week at the Sigma Tau party, Brad and I were dancing. Just as friends. Never did we hook up, or even come close to it.

"This can't be happening. No Tony, I did not hook up with Brad!" I said, stern.

"That is such bullshit Aurora because Emily seen you two together that night too!" he yelled.

"Emily? What the hell does Emily know?" I seethed.

"A whole hell of a lot apparently; I should have known you were running around on me," he stated so matter of fact.

"How can I run around on you when we are not together anymore?" I asked, my anger rising.

"What other explanation do you have for breaking up with me? It's more than a coincidence I overhear the guys talking about you then get confirmation from Emily that she had seen you two. Something isn't adding up here Aurora. You have some explaining to do!" he accused.

"First of all, I don't have to explain anything to you -,"

"THE HELL YOU DON'T," he stepped forward, scream-ing in my face.

I wish I had listened to Ryder when he said it. Tony was belligerent. The sweet, pungent aroma of Jim Beam rolled off his breath in waves. The swerve of his body confirming what I should have known but chose to ignore.

"I should have trusted my gut instinct that you were a lit-tle whore. Using mommy and daddy issues to claim the victim. You can't live behind the shadow of that excuse anymore," he insulted.

"I cannot believe you went there. THAT!" I raised my hand towards him, "THAT is the reason why I broke up with you! You're critical and abusive. You're so full of yourself. You con-stantly tear me down. I'm over it, Tony. WE. ARE. OVER. Just leave me the hell alone!" I yelled, glaring at him. Tears burned hot behind my eyes, threatening to breach the dam.

"Damn straight we are over. If it isn't Brad that you were with, like you 'claim', then who is the shmuck who replaced me?" he accused, using his fingers as quotation marks.

"Damn it, Tony. Nobody. Why can't you get that through your thick skull?" I threw my hands up, exasperated, before slap-ping them down on my legs.

"Because I don't believe you; I can tell you're lying. Emily said she had seen you," he said. He kept pushing the case with Emily, which raised all kinds of red flags. He and Emily were never close.

"SEEN ME WHAT?" I screamed, throwing my hands out as I leaned in towards him. I couldn't take this anymore. His false accusations were only serving to further my anger. I hated feeling this way – like a crazy person, always on edge with him.

My anger only served to fuel his rage, "KISSING! What the

fuck else Aurora?"

"Un-be-lievable! Well, you believed a lie then. How could you be that stupid as to put your trust into *Emily* of all people? You've only known her for a few months. You've been with me for *two* YEARS!"

I'm always on the verge of insanity in his presence. These explosive arguments were nothing new; the jealous cheating accusations were the same. Emily, however, was a new topic I had never seen coming.

"Sometimes a fresh perspective helps you to see things clearer. Don't be mad at Emily because she ratted you out," he stated simply.

"If anyone is seeing anything *clearer*, it's me. Sounds like you have been fooling around with Emily. Have you?" I threw the accusation back at him.

Two could play this game.

Except, he didn't say anything; he stood quiet, fuming.

Shock hit first, then reality, as that short expanse of quietness became all I needed to confirm what I suspected. My heart dropped like an atom bomb into my stomach, knocking the wind out of me.

"Oh, isn't that just SOMETHING? Here you are all high and mighty, accusing *me* of hooking up with Brad, yet you have been fooling around with that *whore* EMILY!" I screamed at him.

I wanted to hit something. I wanted to hit him. I wanted to hit her.

"That isn't the point," he said.

"Where the—who the hell do you think you are?" I yelled as tears threatened to stream down my face. Why was he doing this to me?

"Aurora," Tony said with tenderness as he reached his hand towards me. In his alcohol-induced anger, he must have seen the hurt he caused me. It no longer mattered.

"Don't. You've done enough," I said, raising my hands as I stepped back. He took quick notice of my slow and deliberate movements away from him, as if he were analyzing me. Alarms blared inside my head as the need to leave boiled in my veins.

"We are not done talking," he raised his voice, his anger resurfacing at my attempt to leave. He started matching my steps forward as I picked up the pace backwards, "I just wanted you back. I want us back. Fuck Brad. Fuck Emily. Come back to me babe."

"Well, I'm done talking with you. I've given you answers. It's not my fault you're not satisfied with them. Go have fun with Emily. And go drown yourself in another bottle of Jim while you're at it," I sneered, turning away from the shock on his face.

With each step, I cracked - my mind and heart a mess. It was bad enough trying to get through each day without all of this. Why was Emily spreading lies about me? Why have I become locker room gossip? And why was Tony so deranged?

I heard Tony's quick footsteps running up behind me. I turned around, just before he grabbed for my shoulder, and smacked his hand away from me.

"Don't touch me," I yelled at him.

His face contorted with fury as he grasped my arm, fingers digging in. Adrenaline seized control of my mind, barely registering the sound of feet pounding the pavement together in unison.

"Hey asshole! Keep your hands off my sister," Garrett yelled as he charged at full speed. Tony released me at once as Ryder pulled me back, holding a defensive position in front of me.

Tony staggered back with wide eyes; it must have been past my brothers allotted fifteen minutes.

Garrett was in Tony's face, his jaw muscles tensing back and forth, as he pushed Tony back. "You want to lay your hands on my sister again. Try it with me punk!"

Garrett pushed his hands into Tony's chest before stepping back into his face, moving him further from Ryder and me.

Tony didn't dare try to fight back though his hands were balled into fists at his side. Shock, or was it fear, immobilized him. All the anger he held in his face drained. My brothers had a reputation for being scrappers around here; Tony must still be licking his wounds from the last time Garrett traded fists with him.

"What? Not so tough now, are you? Touch her again and I swear your head will meet your ass. Do I make myself clear?" Garrett's face flushed red. "DO I?" he screamed, veins popping out of his neck with the strain of his anger.

"Yeah. Whatever you say Garrett," Tony dismissed, glancing at anywhere but Garrett.

"Watch yourself Tony. Stay away from her or so help me God." Garrett took one last savage stare at Tony before turning to us, "Let's go."

Ryder nodded, narrowing his eyes at Tony before hooking his arm around my shoulders, keeping me close to his side.

I peeked over my shoulder at Tony, his expression morphing from shock, to anger to...*what? Resolve?* I didn't know what to make of the last expression, but I knew I didn't like it. Chills swam down my spine. Everything about him was off - his stance, his demeanor. He was a completely different person than the guy I met. He was hostile. Unhinged.

"You okay Aurora?" Ryder asked, his hazel eyes staring down at me. I wasn't sure what my face held, too much had happened all at once.

My heart constricted and ached; I knew this feeling well. It was the process of my heart breaking, though it had already been long broken. Tony created yet another missing piece to be mended in my already broken heart, his own personal stamp if you will.

"Yeah Ry, nothing I'm not use to," I sniffed, wiping my tear-stricken face.

"What happened?" he asked.

"He flew off the hinges. I didn't realize how much he had been drinking until we were already at the park. He started accusing me of cheating on him," I said, as another wave of tears brimmed to the surface.

"He what?" Ryder's eyebrows scrunched together, forming a V.

"He said he overheard the guys talking about me in the locker room at school, saying Brad hooked up with me," I said incredulous.

"Did you?" Garrett asked. I gave him the most deadpan, 'give-me-a-break' look I could give him, "Hey, I'm just asking! Girls usually become locker room gossip for a reason."

"What are you insinuating Garrett? Because if it is what I think it is, you better stop right now," my anger flared. I couldn't deal with both Tony and Garrett's accusations in one evening.

"I'm only asking. Cool your jets," he dismissed me, still caught up in his own anger. The solitude of my room couldn't come fast enough.

"Okay, so you didn't hook up with Brad. I wonder why they would say that then," Ryder questioned, more concerned than accusatory.

"I don't know. I have a feeling Emily has something to do with it," I said. It was the only logical explanation.

"Emily?" Garrett spat as an expletive.

"Yeah. Tony said Emily had seen me and Brad hooking up," I still couldn't believe what he said, as if I didn't hear him right, "And before you ask, no. I did not hook up with him Garrett." I glared at him from beneath my lashes. I figured I would beat him to the punch before he said something snarky.

"Hey, judgment free zone here," he said without humor, staring straight ahead. Our house came into view.

"So, you didn't hook up with Brad, and Emily is telling lies? I don't understand it," Ryder said, confused as I was.

"Sounds about right; I found out in the midst of Tony's accusations that he - he had been – he had been hooking up with Emily the w-whole time behind my b-back," I cried through my tears. Ryder tightened his arm around me as we walked in through the front door.

"I should have beat his ass at the park," Garrett growled, becoming further agitated at each admission.

"For what? It wouldn't change anything," I said, solemn.

"Teach that jackass a lesson. To make me feel better. In that order," Garrett answered my rhetorical question.

"Whatever. It's over with. I told him to leave me alone," I sniffled, wiping my face for the umpteenth time.

"Do you think he'll listen? He was pretty riled up," Ryder asked.

"I don't know Ry. I can't live in a bubble in hopes of staying away from him. I-I'm just gonna go to my room guys," I said. Ryder released me from his hold. I could feel their eyes at my back as the weight of the world rested on my shoulders.

"Wait up," Garrett said as he walked over, pulling me into his crushing bear hug. Normally, I would squirm to get out of it. I always ended up with bruises.

Not tonight.

Tonight, it felt like he kept all the pieces from falling apart inside of me as the sobs tore through my chest. "No matter what Aurora, I'm here for you. Ryder is here for you. So is Kate. Remember that. You're not alone. You always have us," he promised, holding my weight. I couldn't answer. I just nodded.

He released his arms around me, only to rest them on my

shoulders as he took a step back to audit my composure. I knew the look well. He was searching for signs of a catatonic episode. I couldn't blame him. Since their death, I haven't been known to cope with major life disturbances.

"Thank you, Garrett. I'm fine. I just need to be alone for a while." This was bad but it wasn't that bad. He nodded his head and released me. I gave him the thinnest smile I could muster and turned towards my room.

Once inside, I shut the door, sliding my back against it until I sat with my knees buried into my chest. Alone, I was free to let go without an audience.

I cried until my eyes were going to bleed. The intolerable pain kneeling on my chest made me immobile. Why did he have to come here tonight? Why did I allow myself to be so affected by him?

This uneasy, restless urge coursed through my body. I needed to do something, anything, than just sit here all night and cry over Tony.

I forced myself towards the closet. In one swift motion, I grabbed all the pictures of us off the mirrored door and tossed them into a shoe box, along with the promise ring he gave me on our one-year anniversary, the earrings he bought me on my twentieth birthday and the small white bear he won at the county fair this past summer.

Everything I had been feeling. Everything I had been through over the past few years; every word Tony had spoken to me over these last few months, echoed in my head. I couldn't escape this nagging pain.

I wanted to run away. Away from all this pain. Away from the constant, knowing stares that I didn't have it all together like I pretended. I wanted to go somewhere I could feel solid ground beneath me, proverbially speaking. I have been unstable for so long. I yearned to feel something other than this sense of hopelessness and loss.

That's what I am – lost.

I didn't recognize myself anymore. I didn't know who I was or where I was going. These past few years I had been ghosting around whichever way the wind blew me.

I have felt so alone; and now betrayed. I caught myself wondering what my mother would say, or if Tanner would have acted the same way as Garrett. Of course, he would. What a stupid thing to question.

I imagined my father sitting on the edge of my bed, cracking jokes to lift my spirits. My heart ached further at their absence. I wanted to get away from this place.

I needed a sense of familiarity. What I needed was home. I want to go home. It had been years since we had been there. The house and ranch were still in our name, just sitting there, rotting.

Thoughts of home brought forth once again the gentle pull I had been feeling to go back, albeit more prominent and forceful.

The gaping holes in my heart needed patching. The only way I knew how to do that was to seek closure in the one place I was afraid to go back to. Do I dare bring it up to my brothers that I wanted to go home? I suppose I should tell them rather than go without saying anything. I didn't want my face to end up on the side of a milk carton because they overreacted.

Formulating a plan was the only thing calming my nerves, allowing me to at least stop bawling. The idea of home resolved itself with each passing moment. With or without my brothers blessing, I am going home. Now, I had to figure out how to go without them.

Chapter Two

Unexpected Chaos

"Maybe we'll meet again, when we are slightly older and our minds less hectic, and I'll be right for you, and you'll be right for me. But right now, I am chaos to your thoughts, and you are poison to my heart." – Anonymous

***

Exhaustion was an understatement.

Sleep and I battled it out, leaving my eyes puffy and red, as I tossed and turned to my thoughts all night. So many questions kept running through my mind. Why was I being lied about? What did I do to deserve this? How long have Tony and Emily been together? That last question stung.

This room was becoming more like a prison with every passing second. With the sun rising, I needed some fresh air for a better perspective. I bounced out of bed, eager to be free from this chamber.

I hurried to change, slipping on my obnoxious orange converse and throwing my auburn hair into a high ponytail before heading out the door.

The house was quiet, but not for long. My brothers were the antonyms of peace and quiet. Luckily Kate was used to my brothers' rowdiness, or else she would never get any sleep around here either.

Opening the back door, I huffed as the unseasonable heat of spring greeted me. *I hated it here.*

My one refuge in this hellish place was the large garden in our backyard. It was my only connection home.

In these quiet moments, when I could dote on my flourishing garden, was when I felt okay being something entirely other. Call me crazy, but I can sense the very life flowing through each stem, radiating out through the leaves and flowers. Gardening was something my mother instilled into me at an early age; her green thumb rubbing off on me.

I stood amongst my heirloom roses, hyacinth, and daffodils, taking in a deep breath of dry *San Diego* heat, and sighed. I missed the cool, damp air of Oregon. I missed my parents and Tanner for that matter.

Garrett and Ryder moved us so far away from home, hoping a change of scenery would improve my mental breakdown after *they* passed. I thought my brothers would at least be reasonable and move us to Idaho or Montana. Instead, they moved us to a landscape that is dead, and people think it's beautiful.

A decomposing Santana rose laid pitiful at my feet, snapped from its stem. I leaned over, pinching the dull green stalk between my fingers to inspect the bloom closer as I stood back up. Its petals were curling in on itself, turning brown and brittle on the ends. Its fire-orange vibrancy was losing itself to the call of death, nipping at my heart for its brutal demise. I sighed at the representation for the 'cycle of life' in my hands.

Where had everything gone wrong? How did I get here?

I didn't have a terrible life. We were well taken care of through the trust fund our parents set up for each of us. We still had each other. No one had any health issues I was aware of. I just couldn't help this perpetual emptiness I always found myself in.

I often think back to my life when *they* were alive. I was vibrant and jovial. We went on hikes and horseback rides every weekend at our family ranch and would play on the beach during the week after school. We spent so much time together as a family.

More than that, my perspective on life was innocent. I never once considered losing any of them. It was as if time stopped, and we never moved forward. We enjoyed each other's company day in and day out.

What a dumb, naïve child I was.

Could that be the draw I'm feeling to go back home though? Did I need to seek closure? More important, am I ready to seek closure?

Tony didn't help matters. With all this chaos, no wonder all I wanted to do was run away. Which begs the question, why had Tony changed so drastically? He loved to party, yes, but never had he been so aggressive, at least in the first year and a half of our relationship. He was sweet and thoughtful.

This behavior was lost on me. He was up one minute and down another. He was fun and carefree, and then the next thing I know he was suspicious and jealous of anyone I talked to. It's like he was on drugs. I wonder if Emily got him hooked onto something.

I plopped down at our patio table with the shabby rose. My head spun with revolving questions as I rested my elbows on the tabletop, holding my face in my hands. The morning dew I hadn't realized covering the table began soaking into my jeans.

Peachy.

Nothing made sense. I have been trying to see things from Tony's perspective, to understand where he was coming from. This only left me with more questions than answers.

I broke up with him to disconnect from his growing hostility and agitation. I could not grasp why he didn't believe me but could trust Emily with such ease. So, he cheated on me. It still didn't explain his overbearing, jealous behavior. *Shouldn't he be less worried about me and more worried about her?* Again, more questions!

He began growing jealous of inconsequential things; a complete one-eighty from the man I first met. The guy I knew was charming and full of charisma. He was the life of all the parties, had been the star quarterback of his high school football team, prodigal player on the college team. He had nicknames here but none of them were negative.

Except from Garrett.

Tony made moving here tolerable. If I were being honest, he had been my paradise in the desert. How he acted now didn't fit the bill.

I lifted my gaze out of my hands and back to the rose. I hated endings. Though I knew it were a necessary evil to this thing called life, I still hated them. If it were within my grasp, I'd erase all endings. Take this once beautiful rose for instance. It didn't have to experience the sting of death. At least for a short while. Not if I could help it.

My heart throbbed with a familiar loving warmth for this unfortunate flower in my hand, radiating the heat across my chest that followed the path of nerves to my fingertips. As if sensing this gentle heat consuming me within, I watched as its petals began to unfurl, waking up as if waking with the morning sun.

The vibrancy it once knew in its short youth began flowing into the dead, brittle ends, bringing forth a soft, fiery luminosity

I loved about these flowers. Why I have this power to give life in ways no one else did, I will never know. All I knew growing up, it was to be kept a secret at all cost from everyone, including my brothers, and for that I was ashamed of it.

"I knew I would find you here," Kate called out as she walked up. My back straightened in surprise as I dropped the rose by my foot, kicking it to the side.

Kate took a seat next to me, pulling her blonde fishtail braid to the side.

"Oh yeah? Am I that predictable?" I glanced at her with an eyebrow raised, trying to slow my erratic heart as I subtly tried to see if she noticed my moment with the rose.

"Eh, to me you are," she smiled her mega-watt grin before letting out a loud yawn. I rolled my eyes at her in response.

"Hey now, what kind of best friend would I be if I didn't know you?" she asked, as if my eye rolling insulted her.

"A less annoying one," I said under my breath.

"I'll just pretend I didn't hear that," she dismissed, picking a flake of black nail polish off her thumbnail. I gave her a side smile.

"Seats wet," I mumbled, obviously way too late for it to matter.

"Yeah, I just found that out. So why are you sitting out here alone with a wet ass anyway?" she asked with a prying innocence only Kate could muster. She continued picking at her nail polish as if she weren't interested at all.

"Enjoying the scenery," I said. I wasn't in the mood to explain myself. I already felt pathetic enough with everything going through my head.

"Riiiigggghhht…." Her sarcastic tone trailed off with a side glance towards me.

"What? Can I not sit and enjoy this *wonderful* San Diego heat in my own backyard?" I asked. Her narrowed eyes left me wary as they meant one of two things; she was fishing for answers she knew she would get, or she already knew the answers and wanted me to cough them up anyways.

"Not when you're brooding," she said, scrutinizing my face with her lips pursed.

"Brooding? Who's brooding? What kind of word is *brooding* anyways?" I said on a tangent, trying to steer the topic away from the bigger issue – no dice.

"A good one. Don't deflect from the question Aurora Marie," she said, crossing her arms as she grew impatient with my dodgy answers.

"What was the question again?" *Why did she feel the need to pry now?* It was way too early for this.

"Why. Are. You. Here?" she pronounced each word as if I was slow.

What is there to say? *I'm obsessing over Tony, his accusations, and heartbroken over just how close he and Emily are. I want to know why he has been acting so manic.* I took a deep breath and huffed.

"I just needed out of the house. I didn't know I needed to clear that with you," I snapped. Defense as the best offense. She didn't need to know how pathetic I had become. I knew I came off bitchy, but then again, she was probably use to that by now.

"Mmhmm, that's what I thought," she said so matter-of-fact, dismissing my tangent, "You need to let Tony go."

"Let him go? I don't think I had a choice in this matter. It seems I've been accused of cheating because of some stupid accusation Emily made. He seems psychotic enough to come around unwarranted too."

She knew everything that had transpired. I overheard my brothers' hushed whispers filling her in when she came home last night. Of course, she knew what Tony said about Brad and I wasn't true. Still, being accused of something wasn't the greatest feeling in the world.

"Listen, I know. I don't have the answers for you. But if he's going to believe Emily's crap after all this time, then it's his loss. The most you can do is move on," she said.

I glared at her with furrowed brows. She backpedaled.

"It's hard to put something like this behind you. I get it. He isn't stable and hasn't been for a while. If anything, he did *you* the favor," she said. It was the most she had spoken on the subject since our breakup.

"How did he do me the favor? He accused me of something he was doing himself, and I'm just supposed to be okay with everything? Let it go like it never happened?" I asked, bitter, because I knew she was right. I also knew it wasn't within my power to let it go. I couldn't help the squeezing ache of my heart every time his name crossed my mind.

"I'm sorry. I know you don't want to hear that, but I must tell you. It hurts me to see you in pain over this jerk. I want my friend back. You have been checked out for a few weeks now. It's time to come back to reality and move forward," she said with sincerity.

It was close to the same thing she had said to pull me out of my mental breakdown when we came to San Diego. I knew her concern was genuine; the connotation still cut deep though.

"So why are you here? How did you know where to find me?" I asked, dismissing her plea for my sanity. I couldn't make any guarantees to move on, at least not until *I* had answers.

"I heard you close the backdoor. Party is this Saturday and I need an outfit. Shopping is not the same without my sidekick so get your wet butt moving and let's go!" she said with uncontained excitement.

Stupid frat party - I completely forgot. I gave her a grimace unable to find it within me to match her level of enthusiasm.

"Rory don't frown. It's not cute. It creates wrinkles. You're going to that party whether you like it or not. You're not going to sit here in this house another minute and mope. It isn't healthy," she said.

She's right. I wasn't going to like it. I had been doing a fair amount of moping in my room since the breakup and didn't have any ambitions of being social now.

"I know what you're doing," I said, narrowing my eyes at her.

"I haven't a clue what you're talking about," she dismissed.

"Don't patronize me. You don't have to get me out of the house because I'm upset about Tony," I said, rolling my eyes.

"I'm not. I need clothes. So do you. Quit your bitching."

"You don't *need* them. You *want* them," I amended

"Same difference," she shrugged.

"I can't go shopping Kate. I have work at two," I complained.

"Could you come up with anymore lame excuses?" she grunted, "It's only eight - *in the morning*. You have plenty of time. Let's go." She pulled me to my feet, locking her arm with mine just to be sure I didn't run back to my seat. She wouldn't relent.

"Can't we just go tomorrow," I whined. Shopping sounded less enticing than the ridiculous party.

"No. Today is the only day I'm free until the party," she stated.

"You know, you can be such a pain in the ass sometimes," I declared, smiling despite my irritation. I dreaded shopping with Kate. She had a thing for wanting to dress me in what she deemed as cute. Not that she had a bad sense of style, quite the opposite. I just didn't like being her human sized Barbie doll.

"Yep, but you still love me!" she laughed.

"That's debatable," I joked with a smirk. She shot me a dirty glance out of the corner of her eye, making me smile wider.

Kate could be bossy at times, and downright demanding at others, but she was my best friend. She's always honest, citing honesty as the best policy. She was also caring and thoughtful. She was more than a best friend to me, she's family – the sister I never had. I will always be grateful for her friendship. Even after that tragic accident, she was there. I think she took their passing just as hard as I did.

When she heard we were moving, she didn't hesitate to pack her bags. She didn't even ask 'where to?' She said she was coming and there wasn't a damn thing we could do about it. If it wasn't for her, I don't know where I would be today. To the day I die, I will always be grateful for Kate in my life.

I was relieved when Kate dropped me off at home after being subjected to her shopping extravaganza. She was meeting Chris for coffee. Luckily, she knew what she wanted, so we were shopping for only three hours instead of four. She found a haltered black shirt with ruffles cascading down the front. She paired it with dark blue jeans and black strappy heels.

Of course, NOT using me as her live mannequin was never an option. She trudged me through aisle after aisle of clothes I would never wear. Kate always wanted me to dress trendy instead of wearing my usual jeans, plaid shirts and converse. I think the plainness of my wardrobe made her cringe.

As I strolled into the house, I passed Garrett sprawled on the couch in the living room. The sports channel blared as he scarfed Cool Ranch Doritos, yelling at the TV.

"Where you heading to Rory?" he asked, eyeing the bags as he kept his attention on the TV. He stuffed his mouth with another handful of chips, his bronzed hair hinting at not seeing a brush this morning.

"Salty Dawg. Don't you have work or something?" I replied, irritated at the mess he made.

"Nope. Fired. Home loans weren't really my thing. Bunch of banksters. What the hell do they know?" he grumbled. "Oh well, onto bigger and better things!"

"You got fired? I swear Garrett; you need to get a life. Mom and dad's money is not going to last forever if you keep living like this you know," I harped, sounding more like the older sibling. If it were Ryder losing his job, I would be more sympathetic. Not Garrett. He only had this job for a year. He was a bus boy before that at the local pub – for a week. He started an argument with his manager over how to clean the tables. Like that was a hard job.

He stared at me in amusement. "Yeah well, that's what I have you for. What good are ya if I can't utilize *your* brains? Besides, I have a plan. Don't you worry little sister," he declared in his usual arrogance.

"Whatever Garrett. If it's anything like your other 'plans' I won't hold my breath," I said, rolling my eyes. "I've gotta go. I'm gonna be late." I headed to my room to change into my work attire – low cut blue jeans and a black V-neck shirt.

"Stop being such a loser," I mumbled under my breath as I walked back past him.

"I heard that!" Garrett yelled from the couch.

"You were meant to," I rolled my eyes as I walked out the door.

"Don't roll your eyes at me!" he hollered, chuckling.

"Oh, shut up. Find a job," I yelled back, slamming the door. He walked around like life owed him something. It's as if our parents passing didn't faze him. I mean it had to be that, or he was masking his pain in utter stupidity. Either way, he was acting like a complete idiot.

I opened the door to my truck, throwing my purse onto the backseat. It landed perfectly so all its contents were strewn across the floorboard.

Just peachy.

I jumped in and turned the key to hear the diesel engine purr to life. This sound could never get old. Garrett's voice on the other hand was a different story.

The Salty Dawg parking lot wasn't crowded - yet. The lunch rush just trickled out, and it was still too early for the spring break crowd. I parked on the outer edge of the large lot where employees are supposed to park. Gathering up the contents of my purse, I headed for the door.

"Hey Chuy," I greeted my favorite chef as I punched in.

"Hey momma, how you doin' today?" he asked with his thick accent, waving hi to me with spatula in hand.

"Oh, you know, same ol' same. How's Rita?"

"Ever the slave driver. I work for nickels so she can go spend dollars. Happy wife, happy life, right?" He smiled, nodding his head at me.

"I guess Chuy. You deserve a vacation," I laughed. Out of all the employees here, he worked the most and the hardest.

"Vacations are only for the privileged. I have bills to pay and three mouths to feed," he smiled, though I could see the heaviness of that statement on his shoulders.

I walked up behind him as I headed to the bar, patting him on the back, "I know. One of these days I'm going to strike it rich, then you can take all the vacations you want," I countered.

"I'm waiting. Ándale! I'm not getting any younger here!" he laughed.

I glanced back as I walked through the large double doors

laughing, "I'm tryin'!"

Three bar patrons sat at the end of the long bar - regulars of Salty. Six tables of the fifteen-table bar were occupied with those finishing their late lunches. The Angels were playing the White Sox on the big screen for spring training. ESPN and various Sports News Channels were on the other screens with their talking heads.

"Hey Charlie, how are ya?" I asked the first shift bartender. She looked worse for wear.

"Dead. Apparently, I thought it was a good idea to finish half a bottle of Jack last night," she croaked, her tired, bloodshot eyes frowning.

"Please don't tell me it's over that jackass Dexter," I said, rolling my eyes. She looked at me with her sad brown eyes and shrugged. She blinked a few times as she choked back the tears threatening to breach.

"Ugh, you're too damn good for him. Don't let him drive you to that," I chided. I'm giving out relationship advice and am the most unqualified to do so.

"I don't want to talk about it right now," her short, midnight-purple hair swayed back and forth as she shook her head, "I've almost made it through this entire shift without falling apart."

"Fair enough but knock that crap off. You can call me anytime you have to deal with him." She dismissed me with a quick nod like I do when I want the subject dropped. "I mean it," I said, giving her a sideways glance to make sure she understood.

"Yeah. I got it. Thanks Aurora," she gave me a tight-lipped smile. I wasn't satisfied with her answer but knew when to stop prying. I hated when it was done to me.

I grabbed the piling cups from the lunch rush and washed them in the sink. It was always tedious trying to find something to do until the night crowd started spilling in. After Charlie's last three regulars closed their tab, she clocked out for her shift. Her demeanor matched mine, empty and hollow - just ghosting through life. It was so much harder seeing a mirror image of me in someone else.

I spent the next two hours cutting limes and lemons, filling glasses into the cooler, wiping down the bar, and helping random patrons while I waited for the night rush to flow in and pass the time.

Why I was always in such a hurry to leave when all I did was sit at home was beyond me. At least this gave me something to do and put money in my pocket.

Once the night rush came, the next few hours passed by in a blink of an eye. For a Thursday night, we were unusually packed. I poured three drinks at a time, took money, closed tabs, and made sure everyone was served in a timely fashion.

I thrived in a fast, high-paced environment. I didn't have to think, I just had to coordinate. It didn't help that we were also short staffed. The other bartender who was supposed to work with me tonight called out sick. It was typical so I wasn't surprised. I worked better solo anyways.

Glancing at the clock; I had two hours before last call. Being in an industrial park, we catered to the surrounding blue and white collars; except for the weekends when we had bands play, would we stay open later than ten. Our manager, Russell, was on vacation and designated me as the one to close the bar down in his place tonight. I wasn't eager about doing it on my own but what choice did I have?

Relief came when I yelled, "Last call. Twenty minutes until close!" I always loved to close my shift like that. It felt like a heavy weight would be lifted off my shoulders every night shift I worked. It meant I was done. Finished. I did my duty and could go back home to be in relative loner-ism.

I worked on filling last drink requests and closing tabs. Once the last of the patrons left, I locked the door behind them to finish my work. I scanned around the now empty bar. It was always eerie being here alone. The kitchen closed an hour before the bar, so they were long gone.

I lowered the volume on the jukebox and turned it to my saved playlist – a compilation of my favorite songs by Imagine Dragons, Breaking Benjamin, and Shinedown, before getting to work.

After a good forty-five minutes, I shut everything off, turned on the alarm, and locked the doors for the evening.

I searched the empty lot as I turned for my truck. It was parked on the far end under one of only three lights that lit this dim lot, leaving the closer spots for patrons.

With my hand buried into my purse in search for my keys, I stayed vigilant. One abandoned car sat a few spaces from my me. It wasn't unusual to see a car or two left here from a few drunks hitching a ride with buddies or grabbing a cab.

My fingers wrapped around the keys as I reached my truck, which was about the same time I heard heavy rustling by the tailgate. There stood Tony, using the truck bed to hold up his weight as he swayed, staring at me.

Correction – glaring at me.

My heart fluttered in terror as I hurried to unlock my truck before he could stumble towards me, but he was faster than I gave him credit for.

"No, you don't. You're not getting away from me that easy," he grabbed me, ripping the keys out of my hand. I froze where I stood, in the death grips of a ravenous wolf.

"Tony, what do you want?" I squeaked out. I meant for it to sound bolder than it did.

"I'm done playing games. I'm tired of everyone getting in my way when it comes to us. You and I are going to resolve some issues *tonight*," he said, menacing. I was terrified to learn what he meant by that.

"Tony, listen to me. You need to stop this right now. You're scaring me," I tried to sound bold. He stood a foot taller than me as he peered down at my face. The deep shadows cast around his eyes made him appear even more frightening. Every nerve in my body wound tight.

"I wasn't done talking to you when your good for nothing brothers stepped in," he seethed.

"That's funny because I distinctly remember being done talkin—"

"*Again*, I wasn't finished," he slurred, raising his voice higher than mine. "As I was saying, I had a lot to think about over these past few days. I think I could overlook your moral—*hiccup*— ineptitude if you'll just confess to me what I already know."

He released my arm, gesturing with his hand for me to stay quiet as I began to speak. "*If* I can finally hear the truth from you, I believe we can move forward with our relationship and move past this or—*hiccup*—deal," he stated, stone-faced.

Did he just *really* say what I think he said? As if he were doing me a favor? How much did he drink?

"What makes you think in your *disillusioned mind* I would *ever* want to continue having a relationship with you? You're a psycho!" I said, my voice strained.

"Oh, *I'm* the psycho but you're the slut that lies, cheats and stabs people in the back! You're the reason I'm losing my mind," he yelled at me.

"I'm the slut? Really? You're the one running around with that *slut* Emily!" I blurted out. It was something I had been stewing on since our fight. It felt good to say it out loud.

"What s'that supposed to mean?" he leaned away with his face scrunched. He held a rigid stance meant to intimidate, though his body wavered.

"I don't know…you seem to be a pretty bright guy. Why don't you figure it out? She has been trying to get into your pants from day one. It looks like she has been doing a damn good job too," I threw back in his face.

I had enough of this – of his persistence in pursing me. I wanted him to move on with what he had planned just so I could be done with this craziness – whatever it meant. That didn't mean I was throwing self-preservation out the window though.

The more heated the argument escalated, the more hyper-aware I became of my surroundings. I searched for a way to escape this madness. I could take my chances running but I knew he would catch me, even in this state. The nearest cross street was a quarter mile away. Even then, it was just as deserted as this parking lot.

I could try to fight my way through except Tony doubled my size in both body and strength.

Calculating my exit strategy, I startled to see a guy with his back perched against a tree, obscured in the cloak of darkness. Tony didn't notice him, but the more my mind became aware of his presence, the clearer I could see him.

The muscles in his arms twitched under his black, skintight shirt. I stared at him with a frightened message screaming '*help*'. He locked eyes with mine, seeming to hear my unspoken plea.

Do I bring attention to this stranger? Do I drag him into my drama? Yes. I knew the answer without even thinking twice. He was going to be my exit. I had no other choice.

"You do not know what you're talking about. Emily has always been a good friend. Don't be mad at her because she called you out," Tony said, leaning towards me.

I shifted my eyes back to Tony, fuming, "*She* has always been a good friend? What, from six months ago? Because that constitutes a long friendship; I have known you a hell of a lot longer than she has."

The plea for help from this stranger was building inside as Tony squinted his eyes at me in pure hatred.

"And by the way, *SHE* didn't call me out on anything. The fact you're so blind to it says something. You know what it says? You have been in bed with her for a lot longer than I realized," I yelled at him, shaking my head.

I was livid at how he was so twisted around Emily's little finger. Knowing this man stood in the shadow's gave me a voice, a boldness, I had lost the moment Tony stepped foot around my truck.

"You have absolutely no clue about anything," he said bearing down on me, getting to within inches of my face. His steel cut eyes were void of any reasoning and filled with rage. His jaw flexed with his aggravation.

My adrenaline accelerated at the uncomfortable proximity he stood next to me - too close.

I glanced to the shadows, where this stranger stood, but he was gone. Dread rushed through me as I scanned the parking lot for him. He vanished.

I was alone. Again. With Tony.

Why would he leave me here seeing what was taking place? He must not have wanted to get involved in our drama. I couldn't blame him, I guess. Despite this realization, I had another more startling realization – I was in deep trouble.

"Who are you looking for?" Tony barked in anger. '*No one*' I said in my mind as I choked back a sob. Ignoring his question, I tried to keep up the bravado in hopes it would help me to stay strong and stand my ground.

"The only one here without a clue is you! Be a good lapdog and run back to Emily," I said, jerking my chin for him to run along. For the first time in all this chaos, I held nothing for him but pure hatred.

"You should also heed the warning from Garrett. Leave me alone and get the hell out of my face," I spat with disgust as I placed both palms on his chest, pushing him away from me. All the good it did; I did a better job at pushing myself away from him.

His hands balled into tight fists by his side. "Screw your brothers. If anything, I owe them a good ass kicking for not minding their own damn business," he sneered.

"I'm their sister idiot. I *am* their business. And you would be like a quivering bunny in the middle of a pack of ravenous wolves with my brothers. You know it. I know it. Everyone else knows it. You should watch your mouth," I said, taking a step back to put more distance between us. His eyes shot to my foot, taking note of my movement, just like last night. He took a step forward. For as drunk as he was, he was extremely observant.

"Tony, look. Why don't we go our separate ways?" I pleaded, unsure if he was capable of letting me go. Panic began to seize my chest. It wasn't me he wanted; it was the control he refused to release over me.

All I wanted to do was leave, to pretend this never happened. My heart tore more with every glare of unadulterated hatred, realizing how a few short weeks were enough to separate our bond to the polar ends of the earth.

Emotions danced across his face from anger and hatred to no emotion whatsoever - as if he suffered from multiple personality disorder.

I glanced back to the tree with false hope *he* would be there. He wasn't. *Was I seeing things? Was there anyone even there in the first place?* Yes, there definitely had been a man there. He looked straight at me.

"What do you keep searching for? There's no one here to help you. It's just you and me," Tony taunted, staggering a step closer. I matched his step back.

"What is wrong with you Tony? This isn't you. What happened to you?" I asked, trying for offense.

"You! You happened to me. You've played me. All I wanted was for you to show me you cared for me the way I care about you. Instead, you cheat on me, you lie to me. I'm falling apart over here. I want you back but at the same time, I want to leave you in a ditch. I can't control these fucked up feelings," he yelled, sounding crazier with every admission.

My heart seized. I cupped my mouth, eyes wide, as he confessed to his murderous intent. Whether it was an idle threat or not, I didn't want to stand around to find out.

During this whole standoff, my body weighed heavy like lead, but now an electric pulse revved up to take flight. Knowing we were approaching the end of the line; I made a dash away from him. I didn't have a snowballs chance in hell to escape him, but I had to try.

His rough hand clasped around my wrist as he yanked me back, slamming me hard into his chest. He didn't move an inch from the impact. He twisted my arm behind me, locking my throat with his free hand. Fear rang through to my core. I couldn't move.

"I refuse to let you walk away from me like you did last time. You can leave when we are done talking," his ice-cold breath seethed with anger against my ear.

Sweat beaded at the nape of my neck. I tried to stay calm, but the bile rose in my throat. I wasn't at all sure he would let me go and couldn't trust all he wanted to do was talk.

"Tony! Let go! You're hurting me," I tried to say with sternness, but my voice squeaked as he squeezed his hands tighter. I strained to see behind me; his eyes were blank. Checked out.

"Why are you acting like this?" I whispered. My ears pulsated with adrenaline as I tried to pull away from him.

He pulled his face away from mine, becoming aware of his surroundings, before turning his agitation back onto me, "We are going somewhere else to talk." He released my throat as he began towing me by my wrist towards the truck.

"Tony *please!* We can talk later once we've both calmed down. Please just let me go," I panicked, trying to pull my wrist free as I back peddled. He pulled harder. I began to protest further, afraid of where he planned to take me, when he stopped in his tracks.

"I believe she told you to let her go; or do I have to break your arm off for her?" a deep, accented voice threatened Tony.

The first twinge of relief rushed over me as I peered around Tony's frame. It was the same man I had seen in the shadows, giving Tony a murderous glare. Tony faced him, dragging me alongside him. *Where did he come from?*

"Mind your own business unless you want to have a bad night," Tony snapped.

I glanced at Tony and back at this stranger. He stood at the same height as Tony; albeit more fighter-like, as his posture broadcasted he meant business. The corners of his mouth curled up, his expression welcoming Tony's threat.

"Afraid I can't do that, you see. The lady told you to let go. Clearly, she is done with the conversation," he challenged, "And the fact you haven't let her wrist go means you do not know how to do as you're told."

His smile faded; his shadowed eyes tensed as he glanced at Tony's hand still locked around my wrist. Even in this dim lot, his expression became noticeably darker, menacing. Pinpricks began radiating from my wrist to my fingertips.

"And who the hell are you?" Tony glared at the man, his body tensing for a fight.

"I'm your worst fucking nightmare," the man promised with a devilish grin, his jaw muscles flexing with anticipation. His demeanor screamed danger though his mannerisms were relaxed. With fierce, calculating eyes, he enjoyed the altercation - it gave him fire. He kept his intense stare blazing on Tony.

"Is that so?" Tony puffed up his chest, stepping forward into this stranger's face, as he let me go.

I grabbed my wrist, bringing it into my chest. It throbbed from the rush of blood. Faint bruising began to appear, shaped perfectly to Tony's fingers.

When I looked up, I caught *him* glancing from me back to Tony; his expression pained before turning lethal. The tension was ready to snap. I had to do something.

"Tony. Stop this!" I said, stepping in front of him with my back towards the stranger. I tried to push him away, as if creating distance between them would lessen the tension. It was useless. Instead, he forced me to the side with a sweep of his arm, tripping me backwards from the force.

I wouldn't let him get into this fight. I didn't know what I was more afraid of, Tony getting hurt or this man getting into trouble on my behalf.

I realized I was hedging my bets in this stranger's favor. Was it wishful thinking? Or the confidence exuding from him as if he couldn't lose?

Tony became agitated I was trying to hold him back, but I couldn't let this continue. I grabbed for his arm, but he smacked my hand out of the way with such violent impact, it unnerved me. My head snapped up in surprise as Tony's back hand landed across my face. My world came crashing into me at the surreal sound of my head meeting the asphalt. A high-pitched ringing screamed in my ears while my vision found itself in a tunnel.

Glancing up through squinted eyes, my protector was mortified. His wide eyes lost the amusement of his altercation and gave way to rage. Tony snapped out a belligerent punch, connecting only with air as the man ducked to the left of Tony's advance, following with a haymaker of his own to Tony's face.

Tony's nose burst with a level of blood I had never seen from anyone before. He staggered back before bringing his hand to the damage, red liquid streaming between his clenched fingers. Pain shot across his face as he swiped below his nose, assessing the damage left on his hand.

"You broke my fucking nose," he yelled with fury pooled in his glossed over eyes. Tony strode forward, bringing his hand down from the carnage before coming at the dark-haired protector again.

The man side stepped as Tony staggered forward with a sloppy right hook, narrowly connecting with his jaw. What happened after became nothing but a blur. Tony whipped around, ready to attack, not realizing his own demise. The man was already barreling down on him, his fists lightning fast before Tony was laid out on the ground, unconscious. In the next instant, this handsome stranger crouched next to me in a panic.

"Aur—, are you okay?" he asked, worry peppering his voice. He sounded distorted to my ears, as if he were trying to speak to me underwater, or through a thick wall. Too stunned to speak, I nodded instead, squinting from the fullness enveloping my brain. He looked me over with uncertainty, his hand gently touching where I had slammed my head.

"Can you stand?" he worried. I nodded to ease his worry, trying to be braver than I should. His lips turned into a grim line as his rough hand engulfed mine for support. I grabbed onto his chiseled shoulder as he lifted me to my feet.

My equilibrium was off.

My head heavy.

As the pain began to spike, everything spun around me.

The adrenaline began wearing off and the enormity of what happened hit me like concrete. The proverbial walls were closing in. My hold on reality imploded until it was lights out.

Chapter Three

Emergency Room

"The worst kind of pain is when you're smiling just to stop the tears from falling." – Anonymous

***

My eyes fluttered to a ceiling with rectangular lights passing behind me. Blue uniforms with name badges walked alongside me.

A slender blond, with her hair high in a tight bun, glanced back before returning her attention forward.

My vision was clouded – like squinting through foggy glass or a smoke-filled room. I lifted my hands to rub the haze from my eyes as a slight tugging on my forearm grabbed my attention. Squinting at the source of the pull, I sat up in a panic to rip the tube from my arm; a forceful set of hands pushed me back down against the gurney.

"Ms. Walker, take it easy. You're all right; we are here to help," a woman's assertive voice said from behind.

I strained my head back to look up at her, her face peculiar from this angle with an elongated nose and small head. Her beady eyes glanced down at me before continuing forward. She had her dark brown hair pulled into a bun – same as the blond nurse in the front. Her nametag read 'T. Johnson.' I took note of the fact she never lifted her hands from my shoulders.

They wheeled me into a bright room with beeping machines as they hoisted me onto a hospital bed. They all shuffled out of the room, except for Johnson. She busied herself with setting up different machines, placing a heart monitor onto my finger.

A short, slender man with a white coat stormed in, standing at the foot of the bed. "Hello Ms. Walker. I'm Dr. Chan. How are you feeling?" he asked without hesitation. He adjusted his large round glasses before placing his hand back onto the clipboard he held, staring with expectation.

"F-fine," I said a beat late. "What happened? Why am I here?" I asked, confused. My memory kludged on as I tried to stitch the pieces of what landed me in here.

"You were in quite an ordeal. It says here you fainted after hitting your head. The paramedic tried to wake you, but you wouldn't come to. Garnering no response, they immediately brought you here. How does your head feel?" he asked in a clinical tone I imagined he learned in med school.

Disoriented, I wanted to say.

"It hurts," I answered. "Can you please explain to me how I ended up here?" I asked again, still confused.

"Can you tell me if you feel pain anywhere else?" he pressed on, ignoring my questions.

"Check her hand. I think it could be broken," I heard the familiar, accented voice coming from the door. My heart skipped a beat. The events from earlier began flooding back, though fragmented as they were. My cheeks reddened with embarrassment.

He stole a quick glance in my direction with worry tormenting his eyes.

"And who are you, young man?" the doctor asked.

"I'm Gavin," he shifted his eyes from me then back to the doctor, "Her cousin." He smirked, elaborating to the doctor his false identity, though the worry never left his eyes.

"Well, Gavin, you will have to wait outside. Patient confidentiality does not allow you in here unless it's okay with Ms. Walker." The doctor turned a speculative eye towards me. He must have seen through Gavin's lie.

What could I say? No? This guy went through a lot of trouble to help me. Besides, he didn't seem like the kind of guy who took no for an answer.

"I don't mind," I said.

"Very well. On a scale of one to ten, how would you rate the pain in your head?" the doctor asked.

"Um, eight I think," I replied. My head felt pressed in a vise grip with a migraine and an aneurism. It made thinking difficult.

"I see," the doctor quipped, scribbling notes onto the clipboard.

"Let me check your hand," the doctor demanded, walking around for a closer examination. A sharp, acute pain I hadn't noticed now spiked from my pinky finger into my wrist. I winced. Dr. Chan laid my hand back on the bed before scribbling notes again.

I glanced at Gavin, standing ridged by the door. The intensity in his eyes warmed my cheeks with embarrassment. I looked back at Dr. Chan to hide whatever my eyes would reveal.

"It is swollen. We will have to X-ray your hand to see if it's a clean break or just fractured. We will also need to take a Cat-scan of your brain to make sure there isn't any unnecessary swelling," Dr. Chan assessed. "And this here looks fresh," he said, poking at the bruising around my wrist. I winced again, remembering how tight Tony held onto my arm. I had been so sure he would snap it.

Gavin stepped further into the room, absolute concern marring his handsome face.

"And you say you do not remember what happened?" Dr. Chan asked, sending a suspicious glance towards Gavin. There wasn't any way to not mistake the handprint bruising over my wrist.

"No. I don't," I snapped, making it clear I did not want to talk about it further. I didn't think he was convinced.

"Right. Well, I will get these tests and X-rays ordered. It will be a few minutes Ms. Walker," Dr. Chan said before making a brisk exit with the nurse on his heels.

"Ms. Walker huh?" Gavin asked with a smile as he stepped to the foot of the bed, resting his hands on the rail.

Something about his presence made me feel at ease, forgetting the situation around me. The irony was not lost on me I would feel safer with a stranger than a guy I had known for two years.

"So, he has a name?" I said, smiling back.

"It seems I do. Gavin Mair. Pleasure to meet you Ms. Walker." His smile pulled to one side as he said my formal name. Was he toying with me?

"Oh, I'm sure it is. I do have a name you know?" I said, agitated.

"Ms. Walker is your name, is it not?" he asked, trying to demonstrate how absurd my irritation was.

"You should know *cousin*," I shot back, raising one of my eyebrows at him.

He lips turned into an impish smile at his little lie to the doctor, "I don't think they would have let me stay here if I wasn't family."

"My name is Aurora," I said, correcting him.

"So, how *are* you feeling Aurora?" he asked with heavy concern in his voice.

"I've had worse," I said, trying to brush off his concern. He grimaced at my nonchalance.

"I guess you could say you had a long day," he noted. More like a long few years but I let that one slide.

"Thank you for earlier. And I'm sorry you had to be involved. What were you doing in the parking lot, I didn't see you in the bar?" I blurted. I know he wasn't in the bar. That face would be hard to miss.

He hesitated, his eyes tightening before humor flashed across his face, "I was waiting for my ride."

Such a normal response; I wasn't sure why it took me by surprise.

"Why did you step in and help me? Please don't misunderstand, I'm very grateful, but most people would turn a blind eye to something like that."

His eyebrows furrowed into a V before he smoothed his composure. He turned an intense, solemn gaze on me, "I'm sorry but is it so wrong I came to help? Is it wrong to believe no one should be laying a hand on you so harshly?"

The ferocity in his voice showed a protectiveness in his words. His intense, dark green eyes held my gaze, showing the deeper meaning his words had spoken. I tried seeing the situation through his perspective, tried to understand how a stranger could feel so deeply for me without ever meeting me. I realized it was all an act of chivalry, nothing more.

"Oh. I see," was all I could say as I played with the hospital sheet between my fingers. I noted the soft gray framing the green in his eyes, giving them more dimension, before I dropped my eyes from his. I couldn't allow myself to become lost in his gaze. The raw emotion in his voice left me unnerved.

"What happened to Tony?" I peeked at him from beneath my lashes, more worried for Gavin's troubles than Tony's pride being hurt.

"Let's just say he will not be bothering you anymore. Not if I have anything to do with it," he threatened with what sounded like a promise, though the last part he said more as a whisper.

His mood changed from light and playful to somewhere distant. A cold veil shrouded his eyes; the distant stare told me his thoughts were anywhere but here. I didn't know what to say to bring him back to the present.

The conviction in his voice made it sound like I would see him more often. I couldn't have heard him right because of the nature of our relationship, or lack thereof. Still, a sense of familiarity hung in the air.

A pixie-like nurse walked in, slicing through the silence, "Ms. Walker—"

"Please, call me Aurora," I said, cutting her off. I was reluctant to take my eyes off Gavin to look at her, transfixed with his expression. I wondered what direction his thoughts took to take him away from me.

"My apologies Aurora. I'm the X-ray technician. My name is Erin. I'll be taking you to your x-ray," she responded in a pleasant, soprano voice. She brushed a strand of light brown hair out of her eyes and tucked it back towards her bob cut.

"Okay," I said with reluctance as I began to sit up.

"Oh Aurora, you can stay where you are. I will be wheeling you up to the X-ray floor," she said. *Great.* This was so embarrassing. I could walk. I didn't break my legs for heaven's sake.

The nurse turned to Gavin standing at the foot of the bed, "You can wait in the lobby."

Gavin nodded with the same distant expression plastered on his face before looking at me.

"I, uh, I will just be in the lobby," he said before turning on his heel.

"Oh-kay," I responded a beat too late. He was already gone from sight by the time I found my voice.

Did I say something wrong? The way his playful banter switched reminded me of when he stood in front of Tony, smiling until he realized I was hurt. What stuck out most in my mind, however, was the way he had been shrouded in the shadows, expectant for something to happen – as if he anticipated Tony's actions.

As for Tony, I have no idea what got into him. Not that he had been stable as of late. I could sense the intense anger he had towards me when he grabbed my wrist. His hatred became so palpable, his eyes pure fire.

The fear he stirred inside me still made my heart race. Just knowing if I had allowed myself to be taken by him, it would only end one way. Surely someone would have figured out what had happened.

I hoped.

"Here we are dear," Erin said, breaking me out of my thought cloud as she wheeled me into the X-Ray room. "I'm going to lay this jacket on you. Just hold still for a moment." She laid a heavy jacket over my torso to keep me from exposure before she walked behind a wall with a tiny window. A light came on, clicked a few times over my fingers and forearm before we were finished.

Being wheeled back like an invalid, Gavin was already waiting, leaning against the wall. My heart skipped a beat, knowing he stayed here for me. How ridiculous I had become for being anxious to see him again. He still had a distant expression, but his eyes softened.

"You're back. And in one piece!" he exclaimed with a teasing shock.

"Yep. Because so much could've happened on my way to take X-Rays," I threw a sarcastic smile back at him.

"You would be surprised," he said in a low voice. I was unsure if he meant for it to be heard.

"Aurora, the doctor will be in to see you in just a few minutes," the nurse stated after fastening the bed to keep from rolling.

"Okay, thank you," I responded. Gavin took the same stance at the foot of the bed as earlier.

"I hope you don't mind but I called your brothers. They're on their way now," Gavin said, eyeing me for my response.

"What? How did you know my brothers' numbers? Or that I even had brothers?" I asked dumbfounded.

"Uh, your phone. When you fainted and didn't wake up, I grabbed it. It was unlocked when it fell out of your purse. On our way to the hospital, I went through your call log. There were only three numbers that were consistent – Ry, Kate, and Dumbass - so I contacted them. Except for one number, Kate, I think it was," he paused for a moment and smiled at himself. "She kept calling nonstop. Was she an earful!" he said without hesitating. If he only knew.

After a long pause, he back peddled, "I'm sorry. I hoped you wouldn't mind. I figured you had family that would like to know where you were."

"No! No. It's fine. Thank you for calling them. I would have wanted them to know," I said, just as I heard Kate's frantic voice berating the nurse to let her into my room.

"I'm sorry miss. She already has a visitor in her room. You'll have to wait in the lobby," an irate nurse said.

"Like hell I do!" Kate said, just outside my room.

"That's my cue. I'll step out and let her take my place," Gavin said turning to step out.

"Hey. Wait. Are you leaving?" I asked, my heart dropping into my stomach. *Could I sound anymore needy and pathetic?* I didn't care. I did not want him to go no matter how pitiful it was. For someone who went through such great lengths to help me, I wanted to at least repay him somehow.

"Yeah. I have a few things to tend to. Now that I know you'll not be alone; I feel better about leaving." The warmth in his voice didn't distract from the tightness in his eyes.

"Okay. Well, when will I see you again?" I asked. My Lord, *kill me now*, I had no control over my mouth. I couldn't have sounded more desperate if my life depended on it. "You have done so much for me I mean. The least I could do is take you out to lunch or something?"

He smirked as if there was a joke said and I missed the punch line. He turned his head, grimacing over his shoulder at Kate all but ripping out the poor nurse's throat.

"You'll see me around. I better go before your friend ends up in jail," he paused in thought, "or in a strait jacket." He smiled one last time at me before stepping out.

I didn't get it. He had helped me, went through great lengths to make sure I had been taken care of, yet he didn't let me know anything about him apart from his name.

"Can you believe these people around here?" Kate exclaimed, storming towards me to wrap me in a hug. "I'm so sorry I wasn't there Aurora. What happened? Are you okay?" she worried.

"Yeah. I'm fine," I said, smirking. I loved my best friend. Growing up in a house full of boys, it was nice feeling a connection with someone I considered more as a sister – even if she was a bit much at times.

"What are you smiling at?" she looked offended.

"You," I giggled.

"*Me?* Why?" she asked, a crease between her brows appearing.

"Because I love you. You're my best friend. That's why," I said.

"How hard did you hit your head?" she questioned, eyeing me like I was crazy. I shrugged.

"Now tell me what happened. I called you a million times because you didn't come home when you should have been. Then a random guy answers it? I find out you're in the *hospital!* I swear I could kill Tony right now. It took every bit of nerve I had to not go find him before I came here," she said, working herself up.

"Honestly, it all happened so fast," I sighed, as I briefed her on what happened. Her face mixed back and forth between anger, surprise and worry as she pushed for details.

"When I see Tony, he will be lucky if a broken nose is all he will have!" she said in her most menacing Kate way.

"Step in line because I'm sure Garrett and Ryder will be on the hunt to put his head on a spike.," I joked.

"Damn straight. Do you blame them?" she asked. "You need to stay away from him. He has completely lost it."

"Trust me, Kate. I won't be going out of my way to find him. He came after me anyways. I can't help it if he is hell bent on stalking me," I said, furrowing my brows as I continued to pluck at the bed sheet.

"Besides, he and Emily are an item now," I added as my voice cracked. Saying it out loud made the pain tangible – Tony and Emily as a couple.

"That bitch! She better watch out who she is messing with.

I will run her over and lay all her crap bare," Kate said, spitting venom.

"Not if I find her first," I glared back at Kate. A devious smile spread across her face.

"Trust me. That won't happen," she promised, "So, what is up with Mr. Handsome? You have been holding out on me. You didn't tell me you had a hot friend!" she pressed for answers.

"Hate to disappoint you but today is the first time we met," I laughed when her face fell.

"And? You didn't get a number? A name? What his favorite color is? What *have* you been doing in here the whole time?" she questioned; probing for answers as if being hospitalized meant we were on a date.

"No, I was too busy arguing with Tony and apparently fainting in this guy's arms to find that out," I exclaimed, throwing my arms in the air. I winced when the IV tugged on my forearm. What did she expect me to do, get his whole life story while I laid here in a hospital bed?

Yes. Yes, she did.

"No excuses! Tell me what you do know," she pried, the hospital surroundings lost on her. If it were her in my position, she would have his whole life story, met his parents, and be planning their wedding by now. At least she provided a bit of a distraction, even if it were to my embarrassment.

"His name is Gavin Mair. Other than that, I know nothing," I said. It was true. I knew nothing about him. I knew the way he made me feel. The way my blood simmered in my veins when his intense eyes locked onto mine. The way I felt damn intimidated by him.

"Did he at least give you his number?" she asked exasperated. I shook my head no with an eyebrow raised.

"Why not?" she pressed.

"I don't know Kate. I asked him when I would see him again. I offered to take him out to lunch for helping me. He just said I would see him around. This *may* come as a total shocker but *maybe* he is just a nice guy trying to help me. Who knows?" I said, exuding part sarcasm and part annoyance. I hated when she pressed for answers like this.

"Aurora Marie, you like this guy!" Kate gushed.

"What? Don't be ridiculous. I don't even know him," I countered.

"Mhm, I know you, Aurora. Better than you know yourself. You're blushing," she exclaimed.

"Kate, you're making my headache worse," I said, dropping my face into my hand.

The doctor stepped in with perfect timing, allowing me to escape her pestering for a short while.

Dr. Chan gave Kate an unwelcoming eyeful before turning to the computer. He must have heard what a pain in the ass she was when she stormed through the door.

"Ms. Walker. We have your X-Rays," he stated the obvious as he pulled the X-rays up.

"You were lucky. Good news is you didn't break your finger. There is a dislocation here in the proximal interphalangeal joint. We may be able to avoid surgery and correct it with closed reduction. Bad news is you will have to wear a soft cast between four to six weeks until it's healed. Even then, your finger may always be weaker than you're used to," he stated as if it were supposed to make me feel better.

Kate seethed at hearing the diagnosis, knowing the reason I was in here. For a moment, I saw Gavin's face and couldn't help placing Kate's expression on his with this news.

"Closed Reduction? What's that?" I asked, ignoring her radiating aggravation.

"It is where we will pull the dislocation until it's freed and then set it back in its correct position. Don't worry. We will give you local anesthesia so you will not feel a thing," he reassured, taking in my worried expression. All I interpreted from his mouth was that it was going to be painful.

"Perfect," I sighed, rolling my eyes to Kate," When do we start?"

"Right now. Miss, if I can ask you to step out to the lobby," Dr. Chan turned to Kate, throwing her out with his eyes. Kate glanced at me then back to him, ready to argue.

"It's okay Kate. Go ahead. Maybe my brothers will be out there, and you can fill them in on what is going on," I said to assure her. She nodded before walking out of the room, giving the doctor one last glare.

Dr. Chan busied himself with getting everything ready. Once he had what he needed, he went to work while I did my best not to focus on the impending pain.

A few hours later, I was sent home with a soft cast on my left hand, a slight concussion and a clean bill of health. My brothers met me in the lobby, fully informed by Kate. They were both furious, naturally, as any brother would be. Mine just happened to take things to the extreme. They wanted to know what happened from my perspective, not just from what Kate had said. I don't know if hearing it from me made it more believable or concrete. The more I went on, the more heated they became.

"That asshole better know what's coming for him," Ryder threatened, "He is a dead man. I'm sorry Rory. I'm sorry you ever met that jackass. You better believe you did not deserve any of this." Unlike Garrett, it was rare for Ryder to let his anger show so I knew how pissed he was.

"Yeah, I know Ry," I replied.

"Damn straight you didn't deserve any of this. Kate if you

see him, relay a message for me. Let that weasel know I'm look-ing for his punk ass," Garrett said, "I'll show him what being left in a ditch really means."

I knew they would be pissed but I felt like I was going to witness a bloodbath in my near future.

"I second that Kate," Ryder chimed in.

"You guys, just let it go. I do not want this to go any further than it already has," I said.

All three of them deadpanned, turning to me as shock spread across their faces. "Look, I'm fine. I am going home," I moved my uninjured hand in the air, up and down along my tor-so to accentuate that I was in one piece. I understood where they were coming from, but I did not want an all-out war breaking out or them to get in serious trouble.

"Like hell Aurora. You can't expect us just to look the other way when some asshole puts you in the hospital. It's not hap-pening. You do not have a say in this. As your brothers, we have an obligation to protect you or beat whoever's ass hurts you," Garrett chided.

"Oh yes I can expect you to," I said with finality.

"I'm with them on this one Aurora. This is inexcusable," Kate said, backing them up. I looked up at all three of them staring at me.

"Fine. Whatever. Just don't end up in jail," I stared at the ground, defeated. I knew between the two of them, and Kate's blessing, I wasn't going to win this one.

"Meh, just call me. I'll bail you out," Kate smirked.

"Thanks sis," Ryder said, throwing his arm around her shoulders.

Once they wheeled me to the car, Ryder picked me up like I was a china doll. "Ry, you do know I can walk? I didn't break my legs," I said.

"Yeah, I know, but with the fainting spells and concussion; I don't want to take any chances," He stated.

"Right. I fainted once," I said, annoyed.

"One too many times in my book," he shot back with a grimace.

By the time we were home, I could hardly keep my eyes open. Ryder continued his overprotective brother role and carried me from the car to my bed, making sure I had everything I needed so I did not have to move an inch. Once he finished worrying over me, I turned out the lights and passed out.

Chapter Four

Kismet

"Do you think the universe fights for souls to be together? Some things are too strange and strong to be coincidences." - Emery Allen

***

Hey. Wake up," Kate whispered, shaking me awake. I opened groggy eyes to her concerned face inches from mine.

"What? What happened?" I asked, my head spinning as I shot up.

"Nothing! I'm just checking on you. The doctor said we were supposed to check on you every so often for the next twenty-four hours with your concussion," she stated. I glanced to the darkened window.

"Ugh, Kate. I was sleeping. What time is it?" I asked, rubbing my eyes.

"Five thirty in the morning," she whispered.

"Why are you whispering? It isn't like my brothers will wake up."

"I don't know. With the house being this quiet, it just feels right. Like being in a library and talking," she shrugged.

"You're so weird," I said through squinted eyes.

"You want to go to The Shack for lunch today?" she asked, expectant. Always thinking about food. I shook my head at her.

"Kate. Seriously? It's five thirty in the morning. All I want right now is sleep," I complained.

"Fine. I'll ask you in the morning," she turned sour and walked out, shutting the door behind her.

"It already is morning!" I exclaimed. I needed to start locking that damn door.

No thanks to Kate, I laid in my bed staring into the dark. My sore wrist tingled from the snug, soft cast. I loosened it, which made my hand feel better - and worse. Blood began to circulate again but without the cast being so tight, it didn't offer much support, giving my hand more freedom to move.

My head didn't hurt nearly as much as it had in the hospital, but it still ached. I touched where it slammed into the asphalt, squinting at its tenderness. I wouldn't be surprised if the bruising took all month to heal, if I let it.

The physical would mend. It was the emotional I stalled to check on. In the grand scheme of things, I was furious with Tony for treating me this way. A part of me wanted my brothers to find him down a dark alley. But the greater part of my heart gave way to sadness, loss and regret for where we were; how far we had fallen apart. How did this become such a mess? What could I have done different on my end?

The physical void of losing Tony spread from my heart across my chest, like tentacles latching itself to my very soul. I couldn't shake it and I did not know how long it would last. I had never experienced heartbreak like this; only the loss of loved ones.

Despite the pain Tony put me through, I couldn't ignore the faint beat in my heart, nor the heat that rose to my face, when I thought of Gavin. I knew the mystery of the unknown was what intrigued me and nothing more. Thinking about him gave me something to hold onto, keeping me from sinking into a deep despair I know I would be in by now.

The only details Gavin left me with were the physical ones – the way his biceps twitched with anticipation in the shadows, his devilish smirk at being challenged, the intensity of his stare.

Moreover, the way the tightness around his eyes never left when he perceived I was in any amount of pain or discomfort. Then there was the way he appeared out of nowhere, and how it seemed there was always a double meaning in his words.

My thoughts ricocheted back and forth between Tony and Gavin. I was processing my feelings from one to the other. If I were hooked up to the Richter scale, it would show the quake of emotions moving inside me.

The sun began to rise until its rays were passing through my windows. Damn Kate to hell. Thanks to her I was wide-awake. With REM and I at odds, I threw my feet over the edge of the king-sized bed. Sitting up too fast, I waited for the vertigo to cease before I slid into orange slippers and headed for the bathroom.

I couldn't hide from the mirror. The cherry of a bruise on my right cheek couldn't be mistaken, nor could the scrape where my cheek skidded on the asphalt when it made contact.

I hesitated, lifting my fingers to my face, as an echo of warning from my mother flooded my thoughts. She wasn't here now, so what did it matter? I finished bringing my hand to the scape, feeling a warming sensation beneath my fingers. Not wanting to overdo it, I dropped my hand.

My mother told me years ago never to reveal my gift, but when I was alone, I couldn't help but marvel at the magic of it all. The bruise lightened, the scrape gone, I lowered my gaze at the shame of what I was – a freak. Even my own mother didn't want others to know what a total anomaly I was. It wasn't normal for people to be able to heal themselves. I flushed my face with water and brushed my teeth before I stormed out of the room.

It was nine-thirty and I was prepared for the day with nowhere to go. No one was awake yet. By now, Ryder or Garrett would be up, but I didn't hear any indication of movement. Figuring payback was in order; I decided to wake Kate to see how she liked it. I walked past the kitchen, down the hall to the third door on the right. I listened for a moment to see if I could hear her stirring. I heard nothing.

With deliberate movements, I tried to stifle the squeaking of the door hinges. Kate sprawled across the bed on her stomach in pastel pink shorts and a white camisole, blankets tangled between her legs. Her face plastered to the pillow she drooled on, as her hair stuck to the side of her face. She was such a heavy sleeper which made her a perfect candidate for pranks, were I willing to expose myself to her sour mood for the rest of the day.

I tiptoed across the plush gray carpet until I came within leaping distance of her bed. I coiled my legs and sprang into the air, bouncing once on her bed before landing solid next to her. Kate jumped five feet in the air; panic spreading across her face before her eyes landed on mine.

"Ahh, Aurora! What the hell?" she growled. I gave her a smug smile.

"Payback!" I sang, holding my pointer finger up.

"For What?"

"For waking me up at five in the morning! I haven't been

able to sleep since, thank you very much," I said.

"You know. You can kind of be an asshole," she griped. I just continued smiling at her. She has never been a morning person.

"Touché!" I giggled. "So, you were saying you wanted to go to The Shack for lunch today?" I pressed on, not the least affected by her ratty hair or the mood that reflected it.

"Is that why you woke me up?" she asked, throwing her arm over her eyes with a sour face.

"Isn't that why you woke me up this morning?" I countered.

"No. I woke you up purely for medical reasons."

"Liar. And you know it," I said. She wouldn't budge from her reasoning but we both knew the truth. She continued to shield her eyes with her arm, but her lips were held in a tight line.

"So?" I pressed on.

"So what?" she spat, rubbing her eyes with the back of her hands.

"Get up. Get ready. By the time you're done, it'll be lunch," I stated, standing up to leave. It would take her forever to get moving, let alone get ready. Anytime she woke not of her own accord, she would always drag ass.

"Wait!" she said before I closed her door.

"Yeah?" I asked, peeking my head through the door.

"How are you feeling?" she asked, sleep still heavy in her voice.

"Peachy," I smiled at her. She smiled back before I closed the door.

My hand still throbbed; my head ached, but all things considering I was okay. The bruising around my wrist had turned to a black-purple overnight. That would be fun trying to explain away. However, I knew that wasn't the question she asked. I just wasn't willing to divulge that information.

I went to the kitchen and poured a glass of OJ. This was ritual. Growing up, our family went through more orange juice than any household in America.

Though Kate was up, the house remained silent, despite Garrett sawing logs down the hallway. I was fortunate my room was on the opposite side of the house. I claimed the master when we first moved here. Nobody protested.

I heard a door close and footsteps shuffling along the hardwood floor towards me. I expected to see Kate turn the corner when Ryder appeared, rubbing the sleep out of his eyes, yawning.

"Oh, hey Rore," he said, surprised to see me.

"Morning Ry."

"Morning," he said back, still half asleep.

"Let me see that," he gestured towards the carton of orange juice. I grabbed it and handed it to him. He didn't bother getting a glass. He opened it up and started chugging.

"Hey! You know there are others in this household who enjoy that carton. I don't think we want your added germs," I chided.

"Aurora. How long have we been siblings?" he asked.

"Too long," I joked.

"Funny. I have been drinking out of the carton since you were a tiny tot. I'd say you're immune to my germs by now," he remarked.

"Gross!" I said, scrunching my face in distaste.

"Get over it," he said, rolling his eyes before putting the carton back in the fridge.

"Get over what?" Kate asked, rounding the corner.

"I was just explaining to Aurora that she has been enjoying my germs from the OJ carton since she was a kid," he said matter of fact.

"Okay. Gross," Kate exclaimed.

"What? We're family. It's not like it's going to kill her," he said.

"Yeah. But I don't want to be enjoying your germs either. I drink out of that carton too," Kate scolded.

"Oh, you know you like my germs," Ryder grinned, dancing his eyebrows at her.

"I think I just threw up a little," Kate joked.

"Whatever. Stop acting like girls."

"Uh, last I checked, we are girls," I said with a pointed look.

"When was the last time you checked to see if Kate was a girl?" Ryder asked, smiling at me with his innuendo.

"Oh my gosh! That's not what I meant!" I screeched, hiding my face with my hands, blushing. They both sat back, laughing at me.

"You guys' suck!"

"That's what she said," Kate laughed, unable to contain herself.

"What is wrong with you two? You're both mental," I said, pushing away from the bar.

"Aww, c'mon! Where are ya going?" Ryder called out to me, still chuckling.

"Away from you until you both can control yourselves," I said walking away.

"Don't be mad. Come back," he laughed as he ran around the kitchen bar after me.

"Leave me alone!" I warned, staring at him in mock horror. When he closed in, I started running. I wasn't fast enough. He tackled me onto the couch and started pinching me.

"Ow! Ryder! Stop," I said, halfway laughing. All three of my brothers use to pin me down and pinch me when we were kids. They never pinched hard enough to hurt, just aggravate. It was their way to pester the young one.

"Are you going to give up and sit with us?" he asked, still pinching. Kate cackled at us, shaking her head.

"Yes!" I laughed until my stomach hurt. "Leave me alone!" I screamed out between laughs.

"Promise?" he pestered.

"Yes!"

"Okay then," he stated, standing to offer his hand. I gave him my uninjured one as he hoisted me up, tucking me under his arm like a football so I made good on my promise. He walked me over to my chair and took his earlier position in front of the bar.

"You're such a pain in the ass Ryder!" I chuckled.

"Likewise," he winked back.

"What time is it?" I asked Kate, glancing down at her rose gold Michael Kors watch.

"Ten Fifteen."

"What time do you want to go?" I asked.

"In about an hour," she said.

"Where are you guys going?" Ryder asked with a teasing tone.

"To The Shack. You wanna go?" Kate offered.

"Nah, I got plans," he said, shrugging it off.

"Oh yeah? What are you doing?" I pried.

"Band practice," he responded like he was talking about the weather, the corners of his mouth downturned.

"You sound amused," I observed.

"No. I am. It's just Derrick is acting like a jerk. We are ready to sign the papers to the label we want, and he is getting cold feet," he vented.

"Why is he getting cold feet?" Kate asked.

"I don't know," he grunted, "He is such a flake. We don't need him as a bass player. We have a perfect backup. Remember Connelly?" he asked before continuing. "Well, anyways, he always practices with us. He knows all of our songs and can play better than Derrick in his sleep."

"So, why don't you guys' kick Derrick out?" I asked.

"Because it's a split fifty-fifty vote. Not that Derrick knows that. Nick and I want him out. Jackson and Aaron want him in because they want to keep the original band together," he explained.

"Understandable. But if someone is holding the band back, it's better to cut the losses while you're ahead. I mean, you guys are ready to get signed! That's kind of a big deal!" I said.

"Yep. That's what we said. They don't get it," he agreed. Kate shook her head in agreement.

"Alright well, I'm going to get ready," Kate said, heading to her room.

"K," I replied.

"Later," Ryder said, still annoyed with his situation. He stood still for a moment, sliding his eyes towards me when we heard Kate's door click shut.

"Hey, promise me something," Ryder demanded.

"What's that?" I hesitated to say yes immediately.

"If you happen to run into that jackass again, don't try to fight him. Or stop him from fighting someone. Call me right away. I don't care what I'm in the middle of. I will be there," he stated, not taking his eyes from mine.

"I will," I replied, dropping my gaze. I knew I wouldn't. It wasn't that I thought they couldn't handle themselves, I knew they could. I didn't want to put them in that predicament.

"I mean it Aurora," Ryder warned, seeing my confliction.

"Yeah. Okay. I will," I stated firmly so he would believe me. I wasn't fooling anyone.

"You can be so stubborn sometimes. Just like Tanner," he

said, shaking his head. I flashed my eyes to him in surprise. We hadn't spoken a whisper of Tanner or our parents in years.

"Hey Ryder. Do you ever feel like you want to go home? You know, just to visit or something," I asked with hesitation. He regarded me for a moment and sighed.

"Yeah. Sometimes. You?" he asked with caution.

"Yeah. More so lately."

"Why is that?" he asked, curious.

"I don't know. For some reason I have been feeling a pull to go home. Just to visit I mean. Not permanently. I know we have created our lives here now," I said.

"Yeah. I know what you mean. I've felt it too," he remarked.

"What? Really?" I was surprised he felt the same.

"Yeah. I've been dismissing it, but I'd be lying if I didn't say it's becoming a nuisance. Maybe we will go soon, for a visit I mean. I can't explain it. Maybe it's just been too long," he shared.

"We can plan a trip soon," I offered.

"Yeah. Maybe," he said with reluctance.

We both knew how it was when we left. I became catatonic from the pain. I wouldn't respond to anyone for months; I didn't eat and hardly drank anything. Regret always gripped at my heart knowing what I put my brothers and Kate through. Not only did they lose our parents and Tanner, but they also lost their sister for a short while in the process.

When they made the choice to shut down the family ranch in Grants Pass and move away from our home in Brookings, I came alive and lashed out with a vicious rage. I did not want to leave. I wanted to hold onto them for as long as I could. Home was the only place I was able to do that. It was all I had left. Leaving home equaled to abandoning them, and their memory, in my mind.

I cried for days before retreating to my catatonic state when we moved to San Diego. I closed myself off in my new room, refusing to come out. I would just stare at the walls.

I remember crystal clear the day Kate came in and sat in front of me. She wouldn't budge from my line of sight. She firmly stated, "They're not coming back. You need to snap out of it. You have grieved long enough for them. We need you back here. We need our sister back. Please stop dying with them."

They had tried to talk to me so many times over those few months, but I couldn't hear a word they were saying. Nothing sank in. I only felt an immense void. My world stopped. When she said those words, time sped and I was reawakened. I emerged on the other side of despair not unscathed, but in the process of healing. I was still troubled by their loss, but it was not crippling like it had been for so many months.

"Hello! Earth to Aurora!" Kate said, snapping her fingers in front of my face. I blinked, turning to her.

"What?" I asked, unaware she was there. She flashed her eyes to Ryder, and then to me, incredulous.

"I've been standing here for the past minute calling your name," she said with disbelief.

"Oh sorry. I must have been daydreaming," I replied, feeling guilty for the direction my thoughts had turned.

"Must have been some daydream. Was it about Mr. Hottie Gavin?" she teased.

"Oh, shut up," I said rolling my eyes, smacking at her in the air. I didn't dare bring up to either of them what I was thinking about. It would worry them.

"Mr. Who?" Ryder asked defensive, playing the big brother role.

"You know. Gavin! The guy that stepped in when Tony was being a dumbass," Kate said.

"Oh!" awareness shot through him with a smile, "You got

the hots for him Rore?"

"You both are done. Are you ready to go to lunch?" I asked, dismissing them. They both laughed as Kate nodded her head.

"Fine. Let's go," I said sour, grabbing my purse. Ryder waved to us as we headed out the door.

We pulled up to The Carnitas Snack Shack, or The Shack for short, in Kate's Mean Green Machine – which backfired before she killed the ignition. I would have preferred to drive but she was so insistent on driving her beat up green Toyota Sentra, making the point she could park easier than I could.

She was in serious need of a new car. The tint on the back window was cracked; the paint was fading in some areas and missing altogether in others. She drove that thing all the way from Oregon; she loved it and would never part from it.

"When are you going to buy a new car?" I asked, rolling my eyes.

"Never," she stated.

"Kate, this thing is a rust bucket. The paint is chipping and fading. Even your window tint looks sad," I harped.

"Hey! No dishing on the green machine okay. This thing has gotten me through more than even you know, so love and cherish it like it's your own," she pointed her finger at me with narrowed eyes. I couldn't help but sigh in resignation.

"I don't know about loving it as if it's my own," I said, scrunching my nose.

"Just think. If something ever happens to me, this will be your inheritance," she beamed.

"No thanks," I deadpanned, rolling my eyes again.

I opened the door to a loud creak and the sound of metal

grinding against metal. There was no talking sense into her. I grabbed my purse and slammed the car door shut, only to watch a few more paint chips fall. I shook my head at Kate's grin, as she waited for me to join her.

"The only thing that car is good for is the scrap yard," I said.

"Pfft, whatever. Good thing it isn't yours then," she chided.

"Thank the heavens for that," I said towards the sky, raising up my free hand.

We sat at the only available table under the overhang. We ate here every other day it seemed. I'm surprised we didn't have a designated spot with our names on it.

"Next time it's my turn to choose where we eat," I said.

"Whatever. You like this place, and you know it," she smiled. I slid into the seat across from her.

"If you say so," I said, arching my right eyebrow. "This place is tasty, I'll give you that. I just prefer to change it up instead of eating at the same place every week," I amended. She shrugged, not caring either way.

"Are you coming home to get ready or going to Chris's tomorrow?" I asked. She usually goes to Chris's house before frat parties and picks me up on the way.

"Home. Chris is grabbing dinner with the guys before the party. He is picking us up after," she said, searching the menu. Chris plays shortstop at SDSU. He has been enjoying the freedom of being a Junior at Alpha Pi. He didn't have to set up the parties anymore.

The "guys" consisted of Aaron Blakely – Chris's best friend and Ryder's band mate, who Kate always tried to hook me up with. It has always been her dream we would date best friends.

There was Scott Livingston – the arrogant catcher. He was a man-whore. I wouldn't be surprised if he was catching more than baseballs.

Then there's Kenji Hoshito – the Japanese foreign exchange student. He spoke great English albeit with a heavy accent. This guy was fast and his swing powerful.

Last of the dynamic five was Elliot Spencer. Elliot and I went on a few dates when I first moved here. Things would have progressed further if it weren't for Tony. At times, I think Elliot still wasn't over it. But that was a whole other story.

All the guys went to high school here, never straying from their circle. You could say the bromance was strong with them.

The waitress came and we placed our orders. When she walked away, I turned to Kate's smiling, scrutinizing eyes.

"What?" I asked, dreading her incoming string of questions. I knew her looks. I was not fond of this one.

"So, Gavin huh?"

"Are you still on that? What about him? Do you know him?" I asked nonchalant.

"No," she said terse, "But you were giddy when you talked about him yesterday." She observed my expression close, "And you were blushing this morning when his name was brought up!"

Seriously, she never quit.

"Kate. I told you. I don't even know him. It seemed like he was there for a split second and then he was gone," I dismissed her questioning. I should know better than to try to brush her off.

"But he was there long enough to make an impact," she stated.

"Not really," I said, taking a sip of my Dr. Pepper.

"Not really? So that means he did. Tell me about him," she pried.

"I. Do Not. Know Him. Kate. Other than physicality's."

She wasn't amused. "Spill it."

"Alright! I'm only telling you this because you scare the hell out of me," I rolled my eyes at her.

I brought up a vision of him in my mind, thinking about what stood out to me the most, "It goes beyond the physical. I have never met someone I instantly felt safe with."

The storm in his deep emerald eyes when he picked me up from the asphalt last night burned brilliant in my mind's eye. I could still feel the ghost of his strong arms holding me when I had been at my most vulnerable. I had this longing to feel them once again.

"And it's not just because of how easy he dealt with Tony either. It's the way he carries himself. He has this aura of confidence and strength that doesn't let you even question his abilities. Like I said, I don't even know him so what do I know," I said, dismissing everything.

Kate stared at me with a huge grin, "What attracts you the most?" She wasn't going to stop at simple details. She wanted every detail. Ugh!

"I don't know Kate. I don't even know if it's the physical I'm drawn to. I mean, I'm not drawn to him drawn to him. I think it's more of the fact he helped me when I was about to be left in a ditch somewhere, according to Tony's words," I said in a rush.

She nodded, fuming in silence, "I swear Aurora, if I see Tony it isn't going to be pretty." I gave her a tight-lipped smile. What could I say?

"Let's lay off of the heavy for now, okay?" she asked, giving me a slight smile. I know she wanted to take my mind away from last night, and maybe hers too.

"Yeah. Sounds good to me," I answered.

"So, tell me, you can't be oblivious to Gavin's charm. Or how in shape he is! I mean, did you see his biceps?" she whistled.

I blushed. "He is the same height as Tony give an inch or so, but in way better shape."

"Is that even possible?" Kate giggled.

"I didn't think so until I met him," I laughed a bit giddy.

"It sucks you weren't able to get his number," she said, bummed.

"Whatever. It is what it is. He left the hospital so fast, I never really had the chance," I said. Kate gave me a disbelieving look but dropped it. Thankfully.

It was still a mystery to me why Gavin was there last night when the parking lot was deserted. Don't get me wrong, I'm thankful he was there. There is no telling where I would be right now if he wasn't. Tony was completely unhinged.

"You should have seen Tony last night Kate. He wasn't right," I said, shaking my head, dismissing her earlier request to lay off the heavy. How could I not? It was on constant replay in my head.

"Tony is lucky I wasn't there to see it," she threatened. Sometimes I wondered if she could act out on her threats. I had never seen it, but she always put such strong promise behind them.

"Afternoon ladies. Aurora. Mind if I join you?"

I glanced towards the new, but now familiar, voice that had been infiltrating my subconscious. At the end of our table stood the main topic of our conversation. Kate's mouth dropped before turning up into her Cheshire grin; I felt like my expression mirrored hers.

I checked my composure.

My mouth didn't hang open quite like Kate's but I'm sure my body language wasn't helping me.

"Of course, Gavin. Join us," she said, grinning when I didn't respond. I kicked her under the table. She wasn't supposed to know his name. Now he will know I had been talking about him.

His emerald eyes smiled at me as I scooted over for him to sit. His black short sleeve shirt exposed strange, tattooed script etched down the length of his arm.

"Aurora, I wanted to apologize about yesterday. I didn't mean to walk out like that," he began explaining.

"Oh, it's fine. You do not have to explain anything to me," I assured him. I glanced over at Kate who was coming apart at the seams.

"Aren't you going to introduce me to your friend, Aurora?" she asked, grinning.

"Kate this is Gavin. Gavin, Kate," I gestured with my hand back and forth as I introduced them. I went for polite, but my voice fell flat.

"Pleasure to meet you," Gavin smiled at her.

"Likewise," Kate smiled back at him. I couldn't put my finger on it, but something with their exchange held a hint of familiarity.

"What are you ladies up to?" he asked as our food arrived. We both ordered the pulled pork sandwich but with Gavin sitting next to me, I was too jittery to eat. My body had become hyperaware of his presence. His cologne wafted off him in waves - fresh hints of rosemary, fruity persimmon, Patchouli with undertones of the ocean and slight musk. Its heady scent made my head spin.

"We were just discussing the Alpha Pi party this Saturday," Kate stated as if it were common knowledge.

"I heard about it," he acknowledged nonchalant. How was that possible? Did he go to SDSU?

"You did?" I asked, surprised. He didn't seem like the frat party type to me. Nor did I know he went to SDSU. It caught me off guard.

"Yeah, of course. I don't live under a rock," he chuckled.

My cheeks reddened as I turned my attention to pick at my food. I lifted my eyes to Kate giving him a strange look. I didn't know what to make of it, but I did know how overprotective she could be. She wouldn't have a problem voicing her displeasure at things said, strangers be damned.

"Are you going Gavin?" Kate asked, her voice thick with implication.

"Yeah, I don't do the frat thing," Gavin stated. He seemed uncomfortable with the question. I had to say, I was relieved he would not be there. I knew I would be making some bad choices in the drinking department, and I did not want him to see me like that. Why I cared so much was a mystery to me.

"I don't do the frat thing either," I said, shooting daggers at Kate. If it weren't for her, I wouldn't even be going to this stupid party. As it was, the only way to make it even worth half a damn was to consume as many free drinks from them as possible.

"Aurora, you're coming regardless. You do not get a choice," Kate said with a devious grin. I knew she had something up her sleeve.

Sensing Gavin's gaze, I glanced up to meet his entrancing smirk. Heat flushed my cheeks. How could a look render me so speechless?

"Well, I guess I could make an exception if you're going," he said, changing his mind.

"You don't have to go because of me. The only reason I'm going is because apparently I don't have a choice," I replied.

"There is always a choice Aurora," he said, too serious for our light banter.

"Not if you're Kate," I said, shooting daggers in her direction.

"That settles it then. We will see you there," Kate laughed, elated.

"I guess that settles it then," he looked at Kate like she was a pain in the ass. He caught on quick.

"Great! We will meet you there?" Kate offered, all too happy to play matchmaker.

"I'll let you ladies get back to your meal. I will see you tomorrow night," he said, winking at me, as he stood up and made his way towards his black sports car. I wasn't a car enthusiast, but I could tell it was of the classic variety.

I followed his movements as he put on his sunglasses and slid into the driver seat before speeding off like he was in some James Dean movie. Rebel without a cause!

I turned back to Kate grinning from ear to ear. "What the hell was that, Kate?"

"That was you needing to thank me for hooking you up," she said, pleased with a job well done.

"Thank you? You practically fed me to the wolves!" I shrieked, embarrassed by the whole exchange. "Newsflash, I do not need you to be hooking me up with random guys I have never met before."

"What wolves? You have met him before," she countered, furrowing her brows.

"A hospital trip doesn't count," I disapproved.

"You were too intimidated to ask him to the party yourself. I did you a favor," she said, pleased with herself. "You should be thanking me."

"Don't do that. Do not try to play matchmaker. I shouldn't have to remind you I broke up with a psycho a few weeks ago who put me in the hospital last night," I said, reminding her anyways.

"Fine. No matchmaker. But I can't promise you I won't be secretly wishing and watching in the distance. He's hot," she said, pushing her bottom lip out.

"Creeper. Mind your own business. Eat your sandwich," I said, narrowing my eyes at her. She smiled, taking too big of a bite. I laughed, shaking my head. There was never a dull moment with Kate, that's for sure.

Chapter Five

PARTY

"Maybe self-improvement isn't the answer, maybe self-destruction is the answer." — Chuck Palahniuk, Fight Club

***

Saturday night came all too soon. Kate and I were getting ready while Chris waited in the living room for us to finish.

Wearing the black halter, jeans, and black stiletto ensemble she purchased earlier in the week, she let her platinum blonde hair cascade down in loose ringlets. She looked perfect as she always did. I chose to keep my auburn hair straight but played up the make up with a cat-eye.

"Let's get this party started," Kate cried out. When we walked out of the room, Chris's jaw dropped. He couldn't take his eyes off her.

"You look stunning," he praised. Kate let out a girlish giggle as I gagged in my mind. It would be a party for two if I weren't here. She had someone she was so infatuated with, and he with her. Tony and I had never been that close.

"Why, thank you!" she blushed. "Now let's go P-A-R-T-Y!" We jumped into Chris's 1968 Canary Yellow Malibu before peeling away like a bat out of hell from our house.

Pulling up to Alpha Pi, a line of people waited to get inside. The place had to be filled to capacity. Walking past the line, a group of girls were screaming 'give-me-attention' with their skimpy attire and propensity for falling into a drag queens make-up box. Didn't they know they had all the right parts for a drunken frat fool to not even care about their clown make up?

Sure, I played up a cat eye, but they caked on the frosting. The guys waiting in line enjoyed the eye candy as they flexed their testosterone to anyone they felt threatened by.

As we took our cuts at the door, Chris slapped hands with Eric who was acting bouncer for the evening. It didn't go unnoticed, the line behind us pissed and moaned we were able to walk in without restrictions. The blaring music drowned them out soon enough as we made it into the room that had become a makeshift dance floor.

The hallways and walkways were crowded shoulder-to-shoulder with people. This was why I loathed these stupid parties. Too many people who moved like cattle in a sardine can.

Finally, we made it to the back of the house where there was more space to move, but not by much. Chris pecked Kate on the cheek before bounding over towards Aaron, Elliot, and the rest of the crew surrounding the cornhole games.

"Keg's that way," Kate pointed to where the football players were all crowding. "Let's go!" she grinned as she grabbed my uninjured hand so we wouldn't be separated.

I spotted Tony the same time he had spotted me. He stood off to the side with a red solo cup in hand and a solid black eye, chatting with a group of guys as if nothing ever happened. He turned away from me and back to his group. Well, two could play that game.

Kate turned to me with wide eyes. "I swear Aurora, I didn't know he was going to be here. We can go if you want," she said.

A part of me wanted to leave.

The other part of me, the more stubborn and dominant part, wanted to stay and have a good time. It wasn't fair to me that I should leave just because he happened to be here. Forget the fact I didn't want to be here in the first place.

"No. It's fine Kate. I'm not going to let my life revolve around him," I said. I refused to let him have the upper hand in my life.

"Good. If he so much as breathes your way, I will karate chop him in the balls," she seethed with pure hate as she shot daggers in his direction. I laughed because I could picture her doing it.

Greg, SDSU's football sweetheart, manned the keg, pouring both of us a drink when we walked up. I could feel Tony eyeing my way, but I did my best not to pay attention and just enjoy the moment. I grabbed my beer and pounded it.

"Woohoo Aurora!" Kate cheered me on. I handed my cup back to Greg who grinned at me as he poured my second cup. I returned a flirtatious smile; very aware Tony was watching my every move.

I didn't care if it made him jealous. I wanted it to. I wanted him to see what his ridiculous behavior gave up. Maybe it was petty, but I wanted to dig at him anyway I could. Kate chugged her beer to keep up with me and handed it back to Greg.

"You girls can drink like champs. Keep drinking like that, you're going to pass out before midnight," Greg laughed.

"Are you kidding Greg? Rory and I here are party champions. We could drink you under the table," Kate challenged him.

I glanced between them both with wide eyes. While Kate and I could hold our own, I didn't think Greg would've been a bet I wanted to take on. He's a towering six-foot-four and solid body mass. There wasn't much he couldn't take.

"We'll see how well you're standing by the end of the night," Greg challenged back.

"Is that a bet Mr. McGuire?" Kate asked playfully, excited to the challenge.

"Sure is. A hundred bucks says you aren't standing by the end of the night," he said.

"A hundred bucks a piece says we are. You lack faith Greg," Kate said, shaking her head in mock sadness. "Now pour me another!"

Greg laughed as he refilled her cup. "I can't wait. I'll be two hundred dollars richer by the end of the night!"

"Correction Greg. You'll be two hundred dollars poorer by the end of the evening," Kate smirked. "Let's dance!" she shrieked as she pulled me back towards the house.

Kate dragged us into the middle of the makeshift dance floor, flailing her arms in the air to the beat of 'Moves Like Mick Jagger' by Maroon Five. The strobe light flashed and froze the movements around us in a dizzying array of snapshots. I shut my eyes, dancing to the rhythm of everyone around us.

Jase came up behind me as we swayed our hips together in harmony. I spun around, caressing my arms around his neck, moving my body against his. He squeezed his fingers against my hip to pull me closer – our legs making their way between each other's to bring us closer. Sweat beaded down my neck, the friction and ambient temperature from all the bodies in the room not helping the matter.

From an outside perspective, Jase and I probably looked like we would be hooking up tonight. I'm sure this wouldn't help Tony's suspicions of me cheating. What did I care though? Regardless, I made sure to keep my feelings in check with Jase. He can be fun and smooth when he wanted to be.

Jase had been my first guy friend when I moved here. He tried to make a pass when we first met but I made it clear we were only friends. Luckily, he wasn't the thin-skinned type. He understood and we stayed friends.

The song ended and I gave him a hug. "Thanks for the dance, Jase. I need to grab a drink," I yelled over the next song. He nodded his head to the beat and moved on to the next single girl he could find on the floor.

I turned to Kate and motioned for another drink. She bounced her head to the beat with her best duck face, following me out. I couldn't help but laugh.

A gush of air hit us as we walked out of the sauna house. It was refreshing yet sent chills throughout my body. Greg still guarded the keg, manning his station. The frat guys must have split duties amongst themselves.

"Ah ladies, back for more?" he grinned.

"Damn straight," Kate grinned wide, handing him our cups. He filled up three cups and handed us each one.

"Alright," Greg said, "Ready to chug? One! Two! Three! GO!" All three of us raced to finish first.

Greg threw his cup down right before me, yelling out he was the victor. Kate finished after me. I could see what Greg was doing. He was making sure we were good and tanked before the night was through, but I refused to let him win.

"I'm just warming up. A war is not won by trying to finish first," Kate said, sour faced.

"Oh Kate. You haven't even entered the battle yet sweetheart. Await to be annihilated!" Greg laughed his boisterous laugh, enjoying his first victory.

"You won by a slight margin Greg. I would hardly say it's a full-scale victory if you ask me," I laughed.

"Right Aurora," he drawled. "You wanna go again? Best two out of three? This time we'll have someone watch it for us. Kenji! Get your ass over here!" he hollered to his teammate. Kenji left his small group and sauntered over to us.

"Listen up, I need you to watch this and tell us who wins. These girls think they can take me in a drinking match," Greg laughed.

Kenji turned to us and laughed, "You're kidding right?"

"Nope. The funny thing is he thinks he can win," Kate said with confidence.

"Alright. Your funeral," Kenji shook his head.

Greg refilled our drinks, "Okay, we are starting over. This is best two out of three. The winner gets fifty bucks." With the terms of the challenge agreed upon, Greg, Kate, and I took our challenger stance.

Kenji turned to us with stone-faced concentration, flipping his black and white Yankees hat backwards. "Players get ready. On your mark. Get Set! CHUG!" All three of us immediately put the cups to our faces and began chugging. I took five big gulps before throwing down my cup at the same time Greg did. Kate was close behind.

"AURORA WINS ROUND ONE!" Kenji yelled like he was a ring announcer. People started gathering around us to join in on the excitement. A few people placed their bets, weighing in mostly on Greg than either of us. That's fine. I didn't mind us being the underdogs. Greg eyed me with speculation while I smiled at him with a devilish grin, as he refilled our drinks.

"Damn girl, you know how to throw 'em back!" Kenji said, smiling. I gave him a smirk. How little did he know – just because I'm a girl, doesn't mean I'm a rookie. Kate and I had been underestimated at all our high school parties.

"We are back and ready for round two!" Kenji swung his right arm forward with his hand in the form of a peace sign, signifying what round we were in. "Players ready! Get Set! CHUG!" We tossed them back again. I tried chugging bigger amounts than the first, but Greg beat me by a second. "Greg is the winner of round two! We are betting for two out of three here folks! Who'll win?"

I glanced at Greg then to Kate who stood in full concentration mode. You would think we were fighting to the death or something. Greg refilled our cups and handed them back to us.

"Alright you three! This is it! Are you ready? One! Two! Three! CHUG!" I chugged as fast as I could, beginning to feel the effects from the rush of alcohol in my system as my teeth became numb. I finished my cup right after Kate. She finally finished warming up. It always took her a minute or two.

"OH MY GOD! OH MY GOD! I CAN'T BELIEVE IT! We have a three-way sudden death match her folks! I've never seen this in my life! Two girls against San Diego States very own linebacker! Who's going to win?" Kenji went crazy, jumping up and down, riling up the crowd. Money exchanged hands while Greg filled up our cups. He stared at us with sheer determination, zero trace of humor on his face any longer.

"Aight playa's! Listen up! Since we have never had a three-way sudden death match before, we are going to do something special. Whoever is the victor in today's drink off will be dubbed 'Frat House Victor' for a year! Now, are you ready?"

All three of us stared each other down while the crowd cheered on who they wanted to win. It seemed minds had changed as the crowd felt their odds had evened amongst the three of us.

"Ready! Set! CHUG!" Kenji yelled.

Furiously, we lifted our cups and chugged, not one of us hesitating to slow down before smashing our cups to the ground at the same time. It was so close, did any of us even win or was it a tie? I didn't think I would be able to do another round of this.

Sure, I could put them back but not this much in such a short amount of time.

We glanced at each other before turning to Kenji. He was being dramatic, staying silent for a long pause before exploding into an uproar. "AURORA IS THE FRAT HOUSE VICTOR! I CANNOT BELIEVE IT!" He jumped up and down, grabbing his head as he lifted his hat, throwing it to the ground.

I was stunned. I knew Kate and I could throw some back but never did I think we could take Greg on.

Greg picked me up and set me on top of his shoulders, parading me around through the crowd. I couldn't help but laugh as everyone cheered me on, chanting my name. Tony stood on the fringe of the crowd, his expression darkening. I couldn't pay him any mind though. I was thoroughly enjoying my victory. We circled back towards the keg as Greg set me down next to Kate.

"Great job Rory. I knew you had it in you. At least one of us had to win," she cheered and sulked at the same time. She hated losing. Turning back to Greg, she said, "see Greg, what did I tell you?" She grinned at him with a brazen look on her face.

"You were right Kate. I will never question you again," he laughed.

"And don't you forget it," she stated.

"We still have a bet though. You both have to be standing," Greg said, hoping to restore his ego, as he pulled out his wallet to ante up the fifty bucks I won.

"You haven't learned. Prepare to be broke Greg," Kate shook her head at him in mock sadness, pulling me back towards the house for a victory dance.

Stepping onto the dance floor, I could feel the rush of alcohol coursing through my bloodstream. My body felt energized by the win, and I let myself ride on that high – feeling alive for the first time in a long time.

I closed my eyes, allowing the music's rhythm to beat

through me as I moved with it. A pair of hands came up behind me, moving along my waist. Soon, the proximity of our bodies danced in sync. Not bothering to open my eyes, I moved along with Jase's smooth moves.

When I opened my eyes, Kate was staring daggers behind me. I turned to see it wasn't Jase as I had anticipated but Tony. Recoiling in disgust, I smacked him hard across the face as I whipped around. Even with the music blaring, it was deafening.

I ran towards the backyard where Greg was. Not only did I need a drink, but I knew Tony wouldn't try anything with him around. Greg handed me a clean cup and I chugged it back, my heart fluttering as I stared at the door.

"You're determined, aren't you?" Greg teased.

"Determined for what?" I asked, half annoyed.

"Paying up," he smiled, wiggling his eyebrows.

"Greg, it would take thirty of these to knock me out. Trust me, I know," I said looking at him from beneath my lashes. I could hear myself slurring but I still had my wits about me. Okay, so I exaggerated on the thirty cups, but I knew my limits.

"If you say so Aurora," Greg chuckled, hearing the bravado in my voice for what it was.

"Well, I do," I smiled back at him.

With a full cup, I sat beside the huge fire ring. It could easily sit fifteen people around it. The guys had set up makeshift seats with hay bales covered in thick Mexican blankets. A few couples sat across from me, as did a lone guy with a hood over his head, concealing his face.

"What the hell is your problem?" Tony hollered. I turned to him as he stormed towards me, his nose bandaged and eye blackened. I sighed, not wanting to rehash this shit show again.

"Other than you, I don't have one. Leave me alone," I snapped.

"No. We were dancing, and everything was fine. Then you just turn around and slap me, hard by the way," he seethed.

"Clearly you have amnesia. You put me in the hospital Tony. Did you forget that one?" I said, lifting my bandaged wrist. "And I didn't know it was you I was dancing with until I turned around, or I would have never let you get that close to me," I spat.

"Aurora. I didn't mean to hurt you," he said apologetic - all former anger gone. His mood swings were making my head spin.

"Save your apology for someone who cares. It's been fun," I dismissed as I stood to walk away. He put himself in my direct path. When I tried to walk around him, he blocked me. Not this again. At least there were more people here this time.

"Tony. Get OUT of my WAY!" I screamed at him. I figured if I made enough of a scene and attracted the attention from the other partiers, I could avoid another domestic violence case.

"I can't Aurora. You're all I think about. I know I've made a mess of everything—"

"You've got that right," I said with disgust, "Now move."

"Let's just talk this out, like two normal people. I don't know how or why I'm hearing all these rumors between you and Brad. Honestly, I don't even know what's true and what's not anymore. I'm losing my mind here," he said.

This admission disturbed him; the turmoil was evident on his face. He stayed in my way, staring into my eyes, as if trying to will an understanding from me. I was too heated to even begin to let that work on me.

"Tony, I do not want to talk things out. We are past that point. I don't even want to be near you, waiting for you to snap, only to send me back to the hospital. I'm done here. You need to leave me alone," I stared at him, willing him to leave. He flinched at the reminder.

"I told you I was sorry. Why do you keep bringing it up?"

he asked, his agitation visible. "It's all because of that asshole we are in this situation. Do you know him? Is that who you cheated on me with?" he began accusing again, this time bringing Gavin into the mix.

"Let me guess, I would be that asshole in question?"

I jolted at Gavin's voice over my right shoulder. I turned to see him standing next to me with unwavering confidence. He had the same smirk on his face from the other night when he and Tony had their confrontation. I'd be lying if I didn't say I felt relieved knowing I stood on Gavin's side of the dividing line.

"Great guess. You're fast," Tony taunted.

"How's the nose?" Gavin smirked, pointing to his bandaged nose.

"Very funny jackass. Thanks for reminding me that a payback is in order," Tony said, taking a step towards us.

"I'd like to go out on a limb here and say you aren't very bright, are you boy?" Gavin asked, placing a gentle hand around my arm to pull me behind him as he matched Tony's forward step.

"Who are you calling boy?" Tony spat, his voice high and tight. He took another step towards us as Gavin matched his step forward. Two more steps in and they would be in boxing range.

"Well, that answers my question," Gavin said. "Save yourself the trouble and run along. Things will only end badly for you here."

I froze like a statue, watching two grown men argue like they were in a schoolyard fight. Déjà vu hit all over again as my mind flashed to the other night when this same scenario played out in the parking lot.

"Boys. I don't think we need to rehash old arguments. What's done is done," a feline-like voice purred from behind Tony.

I couldn't place the voice to a face, as Tony blocked her,

until Emily appeared touching his chest. He relaxed back into his old self as if nothing had happened. What the hell? The power Emily wielded over Tony was borderline magical. If I had any suspicions that she had something to do with the way Tony had been behaving, I now had zero doubts.

Her cropped, jet-black hair and pale features were more distinct in the dark with only the light from the bonfire showing any signs of color on her face. Her dark jeans and black, low-cut top left little to the imagination. Her vixen attitude only backed this fact up.

The impish grin vanished from Gavin's face, replaced with a stone-cold murderous stare.

"Emily. What a pleasant surprise," Gavin said with a tone that said he wasn't surprised at all. I glanced at him in shock that he knew her.

"Gavin! Old Friend. How are you these days? Still looking after things that don't concern you?" she said full of malice, as she shot me a dirty glance.

My blood had been simmering beneath the surface at the very sight of her, but now knowing she has been doing everything within her power to inconvenience my life, it began to boil. She turned back to Gavin as she worked her way between him and Tony.

Leaving one hand on Tony's chest, she reached out to Gavin with the other. If this had bothered Tony, he didn't show it.

Gavin stepped back with utter disgust. "Do not touch me. You'll be sorry you had."

"Oh Gavin. Touchy. Don't tempt me. You were always so arousing when you denied your feelings for me. Kind of like you're doing right now," Emily purred in her most cunning voice.

I glared at her with absolute hatred. I began to see red with thoughts of ripping her head from her very shoulders clouding my vision. With her being on a first name basis with Gavin, it added to the rage that fast built inside of me.

None of this made sense – she knew Gavin well it seemed, but how did Tony come into this equation? I didn't understand how it all fit.

"Why don't you take your pet and go make someone else's life miserable. You know you're not welcomed here," Gavin said with insult.

"Oh, why I fully intend to," Emily said, sneering at me with an evil, mischievous grin. "I heard you ladies arguing over here and came to grab my toy. He's obviously not wanted amongst you two," she pointed between us as she began doting on him like a mother protecting her child.

Tony remained silent as I remained stunned. He didn't care to talk over her or speak on his own behalf. It's like he was a puppet, and she was the master puppeteer.

"You're correct. Run along now and do your best to keep your pet on a short leash. We wouldn't want anything to happen to your new toy now, would we?" Gavin said.

"You wouldn't dare Gavin and you know it," she said in mock anger as she grabbed Tony's hand, walking away with him. Mental images of them together started flashing in my mind and it was all I could do to block them from my brain.

"Remember Gavin, hell hath no fury like a woman's scorn. You'll do your best to remember that," Emily warned over her shoulder.

"You want to talk about a woman's scorn? You just earned mine you two-bit whore!" I yelled after her. I couldn't help myself. I had stood here seething for far too long. My body pulsed with adrenaline, ready for a fight. All I wanted was to rip her to shreds. I reveled in the feeling.

"Oh honey, that's cute. Just be a good girl and speak when

spoken to," she chided like I was some child throwing a tantrum.

"Are you kidding me?" I yelled, propelling myself forward before Gavin crossed his hand over my torso to hold me back.

"Drop it, Aurora. She isn't worth it. Trust me," he said through narrowed eyes as he stared at Emily's retreating back. Emily's response was to laugh – loud – as she continued to walk away with Tony in tow.

I stepped away from Gavin and glared at him. Whatever it was I just witnessed, I knew he couldn't be trusted. I knew nothing about him, yet now knew I was missing some vital information, which set my internal alarms raging.

We stood, staring at each other, testing the mood in the air between us. I had enough. I needed a drink since I kicked mine over trying to walk away from Tony.

As I walked past Gavin, he reached out to catch my arm, but I flinched away from him.

I'm pissed, my teeth are numb, and I'm tired of dealing with bullshit. For one night, I thought I could let loose. I stood corrected.

"Where are you going?" he asked.

"I need a drink. This has been just peachy," I answered, sardonic, before twisting my ankle on the uneven ground, falling to my hands and knees.

"Here, let me help you," he said, reaching down to lend me a hand. Embarrassed, and annoyed with him, I ignored the gesture and stood up on my own.

"Oh, thank you my knight in shining armor. How did you know I was in the market for a bodyguard?" I said sourly.

I couldn't understand how he kept appearing conveniently out of nowhere wherever Tony was concerned. For all I knew, Gavin was a stalker, which only meant I was in much more trouble than the problems Tony presented. What other conclusion could I possibly come to? I didn't know anything about him, and he made it damn hard to find out. Not to mention, he knew the enemy!

"I had my suspicions," he answered.

"It was a rhetorical question," I glanced at him, unamused.

Greg was leaning against the tree, eyeing Gavin next to me as we walked up. "Hey Greg, can you grab me one?" I asked.

"For you Frat House Victor, anything," he said as he bowed, grabbing me a cup. Greg kept glancing at Gavin, whether to size him up or figure out who he was, I couldn't be sure.

"Frat House Victor huh? How did you manage that title?" Gavin asked, curious.

Greg handed me the cup and I chugged it, handing the cup back to Greg for a refill. "That's how," I said, answering his question. I knew I reached my limit. As it sat, my reality was already unbalanced from my consumption. Anymore, I would be paying back Greg his fifty and then some. I took the refilled cup and turned back to the bonfire.

"Hey, why don't you slow down there," Gavin voiced his concern over my heavy drinking.

"Look. While I appreciate you showing up out of the blue every time Tony shows up, I don't need your advice on how to live my life," I snapped.

"Yeah, I can see that," he chided with disapproval. I plopped down on one of the blanketed haystacks laid out next to the fire. He hesitated before sitting next to me.

"What is it with you anyways? Why do you care?" I spat.

"What if I was just a friend looking out for you? And I told you that you were making a big mistake drinking so much?"

"Oh, you want to be friends? That would require knowing something about you apart from your name. For all I know, you could be a stalker," I blurted out, throwing my hand up in the air before letting it slap down on my thigh. I glanced over to see a grimace plastered on his face.

"But if you want to talk about being friends as merely a subjective topic, I will tell you to mind your own damn business and stay the hell out of mine." I eyed him with the continued annoyance I felt towards him, Tony, Emily and the whole damn situation.

He sat in silence, staring into the fire, not making any attempt to defend himself. I had to admit, I did feel bad for being such a jerk to him. With everything going on, I couldn't handle it anymore. What just happened between him and Emily was too much.

"Look, I'm sorry. I'm just," I sighed, searching for the right word, "frustrated I guess." It wasn't quite the word I wanted but to my alcohol-induced mind, it would have to do.

"No. It's fine. I understand," he said.

"I thought you said you didn't do the Frat thing?" I asked him with a raised eyebrow. He glanced at me before smiling and sighed.

"I guess you could say I was morbidly curious. Besides, I heard there were some hot women here," he smiled back at me.

"Oh. There is. Take your pick of any of the brainless twits flitting around here. I'm sure they would be more than happy to offer themselves to you," I said with more bite than I intended. Was he serious?

"Well, I'm sure I could," he leaned back, kicking out his feet and placing his hands behind his head, "but I already have my eyes set on someone who doesn't compare to these 'twits'," he smirked, as he gave me a side eye.

"Hm. Lucky girl," I rolled my eyes.

"Oh. She definitely is," he chuckled.

"You know, I don't buy it," I said.

"You don't buy what?" he asked, puzzled.

"The 'bad boy' bravado. You act so different around me than you do around others. Why is that?" I asked one of the burning questions that had been circling in my head since he had appeared at 'The Shack'.

He turned away from the fire and locked his eyes with mine. "Because you're different. You're not like the others. I know you can see past petty things and how flattery would come off as fake. I don't know how to act around you, but I also feel more like myself around you. I want you to know me but I'm afraid it'll only push you away," he explained.

"You wouldn't push me away. I've met you all of three times and you haven't even given me a chance," I said. I didn't understand how he could come to such a negative conclusion.

"Trust me. If you knew me, you wouldn't like me," he said, somber.

"Why don't you let me be the judge of that? From what I've seen, apart from your attitude, I like what little I do know," I stated with honesty.

I earned a grin from him at this admission, which warmed my numb heart. "Why don't I take you home? It's late," he said.

"Oh crap. What time is it?"

"Two thirty," he said without checking his watch.

"How do you know? You didn't look," I questioned, skeptical, as I pulled out my phone from my back pocket. The light illuminated two-thirty on my screen. I glanced up at him through squinted eyes. Something was very fishy about him.

"I told you," He laughed.

"How did you know that?" I asked.

"I'm psychic," he joked.

"Right," I said, rolling my eyes, "I know so little about you that I might take you seriously. Watch how you joke. Anyways, I need to find Chris and Kate. They're my ride home."

Standing up, I felt the rush of my surroundings flash by my

vision as I headed towards the house, causing my numb leg to misstep. Before the earth came crashing into my face, Gavin's arms wrapped around my torso, saving me from yet another embarrassing landing.

"Whoa. Easy there," he said, locking his gaze with mine as he continued holding me in his arms, our faces intimately closer than I realized. I righted myself with flushed cheeks.

"Um thanks. I think my legs are a little stiff," I said, gesturing with my hand like it were nothing. We both knew the real reason. I had well surpassed my drinking limit. Thankfully, he didn't comment further but humored my ignorance.

"Yeah. Mine too," he laughed. The party had quieted down over the past hour. There were more people passed out on the stairs and puking in the rose bushes than having a dance party in the living room. I found Chris walking towards the front door with a tossed Kate.

"Kate!" I yelled. She turned around with a slackened face.

"Thur yous ars. Wheresss yous been? Wes been looking all over furs you!" she slurred in Chris's arms as she gestured her hands out wide. I couldn't help but giggle. Drunken Kate always amused me.

"Sorry Kate. I was talking to Gavin by the fire," I said back to her.

"Gavin! Oh, yous keep talkin' to him. He's hot! Oh, Hi Gavin," she said without the least bit of embarrassment. Gavin chuckled, both annoyed and amused at the same time. Chris on the other hand eyed Gavin up and down, not amused with Kate's 'hot' statement.

"Hi Kate," Gavin chuckled again, lifting his hand in gesture.

"You ready Rory. I need to get her to bed," Chris asked, as Kate passed out in his arms.

"Um, yeah. I'm ready," I said, glancing at Gavin, "Well, I -,"

"Do you mind if I take her home? I mean, if that is alright with you?" he looked away from Chris to me for approval, cutting me off.

"Uh, yeah. Sure. I don't mind," I said, smiling up at him. I turned to Chris who eyed me as if trying to decide to agree to this.

"Okay. I'll see you back at the house," Chris said, shuffling under the weight of Kate in his arms. The undercurrent of a warning was meant for Gavin not to try anything funny. I should've been more worried about allowing a stranger, who I practically called a stalker, take me home - but I wasn't. I deduced that if he were going to kill me, or cause me harm, he wouldn't keep trying to save me from Tony.

"So where to?" I asked as we walked outside. I didn't know where he parked his car.

"How far is your house?" he asked.

"It's only three blocks that way," I said, throwing my thumb over my shoulder.

"Do you mind if we walk then?" he requested. That's odd. Didn't he drive here?

"Sure," I said, not sure at all.

"Lead the way," he gestured past me. We began walking in awkward silence as question after question wracked around my brain. They weren't the easiest to ask but I wasn't sure if I would have another opportunity. I had to strike while the iron was hot.

"So, do you make it a habit of rescuing girls from their crazy ex-boyfriends?" I blurted out. I hated to bring our talk to a negative topic, but I needed answers and I swore to myself I would get them. I peeked over, expecting to see him offended but was met with a smirk instead.

"Oh yeah. All the time. It's a career choice," he teased.

"Ha. Ha. Very funny. Seriously though, what made you decide to be my valiant knight? And I'm not talking about the first time we met at my work. I didn't realize it was you sitting there alone at the bonfire until you were standing next to me," I said, hoping for a serious answer this time.

"On the contrary, I sat there minding my own business because I don't like crowds. I just so happened to pick a time and place where a show was about to unfold. It wasn't like you two were speaking in privacy or anything. I'm sure half of the party heard your love quarrel," he said without masking the humor in his voice. Why does he always have to go douche mode when it was unwarranted?

"I'm glad you find my drama amusing. I'll make sure to keep it down next time so you won't feel the need to interject," I spat back with pure annoyance. I couldn't believe I was wasting my time with someone who carried the same jerk traits as Garrett.

"I'm sorry. I didn't mean to offend you. I'm not saying I'm not right, but I am sorry. It's rude of me," he smiled with a soft glow in his eyes. Despite his arrogance, I felt myself getting lost in them as I struggled to pull away.

"Why stop now? You're on a roll," I stated.

I couldn't believe I subjected myself to this. Here I thought I would receive some real, honest answers, yet all I received was meaningless bullshit. It was bad enough Tony was idiotic to believe Emily. Not to mention she had some strange voodoo hold over him. But I was talking to a guy I barely knew about my problems which should be of no concern to him.

"I'm sorry. Can we start over? My name is Gavin Mair. I like going on hikes, my favorite color is gray, and I love watching the sunset," he smiled, trying to charm me with his poor attempt at lightening the mood. It worked.

The casual way he blurted it out made me laugh. "What is this? Speed dating?" I asked.

"Nope. But it can be if you'd like?" he winked. Seriously?

Who does he think he is? It would take more than a gorgeous face and chiseled abs to win me over.

"Not a chance. I'm not on the market," I stated matter-of-fact.

"At least I made you laugh," he said, leaning in before pulling back.

"You're incredible," I said, shaking my head in frustration.

"Why, thank you! I think I'm pretty incredible myself too," he grinned.

"Believe me. It wasn't a compliment. Arrogance isn't an attractive quality," I said, furrowing my brows. It was easier to keep my composure around him if I stayed irate.

"Then why are you attracted to me?" He asked, giving me a sheepish grin.

"What? I'm not!" I exclaimed. Sure, he set my heart racing but that was more due to the mystery he presented, not because of his looks. Okay, partly because of his looks but I wasn't going to be admitting that! Especially not to him. His ego was big enough.

"Sure Aurora. Keep telling yourself that," he chuckled.

"You're infuriating, do you know that?"

"I've been called worse," he shrugged.

"Oh, I'm sure you have. No doubt about that," I stated. Been called worse indeed. "This is me," I said, pointing to my house when we were two houses down. Chris's car was already parked in front; thankfully they made it home.

"Well, it was a nice chat Aurora," he smirked.

"Yeah. Likewise," I said, rolling my eyes. "Um, thanks for walking me home."

"Anytime," he said with a genuine smile. When I reached the door, I glanced over my shoulder to see if he was still there.

He was, waiting to make sure I made it in safe. He pulled his right hand from his pocket and waved. I waved back over my shoulder as I fumbled with the lock.

The key turned as I fell forward, smacking the door against the back wall. I snickered under my breath as if that would make up for the loud noise the door made. With a sheepish glance over my shoulder, Gavin was walking away. His shoulders shaking with laughter. I closed the door and tiptoed to my room; a smile spread across my face.

There was something about Gavin, something he was hiding. I could see he was putting up a front and keeping me at arm's length. He would answer questions without answering them — which left me with more questions. I could sense an edge to him. That much I did know.

The way he smiled when Tony challenged him - both times - was different. People don't smile when they're faced with a fight. Even the few times I had seen Garrett and Ryder ready to scrap, they never smiled. Their faces held the fury they felt within.

With Gavin, I could tell he enjoyed fighting. His words always seemed to have a deeper meaning too. Like he wasn't fully saying what he truly wanted to say. I hated this. Why couldn't he just talk to me outright like a normal human being? Why was there always secrecy around him?

I didn't understand but I hoped to find out eventually.

Chapter Six

Home

"Look, I been through so much pain

 And it's hard to maintain, any smile on my face

'Cause there's madness on my brain

 So I gotta make it back, but my home ain't on the map

Gotta follow what I'm feeling to discover where it's at

I need the (memory)

In case this fate is forever, just to be sure these last days are better

And if I have any (enemies)

To give me the strength to look the devil in the face and make it home safe." — Home by Machine Gun Kelly, Bebe Rexha, and X Ambassadors.

***

I didn't need to open my eyes to see if it were daylight. The persistent light filtering through the window made it abundantly clear. What had been unclear was the time of day.

With eyes still closed, I brought both arms overhead and stretched my toes. I needed that stretch but not the spinning accompanying the rush of blood. I had done a number drinking and I knew it.

Peeling one eye open, I gauged how much I was going to hate myself, and my actions, from last night.

Slowly, my tilted room came into focus. So far so good. The spinning didn't continue at least. From experience though, I knew I couldn't depend on a one-eyed test. I braved opening the second eye, hoping full vision would help me to better assess my condition.

I didn't need a mirror to know my eyes would be outlined in red. It felt like someone lit them on fire. I rubbed both, praying for relief but that relief would not come. It was my punishment to suffer through the burning heaviness of my actions for most of the day.

With careful deliberation, I sat up to the aching burden in my muscles. The room began to spin as the drummer boy chose to beat on his drum. I truly cursed last night. If I had half the mind to, I'd curse Kate too. I didn't want to go to that stupid frat party. If I had never gone, I wouldn't be feeling this awful.

In all honesty, I could only blame myself and I knew it. Which was why I no longer drank more than socially acceptable. Temporary fun wasn't worth the next morning's pain.

Yawning, the accompanying cottonmouth was unpleasant as ever. It tasted like the stale version of whatever cheap beer I drank last night, making my stomach churn. My hands clutched the mattress as I leaned forward, waiting for the perpetual rollercoaster to slow its roll. I had hoped today's resulting hangover would've passed me up this time, but I could never have been so lucky.

Feeling the first of the nausea subsiding, the need to brush this taste out of my mouth dominated.

The rest of the day was going to be all about slow motions, so that was how I proceeded to step into my slippers. I stumbled into the bathroom, avoiding the mirror at all costs, to brush my teeth and throw my hair into a messy bun. I was beyond help and didn't need a visual reminder of that fact.

Feeling another wave of nausea rise to the surface, I leaned my elbows against the sink to cradle my face. I knew if I threw up, I would feel better, but I always fought it. If my body wasn't going to do it naturally, there was no way I was going to force it. I wish I could magically heal my hangovers like I could heal my wounds.

As the nausea ebbed, my one-track mind thought of only one thing – water. I'm parched! Rising with shaky legs, I made my way to the kitchen.

"Wow Rory. Looks like you've seen better days," Chris chuckled from the couch. With his ash blonde hair brushed back, and a new change of clothes, he looked fresh faced as ever. Even his sky-blue eyes didn't betray the drink fest from last night.

I couldn't say the same for Kate, however. Her hair was brushed but her face was as ashen as mine.

I strolled past him without a word. I didn't have the energy to produce a comeback. I yanked open the fridge, scouring for anything that would provide relief for this dry throat. My hand went straight for the Orange Juice.

Habit.

The glass be damned, I drank from the carton. It wasn't lost on me the discussion I had with Ryder about this very same thing. Oh well, it couldn't be helped.

Orange juice wasn't helping. I grabbed for one of the small Fiji water bottles and chugged it.

Rookie mistake.

I ran for my bathroom, head spinning as I wretched over the toilet, further igniting my headache. After brushing my teeth for a second time this morning, I grabbed the Advil out of the medicine cabinet and pulled another bottle of Fiji water from the fridge – this time drinking it much slower.

I plopped on the couch next to Kate's other side. Her head leaned on Chris's lap, staring at the TV from a sideways angle, with a green tinge coloring her complexion. I caught a glimpse of Garrett sitting on the loveseat, smirking at me out of the corner of my eye, but paid him little attention. Whatever was going through his feeble mind, I had no energy to deal with.

It hadn't been more than a few minutes of watching 'How States Got Their Shapes' on the History Channel before Garrett couldn't resist any longer.

"Did you have a good time last night Aurora?" he taunted. He knew something about something from his tone, but I didn't know what, and I certainly didn't want to talk to him about it.

"Mhm," was all I said in response, doing my best to ignore him.

"Soooo, what did you do?" he drew out his question, his devious smile widening. I rolled my eyes at him.

What a stupid question. Wasn't it obvious from the state Kate and I were in?

"What do you think?" I asked through squinted eyes. He dismissed my attitude, continuing to taunt me with that same grin plastered on his face.

"Well, by the looks of you two, and the sound of the door crashing open at three o'clock this morning as you stumbled in, I guess it wouldn't be hard to speculate," he chuckled. Kate stuck her tongue out at him.

Why did he always have to be so infuriating? At least she felt the same annoyance with him as I did.

"Whatever it was you were doing last night, it led to an interested party knocking on the door at ten this morning," he smiled, his amber eyes swimming with humor at my expense.

"And? What is that supposed to mean?" I snapped. His attitude was getting to me on another level.

"It meeeeans, someone came by asking for you and left his phone number. A 'secret admirer' if you will," he teased, making a kissy face. I looked over at Chris who failed to hold back a chuckle.

Kate sat up as clueless as me. Her brows pulled in at Chris's chuckling, which he quickly corrected, before she turned her full gaze onto Garrett still grinning at me with that stupid grin.

"Why don't you just spit it out already Garrett," Kate said, cutting to the chase. Thank God for Kate!

"Why don't you go see for yourself Rory? Number's on the counter," he said, throwing his thumb back over his shoulder towards the kitchen.

"What? Who was it, Garrett?" I asked, annoyed. I hated when he did shit like this. Kate and I glanced at each other before bolting for the kitchen. There, a note written in excellent penmanship, sat on the counter by the coffee maker.

I had a great time last night. I hoped we could continue our evening, say dinner on me?

If you want, call me: (760) 490 – 4683.

Gavin

Of course, Garrett being Garrett, couldn't help but add his two cents into an otherwise perfect note…

Oh Aurora. He looked "dreaaaamy"!! Kiss Kiss Smooch Smooch!!!

I slid my eyes to Kate mirroring Garrett's same Cheshire grin from earlier.

"Oh, not you too! Don't start!" I whined at her. She smiled

wider as my cheeks flushed hotter, exposing my embarrassment.

"Is that Mr. Hottie Mair Aurora? You have been holding out on me, you sly fox you?" she said, giving me a knowing grin that barely contained her excitement.

"Oh my gosh Kate, no! Last night was the first time we spent any time together, and it was so brief. We hardly had a chance to talk," I defended.

"Well, you obviously made a great impression on him if he is coming back not even a few hours later to ask you out to dinner. You better call him. It's rude to keep him waiting," she said with such persistence and finality.

"What are you two heckling hens cooing about in here?" Chris asked as he squeezed past me to stand next to Kate. "What's that you got there, Aurora?" he asked, snatching the note from my hand before I even decided to answer.

I glared at him, making it clear my patience was running thin. Not just with him, but all of them.

"Is that the guy who asked if he could give you a ride home this morning?" he asked, smirking.

"Yes, if you must know," I said, trying to grab the note from him but closed my hand a moment too late.

"What's this about random guys bringing you home?" Garrett asked from behind, blocking me in between Kate, Chris, and himself. The kitchen began feeling cramped and I was fast becoming claustrophobic. A kitchen wasn't meant to hold this many people at once.

"He isn't just some random guy Garrett. He is the one who saved me from Tony when that incident happened," I countered and defended Gavin in the same sentence. Garrett's eyes tightened at Tony's name. Though I didn't want to dive any further than I already did with any of them on this matter, I didn't want my brother to get the wrong impression I was sleeping around.

As if it were any of his business anyways, but still.

"I'd like to meet him," he stated.

"Why?" I asked, surprised. "And you already met him this morning apparently."

"I meant officially. Anyone that stands up for my little sister from some punk deserves a proper handshake from her brother. Besides, if he is trying to take you out on dates, I'd also like to know what kind of person he is," he said with such authority.

"Seriously Garrett. I'm twenty-two, NOT fourteen. When will you and Ryder stop treating me as such?" I quipped, my cheeks reddening from more than just embarrassment.

"Never Aurora. We are your brothers. Get used to it. It's our duty to protect you, especially after what Tony has put you through. You better believe we are going to keep a closer eye on whoever comes around you," he stated. I didn't even bother to argue. He was exhausting and there was no point.

"Fine. Whatever. This is ridiculous," I said, circling my hand in the air at the group of us in the kitchen. I took Chris by surprise as I snatched the note right from his fingers. I rolled my eyes at Kate before ducking under Garrett's right arm.

I caught a glimpse of Kate giving me an apologetic smile as I headed straight for my room, away from their prying eyes. I slammed the door and stormed towards the shower to soak under the much-needed hot water.

The clock on the side table registered ten-past-two in the afternoon. I really wasted the day away, didn't I? Setting the note on the side table, I did my best to dismiss the feelings they stirred inside of me. I needed to sort through my thoughts and figure out what to even say to him.

Eyeing the note, I dithered over whether I should call him or not. So much happened last night, leaving open too many unanswered questions. What was his motivation for wanting to be around me?

What was his involvement with Emily? Why was there such palpable malice between them? And why, for the love of my sanity, did he never answer my questions outright? He always had a way of dancing around them.

No, I don't think I will be calling him tonight. Though the nausea subsided; I still didn't have the energy to deal with his Garrett-like personality. I needed tonight to be alone, in my room, collecting my thoughts.

A quick knock rapped on my door as Kate let herself in the room. "Hey. I'm sorry about earlier."

"What's the point of knocking if you're just going to barge in," I spat.

"What's the point of having a lock on the door if you aren't going to use it," she tossed right back at me.

"Fair point," I conceded. It was a fair point. I had to admit. It was a good reminder I needed to use it more often.

"Are you going to call Gavin?" she asked, getting straight to the point.

"Not tonight," I said in a clipped tone.

"Why not tonight?" she asked, sitting on the bed next to me.

"Honestly Kate, I need tonight to relax and be alone. Get some R-and-R if ya know what I mean," I said.

"Yeah. I can understand that one. I need some R-and-R myself. We can't drink like we use to, eh?" she joked, nudging my arm. "These hangovers sure are a bitch."

"No kidding. Thankfully the nausea subsided but I'm beyond drained. I feel like I could sleep for three days," I laughed.

"You and me both sistah! Except I'm still nauseous," she admitted as she began turning a sickly shade of green.

"Maybe you should go sleep it off. It isn't like we have anything to do today," I pointed out, "Honestly, I plan on sleeping it off myself." I didn't want her to feel like she sat alone on the miserable train.

"Yeah, you're right. I think I will. Let me know if you plan on going out. I'll go with you," she said.

"Yeah sure," I agreed, though I didn't know why. It wasn't like I had any plans on going anywhere. The least dramatic place was our home and that was saying something. With two brothers and, for all intents and purposes - a sister, there was always some sort of drama.

She patted me on the shoulder before shutting the door behind her. She must have truly felt sick for not having said a word before leaving. It was so unlike her. Staring after her, my eyes fell to the lock. I made fast work of locking it, mentally feeling better being closed off to the rest of the world.

Laying back, I stared at the ceiling, trying not to let my mind race into anything too complex. It would only boost my headache. I closed my eyes, trying to bring my mind into a meditative state. I focused on my breath.

In. Out. In. Out. In.

My eyes opened for the second time today. I took the rest and relaxation to the max, falling into a deep nap, having slept for what? Five hours? Six? Whatever it was, it was much needed and well received.

Clicking on the light, my stomach began to grumble from the lack of food all day. I knew we had nothing in the kitchen besides water and orange juice, so I'd have to go grab something.

What was open at this hour though?

The café down the street from us; they were open until midnight on the weekends. They made a mean Turkey BLT on sourdough too. My belly grumbled in agreement, making it an easy decision on where I would go.

Without bothering with my wardrobe, I made myself presentable and grabbed my purse. Stopping by Kate's room to see if she wanted anything, I tapped on her door but was met with silence. I cracked her door open just enough to peek around it. Though the room was dark, I could see the bulging blankets where she laid passed out beneath them. I'll just let her sleep rather than wake her. I knew how nice it was to be able to wake up on your body's own accord. I closed her door and headed out.

The café's windows were illuminated from inside, busy for a Sunday evening with laptops and books open at different tables. I scanned the restaurant from my truck to see if anyone I knew was in there. I would prefer to avoid familiar contact at all costs. Thankfully, it appeared safe.

I grabbed for my purse on the floorboard when I spotted a scene that would scar my memories for as long as I had a brain.

There, in the car next to mine, was Tony and Emily sucking each other's face in the front passenger seat. She straddled and grinded against him, barely giving each other room to breathe. Pure pleasure flashed across Tony's slackened face, his head rolling back against the headrest. Emily made quick work of his ear as she sucked and pulled at his lobe between her teeth.

I shut my mouth, realizing I had let it fall open, before throwing the truck into reverse. Screw food. I just lost my appetite.

My heart twisted and ripped apart in a multitude of ways. My mind tried not to comprehend the reality it had just witnessed in order to protect me, though it couldn't come up with any logical answer to deny it.

Burning tears flooded my eyes and streamed down my face. I should pull over and let it out, but I couldn't. I needed the confines of my room to shut the world out, and everything in it, as I had done earlier.

It wasn't like I didn't know they were hooking up, but to

see it with my own eyes somehow made it even more real. After everything we had put each other through, I knew we were both the last thing each other needed. That didn't make seeing him with another woman hurt any less. Our breakup was still fresh. Layer that with the knowledge of him cheating on me long before we separated—well, let's just say that really fucking stings.

I couldn't take it anymore. The precipice I had been teetering on finally gave way to the torturous pain ripping through my chest. All I had held back began surfacing, sending another wave of sobs rushing through me.

With the echo of each sob bouncing in my truck, it only made me cry that much harder. The awful scene kept flashing back at me in clipped form, accentuating each move and action with pronounced accuracy. Would this ever stop?

Pulling up to my house, I took a moment to find composure, only to find myself depleted, raw, and broken. With shaky hands, I made my way inside the house. If anyone were in the way between my room and me, they would see the puffy, lifeless face that I couldn't bring myself to rearrange. As luck would have it, no one was home – save for Kate still passed out in her room.

I bee-lined it for my room, locking the door as I had done earlier. I threw myself onto my bed to allow the fresh wave of tears I didn't know I still had to flow. Five minutes and a wet pillow later, I stared into my room, seeing it for what it was.

My prison.

It was four white, barren walls I allowed to become the only place I could hide away from everything and everyone. Away from prying, pitiful eyes. Away from drama, away from Tony, away from Gavin and the mysteries he presented, and away from the life that didn't make sense after they were taken away from me.

What I had thought of as my refuge had only been a place I could lock myself away. I made it my prison cell.

Feeling my personal prison closing in, and anxiety rising, I needed to get out. I needed to run away – leave. It wasn't enough to leave the house and go to a café or pub it seemed. I would no doubt run into someone I knew, as was tonight's example.

No. I needed to go much further than that. I needed to go home.

Not tomorrow, not next week, tonight - right now.

I refused to allow myself to think a moment more about Tony and Emily. I could only focus on each moment in front of me. The key to maintain sanity is to lose all thought.

No thinking. Just doing. Anything else would leave me paralyzed and that just wouldn't do. I needed to move forward.

I snatched my suitcase and began throwing everything I needed into it – pants, sweats, long sleeved shirts and sweaters, hiking boots, and other essentials. I packed it so full; I had to sit on it for the zipper to close.

I ran to the kitchen, ripping out a grocery bag from the pantry and began shoving any snacks I could get my hands on – protein bars, homemade brownies, the small Cheetos bags from the variety pack of chips. I slammed the pantry doors closed and yanked open the fridge, throwing a few Fiji water bottles into the bag as well. Slamming the door closed, I headed back to my room.

Grabbing my hiking backpack, I threw in the bag of snacks, along with my Chap sticks, lotions, toiletries bag, hats and beanies before wrenching the zipper closed. Snatching the old house keys off the wall hook, I shoved them into my jeans pocket.

I knew I couldn't leave without letting someone know where I went. My brothers and Kate would panic, and I refused to do that to them - to an extent. I could call them and let them know but then they wouldn't let me go. Or worse, they would want to come with me. I couldn't have that. I needed to go alone, and they would never understand why.

I'll write a note and leave it on the bed. At least that way they would know when they came in to look for me.

I'm sorry. I had to go. Don't worry, I'm alright, but I just needed to get away for a while. I'm going home – alone. I don't expect any of you to understand. I just wanted to let you know so you didn't worry so much. Love you all.

Aurora

With that, I grabbed my things and rushed out the door. The faster I left, the less chance someone would come home and stop me.

I chucked everything into the backseat, save for my purse, and drove away as fast as my truck would take me. As soon as tire tread hit the five freeway, I punched the gas and reveled in the whistle the acceleration made.

I rode on some high, knowing I was not only running away, but also running to something. I was running away from all the chaos enveloping my life these past few years. I was running to the past, where I hoped I would be able to find closure. It was such a strange paradox.

It's refreshing knowing I wouldn't have to answer to anyone for a while. Or run into any more scenes like I had tonight. I was leaving it all behind without a second thought. More than anything, knowing I was making this spontaneous decision without anyone knowing, after having mulled over it for so many months, felt freeing in its entirety.

Chapter Seven

The Way Things Are

———— ⌘ ————

"Reality is reality. It is the way things are, not the way you want them to be in your head." — *Dave Sim*

***

By seven a.m., I pulled into the first hotel I could find in Santa Rosa. My eyes were bleeding, and my mind was shutting down. Between the hangover debacle yesterday, and the lack of any real sleep, exhaustion kicked in hard and fast. I could only pray for vacancies and early check in.

Parking by the entrance, I dragged my sorry ass into the lobby.

A shorthaired brunette with an equally short stature greeted me as the doors slid open. She held her pointer finger up, motioning for me to wait while she was on the phone. I nodded, obliging her request as I leaned the full force of my body heavily against the counter. Her raspy, harsh voice belaying that of a smoker kept my attention, or else I would have drifted off to sleep right where I stood.

"Hello. What can I do for you?" she asked as she hung up the phone. It seemed she didn't want to be here as much as I wanted to sleep here.

"I need a room. King bed if you have it?" I requested. I didn't have it in me for pleasantries. The more direct, the faster this would be.

"Do you have a reservation?" she asked, her lips set into a thin line.

"No."

Wasn't it obvious I was *asking* for a room?

"I'm sorry. We are fully booked. We have no vacancies today," she stated.

"What's that? Come again? I could've sworn you said you didn't have any vacancies," I blurted out. Knowing it wasn't her fault; I did my best to reign in my anger.

"Yes. That's what I said," she shot back.

"That's just friggin wonderful," I said, throwing my hands in the air as I stormed out.

What the hell kind of place was this anyways? At least they could display on their marquee that they didn't have any vacancies rather than waste my damn time. How could a hotel have no vacancies in Santa Rosa of all places?

I slammed the truck door and roared the engine to life, peeling out of the parking lot. I glanced over to their marquee to double check their incompetency. Right there - in bright red letters - stated 'NO Vacancies' directly beneath the hotels name, La Quinta Inn. Wonderful. I didn't even bother checking the marquee and now *I* felt like the dumbass. *Insert face palm here.*

I'm not sure what dominated more, my exhaustion or irritation at myself.

In the end, exhaustion won.

I pulled into a Wal-Mart shopping center and crawled over

the front seats, stretching out across the back, as I cushioned up the pillow. Before long, I was drifting.

Tanner and I were strolling in silent harmony, as we often did when we hiked around the family ranch. His lips raised into his classic confidant smirk whenever he thought of something intriguing. His mind always centered on some sort of game of athleticism, or off-the-wall ideas.

"Hey Rory. I'll race you to the stream," he challenged; his eyes lit up with excitement. He always liked to show off his athletic superiority over the rest of us.

"Tanner, now what kind of challenge would that be? You'll just lose," I bluffed. *He turned to me with wide eyes as he let out the carefree laugh I loved so much.*

"In your dreams! I win, you have to clean the horse stalls – by yourself," he wagered.

Our family ranch housed our horses in its stables. Pixie was my favorite girl. She was a dark brown quarter horse with white socks and a patch of white around her left eye. Our ranch hands took care of them when we were not around, but it was our job to take that position over when we came here on the weekends. Tanner didn't care for this job. I didn't mind – I enjoyed being anywhere near the horses.

"And when I win, what will I get?" I asked.

"An older brother who loves you," he chuckled, nudging me to the side.

"No dice. I already have that. In fact, I have three! A challenge wouldn't change that," I smirked at his overstated pout, "Hooow about – when I win, YOU get to clean the horse stalls by yourself! I don't mind it as much as you do," I said, feeling triumphant as he grimaced at that admission. We both knew I didn't mind it. This fact made the challenge even sweeter.

"You're right. I should have thought of something better for you," he

said, pondering what else he could change it to.

"You can't change it now! It's already been set. Are you ready to lose or what?" I challenged, beaming up at him. He wanted a challenge, and I was going to put everything I had into it. I wasn't going to win. We both knew it. We had fun all the same. Tanner's carefree smile was worth losing to every time. Almost.

"Fine," he grumbled. He set himself into an athletic crouch, squinting his eyes, and gave me his best challengers stare. "On your mark. Get set. GO!" he shouted as we both took off into a sprint.

The pounding of our feet over the damp earth beat in unison. I peeked over; astonished I could even keep up with his six-foot one frame. He could overpower me in an instant with his long legs.

What I had failed to realize, it wasn't that I was keeping up with him, but it was he who was slowing down. Was he trying to let me win? *That didn't seem right. It went against his very nature.*

Concern turned to fear when his face twisted and scrunched, his wide eyes staring at me in horror. A shiver ran through every nerve. I didn't know where the danger came from. I was too afraid to look away from him to find out.

He slowed further but I kept my pace, pulling away from him as he continued to slow. When he escaped my view, I didn't bother looking back. It was as if all critical reasoning skills were turned off for fear and adrenaline to take over and call the shots. I didn't know why I should feel afraid, but I did.

"Aurora! No! Don't! Come Back! Stop!" I heard Tanner's panicked yell, his voice becoming a distant echo. I wanted to listen, but I couldn't stop my feet from propelling me further and faster away from him. Soon, his voice grew to a whisper as the forest gave way to darkness.

In the darkened forest, a peculiar buzzing echoed all around me, followed by an aggravating melody sounding oddly familiar. After a moment it paused, only to pick back up with the same cadence. The more I ran, the closer I came to the sound. My heart accelerated at what this sound could mean for me. Regardless, I couldn't stop myself from running towards it — all traces of Tanner now gone.

Up ahead, a pinhole of light shone through in the distance. The closer I ran towards it, the more it pulsed, growing larger and brighter until it engulfed the entire forest. Only a hint of the darkness surrounded my peripheral, as I ran into the bright light.

A sea of white surrounded me - as if I stepped onto a blank sheet of copy paper or crossed over to the pearly gates of heaven.

Am I dead?

Surely heaven wasn't so irritating with that constant stop and go buzzing polluting the airwaves around me.

Every nerve ending vibrated with the high and low pitches of the melody, the feeling of becoming one with the sound leaving me disoriented. My conscience was hyperaware of my surroundings without fully seeing where I was.

Crossing over an unknown and unseen threshold, the bordering darkness caved in as my breath caught in my chest.

I couldn't believe my eyes; I just stepped into…

I shot straight up, hitting my head on the roof of the truck. *Ouch.* I blinked the sleep out of my eyes, taking in my surroundings, as I rubbed my head.

I wasn't in the forest.

I was in Santa Rosa - in the backseat of my truck.

I knew I was dreaming because Tanner was dead.

I let out the breath I hadn't realized I had been holding, my body's hunger for air forcing me to breathe again. What a strange dream that was. *Why did I keep running away from Tanner? And why was he so afraid?* It made no sense. Stupid dreams anyways.

Rubbing the back of my eyes with my hands, I stretched with a deep yawn. The familiar buzzing and ringing from my dream began again except this time I knew what it was.

I scrambled into the front seat, grabbing for my purse to pull out my phone. Buried at the bottom, I couldn't reach it in time. I checked the screen to see twenty missed calls from Kate, nine from Garrett, and four from Ryder. *What the heck?* How in the world did I sleep through so many missed calls?

Somewhere in the back of my mind, I realized that they must have found my note. Or realized I had been missing all night. Maybe both. I didn't have time to wonder any further as Kate's twenty-first call buzzed in my hand.

"Hello?" I croaked, sleep still heavy in my voice.

"WHERE IN THE HELL ARE YOU?" Kate yelled into my ear. I pulled the phone away too late. My right ear rang from the onslaught it received.

"Um, Santa Rosa?" I said. I wasn't normally on the receiving end of Kate's anger but whenever I was, I felt like a little girl being reprimanded by her mother.

"What in the HELL are you doing in Santa Rosa, Aurora *Marie*?" she demanded.

"Sleeping?" I answered unsure, rubbing my left eye.

"Sleeping? Did you find a hotel room?"

"No. They were booked. I slept in my truck," I said. I should have just said yes - my big mouth and I didn't think of just lying about this one.

"You WHAT? Aurora, you stay RIGHT THERE in Santa Rosa. FIND a hotel room! We are coming up," she threatened.

"What? No! Didn't you see my note?" I asked, angry - and nervous, about them reaching me before I could get home. I hated feeling rushed. I hoped to have time to work through my thoughts and find closure, them coming up just hastened a process that didn't need to be.

"Of course, I did. When we didn't see your truck parked, and you didn't answer your phone after a hundred calls, I checked your room thinking someone stole your truck but no. What did I find? A pathetic note saying you were going home. What the hell

Aurora? Did you stop to think about anybody else but yourself about this? About the panic you have put all of us in?

Garrett went out searching for you before I found the note. I have never seen him more afraid in my life. Ryder even called out of work to help us search for you. *Damn it,* Aurora," she scolded me. I didn't realize that they wouldn't think to check my room first before flying off the hinges.

"Kate, look. I'm sorry. This is just something I must do alone. I can't expect you or anyone else to understand and – wait a minute. Didn't you guys think to check my room before taking off and gathering a search party?" I asked.

"Ryder checked your room and didn't find you in there. He didn't see the note either or else I'm sure all this chaos could've been avoided. That's beside the point – you leaving the way you did without talking to anyone is beyond selfish and inconsiderate - to me *and* your brothers," she reprimanded.

"Kate, you're not my mother. I'm a grown adult who can take care of herself. While I appreciate your concern—," I said, but was cut off.

"Oh no you don't Aurora! This isn't about me being your mother – thank the heavens I'm not! This is about me being your concerned friend slash sister, especially when I have to watch your brothers look more afraid about where you could've possibly gone, *especially* with Tony being the way he is. Did you even think to realize that possibility is a reality for you? Luckily, I reached Garrett because no doubt, he went looking for him," she stated.

"Please tell me he didn't," I said, my heart dropping into my stomach. No, I hadn't thought of that scenario. A shudder ran through me even thinking about that possibility.

"No. He didn't. He is on his way back here and he his *livid.* Aurora, I'm not going to even pretend to know why you want to go back home. After we left, you shut down. No one is there anymore. Why do you even want to go back to that?" she asked.

"Kate. I don't know. I can't explain it and I'm not going to even try to. I just wanted to go back home, okay? I didn't think I needed anyone's permission to go back home to *our* house," I spat.

I was done with being reprimanded and questioned. The clock clicked to ten-thirty. If I hit the road now, I would make it there by midafternoon.

"Whatever Aurora. Just stay in Santa Rosa so we can catch up with you," she demanded, more than requested.

"Truly Kate. I wish you all stayed there and let me do this on my own," I pleaded.

"Sorry. The wheels are already set in motion. As soon as Garrett gets back, we are loading up and heading out. Ryder already called out of work and told them he wouldn't be there for the next week either.

With Garrett not having any work commitments anymore, there is absolutely *no* way they're going to sit here knowing you're up there. And I speak for myself on that note too," she said.

"Whatever. I'm not waiting in Santa Rosa for ten hours. I'll just meet you at the house," I said, rolling my eyes. The one thing I needed; they couldn't give me - freedom.

"Seriously Aurora. Just *wait*," Kate sighed. Though she was angry, there was also an undertone of pleading. That makes two of us then. I'm angry they're hasting and disrupting my plans and completely undermining my pleading for them not to do so.

"Sorry Kate. I'll see you at the house," I said before hanging up, letting out a deep sigh as I turned the key in the ignition.

I did my best to not think about the coming reunion with my brothers. Other than the fact I hung up on her, I knew Kate wouldn't be as difficult to deal with. She had gotten most of what she wanted to say off her chest. I just hoped my brothers would calm down by the time they came home.

Pulling out of the Wal-Mart parking lot, my stomach threw a protest of its own at the apparent starvation I put it through. *When was the last time I ate something?* I couldn't remember.

At least that was one problem I could control. I drove through McDonald's drive-thru for a sausage egg McMuffin before pointing my truck North and onto the one-oh-one. I punched the gas, hearing that diesel engine whistle, as I hastened home as fast as possible.

Home at last.

Home indeed.

Here I sat in my truck with the engine turned off, afraid to even open the door. I barely made it to the driveway, yet the house already felt vacant.

I realized I had parked my truck - which use to be my fathers - exactly where he used to park it - on the left side of the driveway closest to the front door. The empty space to my right was where my mother would park her black Excursion, same with the empty space in front of our house by the mailbox where Tanner use to park his jeep. In my mind, I could see their vehicles parked there in vivid detail.

I was surprised to see the grass was still green and well-manicured, no doubt thanks to Mr. Baronski — our next-door neighbor. He was a sweet, widowed man in his sixties who always shared a love for landscape and gardening with my mother. If you hadn't known, you would think someone still lived here without a second thought. You wouldn't even guess that this house, which used to be so full of love and family, was now dead and devoid of all life inside.

Funny, almost identical to how I felt.

No more stalling. It was now or never. As it sat, my brothers and Kate would be here in no time, and I would have regretted wasting even a single minute being afraid to enter my childhood home.

If I had ever hoped my brothers would have calmed down by the time they arrived, that hope was now crushed. I ignored all their phone calls — well just one phone call in particular - Garrett's. He was the only one that had been calling over and over. I didn't bother checking their text messages either. *What was the use in that?* I'm sure I would hear it all once they arrived, I didn't need them clouding this moment for me too.

I slid out of the truck, gently closing the door. *"Take this slow, Aurora. Let this moment wash through you,"* I chanted to myself. I refused to breakdown and cry. I wanted to make the most of this time in the only way that made sense.

Ambling up the walkway, I fumbled for the house key in my pocket that hadn't been used in years. The white paint on the house's exterior began to chip away from the salty air's relentless attacks. My father always made sure to power wash the house to help keep the salt from eroding it. I could hear him saying, "Don't buy - rent, if you don't want to keep your house pristine!" He took pride in his home. It was a shame we were allowing it to deteriorate.

I found myself on the large, narrow porch with its thick, intricate wood posts that led to a decorative sloped ceiling. My mother fell in love with the historic architecture of the homes in Boston, particularly the porches.

We had taken a family trip there one summer and had been caught out in the rain. We were running down the street, laughing hysterically, with our hands over our heads to shield ourselves from the torrential downpour. A sweet elderly lady had seen our ordeal and welcomed us onto her porch out of the elements. It was comical, having all of us dripping wet on her tiny, elegant porch, huddled together like packed sardines.

When we purchased this home, my mother made sure to have this replica porch constructed shortly after. Her vision for things were always grander though, so with our family being as big as it is - or was, a larger porch wasn't even a question.

The four white rocking chairs on the porch had taken on a shade of grey due to the years of dust and sand being kicked up by the winds and storms. They were covered in cobwebs, hinting at their lack of use should someone look that close.

With key in hand, I turned towards our red door and slid the key into the lock. With a turn of the wrist, the key unlocked my past. It was up to me to open the door.

Turning the knob, I let the door fall open of its own accord. A rush of dusty, stagnant air flew past me as fresh air swooped in to take its place. From where I stood, the house was dark and dreary, illuminated only by the light that escaped around the window blinds. With a shaky step and a pounding heart, I moved forward past the threshold and into our living room.

Sheets and dust blanketed the furniture. I'd have thought Garrett and Ryder would have at least sold our furniture instead of leaving it here to rot.

Though my memory was hazy, we left in a haste without thought of how we would handle our lives here. I vaguely remember standing in the very spot I was in now, staring out of the window devoid of all emotion, when Garrett suggested selling our homes and everything in it. Though my episodes were all jumbled together, this one was distinct in that I had woken up with a vengeance.

I lashed out at Garrett, calling him every name in the book, at the mere mention of selling our home. I remember thinking to myself, *how could he?* They weren't even cold yet, and he wanted to get rid of everything as if they never existed. The thought still sent my stomach into knots.

Walking over to the living room windows, I opened the white shutters to allow the natural light to filter in. The kicked-up dust motes swirled in the sun's rays, dancing with happiness now that someone had come home to keep them company. My nose tickled as I let out a sneeze, sending the dancing particles flying in excitement every which way. If we planned on staying here for any amount of time, we would have to clean this place up. It was just *so* dusty.

Turning towards the darkened kitchen, I flicked the light switch on and off. *Why did I even entertain that?* I knew the utilities were off.

I carried on the task of opening all the windows in the kitchen to welcome in the fresh air and natural sunlight. When I opened the long, sheer white curtains that led to our back yard, I was greeted with the sight I missed so much – the slice of beach which held all the memories of my childhood.

The beach bonfires in the summer, the pore-slam challenges we would take into the wintery ocean waters, and the hundreds of failed sandcastle attempts were all reminiscent memories.

It wasn't even that we were horrible at sandcastles. We were all extremely competitive. It was inevitable that someone always ended up having their sandcastle ruined by one of the others. A lot of fights had happened because of our sibling rivalries – it was all comical now.

Of course, this beach held some not so pleasant memories for me as well. Like when Danny Wells decided he wanted to break up with me to go after Evelyn Kohl. He had come by the house while I was on the beach to break my little fifteen-year-old heart. Or when Nolan Davis tried to force me to have sex in his car when all I wanted was anything but that – I narrowly escaped *that* situation.

I remember I ran straight to our little stretch of sand and bawled my eyes out by the water, throwing sand into the ocean as I screamed out his name. I never felt so violated in all my life. He shattered my naïve innocence. I would have told my family, but it was later that day, when Ryder had found me on the beach, that I had learned of *their* tragic accident. Nolan Davis could've done his worst to me, and I would never have cared after that news.

This stretch of sand was one I would not be gracing today.

Shaking my head of the memories, it was astonishing how easy it was to be able to come full circle and remember the events leading up to that tragic day. I had blocked those painful memories out of my mind. Being here, though, unlocked that memory bank. It was like all my memories couldn't come at me fast enough. It was overwhelming. I didn't want to dwell on them and yet it was exactly what I was doing.

I knew I was stalling to the true heart of why I came here. Though the downstairs common areas held so many memories of my family together, it was the bedrooms I have been most afraid of. They were so personal to each of us. It was where we slept, got ready, retreated to when we were mad, lived and grew up in – entering them now almost felt like a violation of their privacy.

I knew it wouldn't matter in the end. They were gone. What would they care? Though I knew this to be true, I couldn't help but to care – and care deeply.

My heart sank when I placed my foot on that first step; hand on the banister, staring up to the darkened stairwell. So many conflicting emotions raged inside of me. I wanted to cry but held a firm grip on the tears I refused to release.

A part of me was eager to rush up there and let the light filter in, but I reserved to the promise I had made to myself to take this slow. With a deep inhale and an audible exhale, I forced my feet forward, taking the steps one by one.

Standing at the entrance of the long hallway, I could see all the doors had been closed. The bit of light filtering into the darkness came from underneath them, as did the small windows framing the French doors at the end of the hall.

This was the one moment where I felt the weight of my decision to come here – alone - was a bad idea.

My chest constricted at the indecision of whose room to start with. My hands folded into themselves over my heart, trying to keep myself in one piece.

If I start with one over the other, would it mean I loved them more than the other? Should I go into all the rooms, or just the ones I was here for? *Should I even go into them at all?*

No, I knew I needed to see them. If not for the mere fact to feel closer to them, then for the closure I hoped they would provide me. I closed my eyes, taking another deep breath, and allowed my feet take me where they may.

I stood at my parents closed French doors. Lined with thick, pewter curtains covering the windows from inside, it added to the suspense of my choices. I was walking in blind. I rested my hands on the crystal door knobs, but froze in my place.

I had to go in.

I knew I had to go in.

I just couldn't.

Chills ran through my body as all the loss, all the loneliness I had been feeling, worked its ways through to my eyes. I wiped the tears away with the back of my hands, furious. *Why? Why did they leave me? How could the forces that be do this to us? To me?*

With my newfound anger, I pushed through the doors.

All the anger faded away.

Their room was precisely as we had left it, or rather just as *they* had left it. I remember that day vividly because I locked myself in their room in the aftermath. I had plenty of hours to study it in my catatonic state.

It was so bright, unlike the rest of the house. The wall-to-wall windows were exposed; the blackout curtains having never been pulled closed. The view of the ocean framed beautifully by the frameless window, which expanded from floor to ceiling.

The wooden four-poster bed with the muted floral comforter, and one too many pillows, was made perfect as the morning they had made it. My dad's blue jeans and signature white polo shirt hung on the railing of their dark mahogany bed. His golfing attire placed out for the next day. A day he never had the chance to live.

My chest constricted as my heart ached at thinking of his bright smile and deep laughter. He commanded respect with his loving nature, his positive energy always drawing the family closer. I imagined him giving me a big, loving hug and telling me everything would be okay. No matter what happened, everything would be okay.

The Verona Persian blue rug still set the stage for the chaise lounge in the center of the room. My mother had often used this lounge as a place to lay her clothes instead of its intended use. I walked over and picked up a black blouse she threw over the lounge in a hurry to find something else to wear. I brought it to my nose, surprised I could still smell her perfume in the fabric — though barely.

I always loved her perfume — honeysuckle, lilac, and lime blossom. I could see her spritzing it into the air and walking through the mist, so it was the perfect hint of scent. I recalled asking her one time why she didn't spray it directly on her clothes.

Her response? She didn't want to smell like she swam in it. It was a valid point.

I only had a very short time with my mother before I lost her again. She had come back to our family after she had abandoned us for a few years. I always missed her and prayed she would come back. To this day, I don't understand why she ever left in the first place. I was only happy when she came home.

The rush of tears I had been holding back since pulling into the driveway hit me like a battering ram. I leaned into the chair as my heart clenched in a way I always sought to avoid.

Mom, Dad, I miss you so much. Why? Why did you have to leave me?

I sank to the floor, my body heaving with sobs. I didn't understand how life could be so cruel. Everything was taken from me. Life as I knew it, and three of the most important people in my life, completely gone. Demolished. Disintegrated into this near lifeless form I could hardly recognize.

Dad, why couldn't you be here when I needed you most? I craved your wisdom and comfort. I always came to you for everything that bothered me.

I squeezed my eyes shut as tight as they would close, wrapping my arms around my torso, in an attempt to hold myself together. This was excruciating. I was robbed of the chance to ever say goodbye.

I was becoming painfully aware of why I had reacted the way I did when Ryder told me the news. I had already dealt with one traumatic situation with Nolan Davis. Learning of Tanner and my parents' death sent me over the edge. My brain tried protecting me, tried protecting itself – however you want to view it.

Which brought me to another painful realization – if only one of my family members had passed away, it would have been hard all around, but we would still have had each other. It wouldn't have been as hard as losing a significant portion of my family all in one go. That was the real tragedy.

Another wave of hysteric sobbing coursed through me. I didn't have the energy or strength to stop it.

Every emotion, every painful memory, every moment I had held back over the past three years, came flooding out of me as if the Hoover Dam had broken without warning. I wrapped myself into a fetal position on the floor, hugging my legs into my chest. I needed this painful sobbing to end but I was not promised any ending in sight.

I was wretched for even thinking it would be better if one of them had passed rather than all three. Wasn't it obvious? The best option would have been to have none of them gone. What kind of daughter was I - what kind of sister was I – to think such horrible things?

It could have been minutes, hours, or days when the tears finally stopped. I felt hollow inside – somehow emptier than when I had first stepped foot into this house. My chest ached at the sobs that ripped through it.

In an odd, twisted way, I also felt better. Not in a happy sense but in the sense, I had finally let out what I had been holding in for so long. I wouldn't call me cured of my depression, but I knew moving forward, I wouldn't allow myself to be a silent martyr to it anymore.

Rolling over onto my hands and knees, I used what little strength I had left against the lounge to pull myself up. I set my mother's blouse back onto the chaise, making sure to spread it out as she had. I couldn't be in here another second. It was too much. Too crushing.

I hastened my way out of the room, wiping my eyes with the back of my hands, not bothering to shut the door behind me. It was stupid, but I'd like to think leaving the formerly closed door open was a sign things had indeed changed.

I hurried down the hall towards the stairs, halting outside of

Tanner's room. My feet froze as I wrestled with whether I should go in or not. A part of me wanted to but knew it was hopeless; another part of me expected to see him lying across his bed reading the latest outdoor sports magazine.

Seeing an empty room would be too much.

After experiencing what I had in my parent's bedroom, there would have been no way I could keep the same episode from happening again. The feeble control I had regained had deep cracks I couldn't hope to repair anytime soon. There was nothing more for me here.

I needed to get out.

I needed to take myself out of this situation. I came here hoping for closure and all I gave myself was gripping pain. This had not gone how I had anticipated it.

Finding life in my legs again, I flew down the stairs and out the door. I had half the mind to at least close and lock it first before I left. I couldn't say the same for the windows and blinds downstairs. I turned, sprinting towards my truck. I didn't want to see any of the neighbors. I wanted to leave without any fanfare.

Okay, so I had been here. Mission accomplished.

I realized now the foolishness of what I had done and what I had just put my brothers and Kate through. I made them pause their whole life to follow me up here on some stupid, misguided attempt to find closure on my own. *How could I have been so igno-rant?* I am the worst sister imaginable.

Knowing there was no way I was going back into that house tonight; I pointed my truck in the only direction I knew to go – the family ranch. That too had long since been abandoned but the memories there were happier and had been reserved for weekends or when we weren't in school. I picked up the phone and speed dialed Kate's number. It rang twice before she answered it.

"Hello! Would it *kill* you to answer Garrett back?" she barked.

"I left my phone in the truck when I went into the house," I gave no further explanation.

"Well, that's just great. What good is a phone if you don't keep it on you?" she asked.

"Sometimes it's healthy to ditch technology," I replied, smiling at the knowledge of no cell service at the ranch.

"Is it healthy when your brothers are Garrett and Ryder, Aurora?" Kate reprimanded.

"Kate. Not now please," I said with a half-choked sob.

"What's wrong? What happened?" she worried into the phone. I knew she wouldn't have missed that.

"What? Something happened?" I heard Ryder panic in the background.

"Nothing Kate. Nothing happened. I'm… just… it was hard for me being back home, ya know?" I admitted. I hated showing my weakness.

She sighed, "Yeah. I know Aurora. Which is why we didn't want you to do this alone."

"Yeah. I know. I realize that now and I'm sorry," I said. "Look, I can't go back to that house tonight. I'm heading to the Ranch. Meet me there."

"What? No Aurora. Stay at the house. We will be there in the morning," Kate snapped.

"What the hell? What now Kate?" Garrett barked at her.

"She says she is going to the ranch and to meet her there," she repeated.

"What? No! Give me the damn phone!" Garrett demanded. I could hear the rustling exchange of hands the phone was going through.

"Now Aurora, you listen to me damn it! You better keep

your ass at that house until we get there all right? Don't make this any more difficult than you already have," he snapped. I hated when he got this way. He wasn't my father, thank God for that. And no one asked him to come in the first place.

"Too late. I already left Garrett," I smiled in defiance.

"It isn't too late. Turn back around and go home," he demanded.

"I will if you will," I challenged.

"Aurora, why do you have to be so damn difficult? Is it that hard to see we want to be up there with you? Do you think you're the only one who has to deal with the pain of them all being gone?" He fumed.

"Whatever Garrett. I already left. If you're planning on coming up then I will meet you at the ranch," I spat as he yelled a string of expletives before I shut my phone off. I couldn't deal with his anger issues right now. I couldn't think about their pain when I couldn't even shoulder my own.

As far as I knew, I was the only one who was screwed up from everything. I was the only one who couldn't move past it. I needed to do what was right by me so I could try to piece my life back together.

I did feel bad for Kate and Ryder having to listen to him the whole way, but I was already heading in that direction. I wasn't changing course now. My only plan was to stop at the country store for firewood and sustenance before heading there. I only hoped I could make it before the sun set.

Chapter Eight

Mystery

———⌒———

"It is only through mystery and madness that the soul is revealed." – Thomas Moore

***

The sun shifted behind the ridge, casting long shadows from the surrounding trees onto the ranch's field. The gravel under the tires made the absence of music blaring. Had I driven the entire hour here on autopilot?

I knew from this point; I still had a quarter mile until I made it to my destination deep in the woods. My refuge.

Though my family and I called this second home of ours 'the ranch', it was just a nickname.

My father purchased this two-hundred-and-forty-acre parcel, many years before I was born, while he still owned our family's logging and lumber business in Eastern Washington. It was his dream, and next venture, to turn this into a full-fledged ranch and vineyard. A place where people could come to enjoy the wines he and his team produced.

He and my mother had worked hard during the better part of their thirties to turn it into what I had always known it as – Walker Vineyard and Ranch.

Driving alongside the pasture, it was hardly recognizable. The forest didn't take long to reclaim our once beautiful field that held two spring fed ponds and rows of vines. The grape vines were overgrown and unruly. Ferns perked up in the walkways between the vines, crowding out the grapes.

It was a mess. A perfect picture of our life – abandoned.

I ached at knowing my parent's years of hard work had been destroyed. To imagine the disappointment on their faces, knowing the state we had allowed their dreams to crumble in, pained me to no end.

The eight-bedroom French Country style manor materialized from a break in the trees, which had once served as a bed and breakfast - another one of my parent's realized dreams. Though I had many fond memories here, I didn't have such trepidation walking through the threshold of this home.

I remember this place bustling with workers, visitors and farm animals. The barn that housed our horses and served as our family loft when guests rented the B-and-B was locked up. No more were the horses I loved so much.

It's a bit disconcerting I hadn't thought of my beloved Pixie in all these years. I had overheard my brothers talking to Kate about their plans to close the family business and sell all our livestock, horses included, before we left. I guess losing Pixie never registered with me on any emotional level at the time, but a piece of my heart ached at the thought of her being in someone else's hands now.

With groceries in hand, I ambled towards the front door - my mother's love for architecture showcased all around. She made sure when they broke ground on the ranch, they would be replicating the rustic and welcoming aesthetic of the chateaus and manors she fell in love with while on their honeymoon in Southern France. It was my favorite home.

Leaves crunched underfoot, disturbing the quiet evening glow. They gathered over a foot thick along the walls of the wrap around porch. I had planned on spending much of my time here knowing it would be the one property needing the most TLC. With the whole brigade hell-bent on coming to rip me a new one, we could get a lot done to tidy up the place.

A similar rush of musky, stagnant air hit me as I opened the heavy wooden door to the manor. An ominous aura from the setting sun and eerie silence rose the hair on the back of my neck on end.

Again, I clicked the switch on and off with false hope, much to my dismay. I needed to find a source of light and heat soon.

Setting the groceries by the couch, which was to be my bed for the evening, I turned to grab the firewood out of the truck. The fireplace in the living room made it convenient to sleep there for the evening.

I quickened my pace to the large stone hearth. Within fifteen minutes, a beautiful fire roared to life, radiating its welcoming warmth. The flickering of the flames danced along the decorative wall molds, casting deep shadows around their borders.

Save for the soft glow of twilight, the rest of the house was near pitch black. Without a flashlight, I had no choice but to use the light on my phone. It wasn't as bright, but it would do in this pinch.

The phone's dim light casted long, eerie shadows down the long hallway as I made my way into the linen room. This was where we housed the extra bedding, pillows, and other essentials for the guests who stayed here.

Across the room, I stacked my bedding for the evening, abandoning it in search of my favorite grey Merino-knit throw blanket. When I was here, I couldn't sleep without it.

In the recess of the cabinet below, the soft fabric caressed my fingertips like a long, lost puppy. I tugged it towards me, only to be met with resistance halting me from pulling it any further. Frustrated, I grabbed for my phone to inspect the problem.

In the far corner, I glimpsed a polished Mahogany box snagging the fabric of the blanket. Crawling halfway in, I pulled both the blanket and the box towards me.

Deep engraving across the top of the velvety wooden box held my interest. Constructed with a hinged lid, it was clasped to the front of the body by an antiquated black lock with a swing arm. The decorative detail lining the inner borders of the staple was an absolute work of art with flowers, filigree, and raised edges.

Burned into the lid was a large tree whose trunk stretched from the bottom of the lid to the top, its leaved branches fanning out across the full expanse of it. The tree continued to cascade down the front, underneath the latch, where a large intricate root system covered the entire lower half of the box.

Above the tree, in small, beautiful cursive, was one word with six letters I could never mistake - **Aurora**. How had I missed this before? This box was mine, or at least it was meant for me.

Why had I never seen it before? Why was it never given to me? And what was it doing in the linen room?

Eager to see its contents, I gathered my blankets. I wanted to inspect this mystery closer in the light of the living room.

What could be in it? For all I knew, it could be empty. Maybe it was meant as a keepsake to store my treasured belongings?

I tilted the beautiful, inexplicable box barring my name to secure it under my arm. Whatever it contained rattled inside as I turned it. There was something in it! My heart pounded at the possibilities.

Dropping everything onto the couch, I set my gaze over the

box placed cautiously on the table. In the soft glow of the fire, it brought to life the tree etched deep into the grain of the wood. The shadows of the depressions were darker, the raised areas more prominent. I was both hesitant and a bit disturbed to find such a rare item, addressed to me, in the most random place I could find it.

Though curiosity overflowed in abundance at this anomaly, I instead found myself making my bed, layer by careful layer, on the pewter Chesterfield sofa. If I were to open this box tonight, and that was a big if, I wanted to feel comfortable and secure.

Would I like what I found? Who was it from? My mother? My father? Probably not Tanner. He wasn't known to do things like this very often.

Sitting cross-legged on top of my makeshift bed, I drew in a deep breath. Controlling the exhale as I reached towards the table, I plucked the box from its surface. The mystery box balanced on my lap as I ran my fingertips over the smooth woodgrain. I traced the trunk of the tree from the roots, towards the elegant cursive spelling out my name. Whoever this was from, they sure went out of their way to have it made for me.

Enough stalling Aurora.

My raging curiosity needed answers; the burning questions inside my head were toying with my anxiety. With an erratic heart, I mentally prepared myself for whatever I would find inside. I grabbed the swing arm that secured the clasp and began to push it open.

It didn't budge.

I pushed harder but again, it wouldn't budge. Was it so old the metal had frozen shut? That seemed unlikely.

With anxiety morphing into frustration, I turned the box left then right in search of some way to open it. There was nothing. Same with the back.

I lifted the box, bringing it over head to search underneath.

Was there a key of some sort?

What I found wasn't a key, but words written in the same elegant script as my name. The dark shadows of the fire made it impossible to read. Flipping it over, I jumped at the noise of its contents rattling in the quietness of the room.

Leaning forward, I grabbed my phone, and switched the light back on. Transcribed beneath the box, in a strange foreign language, was:

Vincit Qui Se Vincit

"Vincit Qui Se Vincit," I whispered, trying to pronounce the foreign words on my tongue. The sliding sound of metal on metal rang through the dark, silent room. Turning the box to face forward, the swing arm unlatched from its frozen state.

Did that just happen?

I swallowed in a feeble attempt to wet my parched mouth. What. In. The Actual. Hell?

Was it voice activated somehow?

With trembling hands, I freed the unlocked latch from its place when an electric pulse fired through my fingertips upon contact with the cool, intricate metal. I yanked my hand back, clenching it into a fist, as the tingling pulse lingered in my palm.

Was the energy surge coming from me? Or the box? Or was it an exchange of currents between the two? I couldn't be sure.

More cautious this time, I reached out again to release the latch. The rush of power came on the same as before, illuminating the bottom roots of the tree with a brilliant glow as it inched its way up the trunk until every branch and leaf radiated.

"Whoa," I whispered.

These energetic exchanges, they weren't foreign to me. No, it was the same pulse I would feel when I tended the garden or healed any of my wounds. It was the one thing I never told anyone about and yet, here it was - the same healing pulse I had come to know. Except, this was stronger somehow, more force-ful.

Try as I might, I knew I couldn't turn away from this now. I had come too far to not know what was in this perplexing box, even if I was freaked out.

As my name became illuminated, the lid cracked open of its own accord with radiant light causing me to squint as it shone through the jarred lid. The electric exchange surged up my arm, into my shoulder as a shiver ran through me at the impossibility, quickening my breath. My pulse hammered to the rhythm of my erratic heart. I slammed the lid shut, all but throwing the box on the tabletop.

That's enough. I don't want to know what's in it.

I steadied my breath.

But didn't I though? I stared at the hell box, paralyzed with indecision. Am I going to sit here all night, peering at this unbe-coming box as its intended recipient? I waited for my pulse to steady, transfixed with the weight of my curiosity and the need for self-preservation of my sanity.

I leaned forward and snatched the box back into my lap.

I paused.

Would I regret finding what was waiting for me?

Snapping the lid open, the light emanating from inside dis-sipated into the darkness like a hundred fireflies being released. It was magnificent.

Peering inside, my throat caught. Tears welled unbidden as I stared down at the last thing I had ever expected to see – an ornate pendant and a note addressed to me from my mother.

Chapter Nine

The Letter

"Better a cruel truth than a comfortable delusion." – Edward Abbey

***

Aurora,

If you are reading this letter, then I know what a shock it must have been for you to receive it. I had this box created for the specific purpose that you, and you alone, would be able to open it. I can safely assume, as well, we are no longer with you.

Honey, I want you to know your father and I are heartbroken we will not be able to be with you moving forward. The future ahead of you is going to be a hard and perilous one, and so the purpose of this letter is to warn you, and prepare you, as much as I possibly can.

You and your brothers are in great danger. There is a dark, hidden world surrounding you that your father and I had worked so hard to keep you all safe from. It had always been my hope and dream you could live and grow normal lives. This dream, I fear, will never be realized.

I cannot go into specifics, as much as I want to share with you the rich history of your lineage, for fear someone else will have managed to take this letter from you. You will need to be always on your guard Aurora. This isn't a joke or something to play around with. Your life is worth much more than you know.

The locket you have found is very special to me. It has always been my good luck charm, passed down to me from your grandfather Daten. It is one I always keep close to my heart, and I press upon you to keep close to yours. Keep it on you always but also keep it well hidden. Let no one know you have this. It is always safest with you.

Once you are done reading this letter, destroy it. I want no one to be able to trace the locket back to you.

You are probably puzzled by the incantation on the bottom of the box - the one allowing you to unlock it. I will explain it to you, but I also want to impart on you my wisdom to be your guide as you move forward.

Aurora, it is easier to take the wrong path in life than it is to choose the right one. The right path isn't always the easiest choice, but it will be the one that counts in the end. Don't stray from this path.

If ever you feel down on your luck, as if your hope is drying up, re-member you are lucky to be alive, breathing, and capable of changing your own destiny. All it takes is courage and perseverance.

My darling, you were born to fly to greater heights along your path than I could ever hope to achieve. When you are down, don't look to anyone else to pull you off the ground. You must be able to rescue yourself because in the end, you're the only one you can rely on. Like the Phoenix, you must find your way. Destroy your old self and come out of it stronger than ever — anew.

As for the incantation - Vincit Qui Se Vincit

This means, 'She conquers who conquers herself.'

Always remember. You are stronger than you think you are. You will prove it to yourself once hard times hit which most assuredly, they will. Do not try to impress others but work to conquer and harness your own power within you. Don't ever be ashamed of your power.

Take these last words of wisdom I have given you to heart. Commit them to memory and never forget them. They will guide you along your path when you need answers but keep coming up empty.

I know you may have many questions – questions I cannot answer. You must find your way, and the information you need, to continue moving forward.

Trust no one. I'm serious Aurora. There will be those who will pretend they can help you. They are liars. Always remain skeptical and trust your instincts. They will keep you alive.

It pains my heart to know I will not be with you when these difficult times arise. I ache at knowing I will not be able to see you grow into the beautiful woman I know you will become.

As much as this letter is a warning to make you aware of the dangers around you, and a guide to help you through them, it is also my goodbye letter.

I love you so much darling. I pray for protection, peace, and a path that will help guide you further.

Love, Mom.

P.S. Do not forget to destroy this letter. Leave no traces of this information behind.

Speechless.

The tears streaming down my face made the letter impossible to read. The love from my mother flowed through these very pages. It was as if she were here now, speaking to me – though the hazy memory of her voice did her little justice.

I unclenched my fists around the letter, leaving crumpled traces of my anguish permanently imbedded into the paper. I missed her so much. I missed them all. A sharp dagger twisted in my gut, doubling me over as I covered my face and sobbed into a tight ball.

Why did this have to happen? What did it all mean?

Lifting my head, I wiped my hands down my face, taking in a cleansing breath to calm my anguish. Through burning eyes, I tried to read through her words once more.

She made it clear a dark danger surrounded our family, more pointedly surrounded me, though she failed to go into any greater details about what the threat or danger was, or what I was supposed to do when it arrived.

How had they kept my brothers and I safe? Why didn't she give me more information than this? Despair at her letter led to indignation at the vagueness of her warning.

Why did she choose to single me out? Why not Garrett? Or Ryder? Did she know Tanner would die as well?

Her words had shaken me to the core. Not only with the box doing the weird stuff it had done but the reality that, in this very moment, my life could be in danger – and I'm alone. Nobody would ever know if something happened now.

Again, Scottie's twenty-twenty comment popped into my head. I had never applied that show to my life more than I had in the past week.

Glancing towards the window, the hairs on the back of my neck stood on end - the feeling of being watched heightened. I couldn't see out, but anyone could see in.

I needed to get a grip. I was becoming paranoid. There was no one out there.

Or was there?

Okay knock it off Aurora. Deep breathes. Inhale through the nose and out through the mouth, repeat until calm.

That shit never works.

Reaching into the box, I pulled out the locket she had referenced. An oval shaped pendant of dark metal, woven into a beautiful labyrinthine of tangled vines and roses, presented itself.

The design was the same on both sides, fixed to a long chain made of the same metal.

I lifted the necklace up by its chain, feeling the solid weight of it dangling from my hand. The glow from the fire shone through where the delicate weaving had openings. Though my mother called this a locket, there wasn't anything to suggest it as such. There were no clasps or sections to show where I could unlock it.

Could it need some incantation to break it open like the box? I couldn't be sure. I had no further directions to its mystery.

I secured the chain around my neck, noting its length had rested the pendant in the center of my chest - above my heart.

Remembering my mother's warning, I hid it beneath my shirt. The coolness of the metal awakened my senses, sending waves of goosebumps shivering throughout my body.

Picking up the letter once more, I read the incantation my mother had written and the meaning behind her words. What language was this? And when did she learn it?

There was much about my mother I didn't know – realized I would never know. I felt betrayed. She had another life I knew nothing about. Was she a secret agent for some underground government agency? What was my father's role in all of this? And what about Tanner? Did he know anything about any of this?

I gasped at the very real possibility that not only did Tanner know about their double life, but their accident probably wasn't an accident at all! Had the danger she referred to caught up with them?

She had stated she and my father had done their best to keep us safe, but Tanner wasn't safe. He was dead, along with them.

What did Garrett and Ryder know - if they knew anything at all? Who were my parents? Did Kate know anything about this?

Tanner and Kate were close friends as well.

Why did I possess the ability to heal things? And why had my mother always demanded I keep it a secret if she told me never to be ashamed of it? I've been ashamed of this power my whole life because of her; because I thought I was other – a freak.

I couldn't understand. The strain of continuous questioning was giving me a headache. I had been so lost in life without them only to learn I never really knew my life with them. I've been kept in a carefully constructed, naïve bubble in some failed attempt to keep me safe.

Was this so much better? That I didn't know about the real dangers and be left with a vague letter explaining the bullshit surrounding my life? If I had known from the very beginning the truth, couldn't I have helped in some way that could have kept them alive?

As it turns out, the trust I had in them had been violently shattered.

I no longer knew if I could trust my brothers and Kate. I certainly didn't trust my parents – they had lied to me my whole life. I didn't know what about, but apparently, it was something big.

No, why would my mother leave this note and locket with me if she weren't trying to protect me still?

I balled my hands into tight fists on either side of my head, squeezing my temples. All this nonsense was driving me crazy. I didn't know which way was up or down. What was the truth and what was the lie? I hated being this confused.

I placed the letter back on the table and crawled under the blankets, staring at the dancing flames crackling in the fireplace. All sense of security and control I held - fled. Left in its wake was raw, open resentment. What am I now other than a pawn in a dangerous game?

Never have I felt so alone than I do now. Even when I had first stepped foot into our family home, I was comforted knowing my brothers and Kate were still in my life. I could count on them. Was that still true? I couldn't be sure.

Exhausted from fighting every unwanted emotion flying through me, I didn't want to think about the dangers lurking in the shadows, or this other unwanted life I had been kept from.

Instead, I focused on the hypnotic flames, allowing their allure to carry me into a meditative state. I found my mind stilled as its glowing aura began soothing me in a way I hadn't been soothed in a long while.

There was no rhyme or reason to the dance of the flames but here they were, dancing in the heat of chaos. Its existence both at peace in its chaos and full of energy in its purest form; this element was fast becoming my living, breathing companion. Was this a message on how to live my life? I couldn't pull my eyes from its irresistible lure.

As my eyes grew heavier, I could only pray for a dreamless night.

A loud thud rocked the house, jarring me out of my sleep as I landed on the floor. What in the world was that?

My heart raced as adrenaline rang in my ears.

The fire I had made hours earlier was now a glowing pile of embers. The once bright living room almost pitch-black again.

I froze, listening in the death throes of silent darkness, trying to hear anything that sounded out of place.

It was eerily quiet.

My breath became the only erratic sound I could hear as I stumbled around for my phone. It was the only light source I had with me should I need it.

Finally, my fingers touched the familiar rectangular shape of my iPhone as I clutched it to my chest. Maybe it was just an earthquake? Those have been known to happen up here too.

I let out a shriek as another loud bang rattled against the front of the house. This time I wasn't going to be a sitting duck. There was definitely something out there. I ran to my father's office and closed his doors, hoping to at least put some barrier between me and whatever was out there.

A third bang, louder than the first two, slammed up against the exterior wall of the office. I bit down on my knuckles, stifling the scream threatening to rip through my throat. Fear trembled through every muscle fiber, pupils fully dilated, like a deer on the wrong side of a lion.

Remembering back to when I was fourteen; my father showed me a secret hideaway in his desk where he kept his gun. He had said if there were ever a true need, I must know where it was. Had he been preparing me to defend myself from this coming threat?

I ducked under the desk, fumbling for the secret latch. My fingers brushed against the piece of wood out of place. Pulling it down, the hidden compartment on the inside of the desk swung open, revealing the forty-five Ruger I had been desperately searching for. I snatched it up to check the mag. It was loaded! Thank you, dad.

I froze. Faint scuffling and grunting of whatever had been slamming up against the house stood right outside the office window. Was it a bear?

My breath caught in my throat, trying to steady my pounding heart. I slid the mag back in and loaded the pistol. Though my adrenaline surged, I had some semblance of peace with the means to defend myself.

The loud grunting outside the window turned into an ear-piercing squeal before dying off in an audible gurgle.

What. Was. That?

The loud ruckus had gone dreadfully quiet. I spanned my hearing as far as it would go, listening for any footsteps, any slight noise which didn't belong, but heard nothing. Was it over? Did a bear just kill its prey?

I didn't want to see the carnage, but I had to check. Though every nerve ending yelled at me in protest, I needed answers. I spent enough of my evening mewling over questions without answers. My mother told me I needed to be courageous, and I needed to depend on myself. This was me doing just that.

My soul felt detached from my body, as if I was an outside spectator watching every movement I made. My muscles protested as I crept towards the front door, every hair standing on end. I tried to steady my rapid breathing, questioning my actions in the process. Should this be the moment I question my sanity?

Squinting to see better in the dark, I peered through the cracked opening of the door. Nothing seemed out of the ordinary. Braver, I opened the door further, raising the pistol, and peeked around the corner. My blood ran cold.

I expected to see signs of a scuffle – that much was obvious. I even expected to see the carnage of whatever had died outside this wall moments ago. What I had not been prepared for, in any way, was the blood splattered across the porch, violently up the walls and onto the dirt driveway, as if part of a scene in a horror movie.

It wasn't the blood per se, but the brilliant blue-green bioluminescence that vibrated with the very life force it had been expelled from.

The odd thing, as if glowing blood wasn't odd enough, was the absence of a body. There were scuffle marks where the blood had been smeared from being stepped on and slid into – but no body.

A glowing, bloody footprint caught my eye at the foot of the door. Were they trying to break in? This wasn't the footprint of a man, but of something other. Abnormal and conical in shape, four sharp toes accented at the top, splayed out in a way too wide for any beast I knew. The size of the print hinted at the immense inhuman stature.

I peered into the darkness before crouching down to touch it. The viscous, gel-like blood transferred to my palm, a low-vibratory sensation dying in my hand as the life force began losing its vivid luminosity before my eyes. I brought my hand closer to my face, searching for clues in the dimming light.

Transfixed, a howling shriek in the tree line cut through my inert state, speeding my mind to the present.

I am in absolute danger.

Rushing back inside, I slammed the heavy wooden door shut and locked it in one swift motion. The fading blood from my palm smeared along its surface.

Backing away from the door on shaky legs, I stumbled in the dark to the back of the couch, pulling my blankets and pillow over. If I were in danger, then being in eyesight of the windows wasn't a place I wanted to be.

I didn't dare restart the fire. Whatever was out there; I didn't want to draw any more attention to myself than I already had.

Instead, I sat in complete darkness and utter silence, too wired for sleep. I kept my breathing shallow and quiet. Not only did I want to hear everything around me, but I also didn't want to be heard by everything around me.

My mind catalogued everything as it overworked to compartmentalize everything it had learned – trying to sort reality from fantasy.

First, I find a strange box not only addressed to me but held closed by some magical seal, which only I could open, as it illuminated in its bizarre fashion. In it contained a letter from my mother explaining she had the box made. I learn not only did she lead a double life but also, I had been lied to my entire life. She knew this language I had never heard before, tells me to trust no one, and leaves me with the absolute worst cliffhanger – my life is in danger. At this very moment.

Then, if everything I had experienced wasn't strange enough, a huge scuffle with copious amounts of glowing blood, or was it slime, had splattered over the entire front porch.

My brain was on overdrive; I was dangerously close to shutting down. This was too much to process. I couldn't compartmentalize any of it except for throwing it into the box my brain marked as absurd.

An eternity passed before the night sky began to give way to the rising sun. The birds began chirping their happy songs to welcome in the fresh morning. Early bird gets the worm. The corner of my mouth turned up. My dad would always wake us before the birds started chirping on the days we planned to go fishing. He loved being there at first light.

Too keyed up, I knew I couldn't stay holed in the house all day. But dare I face whatever waited for me out there? I knew at some point I needed to clean up that mess before my brothers and Kate showed up. They were already worried enough as it was. How could I explain that away?

Oh that? It's nothing. Some unworldly creature was viciously torn apart, and glowing blood splattered everywhere. Nothing to be worried about at all.

Right. I could see that going well. Though, when I brought up all I had learned from mom, it was sure to be stressful enough.

Peeking over the couch, the first light from the sun's rays

had broken through the top surface of the trees, revealing low lying, patchy fog suspended at the tree line. It was now or never.

I peeled myself from behind the couch, folding the blankets and sheets into a neat, methodical pile. Procrastination at its finest. I grabbed for my suitcase to change my clothes, realizing I had left everything, besides groceries and firewood, in the backseat of the cab in my haste to light a fire. I sighed, not prepared in any way to deal with the grotesque scene outside yet.

With tense steps towards the entrance, I took a deep breath to prepare myself while my hand hesitated on the knob. In a surreal sense of facing the death of another being, I cracked the door open and peered outside.

Chapter Ten

The Crossover

"It feels good to be lost in the right direction." – Unknown

***

Crisp morning air rushed to greet my tired, clammy skin, assaulting the warmth I had grown accustomed to. I peeked around the doorframe to further inspect last night's ordeal, except - there was nothing to inspect. The odd glowing blood from last night may very well have been a figment of my imagination. There wasn't a trace of it anywhere. Nor was there a single sign of a struggle.

I walked down the porch to where the first loud bang had woken me. Nothing. Everything was in place as it should be. I know I couldn't have made this entire event up; my mind wasn't that creative. Besides, I have my mother's note, that strange box, and the locket around my neck to prove things are not as they should be right now.

Shaken, I grabbed my suitcase out of the truck and hastened back into the house.

'*Everything is fine Aurora. You're fine,*' I repeated like a mantra to myself to soothe my anxiety. It wasn't working.

Unzipping my luggage, my hiking shoes peeped out from beneath the windbreaker.

I needed to clear my head. Anytime I hiked with Tanner, it always had a way of putting things into perspective. I checked the time on my phone - seven thirty. Kate and my brothers would be here soon enough; a quick trek wouldn't be that big of a deal.

While I should be worried of the dangers lurking all around, what would be the difference if I sat here waiting for it to come to me? I could feel my paranoia increasing and I refused to let that happen. Becoming catatonic was one thing, being someone who was afraid of every little thing was someone I refuse to become.

Throwing on my hiking clothes and grabbing my backpack, I made sure the essentials were in there – snacks from home, a lighter, change of clothes, emergency survival kit, and my father's gun. It was ingrained in me to always be prepared when hiking should something happen in the woods - another one of my father's many lessons.

I pulled out one of the brownies I brought from home, realizing I had been going too long without eating. It was a wonder I had any energy left at all. With a big bite, I loaded the pack onto my back as I wrote a quick note to let the entourage know where I was, should they arrive before I came back.

Before I could complete the first sentence, the magical box caught my eye. The tree was gone, my name had vanished, and it now looked like an ordinary wooden box. No *way!* That couldn't be. I *know* it wasn't like this last night. I snatched it from the table and spun it around so the inscription faced me but that too was gone.

I scrambled for my mother's note on the table to make sure

I wasn't imagining that as well. It was as I had found it. *Whew.* At least I had some hard evidence for when I explained this to my brothers. Without it, I would be two flicks of a lamb's tail from being thrown into an insane asylum.

With brownie still in hand, I darted out of the front door as I stuffed my mothers' letter into the top of my backpack. I rushed past the stables and towards the other side of our property. If I didn't get out now, what state would they find me in when they arrived? Half-crazed and schizophrenic? It would probably appear that way.

There was a distinct dividing line of trees between where our property stopped, and 'Bureau of Land Management' land began. There were many trails leading out of our property and into federal land as well, but I beelined it for one distinct trail – my favorite trail.

I paused for a long moment at the trailhead entrance, taking in the beauty I had committed to memory. My heart squeezed with joy at seeing it again after so long. It was bitter-sweet being here.

I called this the foxglove trail. The moment you walk to its entrance, you are met with a trail flourishing in foxgloves of all different colors - whites, peaches, deep coral pinks, and lavenders. It was the most colorful and breathtaking of any path surrounding us.

The route itself was only two miles long before it curved into one of the larger trailheads leading to the nearby stream. It was one of the roundabout ways to get there, which was why we would hardly use it on family trips. I also recalled my mother saying this specific trail was *pointless*. This was one trail Tanner and I would frequent together most often.

The morning we found this trail, it was much like today - the fog rising high in some areas and obscuring even the brush on the forest floor in others. The sunrays illuminated the surrounding trees as it showered through the misty morning fog, giving the whole area an ethereal jade-green aura. The dewy scent tickled my nose as flurries of damp air rushed in with every breath.

Moving forward, mindlessly taking another bite of the brownie, I recalled the day with perfect clarity, as if I were reliving it all over again.

"Ouch jackass! You know, your bony knuckles hurt!" Ryder yelled, rubbing his arm where Garrett socked him.

Wonderful. Not even half a mile in and they already started.

"Just keeping you tough kid," Garrett grinned from ear to ear. Ryder narrowed his gaze, following Garrett sauntering past him. You could see the cat-like reflexes coil in his muscles as he sprang, tackling Garrett into the overgrown fern bed. He didn't even see Ryder coming, element of surprise — Ryder was good at that. Though, I was surprised Garrett didn't think he would retaliate, or maybe he did and was sending out an invite.

They were rolling around in the ferns, testing each other's strength though we all knew it was no contest. First, Ryder was on top - pinning Garrett's arms down with his knees, poking him in the head with the end of a broken fern stick.

Once Garrett was done letting Ryder have the upper hand, he put his swift ground game to work. Ryder found himself trapped in Garrett's hold; his ear assaulted by Garrett's wet willy.

"Okay! Okay! I give up! Stop! Stooop!" Ryder screamed while Garrett laughed out like a hyena. We all couldn't help but join in on their laughter; how could we not, they were such a circus!

"You both fight like girls," Tanner chided, shaking his head in mock disgust.

"Alright you guys, knock it off. I want to see if this trail is going to lead us to the creek so we can nab some fish before they decide to fall asleep," dad said, chuckling. Garrett helped Ryder up, both covered in bits of fern

and dirt, before he got that look in his eye and pushed Ryder back over. Garrett lifted his knees high as he ran out of the ferns, laughing out loud away from us.

Ryder picked himself back up, wiping the spit out of his ear from Garrett's assault, "Ugh. Gross!" Mom and I shook our heads. For Ryder being nineteen and Garrett twenty-one, they sure did act like they were twelve.

We started back on the trail though we had plenty of time to see where this trail would lead. Regardless, we would find a way to the creek one way or another. That was dad's end game.

Further along, hundreds of tall stalks with colorful bell-shaped flowers stood tall along both sides of the trail. Upon closer inspection, I could see the inside had black and white spots on them, adding to the depth of their beauty.

"Hey Mom! What are these flowers called? They're everywhere!" I asked, enamored by how clustered they were up and down the trail.

"They're called foxgloves," she answered.

"Foxgloves? Why do they call them that? That's a weird name for them," I said.

"I'm not quite sure. Don't touch it!" she panicked, my hand within an inch of plucking a flower.

"What? Why?" I gasped, startled at her sudden outburst.

"They're highly poisonous. Even the slightest amount ingested can prove to be fatal. And besides, it's bad luck to pick them," she said, stern.

"Well, I wasn't going to eat it," I quipped.

"The residue on your hands could still have unpleasant side effects. Just don't touch them, okay?" she said, making me promise with her eyes.

"Yeah. Sure," I said, walking away from their beauty. It would be a shame to pick them anyways.

The restlessness echoing throughout the forest diverted my attention. The bristling cadence of the breeze sifting through the Sitka's and redwoods always comforted me. Fresh air mixed with faint undertones of honeysuckle and myrtle wood tree, crossed with the earthy aroma of damp leaves, smelled like home. I lifted my face to soak in the refreshing misty morning. I felt alive; awakened.

Walking in relative peace, I caught Tanner sneaking up on Garrett before locking him into a full nelson. Garrett struggled to break his hold; Tanner had a few more fighting years on him. You could tell the difference in age just by their body stature.

Ryder, the youngest of my brothers, had a slender build. Always trying the latest fad to gain muscle on his lean five-foot ten body; he often felt at a disadvantage to Garrett and Tanner. He was the natural musician and artist of the family.

Garrett stood at a muscular five foot eleven but was no match for Tanner, who was six-one. With a body builder's frame and the strength of an ox, he was a total powerhouse compared to these two. Everything Garrett knew about wrestling and MMA, Tanner taught him. Naturally, Tanner would be a good fight for Garrett.

"You should learn to pick on someone your own size," Tanner laughed as Garrett grunted, struggling to break free. "Don't you remember anything I taught you, kid?" Tanner said, mocking Garrett's earlier term of endearment for Ryder.

Ryder stood by with a smug look on his face.

Garrett was determined to win but it was as if Tanner were wrestling a kitten. Where Garrett began sweating, Tanner hardly even broke a sweat. "What if you were jumped by a couple of punks? They'd beat you senseless right about now. Seems I have gotten too soft on you in my old age little brother," Tanner chided, toying with Garrett as he flexed his hold. He always knew how to push Garrett to his last nerve.

"Old is right, geezer," Garrett grunted, trying all the moves he could, but every move sunk him deeper into Tanner's submission. Garrett was stubborn and wouldn't tap even if his life depended on it.

"Boys. Knock it off," Mom chided. She knew how easy their little wrestling matches could turn into an all-out brawl. Garrett always tried to one up Tanner, though he never could. Mom always tried to avoid another trip to the hospital like last time when Tanner broke Garrett's nose - which

was Garrett's fault entirely. He was always such a hot head.

Tanner gave one last chuckle before he released Garrett, giving him a wet willy of his own. Garrett began stretching his neck left to right, loosening his muscles as if he were getting ready for a rematch.

"I swear, you guys are like a bunch of teenagers," I joked.

"You should know Rory, you are one," Tanner teased, reminding me where I ranked on the age-totem-pole. He put his hand on top of my head, messing up my hair.

"Don't make me kick your ass Tanner," I said, a playful grin spreading across my face as I swatted his hand away. Mom sent daggers my direction as the word escaped my lips. "I mean butt!" I corrected, my eyes growing wide as my hands flew to cover my mouth.

"Ooooh!" Garrett heckled as I was still receiving the death stare from our mother. She hated cussing of any kind. She always said it wasn't classy and there were better words to use.

"Shut up Garrett before I sick Tanner back on you," I threatened. He rolled his eyes. He knew it wouldn't amount to crap. I rolled my eyes back at him before doing my best to ignore him.

The sight of a young buck in the near distance caught my attention. I slowed, cataloguing the subtle caramel spots in his mocha rich fur. There wasn't anything awe inspiring about his appearance to give me pause. I had seen plenty like him in my life. It was the peculiar way he watched us while plucking berries off the bush, not the least bit startled. With the commotion we were making, he ought to be leagues away from us by now.

"Aurora, are you coming?" Tanner hollered, startling me out of my reverie.

"Y-Yeah, coming," I said, exchanging glances with this buck one last time before jogging away from him.

Soon, we came up to a larger, more familiar trail, our usual trail which led us straight to the creek. We eventually found most trails on this side of the property would weave around in one way, or another, straight to the usual fishing hole. Dad was getting anxious to make it waterside to partake in his

154

second greatest love other than my mother — fishing.

"Such a pointless trail," my mother sighed, shaking her head.

"I thought it was nice," I quipped. It was beautiful and unlike any other I had seen.

"It may be nice Aurora, but I just knew it was pointless," she stated.

"How could you have known?" I asked, questioning her statement.

"Don't worry about it. Let's get to the water," she dismissed with a wave of her hand. I let it go, knowing my mother wouldn't elaborate any further on the subject. She used the "case-closed" tone we all knew too well.

We picked up the pace as dad led the way, the sibling bickering and play fighting over for now. We all had a one-track mind and that was the creek.

I dropped a knee onto the damp forest floor, arms clutched around my torso, as old memories ripped through my soul - I wanted them back. I wanted them *all* back. More than anything, I wanted these memories to be a reality once more.

Hot tears fell unbidden, becoming one with the ground beneath me. The dampened earth soaked through my jeans. I couldn't care less. What was a wet knee anyways? No one was here to judge me or care. There were no walls to close me in; no one to bear witness to the sobs breaking through my chest.

No one was here and that was how I wanted it.

I was free to let go. Not in the way I had in my parents' bedroom, but in a more cleansing way. I was finally able to release the tension I had been holding onto from the moment I stepped foot in our family home. I wiped my eyes with the heel of my hands, sliding them down my face, ridding the evidence of their stain. I hated crying.

Pushing myself up to stand, I lifted my gaze to a creature no taller than the height I was crouched in, staring back at me - its head cocked to the side in curiosity like a dog. My heart thudded once before pausing in its beat.

This prominent, pointy-eared creature stood on two feet much like a person, no more than ten feet in front of me. Its potbelly protruded over the hemline of its cut-off shorts made of leaves. Its sharp chin jutted forward, seeming to balance the foxglove hat it wore with ease, which was auspicious – they were poisonous, and he didn't seem affected by it at all.

What the? *Aurora get it together. Here is this unsightly creature standing mere feet from you wearing foxglove flowers as a hat and you think it's auspicious to be wearing it because it's poisonous?*

The longer we stared at each other, the more I questioned my sanity. Was I having a nervous breakdown and now hallucinating?

No damn it. I grabbed the wrong brownies again! How could I be so stupid? I've told Ryder a million times to label these damn things.

I didn't have time to ponder it further. The creature straightened its head, a mischievous grin spread wide across his face, exposing a full set of razor-sharp teeth. *Whoa!*

My adrenaline accelerated, taking in the possible danger from this otherworldly being. I stood up quick, feeling a heightened sense of vulnerability being huddled at its level. I towered over him, its height not reaching higher than my upper thigh.

Was this the strange creature I heard pounding against the house early this morning? Not likely; his feet weren't the same size as the footprint I had seen.

Neither of us made a move.

We watched each other close, that unsettling smile still plastered on his face. My breath hitched. Amusement rose in this little demon-creature's eyes as he let out a high-pitched chipmunk chuckle, unnerving me to my core. I prepared for this thing to attack but instead it smirked and ran down a trail to its left.

My heart thrummed wild against my chest, my breath faltering as I gasped for air. Should I follow it or make a mad dash to go back home? *Would it chase me if I ran the opposite way?*

Here I am, alone in the woods, hallucinating like some maniac, and debating whether I should even stay out here. I pulled out the bag of brownies just to be sure I hadn't grabbed the wrong ones. My name was written across the white block on the Ziploc bag. So, not the wrong brownies?

The big-eared creature peeked out from behind the bushes, smiling with expectation as if I were to follow it. When I made no move to follow, he lifted his four-fingered hand and curled his pointer finger in the universal "come here" movement. *I definitely grabbed the wrong brownies.* Maybe Ryder switched them on me as a practical joke; it wouldn't have been the first time. Man, these were potent though.

I did what any high, insane girl would do – I followed this three-foot pallor skinned creature down a seedy looking path. As I started forward, the little demon creature trilled and ran away again. *Was it toying with me?*

"Hey! Wait!" I yelled, rushing forward, tripping on an upended root.

Rounding the corner, he stood ten feet in front of me, hands on his hips as he shifted his weight to one leg. It was as if he had been waiting for me for hours to walk those few steps around the bush. I paused, waiting for him to make the next move. I was following him – now what?

His eerie high-pitched laugh echoed through the trees as he turned around and ran in the opposite direction. I picked up the pace and ran after him. Though my inner alarm sounded off like a tsunami siren, my curiosity was getting the better of me. I had never seen a creature like him before, nor did I recognize this trail. If I were to turn back now, would I ever be able to find either of them again?

Through the many twists and turns of the windy path, I lost sight of him. Pausing to catch my breath, I looked around for the first time. Turning and turning, I realized I was truly lost here. The trail I had been walking vanished, covered now by the thick forest fauna. There was no hint of a way back. The only part of the trail visible was what was set before me.

Spinning back to the open trail, it seemed I was already committed to this path. I had no other option but to stay the course. Hopefully, this trail led to another familiar one, like many of the others surrounding our ranch.

With a step forward, a deep rumble vibrated underground, stumbling my feet. Where the trail inclined towards the left, large tree roots scurried across the path, forming steep steps of dirt and gravel where each root intersected. My hand flew to my chest, trying to contain my heart from leaping out of its cavity. What did I just witness?

"Aurora, be brave," I sighed. Was I talking myself into bravery or down from insanity at this point? I couldn't be sure. Eyeing the peculiarity before me, I focused on deep breaths. *What choice did I have but to move forward?* I checked behind me, to be sure the trail had truly vanished. It was now within inches of my back. *Was I being herded?*

With the adrenaline pulsing through my veins, I took a nervous step forward, testing out the solidity of the makeshift stair before me. It felt as solid underfoot as any made by man, I would reckon even more so. I continued up the stairs with trembling legs, cautious with every step I made.

Reaching the top, the elf-like creature sat cross-legged carving pictures into the dirt, bored as a four-year-old with no toys. The moment I stepped off the last step, it perked up with a devilish grin and a sparkle in its eye, floating to its feet before making another mad dash in the opposite direction. It *floated! Floated!* I'm going to *kill* Ryder for doing this to me!

Whatever this creature was, or whatever drugs were laced into this pot, it was on my last nerve. I was done playing these childish games. This creature seemed to be intelligent enough to communicate with me through body language, and it certainly knew how to laugh at me, so why wouldn't it stop and *talk* to me? Without knowing what else to do, I sprinted after it, determined to speak with it - though catching it was out of the question. I shuddered. Who knew what those rows of teeth were capable of?

He came to a sudden halt, long enough for me to walk within five feet of him. At this proximity, I was closer to being a giant, as I towered over its three-foot frame.

"Hey! Why don't you talk to me? What's your name?" I asked in the least nonthreatening way possible. Or so I thought. The pallor creature cocked its head and smiled. In one fluid motion, it whipped around and dashed under the thick brush - a space no bigger than my five-foot four frame lying down.

"Great! Now what am I supposed to do?" I yelled after it.

I spun around to take stock of my options. The forest had enveloped me on all four sides. All signs of the trail were gone. It was as if I were standing in the middle of a clear-cut forest, with no entry in or out. Anxiety sprang like a healthy geyser. This was it, the end of the line for me. I was trapped and royally screwed.

A cold sweat beaded at the nape of my neck as I tried to keep my head. I could try to hack my way through the overgrowth and forge my own trail, but I was guaranteed not to make it very far. This overgrowth was the thickest I've seen. Besides, I didn't want to turn my back on this unsightly creature. What if he came back from that death trap and finished me off out here?

The other option? I could stay here and hope for Kate and my brothers to find me, though I didn't see how it would be possible. *I* didn't even know where I was. I mean - the damn trail closed itself off behind me! This was not okay. I was having one of those out of body moments where I knew I was in my body but also highly aware of everything buzzing around me.

I needed to regain some semblance of reality. Nothing, and I mean *nothing*, has made sense since I got here. Knowing how cornered I was, and out of options, I took a deep breath – crouching down to investigate the cramped tunnel. Despite the dark, I could see light at the end of it.

Was this thing leading me to my death? Was it trying to trap me in that cramped space and eat me with those razor-sharp teeth? That image did nothing for my vote of bravery moments ago.

If I was going to be insane enough to do this, it might as well be now.

I lifted my pack off my back, pushing it through the opening; there was no way I would leave it behind. I dropped down to my hands and knees, cringing at how dirty I was about to become. I thanked my past self for packing an extra set of clothes.

Pushing the pack further into the tight space, I laid down on my belly and army crawled my way through. Once inside, I did my best not to panic. Darkness engulfed me as I blocked what little light filtered in through the other side with my pack.

The space was as cramped as I imagined it and then some. The overgrowth of the twigs and branches pulled at my hair and clothes, lashing at my face in the process. I muffled my cries as a few tore deep into my flesh, leaving trickles of fresh blood flowing in its aftermath. I hope this creature wasn't lured by the scent of it.

Crawling through this darkness, I lost all sense of time and space. I couldn't tell how far I had crawled into this makeshift tunnel. I certainly couldn't tell how far I had to go either. All I knew was the walls were beginning to narrow, making any progress next to impossible.

I had no knowledge of where this creature was either. Was it watching me and bidding its time? Am I not in the right place where it attacks its victims yet? Was it too late for me to turn back now? There was no room for me to turn and look. It occurred to me; I never knew I was claustrophobic until now. Hyperventilating, my mind conjured up the worst happenings where this creature was involved.

I was right. This was it. I was going to die here.

Instead of being torn apart by that evil demon out in the open where some evidence would be found, I was going to be trapped in this hole where my body would decay and fall away to eternity. Maybe this was how the little demon, with muddy yellow eyes, would lure its prey to their death. Maybe he was more scavenger than hunter. He was going to come finish my pathetic ass off once I took my last breath and began reeking to high heaven. *Oh Lord, please, don't let this be how I go! Please!*

Somewhere in the back of my mind, my mother's words of wisdom echoed loud and clear.

"Always remember. You are stronger than you think you are. You will prove it to yourself once hard times hit which most assuredly, they will."

Oh mom. This was one of those hard times. How did I even allow myself to be lured into this situation? My stupid curiosity was how.

She used to always tell me I was too curious for my own good. She was right on both accounts though. Her words gave me the courage I needed to push forward. Yes, it was cramped in here and only getting tighter. I pushed forward anyways. I *needed* to. I *refused* to die here. I had to depend on myself to get out of this situation. No one else was coming. Except for that little devil.

I pushed with all my might against the resistance of the vines and twigs. Instead of making great strides as I had earlier, I inched along. I pushed and pushed until my arms screamed in protest. For all the progress I made, I wasn't getting anywhere fast. *Did this tunnel close too, just like the trail?* I seriously hoped not.

I pushed the pack with all my might, but it refused to budge. I gave it everything I had, locking my toes into the vines for leverage. Instead, I found myself beating the life out of it, letting out my failing aggression until I broke down and sobbed. *Why was this happening to me?*

I gave up, laying my forehead on the ground I had been crawling on. "I tried mom. I'm not as strong as you believed me to be. I'm sorry," I whispered defeat into the darkness. I hated to admit it, but with every move, my muscles cried out in revolt. I didn't have the strength to carry on.

With my hands stretched out before me, resting on my pack, I probably looked like a mole trying to claw its way through the underground tunnels. I was so uncomfortable. What choice did I have but to lay here and wait for a slow painful death? I was trapped, exactly where that little monster wanted me.

Absorbed in my own self-pity and loathing; I nearly missed the pack falling away from my fingertips.

My head shot up, seeing the light filter through for the first time. It was the end of the tunnel! Oh, the irony.

Hope swelled in my panic-stricken chest for the first time since this whole ordeal. I was not going to die here after all! I could go back home and never step foot in this cursed forest ever again. That is, until the little demons face came into view, blocking my exit. *All hope vanished.*

"Don't you come *any* closer! Get away! Get *away!*" I screamed.

This was it. This *was* where it brought its prey to eat them. I tried backing away; my feet only pushed against thick brush.

No! The tunnel closed behind me! Bile rose in my throat.

I was an animal in a cage being prodded, eyes wild at the realization of its demise. I kept my sights on the creature peering in through the exit. He kept turning his head this way and that, confusion settling on its face.

Its once yellow, muddy eyes shimmered gold, like when you flash a light at night into the trees and see a pair of eyes reflecting in response. This was backwards though. There was no light shining into its eyes. I allowed myself this moment to say my silent goodbyes and prepare what fate it had in store for me.

The creature stopped staring at me like a curiosity, instead giving me an impish grin. He opened his mouth and in a piercing soprano voice said, "Sequi me." He jumped down, away from the exit, leaving me here stunned in my own mortification. *So, he wasn't coming in here to kill me?* What else could this hellish creature want from me, if not my death?

I huffed, releasing some anxiety, as the sting of death I expected had been averted. There was no other way but forward it seemed. At least I could see the *light at the end of the tunnel.* How cliché.

Grabbing on to the vines in front of me, I pulled myself from the clutches of this wretched tunnel. I inched forward but my feet were still tangled in its snares. Wrapping my hands around the edge of the opening, eager to be free, I hoisted myself forward with more force than I realized. The tunnel released me from its hold, spitting me out as I came tumbling down on my side with a hard thud onto the forest floor.

Ouch. That one hurt.

The pointy-eared creature leaned up against a tree with its arms crossed, cackling at my graceful exit. I glowered at it as I pulled myself up, brushing off the dirt.

"A little help would have been nice," I said to it.

I grabbed the pack I landed next to as I straightened myself back up.

So, here I am. Its' mission accomplished. *Now what?*

We both stood still for a breath, measuring the opposition. I hated being on the defensive. What move would this creature make now?

He pushed away from the tree and took a step forward. Instinctually, I stepped back.

He stopped, raising his hand to scratch his head. All traces of his earlier behavior were gone; he now showed a seriousness that aged his childlike expression. He brought his hand down, tapping his fingers together with the other, as he lowered his face to the ground. He almost looked remorseful, as if he had his hand caught in the cookie jar.

An empathy I couldn't understand washed over me as I took in his saddened state. The fear I had of him felt suddenly misplaced and undeserved. What could have caused this change to come over him?

He shivered where he stood, terror fresh in his eyes as he lifted his gaze. He shot his hand out to the left, pointing without ever taking his eyes off mine. Reluctantly, I followed the trajectory of his hand, his terror bursting forth an entirely new, unexplained fear.

What stood at the end of his pointed finger was the last thing I expected to see. *How had I missed it before?*

Chapter Eleven

When Destiny Calls

***

The gate stood ten stories high. White vines and multi-colored flowers twisted and tangled every which way in a beautiful display of craftsmanship on its doors; eerily reminiscent of the intricate way my mother's locket was laced.

Light, in a kaleidoscope of celestial colors, filtered through the opening of the canopy and into the circular meadow before me.

Sentinel trees, as tall as the highest redwoods, stood on either side with ancient sleeping faces carved into each trunk. Blocking my entrance were two imposing limbs, which formed an X in front of the gate.

Twisted tendrils, adorned with scarlet leaves, cascaded towards the forest floor like a weeping willow. Its leaves painted the ground in a sea of crimson foliage. The overgrowth of the surrounding forest had grown as high as the gate itself, trapping me within formidable walls.

And here I stood, in awe of it all, as an unseen energy forced my way towards this peculiar, heavily guarded gate in the middle of the forest.

Should I try crawling under the guarding X? Were there traps in place to keep people like me out? How should I proceed from here? I didn't want to make the wrong move.

Inching closer, the shimmer of the opalescent vines wrapping around the crosshairs of the X caught my attention. From the center, they intertwined up the poles until becoming one with the trunks of the trees.

A zinging impulse to touch these vines became overwhelming as I clenched and released my hand. Something so intricately crafted, would it be smooth to the touch? Was there a key hidden somewhere within its vining leaves? A secret passageway, if you will?

I glanced behind me, aware of being unaware of the little demon for the first time. Maybe he would know what to do.

But he was gone; not a trace left where he had been standing. I spun around, searching the meadow in a panic, like a spider you had been keeping an eye on but suddenly lost sight of.

I am alone. Why did he lead me here?

I turned back to appraise the formidable gate shrouded in mystery. *What should I do?*

Remembering when my dad had taught me how to ride a horse; I was nervous in the beginning. His advice, which now echoed in my mind, was to trust my instincts. Listen to the silent voice in my mind, tap into the surrounding environment, feel what it was telling me. It was always talking, guiding, if I would just listen.

166

Raising a trembling hand, adrenaline throbbed in my ears. An impulsive need to caress the vine's surface became unbearable.

With my palm a mere inch from the vines, an impatient energy buzzed in the space between us. All breathing ceased from my lungs as the chaotic pull of this energy invited me to complete the process. The atmosphere grew eerily silent, as if in high anticipation for this connection.

I could no longer ignore the siren call, wanting nothing more than the immediate satisfaction of its promised answers. I closed the gap.

Pupils dilated, and blood boiled, as a violent scream ripped through my vocal chords. A searing pain ignited upon contact with a burst of electrical current, scorching every vein and fiber of my being. This foreign power consumed me.

Information I couldn't comprehend passed between me and these vines. Was it sucking information out of me? Was it sending me vital information? I couldn't know for sure. Nor did I care.

Images flashed in a fury through my mind. Images that made little sense. They all blurred together. The surrounding forest, and the reason for my existence, all a moot point. It's as if I were riding on a high-speed train, focusing only on the objects passing by.

Blurred visions of my parents. Of my mother. I couldn't make sense of the context of these images, only recognizing them through familiarity.

My brothers.

Kate.

They swirled into each other until they became blurred once again.

With a lightning burst, I was thrown back from this frightening torture. The prominent pain and images were gone, though my muscles twitched with the ghosting ache of the residual electric pulses. A high-pitched hum reverberated within my ears, echoing the pulses singing in my veins.

My hand burned bright red from the contact but no longer hurt; just trembled.

Lifting my gaze, the point of my touch illuminated the vines into a brilliant white as it crept up their coils, filling every nook and crevice of the leaves and frills. The resemblance of how I opened the box from last night matched what was happening before me, albeit on a grander scale. Coincidentally, the wood of the box was identical to the bark of these trees.

Standing on shaky legs, I watched the path of the illuminated vines come to its end as it circled around each of the ancient sleeping faces. I stood as silent and still as the wind itself. *What had I gotten myself into?*

I watched in horror as the eyes of these sentient trees peeled open one after another. In unison, they awakened with bolstering yawns, blowing forward the scarlet leaves around them like two wind turbines. I shielded my face as dirt and twigs pelted my body.

"What do we have here?" two curious voices echoed within the meadow. My breath rippled with tremors as I lowered my trembling arms. Staring at me were two sets of large, illuminated eyes - fire burning bright within their irises. I couldn't move, fixated on them as I awaited my fate.

"It's a girl. Poor thing looks terrified," the grandmotherly sentinel on the right said. Though its eyes were lit with fire, its ancient face held a kindness its neighbor did not. I let out a small scream as a vine lifted my chin up. "She's shaking like a leaf!"

"Humph! Serves her right for waking us up. What do you want?" the grumpy left sentinel demanded. I couldn't believe what I was seeing. *Trees were talking.* I *have* gone crazy. I couldn't even blame it on the drugs Ryder laced the brownies with. It was evident I snapped.

"Well dear? What brings you all the way out here?" the kind, grandmotherly sentinel asked.

"I—I don't know. I got lost," I stammered.

"I'd say! Nobody comes here unless they want in through these gates. Why do you want in?" the gruff sentinel asked, cranky as an old grandfather.

"I—I d-don't know," I replied.

"Quit stammering and wasting our time. If you don't know, then why are you here?" the left tree barked.

I was an ant under a microscope with these two ancient faces staring at me with expectation. What should I say? Should I just tell them the truth? This two-foot, pointy-eared demon led me here?

It suddenly didn't seem so crazy to be describing this scenario to talking trees.

"I—I don't know why I was led here, but I-I f-followed a two-foot pointy-eared d-d-demon here," I stammered.

The cranky ancient brought a vined branch to its forehead as it shook back and forth, leaves raining down around me from the movement.

"Oh dear," the grandmotherly tree said solemnly, "it seems you were expected."

"Expected? What does that mean?" I asked, shock emboldening my shaky voice.

"It means you were expected! What are you — *slow?*" the left tree belittled, the vined branch leaving his face and reaching out as if to emphasize its point. The terrified feelings I had were beginning to lose their edge. Anger began seeping through me at *grumpy trees* insults.

"I *know* what expected means. What I don't understand is *why* I'm expected," I exclaimed.

"Don't get sassy with me *sprout!* Who you are?" the left tree bellowed. *Terrified feeling back.*

"A-Aurora. Aurora Walker." I watched as this revelation dawned on both of their faces.

The kind sentinel gasped as a vine moved to cover her mouth. They exchanged knowing glances before turning back to me.

"What? What do you know?" I demanded.

"Could this be?" grumpy tree eyed me with skepticism, squinting one eye closed for a better view.

"I believe so!" exclaimed the gentle sentinel with excitement. "So soon though? How can we be sure?" she asked to the left.

"It's her alright. Did you feel when she laid her hand on us?" the cantankerous ancient asked.

"Yes. That was quite a shock!" the other ancient quivered.

"Stop talking about me like I'm not here," I demanded, "I need answers! Who am I to you? Why were you expecting me? And what do you mean by that shock? Did you feel it too?" I had more and more questions the longer I stood here. My patience was wearing thin.

"Quiet sprout. We're talking," the grumpy tree admonished.

"Quit calling me sprout. Just talk to me!"

"If that temper of hers isn't proof enough, I don't know what is," the friendly sentinel stated.

"Humph," he replied

"The shock when you touched us was quite painful. I wouldn't doubt you experienced it yourself. You are expected; however, you are early. The little 'two-foot demon' as you put it, is a wood elf - mischievous little creatures they are," the kind ancient chuckled. "Those who are expected are led here. Those who are not, are led astray."

"*Wood elf?* I'm losing my mind," I shook my head, burying my face in my hands. I was having an 'Alice-fell-down-the-rabbit-hole' moment.

"I assure you, dear. You are not losing your mind," the kind ancient said.

"Sure. If I'm not losing my mind, then why am I talking to *trees* about a two-foot wood demon, sorry *elf*," I corrected at the admonished look on her grandmotherly face, "about being led here only to learn I've been expected, albeit early, for some unknown reason?"

As I asked the convoluted question, I could only hear the absurdity in my words.

"We cannot discuss the matter further with you. We have been given our orders," the grouch explained.

"What orders? By who? If this is about me, I have a right to know," I demanded.

"You only have the right to know what we have the right to tell you - and that is nothing," he spat back.

"Then what am I even doing here then?" I threw my hands up in frustration.

"You're asking me?" he asked, astonished.

"As we have said, you are early. No matter. Our orders are to grant you entrance regardless of the time of arrival," the gentle ancient explained, passing a disapproving eye to her left.

"Do you have the key?" the grouch demanded.

"What key?" I spat.

"The key to unlock this gate, *obviously,*" he rolled his ancient eyes.

"No, I don't have any key," I stated. How frustrating. Here I was talking to two trees who were more cryptic than my mother's letter. *My mother's letter! The pendant!* Was that the key? My mother said to let no one know I had it. Would that include the gates guards?

"How would I know if I *did* have it?" I asked. I didn't want to freely give away this information if I didn't have to.

"You'd know!" the left ancient barked, looking as frustrated as I felt.

"No. I don't think I would."

"Of course you wouldn't, you subpar intelligent sprout!" he insulted.

"Excuse you," I said.

"You *heard* me!"

"Now that is *enough!* Arguing is not helping," the kind ancient said, raising an eyebrow at its disgruntled counterpart. "Dear, if you had the key, it would only be a matter of placing your hand over it and transferring your energy into these very vines," she said, pointing one of her free vines to the gate.

"Now why did you divulge that *before* knowing if she had it or not?" he asked.

"Because if she has it, it would not matter if we see it or not," the grandmotherly ancient said.

"Doesn't mean you had to divulge information *freely!*" he reprimanded.

"We are here to guard this gate, *not* keep those who are meant to pass through *out!*" the kind ancient said, irate.

"Some guard you are!" the grouch insulted. The grandmotherly sentinel whipped one of her long vines into the left sentinel's cheek.

"Owwwch!"

"Don't mind that old fool, dear. If we know who you are, and you have the key, you are free to pass," she smiled down at me.

"Thank you, but where does this even lead to?" I asked.

I knew one thing; I didn't want to be transferring energy like that again. That was one painful experience I didn't feel quick to relive.

"Oh, you'll find your way, dear. Just trust your instincts to guide you," she advised. My dad's words echoed once again as the strange feeling of them being connected came over me.

"How would I even go about transferring my energy?" I didn't know the first thing about energy transference other than what I did when I healed myself.

"I will guide you," the pleasant ancient said.

The vines around the guarding X began to uncoil and slither away from the center. The massive branches creaked and groaned as they pulled back, revealing on the gates center a tree reminiscent of the mystery box my mother gave me. A circle encompassed it, highlighting it as the main focal point.

I stepped closer, intrigued by the sight of this very same emblem. "Where will this gate lead me?"

"To your destiny dear," she said.

"And what is my destiny?"

"That is up to you to figure out. However, there is only one way to do that, isn't there?" she asked, gently pushing me towards the gate. I would have been like a colt with locked legs if it weren't for the strength of her vine. Within arm's length of touching the gate, the sentinel released me.

They could no doubt hear my wild heart. Did I have no other choice but to walk through these gates?

"What if I don't want to pass through?" I voiced my last thought.

"If you don't want to walk through then why are you wasting our time?" the grouch barked.

"It's a question. Do I have *a choice* in this matter? Is there no other option than to walk through these gates?" I asked again.

"What? Are ya *chicken*?" he taunted.

"Why would you want to walk away from your destiny dear? A whole new set of possibilities awaits you!" the kind sentinel asked.

"That's the thing. I'm walking into this blind. I don't know what possibilities await me on the other side. I don't even know what *is* on the other side of this thing," I said, pointing towards the gate. "And my question hasn't been answered. Is this my *only* option?"

I glanced back and forth between the two ancients. A soft rustling of the leaves caught my attention as the grumpy sentinel gave a tight-lipped shake of the head to the other.

"There *is* another way isn't there?" I deduced.

"Yes. There is," she sighed. "Things are not always as they seem. There is *always* a choice. You can choose to walk through here," the sentinel pulled back what I thought was part of the forest wall, but instead was a curtain of vines revealing a trail, "and go back home. Pretend as if none of this has happened."

"And be a coward. Hide from your destiny," the grouch said. He turned his full attention towards the grandmotherly sentinel. "Why did you have to go and tell the truth like that? A little lie never hurt nobody."

"Those were our orders. Have you forgotten them? She is to know of her choices," she reprimanded.

"Humph. The only *right* choice here is to walk through those gates. Any other choice is a moot point," the left sentinel grumbled.

"The only right choice is *her* choice. If she wants to run away from her destiny, she has a right to it," she argued in my favor. "I must tell you though dear, if you do decide to take this trail back, you may *never* be able to come back here again. The destiny before you now may be lost to you forever."

"Why is that? You said I was early, didn't you?" I asked.

"Well, yes. You are. There are things that must align for you to find your way here. It doesn't happen very often I am afraid," she explained.

From the moment I had stepped foot onto the family ranch, craziness and mysticism has surrounded me. My mother had gone through great lengths to not only protect me but also prepare me as much as she could. I came here under the most impossible circumstances to the most magical place I had ever seen. Though my theory of being drugged and crazy wasn't completely off the table, I knew something greater beckoned me.

If what my parents worked so hard to protect my brothers and I from were on the other side of this gate, was it right to push forward?

What if I can find the answers of their death - the *truth* of their death? Was I prepared to go back to the numb and painful nonexistence in San Diego, knowing what I know now?

Is what stands before me the answer to the life I've been seeking all along?

The internal struggle warred within my very being. To take the trail back home meant conceding to a life of misery, pain, and regret. It was comfortable. It was known.

Beyond the gate was not. Beyond the gate only promised the opportunity of an adventure - nothing more, nothing less. I am promised nothing.

Not knowing what to expect, I expected nothing. The strange pull I had experienced before I came here grew stronger, beckoning me to answer the call of my destiny – whatever that meant. Faced with my old life back on the trail, the appeal of walking away began to lose its luster. I knew my choice.

"Tell me what I must do," I sighed. The kind sentinel smiled as she dropped the curtain.

"There is hope in you after all sprout," the grouch said, giving a smile probably so rare for him. I nodded a tight-lipped smile in his direction, too agitated with my decision to form a proper response.

"Listen to me very carefully dear. Follow my instructions exactly. Where your key lies, place your palm over it." I did as she said, placing my left palm over the center of my chest where the pendant laid positioned over my heart.

"Now, raise your other hand and place it on the center of the circle," she continued. As I raised my hand, I hesitated to touch the emblem. Leaving my hand hovering over the tree, the familiar energy thrummed under my palm.

"Go on dear," she encouraged. I glanced at her before turning back to my hand. Releasing a heavy sigh, I braced myself for the coming pain, and pressed my palm to the gate.

Rather than pain, I became energized. A spark, where my hand laid over the locket, pulsed through my fingertips, up my arm, across my chest and back into my outstretched hand. The trailing sensation pulled my gaze to the pendant glowing bright beneath my shirt. Every nerve ending vibrated between me and the gates tree symbol, which now illuminated before me.

I watched with familiar fascination as the luminous light followed the path of each individual vine that had intricately laced around the other. It wasn't long before the entire gate became illuminated, buzzing with the energy oscillating between my hand and the vines. I glanced up to the grandmotherly sentinel smiling down at me full of wonder.

"Can you feel that energy?" she beamed, "*That* is the energy transference between you and the life force of the forest around you. The gate is accepting your energy dear. Now to unlock it, repeat after me,

"*Ab Aeterno, Ab Intra,*" she recited.

Her counterpart trailed the meaning in English, *"from the eternal, from within"*

"Non Est Ad Astra Mollis E Terris Via"
"The road from earth to the stars is not easy."

"Facilis Descensus Averno"
"Hell is easy."

"Dum Bita Est, Spes Est"
"While there is life, there is hope"

"Alis Volat Propriis"
"She flies with her own wings"

"Alis Grave Nil"
"Nothing is heavy to those who have wings"

"Bis Vincit Qui Se Vincit"
"She conquers who conquers herself."

"What does it all mean?" I asked the gentle elder.

"It is your destiny dear. It is up to you to find out what it means," she said.

That didn't help much.

I remembered the words, the inscription, which opened the box to the letter and the pendant. It was in the same language as what the sentinels spoke. Did my mother create this gate? Was this all her doing? I had no time to ponder further as the vines began to unravel from the gates heart center.

The vines glimmered from top to bottom, like the sparkling curtains of a Vegas Broadway show being peeled back, layer-by-layer, until the brilliance of what the closed doors contained shone through.

The sudden sense of déjà vu hit me; I dreamt of this very moment. I was living the parallels from my dream about walking into heaven, or onto a fresh sheet of bright white copy paper. True to my dream, nothing could be seen on the other side but the brightest white light. Its gentle pull invited me forward, beckoning me to begin my journey.

I lifted my palm flush to the barrier separating me and the light. The familiar energy swirled and pulsed under my palm, stronger than any other time before. Pushing past the barrier, an unseen force pulled my hand from the other side as if someone were grabbing it. I snatched my hand back to my chest, clasping it with my other hand.

"What the?" I gasped, glancing back towards the hidden trail. I could go back. It wasn't too late.

Yet, it was.

I was already in this too deep.

Mentally, I said my goodbyes to Garrett, Ryder, and Kate. I made peace with the life I had lived and the real possibility of leaving it, and everyone I knew, behind me forever. I turned back, both saddened and invigorated, at starting this next chapter – whatever that meant for me.

I took my final breath on this side of the known and stepped forward, allowing the bright void to pull me into the unknown.

Chapter Twelve

Discovery

———— ∞ ————

"You once told me you wanted to find yourself in the world —
And I told you to first apply within,
To discover the world within you.

You once told me you wanted to save the world from all its wars —
And I told you to first save yourself from the world,
And all the wars you put yourself through."
 - Suzy Kassem

***

Crossing the threshold, I staggered at the sight before me.

The trees were numerous; spaced out just enough to see through them. The trunks were wide and, as my eyes traveled up their length, seemed would go on for miles. They could easily dwarf the largest redwoods known to man as their expansive canopies reached out to hug their neighbors.

Imposing ferns covering the ground, between the towering giants, were dwarfed – if one could even call them that. They stood several feet taller than my five-foot four frame.

Something so magnificent, I couldn't be sure if these larger-than-life trees were real. Would the reality of them seep steeper into my mind if I were to touch them? If I could somehow tell my mind through the sensory nerve of touch that what stood before me was truly real and not some illusion?

Resting my hand on the jagged mahogany bark, the rough exterior sprang to life with an overwhelming energy transference, much like the one I experienced when tending the garden at home – albeit, on a much grander scale.

The familiar tickling on my skin, like a feather being brushed across ever so lightly, grew more forceful. Like tiny pinpricks. Not enough to hurt; only annoy. The typical gentle pull of my hand, as if it were slightly heavier, now felt like fighting against gravity to keep it from becoming one with the tree. The usual warm tendrils of vitality flowing from my palm now felt as if my wellspring of healing power had sprung a leak.

I ripped my hand away, cutting off the sensation, only to be bombarded with another. A hyperawareness to the buzzing forest - as if a million bees were zinging all around – dominated my auditory perception. I scanned around to be sure I wasn't standing amidst real bees, unable to pinpoint the source. Turning back to the tree before me, I eyed it with a sneaking suspicion. I pressed my hand once more to the rough bark with cautious awareness.

The energy transfer sprang to life; the auditory buzzing dulled.

The buzzing of nature became hyper focused on this one tree, where I placed my palm. I pulled my hand away once more.

Once again, I became assaulted by the cacophony of low vibratory buzzing. It was a very unnerving experience.

"Well, enough of that," I said out loud, though my voice sounded off. The audible pitch was cut off; dulled somehow. Muted. As if the forest absorbed my tone in the sea of high vibrations. Strange and disorienting.

I rubbed my hand against the back of my neck, leaning my gaze towards the sky as I tried to make heads from tails. The light filtering in through the canopy wasn't the typical shade of jade green I was accustomed to. Instead, prismatic colors filtered in with red and blue hues, greens and yellows, and an occasional purple. I squinted at the oddity, trying to see through to the source of these color combinations from what little openings the forest's canopy allowed, though my findings turned out to be inconclusive.

"Calm down Aurora," I breathed. I repeated this chant as I tried to normalize the atmosphere around me in my mind. I should go back, talk to my brothers about this. They thought I was crazy anyway, at least I would have proof I wasn't completely insane this time.

Besides, I have so many questions; I needed to speak to these sentinel trees before continuing this path.

Turning back, the gate had vanished, as if it were never there in the first place. Was I missing it somehow?

The grandmotherly ancient had said that 'things were not always as they seemed' as she pulled back the curtain of vines. Could this be yet another allusion?

I pushed forward, expecting to be met with the resistance of the gate, though this proved fruitless. I only walked into more forest. Nothing hinted at something otherwise.

Bile rose in my throat. Shallow breaths came in hot and fast. The reality of being lost and alone settled in.

I'm vulnerable. Exposed. Raw. I am not safe.

The words from my mother's letter echoed loud in my head, "You, and your brothers, are in great danger."

I had taken the biggest, and stupidest, risk of all. I walked into the unknown, said goodbye to the life I knew, and now here I wanted that life back. Like the Israelites wanting to go back to slavery in Egypt, I now complained about wanting to go back to my nonexistent life – a slave to my depression.

Utter nonsense. For all I knew, this was the exact thing my parents worked so hard to save my brothers and I from. Yet here I am, gallivanting through an even more twisted scene than Alice's rabbit hole.

I gasped for air, trying to pull myself together. Why was it so hot suddenly?

I ripped off my jacket, slamming it on the ground when its arm twisted around my hand, refusing to release me. The forest felt like it was closing in as the humidity became unbearable, like someone turned up the thermostat in a sauna. How had I not noticed this before? Or was it just me? I wiped the sweat dripping from my brow.

I needed a plan. Yes, a plan would help refocus my thoughts. My father always said, when life fell into absolute chaos, plan and execute immediately. All anxiety and fear will melt away. In order to do that, I needed to calm the eff down. Think with a clear head.

I inhaled a deep breath through my nose, letting out an audible sigh through my mouth. I continued this for a few more repetitions until I felt my shoulders relax out of my ears – my breathing returning to a normal pace.

Think Aurora.

I'm in a place that is larger than life and completely foreign. I don't know which direction to go, but I needed to pick a direction and commit. First things first, find water – a river or stream. Where there is water, civilization would surely follow.

Second, find someone to talk to so I can at least be guided in a better direction than the path I am following.

With a huff and a nod, I swiped up my jacket, forging forward with fear and anxiety wrestling for control over my plan to stay calm. I couldn't let them win.

It couldn't have been over two hours of trampling down this squirrely path around boulders, and under speckled mushroom like plants, before the forest began to darken. How could night already be approaching? It had been early morning when I left the Ranch.

With no signs of water, or civilization for that matter, I had nowhere to take shelter from the elements or predators. I beat the creeping anxiety back down with a stick as I continued to remember my father's teachings - build a fire before nightfall. This will keep you warm and most of the critters away.

I did just that, gathering what branches and twigs I could find. Though the forest was thick with vegetation, I found a small cropping of trees which left a natural opening on the forest floor. After clearing the ground, I had a fire roaring to life in no time.

With the approaching darkness, so came a bitter cold I had not anticipated. It equaled that of a snowy winter night in Oregon, which you would not want to be caught outside in. I huddled as close as I could to the fire – all but sitting in it.

The jacket I abused earlier only kept the deepest part of the cold at bay as a shiver rattled my teeth. I did my best to keep myself warm, the friction from rubbing my arms up and down doing little to keep the chill away.

I scanned the surrounding forest but could see nothing past the glow of the fire. It was eerie, in a Blair Witch Project sort of way, not being able to see what lay beyond the tree line around me.

Stealing a glance towards the canopy, a clear opening amongst the branches revealed a night sky dotted with millions of stars. Accompanying the stars blanketed the most colorful nebula with hues of radiant hot pinks and reds, greens, yellows, and purples. This must be the source of the colors I had seen earlier filtering in through the canopy. It was nice having at least one mystery solved.

A violent shiver pulled me out of my reverie. This wasn't working. At this rate, I'm going to catch a cold, or worse - frostbite. I shuffled through my bag to see if I had packed my thermal blanket, hoping to God that I did.

Digging to the bottom of the bag, a screeching howl echoed against the surrounding trees. I shot straight to my feet. What in the hell was that? It sounded close — too close for comfort.

In the near distance, the heavy flora and fauna of the forest gave way to something large, and fast approaching. A chill, having nothing to do with the bitter cold for once, crawled up my back. Another screeching howl, much louder than the first, echoed even closer.

Searching for a weapon, something to give me a fighting chance, I remembered my father's gun. Falling to my knees, I tore open my bag. I know I packed it in here somewhere.

Finally, my hand wrapped around the cold metal that worked its way to the bottom. I ripped it out of the bag and scrambled to my feet, raising the barrel to the approaching threat.

An unsettling chill rattled through my bones as the eerie howl seemed to multiply, screeching in and out of unison. The forest before me revealed nothing but the crushing sound of a stampede's swift approach. My outstretched hands trembled as I clutched the grip to the gun.

In a guttural whimper, the crashing and screeching went silent. A hitch in my breath, and a laser focus on the darkness in front of me, I readied myself for whatever would find me standing here, shaking violently.

On the edge of darkness, a rustling of the ferns and leaves crunching underfoot sounded deafening compared to the crashing I had heard moments ago. My nerves stretched on a tight wire as the wild glow of the fire made the dancing ferns unmistakable. Something approached, my hawk eye not moving one millimeter away from the impending danger.

An elderly lady, no taller than me, hobbled out of the ferns with a cane and a wicker basket attached to her back. Her gray, straw-like hair hung far past her abdomen, the hunch in her back helping to bring it lower than it typically would be.

She uttered something under her breath; her wrinkled scowl grimacing at the fire before turning a chastised gaze upon me. Her ruthless eyes stared down the length of her long, wart nose as she took in my shocked stance.

"H-hello!" I stuttered, both nervous and elated to have seen someone here for the first time. I lowered the gun.

"What is your problem? You want to bring the howling's upon us both?" she reprimanded in a rough, heavy accent.

"I – I'm sorry? I was trying to keep warm. I'm lost," I explained, before she cut me off.

"I don't need your sob story," she sneered as a wave of her hand extinguished the flames. A shiver rattled through me. I had no logical explanation for what happened. I glanced to where she stood, not realizing she was already on the move.

"Hey! Wait! Let me come with you!" I exclaimed, grabbing my backpack in my haste to catch up with her. She spun on her heel, faster than I would have expected for someone her age, and faced me. By the dim light of the nebulous sky, the menace in her eyes grew perceptibly terrifying.

"No. Get away from me. Go back to wherever you came from," she stated. Her rudeness stopped me short. Not wanting to disrespect my elders, I worked further to explain my case.

"I'm sorry. I can't. You see — you're the first person I've come across. I don't know where I am. Please, let me come with you."

Her eyes fell to my feet before scrutinizing up the length of my body, finally resting on my eyes. "Fine. But keep your mouth shut," she said, reluctant to agree.

"O-kay," I said, unsure.

"Not a peep," she bit back in her harsh accent. She turned quick towards the direction she originally headed. I threw the gun in my pack and zipped it up as I struggled to catch up. She sure moved fast.

We walked in unrelenting silence, not once attempting small talk. I had so many questions burning on the tip of my tongue, though. As my eyes began adjusting to the darkness of the forest, I realized it wasn't dark at all. In every tree, every fern, every vined leaf, a bright bioluminescence radiated throughout each vein.

As if someone suddenly shut the lights off in a room full of glow in the dark ropes and leaves, the entire forest shone bright. Following my gaze up the trees, I could see the bluish-white path of their life essence winding up through the trunk and splaying out through every branch and leaf of the canopy. It reflected a soft glow back down to the forest floor, highlighting the bright pathways of the root systems that ran along the ground, which I now walked.

Every step that landed on the ground became a prism of light surrounding the pressing foot, splaying every which way. I watched in awe as I lifted my foot, the glow slowly faded.

I looked to the old woman to ask about the curiosity but noticed something about her that gave me pause. Walking ahead of me, the luminescence around her faded back into total darkness. The roots scurried away from her, and the ferns shriveled until they were brittle and lifeless. As if the very essence of death herself walked by them. The intuition I should listen to whispered in my ear not to trust her. To stop following her.

As if that wasn't peculiar enough, the vines fast approached, and the ferns sprang to life the moment I followed in her footsteps. The vital life essence restored back to full health. It begged the question, why am I still following this woman?

My dumb reasoning challenged, what choice did I have now? She was the first person I had seen since stepping foot into this strange world. I already committed to following her, no turning back now. I remained cautious, however, as my senses were heightened at the realization, she may be more dangerous than I initially realized.

An opening in the trees ahead revealed the soft glow of light filtering out from a single window of a shanty shack; pieced together by whatever was easily found. Four mismatched walls, an off-kilter slanted roof, and billowing smoke out of the chimney were all what made up the dark and dingy shed. The immediate forest all around was pitch black; the only hint of light coming from within the home.

Following the old woman out of the tree line as she hobbled along on her cane, she made no move to acknowledge if I was to follow or piss off. She continued towards the door, without looking over her shoulder, and said, "Come".

I startled at her gruff voice, as it had been the only thing she said since leaving camp.

"Sure," I replied, not at all sure.

The hair on my arms raised to attention the closer I came to the entrance. I became more unsure and aware than I had ever been. Whoever, and whatever, this woman was; a great power resided here, and it felt ominous. I paused, warring with myself whether or not it was too late to deny her reluctant invitation to join her.

"What are you waiting for?" she asked, staring at me by the doorway.

Rather than shrink back into myself, I had to move forward. I had to face this head on. I'm sick and tired of being afraid; I only hoped this woman could provide me with some answers, whatever that meant.

As she moved from the entrance of her tiny shack, I stepped into a grand, circular foyer that rivaled any mansion back home. A black inlaid compass in the center of the white marble floor pointed towards four rooms before me, rather than in perpendicular lines.

To the right, an enormous staircase curved the length of the room towards the second floor, the marble continuing to adorn the stairs. Carved vines in the ebony wood banister made up the supports as the flowers added to its decorative appeal.

In all of this, the home before me looked nothing of its outside façade. Hundreds of candles were brightly lit along the walls and in the massive chandelier hanging above me.

Pulling myself out of my awe, I turned to compliment the elderly woman about her home, but she vanished.

"Hello?" I called out, listening towards each room from where I stood. I heard nothing and could see no one. How strange.

In the far-right room, closest to the staircase, a shadow flashed along the wall. I hastened towards it, hoping to find the old woman there.

Through the small hallway made of raven stone, a grand

living room with an imposing fireplace opened before me. Two women stood in a lively conversation, stirring the large cauldron heating over the open flames. Just one glance at them was a powerful hit to the confidence. Anyone with eyes could see they held a beauty that would have been prized in Hollywood, rivaling even the most gorgeous on the silver screens.

Both women fell silent before turning a glare onto me.

"Who is this?" the fiery red head questioned, her smooth heavy accent matching the old woman's from earlier.

"An intruder is who!" the brunette stated, alarmed.

"I'm not an intruder," I defended.

"No? Then how did you get in? You weren't let in by one of us," the redhead stated, taking a step forward beneath the flow of her sage green dress.

"I let her in. The nuisance wouldn't leave me be," called out a velvety voice from a door I had not seen. A secret room? Walking out of the shadows was a woman as equally stunning as the other two. Her long, straight blonde hair rested on the silvery blue bodice of her dress. My jaw dropped both at her beauty and at the words she had spoken. This couldn't be the old woman I had followed in here. There was no way!

"YOU let her in! Hmmm," the brunette said, glancing at me with a side eye. "Tell me your name," she commanded, her golden dress shimmering from the fire as she stepped closer to face me.

"Aurora. Would you mind telling me who you are?" I said back.

"Au-ror-a," the redhead sounded out, "where have I heard this name before?" she questioned to no one. She squinted her eyes at me as she cupped her chin.

"What does it matter? The question is, what do we do with her?" the brunette questioned.

"You already know what we are going to do with her," the blonde stated.

"Do with me? What do you mean?" I demanded, inching back towards the front door. What did they intend to do? I wish I knew more about what I had gotten myself into. It would be easier to know how to respond.

The sound of a large book slamming shut startled me. A large hand grasped my shoulder, whipping me around to face the opposite side of the room. A man in a scarlet overcoat, with piercing grey eyes, scrutinized my face. His expression wasn't as intense as the three behind me, but were calculated. Leery.

Under the microscope of his watchful eye, I felt exposed in a way I hadn't with the others - as if he were boring into my very soul; searching for something that would give him clues.

"She's mine! I found her! Muta puella! Incipiens Ignes!" the blonde barked out.

Without taking his eyes from mine, he raised his cloaked arm and snapped his ringed fingers at her, silencing her from speaking further. After a moment, he released me, motioning towards the chair by the fire.

"Come child. After the long journey you have had, you are no doubt tired. Sit," he enunciated his words slowly in a heavy Slavic accent.

"How do you know I'm on a long journey?" I questioned. He couldn't have known that.

"Merah told me you started a fire in the forest. Clearly you are not from here, as everyone knows that is a death sentence," he answered. I glanced towards the seething blonde.

"Why is that?" I asked, slipping my bag from my shoulders as I sat in the tall chair he offered.

"Howlings. Smart creatures. They work in packs and are most attracted to light and fire," he simply stated, as if this were common knowledge.

"I didn't know. I've never seen one," I said.

"Which is precisely why I know you are not from here. Tell me, where are you from exactly?" he asked, calculating my every move.

The three women converged, standing next to the caped man. Should I answer truthfully? How much should I divulge? I didn't trust them. My senses, and gut instinct, telling me they were not safe. I surely couldn't tell them I crossed through the gate into this strange place from earth – that would let them know far more than I cared to share.

"I don't know. I went on a hike and then I was here," I stammered.

"She's lying!" the redhead's sharp eyes glanced back and forth between the man and me.

"No, I'm not," I defended.

"I can tell that you are. Give up these games and tell us who you are," she demanded.

"My name is Aurora. I went on a hike. I got lost. The next thing I know, I was here." I said, my voice raised an octave higher than I intended.

"What is a hike? And where did you find such strange attire?" the blonde asked, puzzled.

I was being backed further and further into a corner. I didn't have enough knowledge of this place to lie effectively. Damn it, mom! Why did you leave me at such a disadvantage?

"Well. If you don't want to tell us, that's fine. We have ways of extracting the knowledge we want to know," the man stated calmly. With a flick of his hand, icy metal cuffs clasped around my wrists and the arms of the chair, securing me in place of their own accord.

"Check her bag," he commanded with a nod of the head.

The brunette fell to her knees, lifting my bag from the bottom and dumping its contents across the marbled floor. "We could have done this the easy way. Seeing as how you don't want to tell us who you are, you have chosen the hard way," he said with a smug gleam in his eye.

"Who are you people?" I screamed, my nerves taking over. This couldn't be happening. This wasn't real. People didn't put out fires with a wave of a hand and inanimate objects didn't move of their own free will.

"People? We are not people!" the redhead spat, as she rifled through my things. "We are Teykin. The most superior race you will ever come across. Never confuse us with those stinky, simple raced maggots."

"What Sharsee is trying to say is we are considered the more superior beings in our land. We are occultists," he answered with a sense of refinement the women lacked. Though by appearance, you would think they were all part of a higher society; the women lacked the social poise that came with those dresses.

"Occultists?" I asked, skeptical.

"Yes! Occultists. You know, witches, warlocks," Sharsee said with her head down, continuing to ruffle through my things. "I found something!" She stood, my blood running cold as it drained from my face.

In her lifted hand was my mother's letter. In my haste to escape from the craziness I had been experiencing back home, I forgot to destroy it as she had directed. Now, it's in their hands!

I watched with trepidation as she unfolded the words that would become my undoing. The other women peered over her shoulders to read what was written.

"What is this? I can't read it apart from what is in our written language," Sharsee said, frustrated. I sighed in silent relief.

"Give it here," the warlock stretched out his cloaked hand.

Sharsee did as he asked, placing the letter into his hand. He scanned through the words in a fury, both hands gripping the letter. When he reached the end, he focused on my face as the pieces clicked into place. My heart skipped a beat.

"Who is your mother?" he asked, our eyes locked.

Shit. He knew too much. I licked my suddenly dry lips as I stalled to answer.

"Marie," I said through clenched teeth.

"Marie who?" he questioned further.

"Walker."

The sharp gasp from all four occults dropped my heart into the deepest depths of my stomach. They knew my mother, or at least enough of her. What did this mean for me? What are they going to do with me now that they know who my mother is? What were they planning on doing before they had found that out?

"Could this be?" Merah questioned, turning to the brunette.

"It couldn't... how could it? Unless..." the brunette replied, scanning me up and down.

"She was granted access," Sharsee said, eyes gleaming as if she had won a prize.

"The key! Where is it girl?" the brunette barked.

"What key?" I asked.

"Don't play dumb with me. Where is it?" the brunette screamed.

"Calm now, Asha. Don't lose your head. We will get the answers we seek," the warlock said.

"Sharsee, get me the druggards and pestle. Merah, grab the amulet. Asha, bring me my table," the warlock ordered.

"Yes Sonat," the three females said, giddy as they hurried to gather the items.

"What do you think you're doing?" I half yelled.

"It's not what I think, it's what I know. And as I said, we are extracting answers," he said with a devilish grin. Before long, they stationed the table Sonat requested to my right, along with a dark speckled mortar and pestle.

The rectangular table held the same compass markings as on the foyer floor, inlaid in the center. Situated at the end of each extending line from the compasses circle were smaller etchings and symbols - all facing me.

Merah handed Sonat a deep crimson-plum crystal, not quite ruby and not quite amethyst but a combination of the two. He placed the crystal in the center of the circle, at the point where all of the lines came together.

Sharsee followed with four jars, some containing grotesque contents I wish I could unsee. Of the first jar, Sonat pulled out a small bird skeleton. On closer inspection, the jar was full of them!

"Alis de Phoenix..," he called out, carefully laying the bones across the symbol closest to me. The moment his hand released, the length of the line illuminated in bright white, stopping at the outside of the compasses circle. I released a jagged breath.

In a low voice, Sharsee began to chant words I couldn't understand the meaning of.

The second jar held a medley of random twigs and herbs. He pulled out a calculated amount and placed them into his mortar, hovering all five fingers together before flicking them at the dried contents. Blue flames licked up high towards the ceiling before losing its fuel and dying out altogether. With pestle in hand, he worked in a fury to grind up what he could of the ashen mix.

"Dulcis Melodiam Terrae..," he sang out, pouring the contents of the mortar over the second symbol. With this, a fire raced down the second line, igniting into a brilliant obsidian flame before stopping at the outer circle as the first. Merah then joined Sharsee, their chants growing louder. Shivers ran through my body, leaving goose bumps in its quake.

Bile rushed up my throat at the sight of the third jar. Eyeballs pressed against the glass, blinking in and out of unison, staring at me. What the hell?

He put his slender ringed fingers into the jar, grabbing a set of blinking orbs and placed them on the third symbol.

"Fiat Mihi Videre Verum…," he chanted louder, as the line illuminated green.

He grabbed the last of the contents from jar number four - a disembodied, beating heart.

Asha joined Merah and Sharsee, their chants deafening as they each fed off each other. The heart in Sonat's hand beat to the rhythm of their song.

"Voluntatem Cordis Mei," he shouted, as he placed the beating heart on the last symbol. A deep violet irradiated along the line, much like the first three, albeit slow - viscous, as if blood were oozing back into its chambers.

Once the light reached the outer circle, all four lines traveled along the single path towards the amulet, cascading a prism of dark colors through the center once they reached it. I watched in trepidation as the crystal melted into a life force of flowing plasma. With the mortar that Sonat used earlier, he placed it under the single line carved on the opposite side of the amulet, capturing the flowing contents into the indented space.

With the newly created potion now sitting on the table, Sonat reached into his coat and pulled out a pointed dagger with a diamond tipped handle - coating it with the potion's essence. He turned to me, bringing the blade to my throat - the cold steel resting on the delicate skin above my artery.

The first trickle of blood oozed from the stinging cut into my flesh. He didn't leave his blade there long, continuing to slice fresh cuts beneath each side of my clavicle before bringing his blade beneath the right arm of my jacket. With one flick of his wrist, my skin became exposed and assaulted once more by the cold, dark metal of his blade.

With each controlled movement, he exuded joy, as if he lived for the torture. With both arms exposed, he pulled down the front of my jacket, exposing my shirt where I hid my mother's pendant. I trembled beneath his heathen touch, the slow anticipation of his every move leaving me guessing when the final blow would seal my fate.

"That! There!" Sharsee said, pointing to my chest. I dropped my eyes to where she pointed, noting how the blood trickled down from my neck, settling snug around the pendant - not a drop going past it. A Cheshire grin spread across her face as she ripped my shirt down the center, exposing my chest and the pendant placed there. Panic flooded in as their faces lit up. They found their pot of gold. What do I do? I can't let them take it! Why did I have to be so careless?

Merah's hand snapped out to grab the pendant off my neck, only to snap it right back, cradling it into her chest as she let out a wail. "Owwwwch! The damn thing burned me!"

"Burned you?" Asha asked, surprised.

"That's what I said! Are you even listening?" Merah snapped.

"It's a clavis. Just take it off her," she replied.

"You do it if you think you can!"

Asha turned to me; her eyes wary as her hand trembled towards my chest. She hesitated only a second, her greedy eyes never leaving the prize she sought, before her fingers wrapped around their reward. A curdling cry escaped her lips as she continued to hold on, unable to let go. The pendant itself emanated vibrations across my chest, drawing closer to me, not allowing the fiends to move it one iota. Though it didn't hurt me, I could feel the percussive shocks it placed into her.

Merah and Sharsee grabbed Asha's shoulders, letting out their own crying pleas as they attempted to pull her away from me. I could only guess the defense mechanism of the pendant reverberated through them as well.

They collapsed to the floor as the pendant released them with a healthy fear for its power. A power that wasn't meant for them.

"We can't get it this way!" Asha panted, rubbing her hand like Merah had. "How are we going to get it?"

"You can't. This pendant is mine, and there is no way you can take it!" I yelled, smug at their failed attempt. Knowing they couldn't get their hands on what they wanted gave me the confidence I needed. It meant they couldn't kill me. They needed me alive if they wanted to use its power. I had a bargaining chip.

"You think you are so clever," Sonat sneered, "Do not underestimate us!"

He turned to the witches. "Get up you lazy hags! We continue with the original plan." The three women scrambled to their feet, falling over each other in the process. Sonat shook his head at the spectacle before him.

"What original plan?" I asked, shrinking back into myself.

"What's the saying? There is more than one way to skin a caballus?" he mused. "The pendant is drawn to you. No one in the universe can hope to take it from you. That is - unless you're dead," he stated, pointing at my chest. So much for my bargaining chip.

"So why not hurry and kill me already? Get it over with!" I challenged. He clicked his tongue.

"Patience child; all in due time. What is the sense in expediting your death when your very essence can be of great use to us," he stated, giddy with this admission.

"What do you mean?" I whispered.

"Us occults find life very - precious. Waste not, want not. Don't worry, your life will go to good use," he smirked. I could say no more. With each diabolical admission, I came to accept this startling conclusion – tonight, I die.

If I'm to meet my demise tonight, it won't be swift. I couldn't afford myself to hope someone would rescue me from this. The only thing I could do is accept what was – and what was, I feared, would be torture.

All four converged on me once again, surrounding me from left to right, with Sonat and Merah in the middle.

Asha handed Sonat the black dagger he had placed on the table earlier. When he rested his smoldering grey eyes back on mine, he let out a soft chuckle, "Let's begin."

Approaching with dagger in hand, I kicked my right foot high into his gut. He rocked back, dropping the dagger with an audible clank on the marbled floor. The witches gasped.

Merah stepped closer, lifting her back hand towards me. I raised my left foot in time to keep her at bay, using the leverage of the chair. My arms may be strapped but they forgot about my feet.

"Grab her legs!" Sonat yelled, pointing at me with anger flashing in his eyes. The kick to the gut had been a lot harder than I thought, as he rested on the table, doubled over.

The three women weaved and dodged out of my kicking range. Asha and Sharsee came around the sides of the chair and grabbed my legs from behind, pulling them hard into the chair. I thrashed around with all my might, trying to break their hold. It was no use.

I soon realized they had stopped holding my legs and were now standing in front of me. I dropped my eyes to see the famil- iar metal cuffs strapping my legs to the chair, just like my wrists.

When I lifted my gaze, Sonat back handed me with his heavy ringed fingers. Blood trickled from the stinging pain on the left side of my mouth, seeping into my lips. Salt and iron dominated my taste buds. A moment of insanity bubbled inside of me as I let out a chuckle, allowing the steady flow to pool inside my mouth.

"What are you smiling at?" he jeered, pushing his face closer to mine. I glared at him in defiance, putting all I had into spewing the glob of sanguine fluid in his face.

Shock dominated as he pulled back, a smirk spreading across his face. His smiling eyes mocked me as he licked the trickling blood off his lips and hummed.

"Such sweet blood. A rare delicacy – Maeshiren," he said, wiping the blood from his cheek with his fingers. He closed his eyes in pure bliss as he wrapped his lips around his bloodied fingers. Not the reaction I expected at all.

I had hoped for repulsed. Disgusted. Thoroughly sickened. I had hoped my defiance would be the one redeeming quality in this whole turn of events. It seemed even that was something these twisted freaks got off on.

With the wind out of my sails, and fresh out of options, I worked on shutting down my brain like I did so many years ago. While I knew I couldn't go catatonic, I had plenty of experience going numb and shutting myself off to the world. In the grand scheme of things, what did I have to live for? I was a constant pain to my brothers and Kate. They could at least move on with their lives and stop worrying about me.

As he finished enjoying the last intoxicating pleasures of my blood, he strode forward to proceed with their plan – whatever that plan may be. Strapped and cornered like a wild beast, I could only be a spectator, an unwilling participant, in this messed up game. I was a broken, caged animal, accepting its lowly lot in life.

Though I already resigned myself to the truth of my pending demise, my heart still hammered out of my chest.

Asha handed Sonat the potion they had created earlier. He dipped his finger into the gobbing mess and began painting my skin with it; over the cut on my throat he made earlier, under the fleshy part of my clavicle bones, on the inside of my elbows. He flipped my hands over and proceeded to place three slits across both forearms.

"Unclench your fists," he commanded.

Subconsciously, I had clenched my fists into tight balls, my thumbs tucked over my fingers. In my last act of defiance, I stared into his eyes and closed my fists tighter, my fingernails cutting into my palms. If he wanted something from me, it would be over my dead body.

Sonat snapped his fingers. Asha and Sharsee jumped to pry my fingers open one by one. The moment they pried one open, I closed another. It became a game they weren't thrilled to play and one I would end up losing in the long run.

"You will regret this Aurora," Merah said, annoyed. "Secure them in place," she barked at the other two.

Despite struggling against their assault, their teamwork won in the end. Merah grabbed what looked to be a barbed fishhook from a rolled-out tool flat with various torture devices.

"You should have listened," Merah spat as she pierced deep the fleshy pad of my left pointer finger. A guttural shriek echoed from my throat as she pulled the attached string down, hyper-extending my finger back to secure it to the chair. Nausea ebbed and flowed in waves as tears streamed down my face. I wanted to grab my hand, I wanted to find relief – it wouldn't come.

I cringed as she grabbed for another barbed hook, swallowing deep before she pierced it hard and slow into my middle finger, wrenching it back as the first. I wanted to fight, but it was no use. The strength had been taken out of my grasp. One by torturous one, they pierced my flesh with the barbed hooks, a wailing scream ripping through my chest from each pull of a string.

Bile rose and my head spun as I stared at the sight of my flesh pierced through - bloodied and splayed out like they wanted them.

Lord, please, let this torture end. Please take my life now.

I had never been one to pray. Maybe that was my first mistake, but I'm praying now. Take my life. I don't want to be alive for whatever else they have in store for me. What did I do to deserve such a fate?

In the dim awareness of my mind, it struck a chord that this was not the first time they had done this to someone. They were well prepared for events such as this. It brought on a fresh wave of nausea and tears as I cried out to the throbbing pain radiating through my hands.

Sonat proceeded to paint my injured fingers with the concoction he placed on my body earlier. Just the fingers; not the thumbs.

"Grab the apothecaries, I don't want to waste another drop of this precious essence," Sonat demanded with urgency. I swung my head as Sharsee grabbed for the three apothecary glasses on the mantle of the fireplace. She gave one to each of the other women, as both she and Asha held the glasses under my fingers.

"Now, let's begin," he said. That wasn't the beginning? I didn't think I had any hope left to speak of, but I found it hit a new low. I was slipping closer and closer to shock.

The loose fabric of Sonat's cloak pooled down towards his elbows as he lifted his hands high towards the sky. With dagger in hand, he spoke in tongues I couldn't understand,

"Septum Coeli...

Dona mihi hoc votum…

Luvenis Infinitum…

Magicae abundavit delictum…

Trahere a Sanguine…

Da Mihi Vitae Essentia!"

His painted creations began to melt into my skin with a searing black smoke. The darker it became, the hotter it burned until it burst into flames, the scent of crackling, charred flesh assaulting my nose. The scorching pain of the flames no longer stayed isolated outside of my body. I felt their entry through every exposed nerve ending, desiccating and smoldering from within.

With eyes clenched, I prayed to God for the torture to end. The tension in my throat strained against the earsplitting scream escaping my vocal cords. I vaguely heard shattering around me as my screams grew in octaves.

"The holding glasses. They've shattered," one witch yelled out over my wails.

"Grab the others!" another shouted.

Every muscle, every vein, every living fiber that made me a human being became lit with this flaming inferno. No longer was I worried about defiance, or even making it through the next moment. The screams ripping through me became muffled as I pleaded for death.

Soon, my prayers were answered. The fires were being quenched, one by one, as cold steel sliced across soft flesh. In some process of my mind, I was aware that Sonat was continuing the ritual, but I didn't care. I only wanted peace – I only wished for death.

All the fires were out. I no longer had the energy to scream. I lifted laden eyes to the room spinning around me, my head heavy as it swayed whichever way I looked. Glancing at my arms, they had replaced the torturous fire with deep gashes that seeped blood into pools at the bottom of metal vases on the floor. This was it. As the seconds ticked, I knew I wasn't far from meeting my end.

A tingling sensation overwhelmed me, as particles of light seeped from my wounds and into a clear crystal Sonat held in his hand. A tinge of red colored the crystal with the very essence of my vital life force. This is what was to become of me?

A powerful surge of frigid air slammed against my body, rustling leaves across the marbled floor. The crackling of the fire blazed high from the rushing fuel source, illuminating the room in a flash before dimming to its normal flicker.

Sonat turned over his shoulder, feeling something amiss. His face morphed into anger as he yelled at Merah. "You left the door unlocked, you dimwit. The wind has kicked up. Go close that damn door and lock it!" he ordered.

Merah did as instructed, slamming it shut as she pulled down the wooden latch, securing it in place.

In their distraction, my life force stopped fleeing from my body. Instead, it began returning to its rightful place, as the color leached from the crystal.

"Apologies," she said, walking back to her original place.

"Now, where were we?" he said. "Oh yes. Sharsee, go get…" he began his next request before a slow, beckoning whistle echoed. All four heads snapped up as they scanned the room, weary they were not alone.

"What was that?" Asha whispered, startled.

Nobody said a word as they listened for the sound. After a few moments of silence, they brushed it off and turned their attention back to me.

"Must have been the wind," Merah stated.

"That was some wind," Sharsee commented.

"You three. Time is of the essence. We cannot allow her

a moment to recuperate, or all of this is for not," Sonat stated, bringing their focus back to task. "Asha, bring me the sealer for the amulet. Once we have what we need, we don't want this to leak out," he stated.

"Sure," Asha said tersely, glancing at Sharsee through squinted eyes. She didn't like to be asked to do Sharsee's work, it seemed. Asha began to shuffle out of the room towards the foyer when a long and deeper whistle echoed through the room with a menacing edge. Everyone took pause as they stood ram-rod straight, thoroughly inspecting the darkened room.

In the corner, where Asha had been blocking my line of sight, stood a figure in the shadows with crimson eyes ablaze in contrast with the darkness surrounding it. I summoned all my weak strength to bring my head up, trying for a better view of this figure staring down the five of us without moving an inch. Was this a howling? Sonat said they were smart creatures.

"Who are you?" Sonat demanded.

In the corner, the cloaked figure clicked his tongue before all but disappearing.

A blur whooshed past, the dark figure now on the other side of the room with the warlock in its clutches. Sonat was pinned by his neck against the wall, his feet dangling two feet from the ground.

With pure elation, I watched as this broad-cloaked figure tightened his hand around the warlock's neck; the choking and gurgling being strangled from Sonat's air passageway music to my ears. Whatever fate held for me here tonight, I could rest in peace, knowing justice had been served.

Merah ran to Sonat's defense, yelling at the cloaked figure along the way. "Leave him alone! Release him. Dracones et unguibus Galli oculos…," she chanted as she raised her arms to unleash whatever magic spell she summoned. The cloaked figure turned at the right moment, grasping her by her very neck and lifted her off her feet – much like Sonat, who was still within his other grasp.

In one swift motion, Merah was slammed into the wall with a hard force that reverberated through us all. She knocked out in an instant as she crumbled to her knees, balling over to her side.

Everything changed.

I no longer sat in a grand room by a large roaring fire, surrounded by white marbled flooring and gorgeous people (er… occults) in front of me. Instead, I was transported to the pitiful, rickety old shack I had seen from the outside. The dirt floor ran wild with large, cockroach-like bugs scurrying about. The shack was dark, the only light from the scant fireplace casting a glow to break up the darkness.

Asha and Sharsee were not the bombshell redhead and brunette women I had come to know. By the glow of the fire, I could see they were bloated, bitter old hags; the color of their hair the only way I could tell them apart.

Sharsee still stood tall but had the largest protruding potbelly I had ever seen, hanging over twig-like legs too frail to be bearing the weight of her upper half.

Asha stood short and bloated, with folds folding over folds - her legs blending in with the weight of her midsection.

Both witches had gangly teeth that drooled over the protruded under bite they both possessed. With elongated noses and growths in various places on their face, I could not see how they were the same women I met.

Though I couldn't see Merah crumpled on the floor, the table concealed her, I could see Sonat - he too had changed. Shrunken in, he resembled more of a skeleton than the full-bodied warlock that filled out the cloak he had worn.

By the light of the fire, his left eye appeared much bigger

than his right and his teeth stuck out every which way. The clothes he wore, in fact the clothes all of them wore, were tattered and nothing even comparable to the beautiful garb they had worn.

"How dare you come in here and…" Sonat began hurling his idle threat.

"How dare you threaten me," the cloaked man growled. Even in my half dead state, the deep hostility in his voice sounded familiar; safe. I couldn't place where I had heard it before, if I ever had. In this moment, my mind registered it as being safe. That would have to be good enough for now. Whether this man came here to finish me off himself, or rescue me from the grim reapers, I would be okay with either one – if only this torture ended.

The mystery man lifted his free hand and released the mask concealing his identity. Though he faced away from me, I watched as Sonat's eyes widened with acknowledgement and horror.

"But… but how? You have been locked out for…" he squeaked out from under the man's stranglehold.

"That is none of your concern. Not anymore," the man snarled, squeezing Sonat's neck tighter. The air supply cut off from his brain as his terror-stricken eyes grew wider at the realization, he was meeting his end.

Asha and Sharsee stood forming a plan for a double attack when the bone crushing reality of Sonat's life crumbled into the man's hands; every neck bone under his grip popped and cracked. No longer with us, the death dealer threw Sonat into a piling heap next to Merah as he stared down at his lifeless corpse.

"Two down, two more to go. Who'll be my next victim?" he taunted.

Slowly, the man turned towards Asha and Sharsee. Through heavy eyes, I watched this man depart from the shadows and into the firelight. For the first time in this torturous evening, the wellspring of hope bubbled inside of me. Though I writhed in bitter pain, the minute hope of rescue sprang out for its lifeline. I thanked the Lord above for the bit of fortune he bestowed upon me.

Gavin stood before me; his face etched with murderous intent. He never looked my way, never stole a glance. The red malice in his eyes meant only for the two occults standing before him. The former smirks I had seen when he stood toe-to-toe with Tony were erased. In its place, a savage glare, hell bent on meting out justice. "Who wants to try me?" he sneered.

"How dare you come in here and steal our bounty," Sharsee shrieked. In a flash, Gavin had both women strung up by their necks, held high in the air overhead.

"And what bounty do you have claim to if you are dead?" he seethed through clenched teeth.

"We are sorry. Please, take the girl. We won't cause any trouble," Asha pleaded. Sharsee sent a murderous glare at Asha for opening her mouth.

"Tell me, do witches bleed?" he cocked his head, as if to observe these unsightly creatures better, "Or do they just ooze disease?" Neither of them made a peep, though Asha answered by urinating on the floor. Disgusted, Gavin threw them back. They may as well have been trash.

"If you ever involve yourself with Aurora's life again, in any way, you'll answer to me. And if you ever harm her again, you will die the most gruesome death imaginable. Do I make myself clear?" he both threatened and promised.

"Is that a threat?" Sharsee piped in her harsh, heavy accent.

"No. It's a promise. In fact," Gavin moved to Sharsee, pulling her vocal cords out of her gelatinous neck. "I mitigated one problem for the future," he said to no one in particular, as he threw her lifeless body back to the ground.

"Do you want some too?" he glared at Asha. She shook her head quickly.

"Good Teykin," he stated.

He turned to me but stopped midway, something on his hand catching his eye. "Well, what do you know," he said, turning back to Asha, "witches do bleed." He laughed as he wiped his bloodied hand on his cloak.

Watching his every move through heavy eyes, Gavin's amusement turned solemn as he faced me, seeing me for the first time. He rushed to my side, yanking free the bindings around my wrists. "Fancy seeing you here," he tried to joke, but no humor colored his voice.

He bent down, breaking free the straps around my ankles. Through the illusion, the bindings had been metal clasps. In actuality, they were no more than tattered old ropes I could have easily broken. I had no response for him. I hadn't the energy, nor the strength to hold the weight of my own head up.

His eyes scanned my body, anger seething through his crimson eyes as he took in the torture the occultists had subjected me to. When his eyes landed on the hooks through the pads of my fingers, he let out an angry and torturous moan.

"What did they do to you?" he broke down, falling to his knees. He bent forward for a closer inspection of my wounds, inspecting them from all angles.

"They're deep. Do you want me to pull them out now, or wait for medical help?" he asked, searching my face for a direction. I pitied the look in his eyes. The torture I had gone through seemed to torture him the same. His expression pained and lost.

"Pull them out," I squeaked.

"It's going to be painful. Some of these have pierced all the way through," he sighed, regretting the thought of putting me through more pain.

"I know," I said, my voice shallow and hoarse.

"Don't look," he said. I turned my face as the first of the pain ripped through my right pinky finger, the barb tearing more flesh away from bone. I screamed at the pain lancing through my hand - one down and seven more to go. He began yanking free the hooks out of my right hand, the pain of each pull and tear felt at a magnitude greater than when they had sunken in.

"STOP! Please, stop!" I cried out. Despite being tortured throughout the night, this pain was unbearable. Earlier, when I had cried out for Sonat to end the torture, I had been mentally at peace with my demise. To subject myself to this torture once more, even though it meant being saved, I could no longer bear it. I could feel my spirit slipping; no longer was it worth the fight to continue.

"Please, just kill me," I cried.

"Over my dead body. Aurora, look at me! You can do this! See," he picked up my right hand to show me, "this one is already done. You have only one more hand to go." I stared at the meaty, shredded exit holes bleeding profusely from my fingertips. It looked as if someone had taken a jagged hole punch and pierced a hole through each pad – some going all the way through, some not.

Nausea hit hard.

"You can do this," he said again with such strong conviction, pepping me up to finish what we started. His emerald eyes pleading with me to fight. I couldn't do this, but I had to. There was something in his expression, in the way he believed in me, which made me want to continue to fight. I conceded, nodding through the tears streaming down my face.

"Okay. I'll make this quick," he promised. I stared into his eyes, not bothering to turn away this time. He dropped his apologetic gaze to my left hand. "Ready?"

I gave him a nod.

He pulled out the razor-sharp barbs faster than he had the others. The pain just as excruciating, my screams just as torturous, but it felt uplifting to be freed. The pain itself never subsided. Though the hooks were out, my fingers throbbed with a pulsing pain which radiated through my hand and up my forearm.

"Let's get you home," he said, speaking the most heartwarming words I had yearned to hear. Home! A place where everything made sense, even if life was less than ideal.

Gavin paused, taking in my disheveled sight. He shouldered off his cloak, wrapping it around my half naked torso, helping my arms through the openings. Though I swam in it, I welcomed the warmth.

"My things. My mother's letter," I slurred. Gavin snatched up my bag, rushing to throw everything back in. He slung it over his shoulder before tending to me, helping me forward out of the seat and onto my feet. The moment I bore weight on my legs, I crumbled towards the floor. I didn't have it in me stand.

"Leave me," I said, as Gavin held my weight up with his body.

"Nonsense. Leave you? Are you insane?" he questioned, staring into my eyes.

Gavin bent down, sweeping his arm under my legs, and lifted me into the comfort of his hold. He cradled me close to his chest, resting my head onto his shoulder as he walked out of the torture shack.

He paused before the foyer, not looking at Asha but speaking directly to her. "I spared your life because you didn't cause me trouble. The moment you do, your life is forfeit. Pray you never cross me again." With that, he strode forward.

I whimpered with the pain of being jostled from his movements. The lacerations in my flesh throbbed with my pulse. I sobbed as everything came crashing down around me. The pain, the torment, the torture – it was all too much.

Lifting my head to see Gavin's face, I was confused as to why he was here. Was he another illusion?

"Are you really here?" I asked, though I couldn't be sure I said the words right.

"Shhh, it's okay. You're okay now. Sleep. The pain will be gone soon," Gavin soothed, though the strain in his voice was evident.

Unconsciousness kept beckoning me, drooping heavy lids, only to bring me back to a hazy awareness. Despite the safety of Gavin's arms, I was terrified of closing my eyes. I didn't want to relive this nightmare over in my sleep, but I lost too much blood. I was near drained. My head refused to stay up, despite my willingness for it to do so.

Conceding to the will of my body, my head fell back, slipping me into total darkness.

Chapter Thirteen

Fact From Fiction

<hr>

"Fact and fiction are different truths." - Patricia MacLachlan

***

Floating in a state of dream-like awareness, the hushed whispers from another room infiltrated my thoughts, dragging me into consciousness. The faint throbbing in my fingertips became the first of many pains that registered. I squeezed my eyes shut, praying for the unconscious darkness to envelop me once again. My body – it hurt. The more aware I became, the more my nightmarish ordeal flashed through my mind.

Cold, dark steel against virgin flesh. Hooks pierced through meaty fingertips. An intense inferno blazing through my central nervous system.

Relenting, I opened heavy lids to dark vaulted ceilings accented by large wooden beams. The flicker of the fireplace teased against the iron of the four-post bed. *Where am I?*

I didn't move, yet the room spun. Vertigo. A once remembered experience from long ago. Lovely.

The hushed voices I had been hearing came to a sudden halt. "She's awake!" a heavy whisper exclaimed.

"Aurora!" Ryder's voice called out before he fell through the doorway. My gaze fell to the commotion of Ryder picking himself up from the floor. I would have laughed if it didn't hurt so much. Behind him, others piled into the darkened room. Their faces near unrecognizable in the dim light of the fire.

"Can you hear me?" He walked forward, squatting down to place his hand on my forehead. "Kartcher, she's burning up!" he cried out over his shoulder. Am I burning up? I didn't feel like it. In fact, I was freezing.

I stared up at my brother, wanting to smooth the worry lines forming between his brows when he turned back to me. It wasn't a good look for his handsome face. I lifted my heavy hand to smooth the lines before he caught it in his own.

"Aurora. Can you hear me?" he asked again. "Say something. Blink three times. Do something to let me know you understand me," he panicked.

"I hear you," I croaked, as I tried to soothe his worry.

"Oh, thank God," he whispered, closing his eyes and bowing his head to my hand.

"Aurora, I thought we lost you," he choked, a single tear glistening down his cheek. With my free hand, I placed it on top of our gathered hands to reassure and comfort him.

"You can't get rid of me that easy," I joked, pulling my lips into a side smirk.

"Thank God for that," he chuckled, the worry never leaving his eyes.

"Help me sit up, please?" I asked, as I struggled to push myself up to a seated position. Ryder realized a bit late what I was doing before helping me to sit up the rest of the way.

I didn't know which was worse – laying down or sitting up, but I wanted to assess the damages. I needed to see what I could heal and what would take weeks to heal.

Garrett came forward, hovering over Ryder's shoulder with a worried frown rivaling our youngest brothers. "Welcome back from the dead." Ever the sensitive one.

"Gee, thanks," I responded, kicking my leg over the side of the bed to stand.

"What do you think you're doing?" Ryder cried out, pushing my shoulders down.

"What does it look like I'm doing, Ryder? I'm getting up!" I rolled my eyes.

"Oh no you don't. You lay there and rest," Garrett said, "I don't even want to begin by asking what you have been through but whatever it had been, you need your rest." His remorseful eyes looked away as he brought up my harrowing experience.

"I can't keep laying here Garrett," I said, lowering myself down from the tall, plush bed.

As my feet touched the chilly stone floor, the shakiness of my legs gave out. The room spun out of control as the heart wrenching experience of a free fall travelled through my stomach, my hands slapping down hard before my face contacted the solid surface of the floor. The room fell quiet before a cacophony of voices, in various degrees of gasps, said my name.

"I'm okay! I'm okay!" I chanted, as multiple hands worked to lift me off the floor. You would think I had forgotten how to use my legs at all.

"Stop. I got her."

A pair of strong, familiar arms pulled me away from the many helpful hands. I turned my head, only to find myself in the intimate space of Gavin Mair. His troubled emerald eyes bore into mine, locking onto my gaze. The rest of the room fell away;

he and I sharing in this personal exchange alone.

"*Are you okay?*" his unspoken question asked. I tried to relay to him, "*I am now.*" I gave him a small smile, grateful for his perfect timing at the occultists.

Someone cleared their throat from behind the crowd. "Gavin," said the new voice, "if you will. Please place her back on the bed." Gavin's body blocked the source of the man's voice as he shifted towards the bed.

"Ahem," the man cleared his throat once again, making the others move out of the way. "Now that she is awake, it will be easier to tap into her latent abilities to continue the healing process," said the voice in question. A man, no – not a man, a talking lizard on two legs, came forward. His graceful aura made him seem as if he were floating under his white cloak.

"W-what are you?" I asked, alarmed at his appearance. Am I hallucinating?

"I'm Kartcher. I realize my appearance may be unsettling to you, but I assure you, I mean you no harm," he said.

"I-I'm sorry. I didn't mean to be rude. It's just…" I said, trying to formulate my thoughts into words.

"I know. I understand. Please, you have not offended me in the slightest. Even among my own world, my species is quite a sight for some," he said, his eyes smiling behind bifocals.

"Freaky, isn't it?" Garrett joked. Kate backhanded his chest, giving him a dirty look. "What? It's true!"

"Where am I?" I asked

"You are in Gavin's home," the lizardman answered, taking a passing glance at Gavin who was fixated on me. I remembered Gavin saying he was taking me home before I blacked out.

"And why exactly am I in Gavin's home?" I croaked, glancing back and forth between Gavin and Kartcher. The question seemed unsettling to Gavin, his eyes tightening before closing all together, pinching the bridge of his nose.

"Let's finish your healing process, shall we? We will have more time to answer your questions afterwards," Kartcher said, his soothing tone spoke to a bedside manner reserved for good doctors.

"Wait. No. What do you mean about my latent healing abilities?" I pressed on. How did he know about that? It might be best to play dumb for now.

"Aurora, just listen to Kartcher. We will square everything away in a few moments if you'll allow him to finish healing you," Kate said. Her impatient tone was one of finality, which I knew all too well.

I narrowed my eyes, wondering what her role was in all of this, but let it go for the moment. My head ached, as did every inch of my body. I conceded but resolved to getting answers.

Sighing, I brought my eyes back to Kartcher's, "And how exactly did you plan on healing me?"

"Actually, I'm not. You are," he stated.

"Come again?" I deadpanned, glancing over to Ryder and Garrett, who were as lost as me. Ryder shrugged his shoulders.

"Aurora, within you is a healing power unlike any within this realm. Now, it is latent, as you have yet to fully realize this true power. While I cannot unlock your full potential, I can help draw some of it out. When I do this, I want you to pull that power into every cut, bruise, and puncture wound," Kartcher explained.

"You want me to do what? You can't drop something like that on me and expect me to know what to do," I exclaimed.

"Surely, by now, you have experienced those healing powers yourself. Have you not healed your own cuts before? Have you not brought back to life the very flowers in your own garden at home?" he asked with such fervor. "Playing a fool's errand is not your style and will not help you in this moment, I assure you."

"H-how did you know about that?" I whispered. No one knew about my *gift*. My mother made sure no one knew about it. How did this man-lizard *thing* know anything about that?

Throughout my life, I had been told to hide it. I had been ashamed of it. I'm a freak – an outcast. What would my brothers think if they knew I was anymore different than I already was?

"As I have said, we have much to discuss. However, healing your wounds is of utmost importance. Any further strain, emotional or otherwise, will only lessen the effective ability of your healing power. And hiding your truth will only seek to undermine the process altogether," Kartcher admonished.

I knew how to heal minor cuts; I had done it before as he had stated. I knew the warm sensation of a small wound sealing itself up, the tight pulling of the skin stitching itself back together. What he asked of me was different. I had never healed deeper wounds than that, and never in front of the watchful eyes of others.

"I've never healed my whole body before," I whispered back. My eyes shot to Ryder's as he and Garrett gasped at my admission.

"What are you saying, Aurora? You can heal yourself? So, what Kartcher has been saying is true?" Ryder asked, throwing out questions.

I stayed silent, only nodding my head as I watched his wary reaction. His eyes went wide with a blank stare, his posture rigid. His mental process seemed slow before his lashes fluttered as he shook his head. "I guess I shouldn't be surprised. With as many crazy things we have witnessed and heard about, who knows? Maybe Garrett and I have latent abilities as well." He chuckled without humor.

"You do," Kartcher said without looking at them.

"WHAT?" Garrett and Ryder screeched, eyes bugging out

at Kartcher. I was just as shocked to hear this as they were.

"Now is not the time. We have already taken too long discussing what we can hold off for later. You are right to be cautious about doing this, Aurora. If you do not find a way to pull this healing energy back into your being, it can be disastrous. As it is, you are very weak and have suffered quite an ordeal. However, I believe you are strong enough to make it through," Kartcher said.

"What do you mean by disastrous?" Garrett asked

Kartcher flashed Garrett a solemn frown. "She could die."

"No! No way! That's out of the question. She's not doing this," Garrett stated.

"There's gotta be some other way," Ryder chimed in.

"There is no other way, I'm afraid," Kartcher said.

"Aurora, don't do it. It's not worth it," Garrett said.

"And what is? Her suffering for weeks on end while she heals naturally?" Kate said.

"You support this?" Garrett shot daggers at Kate.

"I support her getting better. She is strong enough to do this. Have some faith in her," she said.

"Aurora, are you ready?" Kartcher asked.

Garrett slowly shook his head, the fear in his eyes marring his handsome face. While I didn't want to die, I also didn't want to feel this pain anymore.

I slid my eyes to Gavin's. He gave me a gentle nod with a confidence in his eyes that said I could do this. His belief in me was all I needed to go through with this. With a deep inhale, I glanced back to Kartcher and nodded my head.

"Remember, when I begin to draw the energy out of you, fight against it and pull that energy back in. When you do, your power will automatically know where to go," he said. I nodded my head once, trying to wrap my mind around his words.

"Repeat after me: *lux sanitatem, da requiem, sana afflictions, effundam in me!*"

The words were foreign to my tongue. I wasn't even sure I was saying them right, but we kept eye contact as we repeated the words. He hovered his scaly hands mere inches from my deepest wounds, his talons becoming prominent for the first time. With a sharp inhale, the shock of a too recent memory shot through my body in an intense inferno. Eyes clenched; I prayed for it to be quick.

Sonat was standing over me, a clear amulet held in his hand, as my light - my life force - seeped out of me. The strange sensation, searing and pulsating with every outflow of energy, was back again. I screamed out as the force of each pulsation becomes more intense than the first - the pain reaching new heights.

In the deep recesses of my mind, an alternate path opened before me. Within its darkness, it beckoned me to follow. It promised peace – peace away from the excruciating pain. Away from the chaos and noise chattering in another space of my mind.

I took a step towards the promised peace. Anything to cease the unbearable torture I was experiencing yet again. Anything that allowed me to slip back into oblivion. My foot faltered.

"Kartcher, you are losing her!" I heard Gavin's muffled yell in the distance. My heart beat.

"No, I am not! Aurora, stay with me. Listen to my voice. Pull your energy back into you. You must do it now!" Kartcher yelled. But I didn't want to. I wanted the promised peace this darkened path was promising.

A militant whisper beckoned me to reach out; its insistent intrusion pushing me to grasp my powers and reel them in. *But how?* I turned to the path at my right - agony flashed towards me of what those witches put me through. Every slice, every hook, was fresh and raw.

I kept being pulled in different directions. The pain I couldn't escape from. Peace, the darkness beckoned me towards. This new demanding voice whispering for me to fight. Why can't they put me out of this agony? Why did I have to wake up?

"Aurora, don't lose yourself. Listen to Kartcher, damn it," Garrett yelled so close; I could feel his breath.

"Aurora. Pull against the strain of your power being drawn out. Do it now!" Kartcher pressed.

Try as I may, I didn't know how.

"Aurora, it's Gavin. Listen to me," he demanded, his hand grasping mine, sudden and firm. "Can you feel my hand?"

I couldn't respond.

"If you can, grasp onto my hold. Don't lose yourself in there. Hold on to me. Don't let go," he pleaded, his voice trailing off towards the end.

That agonizing plea from Gavin, I never wanted to hear again. I wanted to pull him into my embrace and let him know I was all right. Every inch of me wanted to do as he asked – to hold on and not let go.

I reached out with my mind, three paths still emerging – the one of prominent pain, the one of promised peace, and the place of the curious voice beckoning me to stay and fight.

"Kartcher, her wounds are opening!" Kate cried out.

"I know. Listen to me, Aurora. Deep within your mind, feel your power. Find a tangible cord you can feel and wrap your mind around it," Kartcher's panicked voice guided. "You only have a few more seconds before I have to stop."

"You should stop now," Ryder yelled.

Beyond the pain, I tried to do what Kartcher asked. Behind closed lids, all I could see were the three paths before me as darkness continued to layer upon itself, offering continued promises of peace.

Within my grasp, I could feel the pull of Gavin's pleas. I was being torn into thirds with Gavin's grasp barely keeping me grounded.

"Look close," I heard that same whisper again, sharp and forceful. I did what it said. In the distance, a bright string of red light waved in the air like a flag waving in the wind. All around was enveloped in darkness, save for this string of light.

"C'mon Aurora! Fight!" Gavin pleaded again. I wanted to do as he asked. I assessed the three options in front of me before taking off towards the string of light – my legs heavy, movements slow.

"Damn it, I said stop it! Can't you see what you're doing to her?" Ryder yelled.

"The bed is soaking with her blood," Garrett panicked before a loud crash of furniture and breakables dominated in the background. The absence of Gavin's hand was jarring. I faltered in my stride.

"Get him out of here," Gavin yelled, to whom I couldn't be sure. "Unless you want to be next, I suggest you don't pull any of that shit. Kartcher, she doesn't have much longer," Gavin's calloused hand was placed back in mine.

"Yes, she does. Just a few more moments," he strained.

Though my movement's felt like trudging through muddy water, the string of light grew bigger and brighter as I drew nearer – a few more slow strides.

My resolve built with each step. Answering Gavin's pleas to fight became my focus. The pain and darkened peace reached out their tentacles, trying to pull me back, slowing me further. They were fighting for domination against my new resolve.

"Kartcher, I'm pulling the plug on this. Any further she will be dead," Gavin stated.

A few more feet – I reached my hand out and forward as I

readied myself to grasp the cord.

"Kartcher, do you hear me? Stop this now or else I will end this for you!" Gavin threatened.

My fingertips were mere inches from it. I could feel the power pulsating from its center as it flung wildly through the air. I couldn't grasp it.

"Damn it Kartcher! Now!" Gavin bellowed.

With sheer determination, I stretched myself to the opposite ends, lengthening my reach as far as possible, when my fingertips finally made purchase.

"NO!" Kartcher yelled back. "LOOK!"

With one hand fully grasped onto the cord, it made it easier to pull my other hand in for a better grip. The moment both hands held it, the bright cord straightened out in an endless length. No longer did it flail about. With it, I could feel the power flowing back into my body at an accelerated rate, the searing pain and promises of peace falling away into nonexistence.

The light energy pulsated through me, overpowering my very being. I became warm, and light, and peace balled into perfect harmony. I concentrated on this new feeling into the prominent areas that hurt. From head to fingertips, heat emanated from every contusion and open wound. The familiar tightness from skin stitching itself together echoed from cut to cut.

"I'll be damned," Gavin breathed out a heavy sigh.

Not wanting to lose focus, I kept my eyes closed until the last of my wounds finished the healing cycle. Sweat dripped from my brow at the exertion, my heart pounding in my ears deafening, but I never felt better. I raised my lids to Gavin's penetrating stare.

Though others were standing next to him, his eyes were the only ones I could see; his hand still held onto mine like a lifeline. The room fell silent. You could hear a pin drop if it weren't for my ragged breath.

"Well, I'd say that went much smoother than I had originally thought," Kartcher huffed, smiling as he turned towards Gavin. A murderous glare flashed through Gavin's eyes before he turned and punched Kartcher square in the nose.

"You thought she wouldn't make it through that, didn't you?" He yelled, standing over a kneeling Kartcher holding his bloodied nose.

"Of course not. I didn't know what to expect! Must you *always* resort to violence?" the lizard stood, still rubbing his nose. "All I am saying is she did much better than I had expected. For being as weak as she was in both latent ability and physical demeanor, she has made a complete and full recovery."

All three turned to stare at me at once. Did I make a full recovery? I sure felt much better. More than I had in years, actually. I rode on some strange high, as I could feel a vibration buzzing through every limb and vein.

I lifted my hand above my face, all traces of my wounds gone as if they were never there. Opening and closing my hand into a fist, the throbbing ache coursing through it was nonexistent. A quick glance down my arms, where Sonat had left deep gashes, a distance memory. I moved to sit up, Gavin's hands coming out to help but stopping as he realized I didn't need it.

I glanced at Kartcher, still taken aback by his appearance. "Thank you."

"No thanks needed. I am just happy you are alright," he smiled with relief, dabbing his nose. He gestured for me to stand, holding out his clawed hand to help me to my feet. Though hesitant, I took his offer. I had expected his hand to be rough, but instead was met by smooth, warm scales.

Carefully, I lowered myself to my feet. No longer shaky and needing the support of others, I stood firm on my own for once.

I beamed up at him, thanking him again in a silent exchange. He responded with a bow of his head, bringing his hand to his chest, and closing his eyes.

I shifted my eyes back to Gavin's, a hint of remorse coloring his expression. I couldn't understand why.

"I should also say thank you as well," I said to Gavin. Without him, my life would be lived inside of a crystal.

"Anytime," he smirked. The way his lips pulled to one side, highlighting the dimple in his cheek, had my heart racing. It was such a handsome expression on his otherwise gorgeous face.

"Shall we move this to the living room so we can discuss everything as a group?" Kate cut in as she walked back into the room, fidgeting.

"Yes. You haven't told us the entire story yet. Like our latent abilities, apparently?" Ryder admonished. He had been so quiet; I almost forgot he stood behind Kartcher.

"There are other people in this room who needed to be brought up to speed *with* you. Don't be so selfish," Kate reprimanded before she whipped her long blond hair behind her and strode out the door.

"Well, you heard the woman. Everyone hasten your way out," Kartcher stated. Ryder walked over to me and threw his arm over my shoulders.

"C'mon sis!"

I let him lead me out of the room and down the short hallway. We walked into a well-lit living room with river-stone floors and a large hearth roaring. Garrett sat next to the fireplace in a single chair, unnerved. The moment he heard us walk in, he shot to his feet.

"Oh, thank God Aurora," he rushed over, wrapping me in his tight bear hug.

"Too. Tight. Garrett," I squeaked out underneath his arms.

"Oh. Sorry!"

My breath caught as soon as he released me, still never letting his hands leave my shoulders.

"You will NEVER again do what you did to me these past few days. Aurora, you have no clue how many times I thought I had lost you while you were laying lifeless on that bed," his voice cracked.

"I'm sorry Garrett. Had I known what a shit show I would've walked into, I never would have come here in the first place," I apologized.

"Yes, you would've," Kate said, matter of fact.

"Excuse you?" I deadpanned.

"I *said* Yes. You *would* have," she reiterated.

"I know what you said. Are you insinuating I would have knowingly walked into that psycho den knowing I was about to be *tortured?*"

"Calm down. No. That's not what I'm saying."

"Then what *are* you saying?" I spat. With everything going on, Kate's typical nonchalance was about as much as I could handle at this junction.

"What she means is that you would have come here to Elderon regardless, whether or not you knew of the consequences. Whether by your own two feet or through force, you would have come to this world," Kartcher elaborated.

"Can someone please speak English here?" Ryder chimed in.

"It was fucking fated alright!" Gavin snapped. "You all would have ended up here, eventually." This admission put him on edge. He didn't like it any more than the rest of us.

"Can you elaborate on that further?" Garrett deadpanned.

"I think it is best if we all sat down," Kartcher said, gesturing to the seats surrounding the hearth. Though the surroundings were different, my mind flashed back to when Sonat had told me to sit down. I shiver ran through my spine as I contemplated on standing. Ryder challenged my decision when he pulled me close to him and sat us on the loveseat facing the chair Garrett sat in earlier.

Garrett sat back in the single chair as Kate and Kartcher took their positions on either ends of the couch facing the fireplace. Gavin opted to continue standing in the background, the shadows partially concealing him. He leaned against the post behind the couch in the classic posture I had come to know, arms crossed and vigilant without being noticeable. Except, I noticed.

"Where to begin? I suppose from the beginning," Kartcher said, staring deep into the fire as he tapped his chin.

"You - Aurora, Ryder, and Garrett, are of a royal bloodline known as the Maeshiren of Elderon," he addressed each of us. I gasped as my mother's words all flooded back to me. She warned me we were all in great danger. Sonat's voice echoed in my mind when he called me *Maeshiren.*

"Why weren't we told?" I demanded.

"Please, if you will be patient," Kartcher admonished. I sighed before nodding my head for him to continue.

"Many years ago, your grandfather Daten ruled in Höllengrad with his sister Johannes by his side over these lands. A sickness began to spread at a staggering rate. Dark forces worked to overtake the entirety of this world and yours," he paused, making sure we understood the gravity of this history – *our* history.

So many questions sprang into my head, but they were all disjointed. What dark forces? What is this world? What is Gavin and Kate's role in all of this? Or my parents? Why were we never told? So many questions, I feared they would go unanswered.

"The Maeshiren are an ancient race, appointed many millennia ago to rule and protect the kingdom of Elderon. They are bringers of light to this world by mercy but also by meting out justice when the need fit. A strong warrior class who upheld virtue and honor as their code of conduct. When a Maeshiren rules, they bring about times of peace. During war, they bring about times of strength," he continued.

"So, if that's the case, what happened to the Maeshiren? It shocked those witches to know I was a Maeshiren," I asked.

"Witches?" Garrett stared at me, confused. *Did he not know?*

"Did you not tell them?" I asked Gavin, who hadn't moved an inch since Kartcher began.

"No. I didn't," he said, cold and distant, staring into the fire.

"What haven't I been told?" Garrett asked, irritated.

"Why not?" I asked, staring at Gavin.

"I wasn't of mind to," Gavin answered, continuing to look away from me. Whatever that meant.

"What the hell, you guys! What are you hiding from us?" Garrett demanded, standing up.

"Garrett, sit down. We are not hiding anything from you. If you'll calm down, I'll tell you," I said, raising my voice.

He sat back on the edge of his seat, folding his hands under his chin, as he glared into my eyes, "Go on".

I didn't want to relive this again. I didn't have to tell him all the gory details though, just enough information to satisfy him, "When I first came here, I entered through a gate. When I turned to walk back through, the gate vanished. It started getting dark, so I made camp and a fire. I found out that wasn't the best idea, as an elderly lady approached and put the fire out with a wave of her hand. As she was the first person I had seen, I followed her back to her house," I paused when Gavin scoffed.

"Do you have something to add, Gavin?" I spat. Though grateful, on the same side of the coin, I couldn't help feeling irritated with him. There was so much I didn't know, and way more that he *did*.

"They're *not* people, Aurora. They are filthy vermin that walk this earth. Remember that," Gavin corrected me.

"Yes. I'm well aware, Gavin. Excuse me for not knowing the correct *verbiage* of *your* world," I spat back. Instead of coming back with a retort, he stayed silent.

"Please Aurora, go on," Kartcher urged me to continue. "How did they find out you were a Maeshiren?"

"My mother's letter," I answered, unsure if I should be telling them about it. Gasps were heard all around - from my brothers, because of shock - from Kate and Kartcher, because of awareness.

"She told you of your lineage in a letter?" Kate gasped.

"Not exactly. Sonat read the letter and deduced who I was by asking *who* my mother was. I didn't know what else to say. I knew nothing about this world, or that I'm of a royal bloodline," I said, defending myself. "Even at the time of Sonat finding out about my mother, I still didn't know what that meant."

"This can't be good," Kate said to Kartcher, who held my gaze.

"This can present a problem," Kartcher said. "If more people know you all are here, word will travel fast and fate will be set in motion faster than can be expected," he said, closing his eyes and shaking his head.

"What do you mean?" Ryder asked.

"When Daten and Johannes ruled, many Maeshiren also reigned supreme under them. When I say the Maeshiren lineage was strong, I mean it. However, they were met with a force unlike ever before. A heathen by the name of Braeden used many unconventional tactics. You see, it wasn't the Maeshiren's sole duty to protect Elderon but to protect the crossings into Earth as well.

"The great battle raged on. Every able-bodied person, including Daten, was needed on the front lines to push back the enemy from entering the opened gate. Battle by battle, we lost more and more Maeshiren by the hundreds. With explicit orders, should we have failed, the council was to take Daten's place in Höllengrad until the Maeshiren could rule again. The Niveh gates between this world and yours were to be sealed off to all travel, save for a select few who carried the key," Kartcher explained.

"My mother's necklace," I said, looking down at the chain disappearing beneath my shirt. I realized, at some point, someone had changed my clothes. I hoped it was Kate, or else this would be awkward.

"You have the key?" Kate asked, eyes wide.

"I suppose. My mother left this with the letter in a box," I lifted the pendant from the chain. "The witches tried to take it from me, but they couldn't. Instead, it fused to my body. They couldn't pull it even an inch away from me. In fact, it burned them when they tried," I said.

"That's because the key has been passed on to the rightful owner. That pendant you possess was your grandfather Daten's. He had passed it down to your mother who, in turn, passed it down to you," Kartcher explained.

"I don't understand. Earlier you said it was fated we would end up here eventually. How so?" Garrett asked.

"As you can imagine, the Maeshiren had lost for the first time in many millennia. With that, the gate had been sealed, but not before Daten had made his way to Earth. He was the last Maeshiren known who had survived the great battle. For the sake of this world and yours, he had to protect himself so he, or someone in his lineage, could come back and rule once again — restoring order from chaos and bringing about the destruction to darkness." Kartcher said.

It saddened me to know that his sister didn't make it with him in battle. I catalogued that for a later discussion to find out what had happened to her.

"Okay, so why didn't he come back and take his rightful place?" I asked.

"That – is complicated," Kartcher said. Gavin and Kate shifted as Kartcher did. Clearly, they were uncomfortable with this subject. Kartcher became hesitant when he had been so forthcoming with everything else. Kate kept fidgeting, which was classic Kate when she had something to hide. Gavin held his gaze to the floor with tight lips and narrowed eyes. The expression was unmistakable.

"I don't see what is so complicated about it," Garrett said.

"Well, first of all, he's dead," Kate spat, staring daggers at Garrett.

"Okay, well then why didn't our mother—," I started to ask.

"That is complicated as well," Kartcher said.

"We have a right to know what happened. If it's true what you're saying, we are of royal bloodline, then this concerns *our* family! That is *our* mother you're talking about *and* our grandfather," Ryder stated.

"Yes. We understand the gravity of this situation, much more than you realize, young Ryder," Kartcher stated, staring at Ryder with the superiority of age and wisdom Ryder lacked.

"Will someone please get to the point then? How is our mother involved in all of this?" Garrett asked.

"Your parents are both from this world. Your mother came here when she came of age to take her rightful place as ruler of the Maeshiren. Instead, she was met with hostility from the council, much as you will face should you meet them yourselves. She was only half Maeshiren, and half-human," Kartcher said.

"When she became pregnant with Tanner, they grew more hostile as they considered her in a fragile state. There were attempts to end her life. Your father would have none of it. With the possession of the gate key, they fled back to earth to raise Tanner, and much later you all, in a world without magic and chaos. They chose to give you a normal life, knowing someday fate and destiny would pull you back here once again," Kate finished.

The gravity of our parents' past weighed heavy on my shoulders. Realizing what dangers they had been through, but also coming to terms with the fact there was so much we never knew about them, both saddened and angered me.

"What is all of your roles in this?" I asked. I squinted at Kate, who held my gaze for only a beat before dropping hers to the floor. Was she ashamed? I glanced at Gavin, but he refused to acknowledge me.

"When Daten crossed over worlds, we were with him. We were his guard, so to speak," Kartcher answered. My heart dropped into my stomach and for a second time in so many hours, bile rose in my throat.

"You *lied* to me," I whispered, hurt and shock coursing through me as I stared at Kate. Tears welled at the realization everything I knew was a lie. Every. Single. Thing.

"No, I didn't. I'm still exactly who you know me to be," Kate looked at me with pleading eyes.

"No, you aren't. Our whole lives have been fabricated. You weren't there to be my *friend*," I sneered, "you were there to be our bodyguards. Both of you!" I glared at Gavin, who turned to me with remorse. "It wasn't out of a sense of friendship but out of duty. What kind of friendship is that?" I spat.

"Please Aurora. Listen to me," Kate stood up the same time I did. "It may have been out of a sense of duty at first, but it became more than that."

"I don't want to hear another word. I can't trust a thing you say," I spun around, unsure of where else to go as I held back tears, not wanting to cry in front of the others.

"Where are you going?" Kate asked, exasperated.

"Anywhere but here with you. Leave me the hell alone," I screamed, running back to the bedroom I had woken up in. I slammed the solid hardwood door, pulling the large wooden beam across to lock it in place before throwing myself onto the bed I had woken up from only an hour prior.

How could my entire existence have been a lie? I'd accuse my brothers of being in on this, except they were as shocked by these admissions as I was.

"Aurora?" Ryder knocked.

"Go away Ryder."

"Please let me in. Let's talk about this," he soothed. I didn't answer. I couldn't answer. Anything I wanted to say kept getting choked up in my throat. After a few minutes, he gave up and walked away.

I sat in the center of the bed, pulling my legs into my chest as I cried into my knees. I rocked myself back and forth, trying to quiet the hurt, the anger, and the betrayal I felt, though little could help that.

A few moments later, Kate knocked on the door. "Aurora, *please* talk to me," she pleaded. She, of all people, was the last person I wanted to speak with. How could she have kept this from me for so many years? We were sisters! At least, that's how I thought of her. The title was misplaced. I cried harder as a new anguish ripped through my heart.

"Aurora, please understand. Daten *ordered* me to be in his guard. That is my duty. It's my *free will* to be your friend, your sister," she cried on the other side of the door.

"Words," I growled. "Just. Go. Away. Kate," I said loud enough for her to hear. I couldn't listen to anymore of her lies. Maybe what she said was true. Maybe it wasn't. In the state I was in now, there was no way I could rationally think straight.

It felt like I had tripped and knocked myself out, only to wake up in some upside-down nightmare. I found myself in a place where mythical creatures were real and nonsensical matters ruled rather than logic. I rested my chin on my knees, losing myself in the mesmerizing dance of the flames in the fireplace.

Talking lizards. Royal bloodlines. Gates that disappeared and witches that tortured; I must be in a nightmare.

"Damn it, Aurora. Open this fucking door," Garrett hollered, making me jump six feet in the air at his pounding fist. "Don't you think we are all freaked out?" When I didn't answer, he stomped back towards the living room.

Would they never quit? Were they going to keep revolving person-to-person to see who I would give into first? I needed to get out of here. I needed to get away from them and get some fresh air.

I focused on the only way of escape – the floor to ceiling stained windows. Crawling off the bed, I noted the traces of blood soaked into the white sheets where I had been laying earlier. A shiver ran through me, giving me a moment of pause to question whether I should even leave the protection of these four walls. When I heard footsteps echoing up the short hallway, I decided I didn't care. I didn't want to be around this craziness any longer.

Catching my backpack left on the chair by the fireplace, I flung it over my back as the next knock rapped on the door.

"Aurora?"

Kate again. Just her voice grated on my nerves.

"Aurora. Please let me in," she pleaded. I ignored her, pausing with shallow breaths as I listened for her steps to fade away. Couldn't they take a hint and leave me alone?

Grasping the cold metal hinges that locked the windows in place, the hope I had for them to open without a sound became a lost cause. They creaked with each deliberate, downward movement of my hands. It was like they hadn't been opened in over a century.

I stopped with each creak, listening to see if they had caught onto me. It didn't seem to be the case, as I could still hear them all talking amongst themselves in the living room.

With one final downturn of the handles, the windows swung out rather than in, nearly toppling me through the opening. I swear! *Did nothing make sense here?*

I glanced over my shoulder, silent, listening to them converse in the living room. My heart pounded, as if I was making a jailbreak. With one final deep breath, I peered over the high ledge. I would have to make a small leap to reach the ground.

Lifting my leg over the ledge, I held onto the metal window support. I lifted my other leg over and leveraged my weight against that of the house so I could walk my way down before jumping.

"Where are ya going?" Gavin asked, making me whip my head and lose my grip at the same time, landing me square on my ass with an "oomph." I turned to him, leaning against the house with one foot holding him up and his arms crossed - a Cheshire grin lining his face.

"I – I – I needed some fresh air is all," I stuttered, knowing full well I was caught.

"There are better ways to get fresh air than falling through a window," he chuckled. He knew what I was doing.

"How did you know?" I squinted at him, sheepish about getting caught.

"I know many things Aurora," he toyed, chuckling.

"Yes. I'm fully aware of this fact," I deadpanned. He lost his smug grin, realizing the corner he placed himself in.

"C'mon. I'm going to take you somewhere," he said, pushing off the house.

"Huh?" I asked stupidly.

"You said you wanted fresh air. To be honest, I could use getting away from annoying, prying eyes too. Let's go," he said, offering me a helping hand up.

I stared at his hand, debating whether I should grab it or stand on my own just to prove a point. Glancing into his inviting eyes, I grasped his hand without thinking, feeling the strength in his arm as he hoisted me to my feet.

My heart galloped as he let his hand linger in mine before pulling away. Warmth flooded my cheeks, the yearning to fill the void with his hand once again prominent. It made little sense for me to feel this way. Why should I be disappointed he no longer held my hand? I wasn't some schoolgirl with a crush. *Or was I?* Besides, I reminded myself; I'm just as pissed at him as I am at Kate.

"Where are we going?" I asked.

"You'll see," he smirked, saying nothing more.

Chapter Fourteen

Confessions

⸻ ❧ ⸻

"I refused to allow myself to accept any of it in my heart, because I was afraid of a headlong fall, but I was hanging in suspense which was more likely to be fatal than a fall." – St. Augustine, "Confessions"

***

A lake, with an unending horizon, shimmered bright against the contrast of the evening sky. The illumination of the water moving about, with the gentle ebb and flow of the lake's natural tide, swirled about a kaleidoscope of colors – variations of blues, pinks, and purples with a glistening white in between.

Without the obscuring trees above, the darkened sky displayed a brilliance all its own. Two massive, planet-like orbs, askew from one another, radiated with deep magentas, oranges, purples, and greens. The sky danced in a dizzying array of lights, rivaling that of the Northern Borealis.

Tiny fireflies danced along the water's edge, as freesia and hints of tropical fruits wafted towards my olfactory senses. Nightingales sang deep into the night, turning a romantic setting into a heavenly dream.

"Where are we?" I whispered, afraid to speak with any audibility as if the place would disappear.

"My private lake," he answered with a humbled humility.

"Your what?" I choked with wide eyes. He answered with a sheepish grin.

"It's the one place I can come and experience true peace," he said, his eyes following my every move as I bent down to pick up a rock. Skipping it along the lake's surface, it created a prism of colors in its wake.

"Wow. It isn't every day you come across someone who has their own giant private lake," I teased.

"Perks of being part of the guard," he said, bothered by this admission.

"Yes. About that." I let my words hang in the air as I collected my thoughts. Being in this place made it difficult to remember why I had become angry in the first place, but just so.

"I'm done with the lies and the secrecy, Gavin. I need answers and I need them now," I demanded. I stood my ground, lifting my chin to better see his face, fighting the urge to become wrapped up in his intoxicating presence.

Silence defined this moment as we gauged each other's intentions, searching desperately for answers – for permission – to be vulnerable and forthcoming. *Do we trust each other enough to be honest?* That remained to be seen. I believe the bigger question is *'would he divulge the answers I so needed?'*

He took a deep breath, closing his eyes as he exhaled, cutting off our silent exchange. When he opened his eyes again, he turned his face away from me and towards the allure of the lake. My heart dropped at any hopes of getting answers when he continued to stay silent and walked away.

I stared at his retreating back, wondering if he would leave me standing here without another word. I prayed that would not be the case.

Only a few feet away, he took pause.

"Come sit," he gestured toward a large, fallen tree by the water's edge. "It's going to be a long story."

When I didn't answer right away, he glanced back. Though he seemed relaxed, his eyes held a different story, as tight and somber as they were. I hesitated, unsure if I was ready to hear all he had to say, but resigned to the truth, I would never be ready.

Ever the gentleman, he stood, waiting, as I ambled towards him. The reluctance of his unspoken admissions was clearly visible in his eyes, though he graced me with a dimpled side smile I had grown fond of. Butterflies fluttered in my belly, awakening a carnal need to close the gap between us, taking me by surprise. Could he sense my growing infatuation? Or was this just a one-sided experience?

He turned and sat on the makeshift bench. Taking a steady breath, I focused on calming my nerves before sitting a safe proximity away from him – one foot planted on the stump as I rested on my knee.

"Aurora, there have been many times I wanted to step into your life and share with you your history - your future, and who you truly are. Every time I was prepared to do so, something would remind me why I should wait a little longer," he started, but made no attempt to elaborate.

"Why should you have waited?" I pushed on. He released a heavy sigh before continuing.

"Because the knowledge of what I'm about to tell you would have set everything in motion much faster. It would have collided you with this world much sooner than I was ready for. It would have put you in more danger than you already were," he said. As he scanned across the lake, his lips morphed into a grim line.

"I don't understand. You said earlier it was fated I would have come here one-way or another. What did you mean by that?"

"This is so much harder than I realized it would be," he said, more to himself as he swiped a hand through his hair.

"Aurora, you know a bit of your lineage from what Kartcher and Kate said earlier. What they failed to mention is that a direct descendant of Daten's lineage must be the one who retakes the throne.

Before he died, he set everything up for your mother to take that place – his only living heir to the throne. For various reasons, your mother couldn't do so. She had to choose who would be the one who took that coveted place, and she chose you," he said, staring intently into my eyes. I didn't have to understand everything to see he did not approve of her decision.

"Why? Why would she choose me over my brothers?" I asked.

"My guess is because you're the one with the more powerful latent abilities. Last I was here with your mother, the night before we fled, I found her panicked in her room alone. She kept mumbling something about a seer visiting her, saying her children were in danger," he said, staring off into some distant memory with his brows turned in.

He continued, "Before we left, she made me promise to watch over you as I had done for her. It's then I realized she chose you to take this place. When I asked her why you, she said she believed you would be the one who could restore the Maeshiren order and bring times of peace once more." He watched me carefully. Shocked couldn't even describe what I felt.

"I-I'm to do what now?" I choked out.

"And she isn't the only one to think this. In this world, everything and everyone is under the careful eye of others. Even more so since everyone is awaiting the arrival of the Maeshiren who will retake the throne. It is highly suspect. Your mother, and in effect you and your brothers, have been well watched by both the enemy and the council alike," he divulged, almost pained in his expression.

"I thought the gates were closed. How is that even possible?" I asked, my voice raising a few octaves higher than I expected.

"They're closed to *most*. Those who have the means to get through still do," he said.

"How?" I asked.

"How did you get through? Much the same way. You don't carry the only key to go back and forth, you know," he said, as if the answer should have been obvious.

The raw truth is I've been in danger my entire life. I was wrapped in a carefully crafted, naïve bubble, though exposed to this world in plain sight.

Knowing my family has always been under the watchful eyes of our enemies was jarring. Not to mention, the realization my whole life had been an utter lie. Everything I knew, I viewed through half-truths.

I groaned, as my hands slid down my face, trying to process all of this information. "This isn't happening - so where do you fit into all of this? Why have you decided to make an appearance into my life after all of this time?"

So many burning questions; I couldn't get them out fast enough.

He hesitated to answer at first. Or maybe he was trying to figure out the best way *to* answer. I hoped there wouldn't be a line I would cross. I needed to keep him talking.

"I'm a part of Daten's guard. It's my job to protect your family," he said.

"Yes. I know that already. What I *want* to know is where *you* fit in with all of this when it comes to *me*?" I asked; making sure he couldn't dodge my questions. As of recent, wherever Tony had been involved, he was there. Out of nowhere.

I couldn't help but feel slighted. He has known me my whole life, probably knows close to everything about me, yet here I remain, still knowing next to nothing about him. In the grand scheme of things, maybe it was childish, but I was angry about it. He remained silent.

"Are you not going to answer me? Is it that bad?" I asked, now expecting the worse. I regretted asking but also knew the regret of *not* knowing would weigh even heavier.

"I *am* answering you. If you'll give me a moment," he bit back. If he was collecting his thoughts, I could afford to be patient. I watched as a multitude of emotions flashed across his face – reluctance, anger, fear, and ultimately, resolve. He turned the full force of his gaze onto me with purpose.

"Being a part of Daten's guard is something I took pride in. I wasn't just his guard, but his friend, his confidant. Before he died, he asked me – no, begged me, to continue serving the Maeshiren long after his passing. This, of course, extended to your mother, then you and your siblings. Do you remember when your mother left for a few years?" he asked. I nodded.

"We were here. Things had taken a bad turn with the council. Instead of ruling in the Maeshiren's stead, they overthrew the checks and balances set in place and took on the rule for themselves. They upset the balance, leaving thousands starving and impoverished. Your mother came here to correct that order. We barely made it back to earth alive.

When I came back, you were no longer a child but a grown

woman. I was charged to be your mother's sole protector, but when we came back, I was drawn to you. Marie noticed," he said, grinning at a silent memory, watching for my reaction. My heart galloped; I urged him to continue with a small smile of my own.

"Even without promising your mother to watch over you, I wanted to be an important part of your life, but was always reluctant. I wanted you to know me, but I never wanted you to be in any more danger *because* of me. Kate was as drawn to you as I was.

Before we left, she begged your mother to be in your life because she had always seen you as her little sister. She didn't realize until much later how close you would both become in the end," he stared at me, pointedly. I didn't want to think about Kate now. I was still pissed at her, yet this glimpse into Kate's past did soften my anger towards her a bit.

"With Kate there, you were as safe as you ever would be, so there was no immediate need for me to step in. I can't say it didn't bother me in the end though," he admitted, his voice falling to a whisper as he lowered his gaze.

"Why did it bother you?" I whispered back, searching his face for answers.

Leaning forward, he lifted his smoldering gaze beneath the veil of his lashes. "I wanted it to be me. I wanted to be the one near you, protecting you, knowing you," he said, his voice thick, "You always had this aura that drew me in like a moth to a flame. Shortly after Marie and I came back, after *that* tragic day, I wanted nothing more than to hold you in my arms and reassure you everything would be okay." His voice cracked as his brows drew in. He gulped back the pain we both shared.

Everything felt heightened, raw. Bringing my parents and Tanner into the foreground, through the eyes of someone who was there, made it all real again.

That wasn't all though. There was a layer I never thought I could add - Gavin's pain. It was so palpable; I could almost take it as my own. The unimaginable guilt he has carried, imagining myself in his shoes, caring for a person so deeply yet not being able to bring myself to be a part of their life. Watching their struggles and taking them as my own, it was more than my heart could bear.

"You were never the same after that. It killed me inside. Still does to this day," he added with such compassion as he wiped away a tear streaming down my cheek. Without another word, he pulled me into the safe harbor of his arms, holding me tight to his side as I let the tears fall from each confession playing in my mind.

The warm cocoon of his embrace helped to soothe the ache deep within my soul. More than the pain we shouldered on our own; this was a pain we shouldered together. Internalizing the depth of each revelation, neither of us moved to break the companionable silence. As my heart simmered down in its despair, a new welling emerged with a deep heat smoldering in its place. It became harder not to nuzzle into the comfort of his chest.

"Why now?" I cleared my voice. "I mean, I understand why you waited, but what happened since to make you decide to step into my life?"

"Our enemies have become bolder. While it's true, the gate is sealed, there are still ways to pass information. Not everyone who seems to be on our side *is*. There is corruption everywhere. When you moved to San Diego, our enemies had a hard time finding your whereabouts, but it was only a matter of time. Once they did, they found ways to get closer to you and your brothers. It was time I made my appearance so I could protect you," he said, matter-of-fact.

"How did you find me with the witches, then?"

His muscles tensed before he relaxed enough to speak. He released his hold, bringing his eyes to my level, never fully letting me go.

"Aurora, I've never been so afraid of losing something or someone in my entire life. Nothing in my life has ever meant as much to me as you do. When I found out you were missing, when I no longer felt your presence on earth, my entire world froze.

I followed your spiritual essence to the gates, confirming my worst fears. When I followed you to the witch's lair, my heart dropped. But when I had seen the torture they submitted you to, my entire world fell apart. I almost lost you," his voice cracked as he squeezed his eyes shut. He tightened his hold, bringing me back into his side, embracing me as if I were going to disappear. I turned to comfort him, but he held me in place.

I remembered the pure anger and sheer panic on his face when he found me with the occults. I remembered the dark shadows obscuring his figure, the red glow of his eyes being the only tell giving him away.

The nagging question I couldn't bring myself to ask - *what was he?*

A part of me didn't want to know. Would I be afraid of him if I knew? How could I be, though, after the confession he laid at my feet?

Was he dangerous? Unequivocally. Was he a danger to me? I'd like to think not.

"Spiritual Essence? What's that?" I asked, trying to keep him talking.

"Everyone has a spiritual essence, a spiritual thumbprint, if you will. Each is unique to the individual and if you know what you're searching for, you know how to track someone. With you, it's so easy for me. I'm so attuned to your essence. It's the most powerful thing in my life. So, when I no longer sensed it, when I could no longer feel your presence, I knew something terrible had happened.

I traced your steps from your family farm, which led me directly to where you crossed over. I didn't hesitate. I crossed over the moment I figured out where you went," he stated, still living back in that moment. The way he described it; I could see the exact moment playing out in my mind.

"How did you cross over? Do you have a key too?" I asked.

"No. The gate stays open for undetermined amounts of time from the side you open it. It's a major flaw no one has been able to figure out how to fix. This is why crossing back and forth for those who do have the key should only be done under absolute dire circumstances. It allows for other opportunistic beings to take advantage of this fact, should they know about it," he said, his eyebrows pulling in.

The more we talked, the darker our conversation turned. I tried to think of something to steer the conversation into happier grounds, but kept coming up empty. I have questions, oh believe me do I have questions, but none of them seemed right to ask in this moment.

"How old are you?" I blurted out. I kept it simple. With him knowing my grandfather, whom I never met and rarely heard about, he appeared nothing like the age he should.

He chuckled, "In your world, the equivalent of twenty-three."

"And in your world?"

"Honestly, I'm afraid to answer that one," he replied, eyeing me from the side.

"Why?"

"I'm afraid of what you'll think," he said, releasing me from his hold. I sat up, facing him once again.

"You can't scare me that easily," I smirked. "Besides, with all the other craziness I've experienced, that would seem the most normal to me."

"Don't be so sure," he huffed. "I'm technically four hundred and thirty-one years old."

I gulped, trying to maintain my composure. Apparently, I was doing a stand-up job at it.

"I knew you would freak out," he said, closing his eyes and shaking his head.

"I'm not freaking out," my voice went a few octaves higher than I meant it.

"Sure, you're not. If you aren't freaking out, then why do you look constipated all of a sudden?" he stated, snapping his eyes open.

"I do *not* look constipated!" I wailed; my cheeks flushing crimson. He laughed at my embarrassment.

"It's okay. I know it can be a lot to take in," he chuckled, his cheeks flushed himself. "You should have seen your brothers when they learned how old Kartcher is." His tight-lipped smile amused at the remembered reactions.

"How is it possible? You still seem so young," I asked.

"Hey, I *am* still young! Even in this world, I'm considered barely an adult," he exclaimed, offended.

"Wow. How does that work?"

"How does age work in your world? Who knows? Some age faster, some slower. It's how this world operates. Some philosophers here believe our time moves much slower than on Earth, halting accelerated aging," he said, explaining his philosophical reason.

"So, does everyone live as long as you have?" I asked.

"No. Which is why I don't believe in some of these philosophers. As I've said, everyone ages at different rates here," he responded.

I turned over in my head how it all worked out. I kept coming up empty, so instead I settled on the notion of him being more my age regardless of number. By appearances alone, I could see this to be true.

"What are you thinking?" he asked when I gave no further inquiry into my musings.

"Pfft, honestly, I'm thinking about how crazy everything is. I keep thinking I'll wake up and this entire experience will be one big, convoluted dream," I explained, shaking my head. He sighed.

"As much as I wish I could tell you it's a dream, it's not. More like a nightmare," he chuckled at the absurdity of it all.

"Yeah, maybe you're right. Though, I don't see you being part of any nightmare," I laughed, rolling my eyes at his dubious expression.

Despite the light banter our conversation had turned, Tony's face flashed in my mind's eye. The association between Gavin and Tony left me puzzled. Why had he always been there where Tony was concerned? Was it due to jealousy? Or something else?

"Not to steer us off topic, but can you tell me what happened to Tony? Who is Emily to you, and why is she so involved with Tony?"

It seemed like a lifetime ago, rather than a few days, what happened between us. It still pained me to think of his name. However, there were too many holes in my understanding needing to be filled. While I trusted Kartcher and Kate to tell me these answers, if I were so inclined to ask them, it was Gavin's lips I wanted to hear them from.

He inhaled, running a hand through his hair. "I knew this would come up sooner or later."

"Of course."

"Of course," he replied, as he cleared his throat. The playful smirk he had only a moment before turned frigid. "The day I stepped into your life is the day Tony was prepared to take it from you."

I gasped, a sheen of sweat beading at the nape of my neck. I remembered the night Tony said he wanted to put me in a ditch. While a part of me hoped it was an idle threat, a larger part of me knew it wasn't. Bile rose in my throat, knowing how close I had come to being a goner at the hands of someone I used to love.

"Why?" I breathed without a sound.

"As I said earlier, our enemies were getting too close for comfort. Kate, Kartcher, and I were on overtime trying to track their movements, to see what angle they would attack from. When I had seen Emily enter the scene, I knew the gravity of our situation had become grim," he explained.

"Emily is Braeden's right-hand assassin," he seethed. "She can unleash a power that is absolutely lethal, if she were so inclined to use it that way."

"What power?" I asked, the knot in my stomach winding tighter.

"With the power of touch, she can control you. Make you do her biding. It's close to that of a master puppeteer," he said.

"Wait. With just one touch, she has that kind of power?"

"Not just a single touch," he said. "She must be in physical contact with you for a period before it takes hold, intimate or otherwise. The longer she touches someone, the more control she has over them. Once she has her clutches into someone, it tends to run deep," he explained.

My mind halted on *'intimate or otherwise.'* A heaviness overcame me at the realization of how intimate Tony and Emily had truly been. The flashback of them all over each other in Tony's car flashed vividly in my mind. Anger and pain rolled through me in waves as I worked hard to gain composure over myself.

I dropped my eyes towards my twisting hands. My face flushed with anger and embarrassment at the knowledge of everyone else knowing what was going on except me. The irrational side of me was prepared to snap out in anger, but a small whisper inside my head told me to see it differently. I tried to listen, view things in a more constructive light. I understood what they did was in my best interest – I still wasn't happy about it.

The anger simmered to a controllable level. While I had every right to be angry, I knew I shouldn't be. I lifted my eyes to Gavin's patient gaze and gave him a gentle nod. "I guess I shouldn't be surprised. I suppose a part of me always knew he was cheating on me. The night you showed up, I knew I was in danger. I never knew how close it had come to *that* though," I admitted.

It was humbling to know if it weren't for Gavin, I wouldn't be here. I would probably be on a murder mystery special or something.

"What I can't wrap my head around, though, is *why*? Why go through Tony to kill me? Why not do it herself?" I asked.

"Emily toys with her prey. She gets off on creating drama before the final drawing of the curtain, so to speak," he said, leaning over to pick up a rock and roll it in his hand.

"At the time, Tony had been the closest to you who she could control. She knew she couldn't get to your brothers with them being so heavily guarded by us. It was a no brainer for her."

"That's disturbing," I shuddered. "If she has such amazing control, why had Tony become so manic? It's like he was on drugs." I remembered how disheveled and crazy he was.

"He was fighting against her hold, though he probably didn't know it," he said, still focusing on the rock like it was the most important thing in his world.

"That's possible?"

"Yeah. When someone is too headstrong, or when Emily hasn't had long enough contact with her puppet, the will of the person fights against her power. You could say it's one character flaw with her abilities," he smirked without humor.

"Well, I know the contact part wasn't a problem for her with Tony. So, he must have been fighting against her then?" I asked and stated at the same time.

"You could say that," Gavin said.

"I feel bad, he didn't ask for any of this," I said, remorse prominent at knowing everything he had done was against his will. And I was to blame.

"Hmpf, I wouldn't feel too bad for the shmuck," Gavin said, rolling his eyes.

"Why is that?"

"How do you think Emily got to him in the first place, Aurora?" he turned away from the source of his fascination and stared at me like I missed the point.

"I guess I know. I can't help but think this happened against his will," I said. He gave me a dubious look but left it at that.

"So, what does Emily plan to do with him now that I'm no longer home?" I asked, afraid for Tony's wellbeing.

Gavin's eyes tightened before turning away towards the water's edge. "I have no idea." He skidded the pebble across the water's surface, casting colorful swirls as I had earlier.

He looked as bothered by the unknown for his safety as I was. Or maybe he truly didn't care. On second thought, from everything Gavin has said, I don't think he would think twice about taking Tony out if he remained a threat to me, or my brothers. I shuddered once at the thought before kicking it out of my mind.

We sat in companionable silence. So much we had discussed

and yet, we hadn't even breached the surface. One thing I knew for certain, he cared for me enough to want to be in my life. In what capacity, I couldn't be sure. This unknown still did little to keep my heart from pitter pattering when I was near him.

Though he continued to look away from me, I couldn't tear my eyes away from him. It's as if I were seeing him for the first time in the right light. His strong jawline and subtle five-o'clock shadow accented his tan complexion perfectly. And the way his emerald gaze would settle on me, as if he were sharing an intimate moment with my soul, set my body ablaze.

The image of his full lips on mine stole my breath. Was he a good kisser? What would he taste like? Shivers ran through me as I bit my lip, trying to contain these urges I kept having in his presence.

He turned, giving me a smile that nearly knocked me off the stump. It wasn't fair. How could anyone have this kind of hold on me?

"What?" he smiled wider.

"Nothing," I blushed, turning away from him as my traitorous lips turned up on their own. What is wrong with me? Sure, he is attractive but *pull yourself together Aurora!*

Watching my hands knot in and out of themselves; I tried to calm my racing heart. I didn't want to be absorbed in these feelings. They were irrational. Unnecessary. The wounds Tony had inflicted were still too fresh; I couldn't allow myself into a headlong fall for Gavin – if that was where I was headed. I could not handle another heartbreak, another blow to the soul.

Which brings me full circle to the many questions I have yet to get answered. He was close to my parents and Tanner, close enough to know what happened the day they passed away.

"If I asked you a question, would you be honest with me?" I know he had been answering my questions since we got here, but I also knew he edited.

"Of course," he replied, unsure.

"My parents and Tanner didn't die in a car accident," I stated, locking his eyes with mine. I waited for him to tell me the truth I didn't want to hear. The moment I had found my mother's note, it had been on my mind. Her knowing we were all in danger, knowing she would no longer be here to help us, meant only one thing. She knew of her impending death.

"That's not a question Aurora," he said, stalling.

"I know. You know what I'm asking though," I said, not willing to drop his gaze for even a moment.

"No. They did not. That was a cover up," he said, warily. Fury welled inside at having my suspicions confirmed. They were murdered. Someone was responsible. I wanted to find them.

"How did they die?"

"Aurora, I don't think right now is a good time –"

"How?" I yelled, cutting him off. A blast of air swirled the ground leaves around us as an unexpected energy surge left my body. Gavin leaned back with eyes wide.

I dropped his gaze, paralyzed with fear and an excited foreign sensation coursing through me. Never had I been able to alter physical objects around me other than to heal them. It felt empowering, yet chaotic. *What changed?*

The familiar heaviness sitting on my chest took hold as I reminded myself what an anomaly I was - a freak. I wasn't normal, and this was clear evidence of that.

I peeked at Gavin from beneath my lashes, afraid to see the same startled expression plastered on his face. What I had seen, though, was nothing but compassion.

"I don't think you can handle the truth right now, Aurora," he said, continuing to watch me as one hand hung in the air before falling back onto his lap.

I was trying to keep it together. I was trying to be strong enough to hear what he had to say. This was as close as I was ever going to get to the truth, so I needed him to see I could handle it.

"Please. I need to know," I begged through clenched teeth. I turned away, unable to look him in the eye and continue to hold it together. He could see right through me.

"For what it's worth, I'm sorry. It should be me in their place," he said, his voice cracking with his confession. I flashed my eyes to meet his silent grief imploring me to understand, his watery eyes carrying the agonizing burden of shame. With this one look, he punched a hole right through my heart.

Never again did I want to witness this disturbed look marring his handsome face. With the inaccuracies surrounding the death of my parents and Tanner confirmed, it opened fresh wounds I knew would come. However, hearing Gavin speak those words with such finality tormented my very being. It was irrational, but to think of Gavin no longer existing would be a pain I couldn't endure.

"Don't say that," I said, horrified.

"It's true Aurora. If I had been a second faster, I would have–," he cut himself off, shaking his head in the sea of guilt consuming him.

"Stop it! Stop it right now, Gavin!" I exclaimed. "I don't want to hear you talking like that anymore. If you believe in fate, then what happened to my parents and brother is not your fault. It was their fate. If you don't believe in that, then believe this. You can't control everything. You can't be everywhere for everybody. Sure, the pain of missing them is still fresh and I fear always will be. But they're gone Gavin and we can't keep staying stifled in the past," I said, willing him to see my point. I don't know who I tried to convince more, me – or him. Maybe both? Who knows?

Seeing my pain doubled in him was too much. I grasped both of his hands, willing him to understand. If I could see the conviction of my own words take hold in him, I could finally allow it to take hold in me too. He lifted his sorrowful gaze, a small sympathetic smile capturing my breath. Between the hard discussions and the newness of his warm touch, I was fraying.

He pulled one hand out from underneath mine, brushing the back of it against my cheek. I leaned in, relishing in the close contact of his touch.

"I wasn't there when it happened. I made it only in the aftermath. You will never know what that day did to me. Not only did I bear the pain of losing them, but I felt yours just the same. You could say I received a double dose of my failure," he admitted, a tear escaping his dark and saddened eyes.

My heart faltered at the dripping pain of his admission. I wanted to know more. I wanted to know every single detail but how could I? How could I press him for more when I could see the pain it caused him to remember? The pain it cost him to relive that horrible day out loud and to the one person he knew felt it on a scale that he did. No doubt, he knew of my mental breakdown. Why else would he know not to broach the subject without sensitivity?

The pain emanating from him was so much more than I could bear. Every nerve ending on fire, and the swelling urge to hug him tight, became overbearing. Before I knew it, my brain malfunctioned as I threw myself at him, hugging his neck tight with my wet cheek pressed firm against his.

"I'm so sorry," I sobbed. Three years of numbness, three years of repressed pain, three years of ignoring everything I had felt instead of dealing with it broke free. I didn't mean to become a blubbering mess, but the dam broke. There was no hope of putting that wall back up again.

Taking him by surprise with my emotional attack, he paused before wrapping me tight into the enclosure of his arms, holding me together. Hell - he was holding us together, but it was exactly what I needed.

"Aurora, I promise you. I will never leave you. I will never allow what happened to them to happen to you. It will be over my dead body and not even then," he said as he buried his face into my hair. I felt the conviction in his words as he swore his oath to me. "I know I've done little to earn your trust. I know I don't deserve it either, but please believe me when I say you can trust me. Always come to me for anything. I get to be in your life now. I'm the one you can confide in now," he said, seeming more to ask for my permission than extracting it.

We released each other's hold, searching one another with a renewed sense of what? I couldn't be sure. But the light I felt in my eyes, and the strange hunger I had seen in his, told me we crossed a path of trust, of connection, however strained it may be.

"I'll try to remember that," I smirked, wiping my tear stricken face.

"You make sure to do that," he smiled, pushing a strand of hair out of my eyes and behind my ear. A shy smile traded places with my smirk as I found myself self-conscience in his presence.

Much had changed since crossing the gate. All the events and revelations leading to this point had only left me confused and frayed. There had been no sweet release, no safe harbor I could pull into. The way his eyes now smoldered into mine, and the way his fingers lingered for a moment longer against my cheek than was socially acceptable, told me I had finally found one.

Could I trust it? This connection blossoming between us?

The conviction in his words wanted me to say yes; my heart

wanted me to believe in his every word so I could feel safe. I didn't want to think, I just wanted to feel – something. Anything than what I have been. And so, I would allow my guarded heart to crack open the door to this dark protector. I would revel in this feeling of falling, wherever it would leave me. I would allow myself to trust this man, though it went against my better judgement to do so.

Before I had formulated my thoughts into coherent words, fear replaced the adoration in Gavin's eyes. He grasped my hand, pulling us up with our backs facing the lake. Taking a protective stance in front of me, he scanned the darkness, his hand never leaving mine. The lake illuminated the side of his face, exposing his anger.

"Whatever you do, stay behind me," he growled in a hushed whisper. My knuckles were white as I clenched his cloak from behind. Fear shivered down my spine, making my hands tremble with it. I tried to scan the shadows for the threat but could see nothing, the brilliance of the lake doing nothing to help my vision focus on the darkness.

The cracking of a large branch from the left made my head snap in its direction. I couldn't silence the uncontrollable nerves taking my body hostage. With my hands so close to Gavin's back, I could feel the deep growl rumble within him before he released it for whoever dared to threaten us.

Chapter Fifteen

A Quandary

———⟡———

"The voice of conscience is so delicate that it is easy to stifle it;

but it is also so clear that it is impossible to mistake it." – Madame de Stael

***

Do not take one step closer," Gavin threatened through gritted teeth.

"Gavin Mair. You do not intimidate me," a deep voice boomed from the darkness. "You are required to bring the intruders to court, as ordered by the high council. To disobey is treason; punishable to the highest extent of the law." My eyes narrowed as I struggled to see the shadowed figure standing within the line of the trees.

As if whoever spoke took pity on my lack of vision, a large, grotesque figure stepped forward into the illumination of the lake. He looked every bit like a man, but he dwarfed any human

I had ever seen. Covered in Kevlar, the blackest breastplate covered his torso; it was a wonder how he moved so quietly through the trees. He carried his helmet on his side, exposing tattered dreadlocks woven into thick braids, cascading from the middle of his scalp and down his back - the sides' shaven clean. His eyes held a menace that had me shrinking behind Gavin.

"Who sent you?" Gavin asked, angered.

"The high council," he responded.

"Don't play games with me, you ugly baboon, *who* on the high council sent you," Gavin demanded.

"As if that will matter, but it was Servius Vasuvius."

"Huh, as if his opinion matters," Gavin insulted.

"All opinions of those who sit on the high council matters," he stated.

"Except his. Run along now. Tell Servius not send his lapdogs out to his dirty work," Gavin taunted.

"Should I take that as a threat?"

"Take it however you want. Just take your sorry ass away from here or else I won't be giving you the option," Gavin threatened.

"Bring the girl," he demanded.

"Over my dead body."

"That can be arranged," he said, waving his hairy hand forward. As he gave the signal, a group of eight masked men converged forward, surrounding us in a semi-circle. I was scared for Gavin. I was nervous for me. What did they want with me? How did they know we were here? Did they know my brothers were here too? He said *the intruders.*

"Oh, you're going to make this fun for me?" Gavin asked, his face radiant.

"Come quietly and I may let this slip from my memory when I brief the high council," the man said.

"No. I think I like these odds. Why don't we settle this *quietly* here you big ape?" Gavin said, overconfident, as his eyes flashed red.

"Gavin? What are you doing?" I whispered through clenched teeth. Though I had seen him in action on a few occasions, it was always with the element of surprise. I feared for him. I didn't want to see him hurt, especially not over me.

"Shh. Not now," he said over his shoulder, not taking his eyes off the threat. "Aurora, I want you to stay perfectly still when things pop off. I mean it, stay exactly where you are. Don't move a muscle," he demanded.

I nodded before squeaking out, "Okay," when I realized he wasn't looking at me.

"Well, c'mon! I don't have all day," Gavin taunted.

As he finished speaking, a masked figure jumped out from the big guy's flank, slashing his sword through the air. Gavin sidestepped him, blocking his sword arm, as he shoved the heel of his hand into the assailant's nose. Without giving the attacker time to recover, Gavin pushed his hands towards the man's chest, throwing him back through the air until he slammed against a tree; its life force exploding on impact.

The explosive energy reverberated against the surrounding trees, dying with a deep echo being swallowed into the darkness. Three more assailants took the dead man's place.

We were surrounded. My violent heart crashed against my chest at possibly witnessing Gavin's death. I couldn't bear it. Shadows swirled around Gavin as he let out a throaty laugh.

With eyes glowing red, he ripped out the throat of the masked figure to his right before unsheathing a curved sword from underneath his cloak, splitting the man to his left from belly button to chin. The third man, too stunned at Gavin's swift moves, couldn't react fast enough to Gavin's hand slicing through his chest and ripping out his heart. All three men staggered before crashing to the floor, all life drained from their bodies.

Gavin stood from his slight crouch, dropping the heart, and turned to the next wave of masked men prepared to take him down.

His devilish smile and red eyes flashed with excitement as he pulled out a second curved sword from under his cloak. "C'mon you *sonsofbitches*. Come at me with all you've got!" he grinned, his face dripping from the blood of his enemies. He crouched, preparing for his next attack when we heard Kate yelling in the distance.

"Gavin! Stop! They have them! Stop or else we are all dead!" she yelled, as she ran up to the battle scene unfolding. Gavin took pause. *Who had my brothers?*

My head spun at how fast everything had unfolded. Fear for my brothers took over whatever fear I held onto for Gavin and me. I needed to get to my brothers, *now.*

I turned from Kate to Gavin, anger mixed with bloodlust plastered on his face as he took in Kate's approaching sight. He warred with himself, weighing the options playing out before him.

With eyes trained on Gavin, staying in perfect stillness as he had asked, too consumed with the thought of my brothers in danger; I let out a muffled scream as a heavy hand wrapped around my mouth. I was pulled backwards, knocking the air from my lungs as they slammed me against their hardened torso.

My arm yanked back painfully with my head pulled in the opposite direction, cutting off any hopes I had of fighting back.

With frightened eyes, I strained to see Gavin whip his head around to see why I screamed. I heard Kate gasp in horror. The blood drained from Gavin's face as all reasoning left his body. In a blink of an eye, Gavin stood in front of me ripping the man's arm off his body at the same time plunging his sword deep into my captor's forehead. The hold he had on me released before Gavin pulled me into his arms, stepping away from the remaining threats.

"And where do you *think* you are going to go?" the colossal beast asked, taking a step towards us.

"Gavin, listen to me. You must stop this now. Think about Ryder, Garrett, and Kartcher. Neven has them!" Kate yelled at him. She wanted him to concede. Something about that felt wrong. If Gavin was fighting this hard against bringing me to the high council, why did it feel wrong to back down now? Whoever this Neven was, it seemed he wasn't someone they wanted to fight.

"Gavin?" I whispered, trying to get his attention. He broke away from Kate and the approaching beast before glancing down at me. His fierce state softened when he took in my frightened expression, the red glow of his iris' fading back to his normal shade of green.

"I'm sorry you had to see that," he said, taking me off guard.

"Alright. I'll come but no one, and I mean *no one*, fucking touches her or else they *will* die," he threatened as he pulled me tight into his side, scanning the approaching threats.

The beast stopped his approach, stepping to the side as he swept his arm for Gavin to lead the way. Gavin pulled me to the opposite side, away from the intimidating man, as I shuddered. He grew impossibly larger the closer we were to him.

Gavin's murderous stare bore into the beasts' eyes as we passed. When a shudder rolled through my body once more, he tightened his hold and walked faster towards Kate. He shot his arm out, grabbing her shoulders to bring her along with him.

"How did you get away?" he asked Kate, subdued.

"Let's just say, I barely escaped unnoticed. I was searching for you when I heard them approach. When I rounded the corner, they already had the guys captured in front of the house," Kate said.

"I see," was all Gavin said, as he stared straight ahead. No humor colored his voice, no hint of sarcasm, only the subdued simmering rage he was trying to control. I hated walking into this blind. From Kate and Gavin's exchange, I could tell one wrong move would have dire consequences.

Everything was heightened. I felt like a panicked lamb, knowing it was being brought to slaughter. If it wasn't for Gavin holding me close to his side, my feet would step on the brakes as I did my best to backpedal away from the impending danger.

Rounding the corner of the river stone house, the sight of my brothers and Kartcher bound on the hard packed ground came into view. Ten men, dressed in ivory plated armor, stood over them as they glared at their captors. Kartcher shot daggers at someone beyond the line of men, not blinking once in his stare.

I barely noticed Gavin restraining me as I locked eyes with Ryder. My blood boiled at them being rendered helpless under the thumb of these tyrants. I wanted to run to my brothers and save them somehow.

"Do not leave my side," Gavin whispered in my ear. I looked up into his darkened eyes, conveying to me the severity of his demand. When I nodded in agreement, he turned a grimace toward the armor-clad men. These men before me held zero resemblance to the masked men who attacked us moments ago. They were more fit for a royal guard.

Three horses, adorned with the same ivory armor as the ten men before us, pulled a large carriage. Elegant filigree in accented gold covered every inch of the enclosed cabin. It weaved and vined its way into such intricacies, reminding me of the gate before I passed through to this world. Attached to the backend of the carriage was an open coach, just as ornate but resembling more of a pen for parading prisoners than a comfortable ride from point A to point B.

Drawing closer, the horses were unlike the horses back home. They stood more deer-like, with long antlers protruding from their foreheads and cascading back into giant points. Bony protrusions continued inline down their neck in the opposite upward point of their rack.

Each one was bright white with an iridescent glow, standing strong and proud on eight legs. Close into their bodies, as if they weren't even there, were long wings that spanned from shoulder to tail. Their shimmering manes hovered over the floor despite being intricately woven with strands of pure gold. They were, by far, the most fascinating creatures I had seen yet.

"Ah, good job Einar. You brought them all in peacefully," a man said, as he stepped around the other side of the carriage, clapping his hands together in approval. He dressed in ivory as the rest of the guards; except his highly decorated suit showed the status his edge of refinement failed to capture.

"I wouldn't say it was altogether peaceful," Einar replied. The man inhaled before letting out a deep, exaggerated sigh.

"No, I would suppose not," he said, shooting Gavin a hard grimace. "And what do you have to say for yourself, Gavin?"

"They attacked first. It was self-defense," he smirked, shrugging, covered in his enemies drying blood.

"Highly unlikely," the man said, disapproving.

"I'm not surprised you don't see it that way, Neven," Gavin stated, staring directly into his eyes.

"There is no other way to see it. You all are fugitives, according to the high council. If one of our men attacked, it must have been provoked. This is the only explanation. How many of them fell at this traitor's hands?" the man asked, directing the question to Einar.

"Five, my lord," Einar responded, glancing at the remaining three attackers carrying the injured guard who first challenged Gavin. This *lord's* eyes followed the men bringing him to the carriage.

"Five of the high council's well-equipped assassins fell at your hands?" he admonished, staring hard at Gavin.

"They must not have been that well equipped if they fell so easily," Gavin retorted, challenging his stare.

"I see," he brought his hand to his chin before turning to his guards. "Lock them up! Throw them in the back! We will let the high council decide their fate," he ordered.

The men in front of my brothers forced them up from their bound hands. Panic gripped me.

Kartcher used the force of his body to knock down one guard as my brothers struggled against the force of the others, pulling them to the back of the coach. The rest of the ivory clad guards, along with the remaining assassins, converged on me, Gavin and Kate.

My body trembled.

One guard grabbed Kate's wrist and yanked it back. Frozen in place, I watched Gavin smash the guy in the face before two guards were on him, struggling to subdue him.

Everywhere I looked, everyone I loved or cared about struggled against their opponent.

Heat rose and coursed through my torso, expanding out through my limbs. I was powerless.

Despair rocked me.

Tired of the struggle, the guards drew their swords at Neven's command.

Blood boiled beneath the surface.

Fingers dug into the back of my arm in a tight hold as a small voice whispered, *"unleash."*

Time slowed. The only audible sound was a hitch in my breath.

Everything became hyper focused – the hot air billowing from the horses' nose, the symbol of a dragon eating its own tail adorned on the right side of Neven's breastplate, the hidden dagger Kate pulled from her side.

Heat within me rose to unbearable levels, my peripheral vision becoming distorted. I closed my eyes as a hand yanked me back, throwing off my balance. On the verge of imploding, I unleashed the pent-up frustration and fear in a loud, piercing scream.

I stood alone, trembling in its wake.

Slowly, I opened disoriented eyes, no longer sensed myself being held in place. No longer were the converging men near us. Some were laid out to the tree line, getting their wits about them. Others did not fare as well, being skewered by the tree branches themselves.

No longer were Gavin and Kate standing where they stood moments ago. I searched the yard; anxious I had hurt them.

I spotted Kate, her hair disheveled, as she picked herself off the ground. I searched her over, but she seemed to have fared fine.

Gavin strode towards me from across the large yard, his face a mix of horror and fascination.

"Are you okay?" I asked as he drew closer. He didn't say a word. He pulled me into his arms, leaving me with little option but to do the same. In any other scenario, I would have lost myself in his embrace, but my worry turned towards my brothers.

"My brothers?" I said, all but pushing myself away from him. I found them laid out on the ground, barely coming to. The guards who were wrestling them no longer there. I ran towards them, making quick work to release their hands.

"Aurora, are you okay?" Garrett asked, cupping my face after I released his bindings. I looked into his wide, shocked eyes and nodded.

From the corner of my eye, Kartcher released his bindings with a flick of his tail before undoing Ryder's.

"Are you sure?" Ryder asked, putting a hand on my shoulder with wide disbelief.

"Yeah, of course I am," I replied, nodding my head as Garrett dropped his hands.

"My God Aurora," Garrett whispered, before wrapping me into his bear hug. "Whatever that was, never do it again," he shuddered. It was disorienting to feel the chaotic power within me release, but a whole other entirely to have others bear witness to something I couldn't comprehend myself.

"I can see using force will not work," Neven said. "Let's start on better terms, shall we?" While the rest of the guards were stunned, this man stood hardly fazed.

"By better terms, do you mean you leaving and us going our separate ways?" Kate spoke, still shaken by what transpired but commanding herself well.

"No. You, of all people, should know better than that Katernius. All I mean is it is obvious you have a powerful force with you I am unwilling to subject my men to any further," the man raised his hand to me. "I am merely asking for you to comply."

"Yet, only moments ago, you were willing to remove us by force," Kartcher stated.

"Hm, yes, well. As you know, these are delicate times and as such, any threats must be handled accordingly," he stated.

"Threats?" Ryder questioned.

"I suppose 'threats' is the wrong term," he used his fingers in quotation. "*Unknown* may have been the better verbiage. Regardless, the high council doesn't approve of any outside factors beyond their control. They seek your prompt attendance to discuss the matters of you all being here, given the high security nature at hand," he explained.

"Now, Neven, we know this isn't true. The high council is about as corrupt as you," Gavin stated.

"Says the traitor to his own people. Were you three not last seen with Daten before the closing of the gates?" Neven asked, his accusing eyes glaring at Gavin, Kate, and Kartcher. "Now here you stand without Daten, the rightful ruler to the throne, and last Maeshiren who could have secured peace to our nation. Instead, you stand here with three other unknowns who, by all means, is. a. threat," he finished as his eyes slid to me.

"*Threats. Unknowns!* Why don't you tell us what your real motives are here instead of spewing bullshit you know nothing about," Gavin scoffed.

"That isn't for me to decide. This is for the high council to decide. So, I ask, stop this ridiculous standoff and come peacefully so this can be resolved," he demanded.

"How did you find us?" I spoke for the first time. Through all this turmoil, it was the one question on the tip of my tongue. How did they even know we were here in the first place? Not only that, how did they know *exactly* where we were?

"We have our ways," he smirked. Evasive yet confirming what I needed to know. Someone must be following us at this council's command.

"Now, if you will all comply," Neven said, sweeping his arm towards the ornate wagon.

No one moved. Gavin fixed a murderous stare squarely on Neven. Kate and Kartcher were about as pleased as Gavin, but more apprehensive. My brothers were weary and confused.

And me? What was I? Incredulous, mostly. There was a reason Gavin didn't want to go to this High Council. There was a reason Kartcher and Kate were apprehensive about the place that was supposed to be rightfully ours by birthright, according to them.

So, what was the reason I felt this push to go? I should take their reactions as a warning. However, the same commanding voice that told me to *'unleash'* now beckoned me to *'just go'*. Do I listen to this foreign voice inside my head? Or trust those who are standing their ground around me?

"Trust yourself," this voice whispered.

What I was about to do went against my better judgement, which seemed to be a common theme for myself as of late. No one will be pleased by my speaking out for the group, that I was sure about.

"Gavin let's go. All of us, let's go and get this over with," I said.

Gavin turned an icy stare onto me, making my blood run cold. Never have I been on the receiving end of the rage in his eyes. It was downright frightening.

"No," he said in finality.

I wanted to back down. I wanted to agree and go along with what he said, but the inherent need to find answers became too pronounced for me to ignore.

This was supposed to be the Maeshiren's kingdom. *Our* kingdom. *Not* the council's kingdom. My parents and Tanner died protecting us because of this place. My mother went through great lengths to ensure I could cross into this world. I *needed* to find answers!

"Listen. They're going to keep pursuing us, whether in this world or the next. The best thing we can do at this point is to face it head on," I reasoned.

"I WILL NOT bring you to those murdering scumbags," he yelled, the strain palpable in his eyes still zoned in on me. *What made him say that?* There was still so much I didn't know. So much he hasn't told me. A moment of doubt crept in at my stance on this situation. I was out of my scope with this. Regardless, meeting this High Council felt to be the right thing to do.

I sighed. "Then I will go alone." The fear replacing the anger in his eyes was not something I expected from Gavin.

"What are you saying, Aurora? You think we would let you go off by yourself to these savages? You don't even know them," Garrett rebuked, getting louder by the second.

"You're more than welcome to come Garrett, but we will never be at peace, nor safe, as long as we know they're on our tail," I said, feeling calmer about the situation than I probably should.

"Could we escape them this time? Maybe. Who's to say they won't come back at us with more guard's next time? Are you willing to postpone this for another time when we will eventually be taken in by force? Possibly at the expense of our lives?" I glanced back and forth between Garrett and Ryder, trying to get them to understand where I was coming from.

They understood, but they weren't happy about it.

"I don't like this, Aurora," Ryder said.

"Neither do I, but what choice do we have?" I asked, looking to Kartcher, who only gave a nod in response.

"Fine. You stay close to me though, you got it," Garrett stated, eyes hard. Ryder nodded in agreement.

"Okay," I said, giving him a small smile. I'd be lying if I didn't say I felt relieved knowing I wasn't going into the unknown alone again.

Reluctantly, I forced myself to face Gavin, whose eyes continued to bore into mine. Anger was an understatement; he was furious. Whatever his reservations were about me going to the High Council, I dismissed. His anger only fueled mine. It was his fault he didn't tell me what I should already know at this point.

From the moment I stepped foot into this world, I've been walking around blind. I have literally been beaten, misled, and confused. No longer did I want to be without answers. If I had to continue walking around blind until I received the answers I needed, so be it. If he will not help me with this, then he was hindering me.

The power I possessed my entire life has taken on a different form, or at least an out-of-control form. If the two guards lifeless on the tree were any indication, I'm becoming a liability. Gavin sought to protect me from the outside world, but what he was failing to do was protect me from myself.

I glanced at Kate staring at Gavin. *Was she waiting for his answer before she decided herself?* That wasn't like the Kate I knew. Then again, what did I know of her anymore?

In one heartbeat, he closed his eyes and nodded his head. *He conceded?* Relief washed through me in a tidal wave of peace. Though I was willing to walk into this head on, I knew I didn't want to do it without him.

In him, I sensed controlled chaos. In me, I was in constant danger of imploding. With him near me, I felt more stable. Call it crazy. Call it what you will, but I knew a large part of my soul needed him so I could keep a firm grasp on reality.

"Sorry Garrett, but she is staying with me," Gavin stated, opening his eyes and stood by my side. Garrett began to argue the point when Gavin cut him off. "I don't care if you're her brother. You are not equipped enough to protect her," he said with such finality. Garrett no longer continued his argument, chagrined.

"Shall we then?" Neven asked, smug at the turn in his favor. Since I was the one who initiated it, I made the first move towards the prison pen. Gavin held my shoulder and glanced at Kate, giving him a nod. She slid her eyes to me with a tight smile and walked ahead of us, my brothers and Kartcher following us in tow.

Once in the wagon, the doors shut of their own accord before the horses jolted forward. Whatever awaited us, it was sure to be unpleasant. However, I could not begin to doubt the decision that put everyone at risk now. I needed to continue to be brave. I needed to be strong. More importantly, I needed to remember the words my mother left me and never let go of them. As long as we were all together, we could get through anything.

Chapter Sixteen

Standing Trial

———— ✤ ————

"It's hard to prove your innocence when you are already deemed guilty."
— Brittany Lou

***

Whoa!" Ryder echoed in words the silent sentiment plastered on my face.

Tall, stony arches stood proud at the gate's entrance as a marbled white bridge allowed us passage over a radiant turquoise river. Flames in various colors floated above each lantern's cradle, casting shadows onto the bridge in the sun's fading light.

Beyond the gate's entrance laid a bustling town at the foot of a towering glass castle built high into the cliff face of the mountain. Hugging the castle, a scenic waterfall reflecting the remnants of the sun spilled over into a glimmering body of water. There wasn't an end in sight past its horizon.

Beings from all different walks of life stared at us in amusement and curiosity. I was equally enthralled.

Their opulent and colorful clothing held the edge of refinement I had glimpsed in the armor of the high council guards. I suddenly felt all too underdressed to even step foot into this ostentatious city. Be it men, women, or otherworldly beings, their everyday garb was something you'd see on a New York City catwalk. It was that, or there was some event taking place I wasn't privy to.

"Their clothes…" I said, trailing off as I glimpsed a woman with a foxlike face. Her dress flowed every which way in a beautiful shade of viridian. As she moved, it sparkled as if a million fireflies were attached to its fabric.

"Are hideous!" Garrett said, gagging with exaggeration as he glared back at them.

"Hideous? They're beautiful! How could you say that?" I rebuked.

"Ha! Yeah. About as beautiful if Picasso himself threw up and it landed on these freaks," he said, staring down all those who dared to stare back at us.

"Well, these *freaks*, as you call them, are *your* people too," I said, smirking.

"No Aurora. They're not. These are my people." He stared at me with purposeful intent as he circled his hand around our little group. I turned away from him. His negativity and stubbornness wasn't something I wanted to deal with.

"Gavin, why are they all dressed like this?" I asked, speaking to him for the first time since they put us into this cage. He hadn't said one word the entire way, instead choosing to glare at nothing but the floor.

"Gavin…," I said again, vying for his attention.

"They're always dressed like this," Kate said. The seriousness in her tone matched the tightness in her eyes. As if the puzzle pieces clicked together, I realized being here made both Kate and Gavin on edge, which brought me back down to reality.

The severity of the situation was about to come to a head and here I was, getting caught up in the superfluous apparel of another world's culture. If I could slap myself hard enough, I would have.

I glanced at Garrett and Ryder, giving me the pity look I hated. I looked away, feeling like a sullen child, and continued to take in the sights of the city in silence. A dirty child scurrying along the shadows of the buildings caught my attention, her eyes sunken in and cheekbones prominent. She gave me a ghostly stare as she watched our caravan roll by. I followed her with my eyes as she slinked away into the darkened alley she headed to-wards.

What was she doing so hungry and filthy in a city filled such with opulence and charm? She couldn't have been more than six or seven, at least by my world's standards. I found myself pitying her as if I were passing the buck my brothers bestowed upon me to her. My irritation fueled into anger.

What kind of justice was it for a city such as this to not take care of its own citizens? Has it always been like this, or just since the Maeshiren no longer ruled on the High Council? I'd hoped for the latter and not the former, or else I had little respect for those who came before us.

The slowing of the horses brought me to the present as we rounded the floral courtyard of the castle's entrance. As the doors to our cattle cage opened, six guards stood ready for us to exit with golden shackles.

"Come along now. We don't have all day," Neven called over his shoulder as he raised his hand for us to follow.

As Kartcher stood, a guard moved to restrain the shackles to one of his wrists. His tail slithered from beneath his cloak, smacking the shackles out of the guard's hands, flinging them into the large fountain. "Is this necessary?"

"Kartcher, you know the rules of the High Council. Prisoners must be subdued for the safety of the council members," Neven responded.

"I am aware of the rules, Neven. However, we are not prisoners. Not yet. We came here willingly and as our codex thirty-four-sixty-one states, 'those who come by freewill are not considered prisoners until deemed so by the High Council'," he challenged.

"Hm. Yes. It would seem so. Yet, the High Council has already deemed you as intruders and traitors, so that by default makes you all prisoners," he retorted.

"I disagree. Unless you want to make a show of what happened back at Gavin's, I suggest we move forward with the codex," Kartcher pressed.

"Is that a threat?" Neven asked, his voice turning hard.

"No. It is simply an observation," Kartcher responded, as Neven weighed his options. He knew what we were capable of more than I. Saving face in front of the city's castle held more importance than the High Council's unlawful detainers, it seemed.

"So be it. This will not bode well for any of you in the High Council's Chamber," Neven said, before spinning back around and stomping towards the castle's doors.

"I would presume not," Kartcher smiled back at us.

The guards stood dumbfounded, but no longer made their move to restrain us. Instead, they marched by our side, up the diamond-like stairs that appeared to never end. At the top, tall glass doors opened to a large, vaulted hall with chambers snaking every which way. Thick, stained-glass windows arched along the ceiling, adorned with pictures of leaders and dragons, telling a story I had yet to learn about.

"Keep it moving," one guard said, pushing me forward when I had stopped.

"If you enjoy your hands, I suggest you keep them off of her," Gavin glowered at the guard, giving him pause. Gavin reached out and brought me next to him, away from both guards, who continued to march with us.

"Stay with me. Don't leave my side," he said, detached as he continued to stare forward. I couldn't respond to this change in him.

Before we reached the end of the long hall, we veered right, crossing into a smaller hall before entering a large circular chamber where nine men, and three women sat at an imposing obsidian-marbled table. In the center, a glass orb spun in the air above vibrant water. The room itself was encased in thick glass, accentuating the magnificent waterfall flowing freely outside.

With our backs turned to the beauty outside, the collective expressions of those sitting on the council's table were fierce as they watched us shuffle in and stand shoulder to shoulder before them.

"Why are they not in chains?" a man asked, whose snowy beard masked the downturn in his lips.

"Sir, they have called on codex thirty-four-sixty-one," Neven said, bowing before the council.

"That codex does not apply when they are already deemed prisoners," he admonished, his hand engulfed in the purple sleeve of his robe as he threw his arm out in front of him.

"We came willingly, which puts the codex into effect," Kartcher calmly explained.

"How so when you were apprehended by our men?" the man stated, staring at Kartcher full of scorn. Einar's movement caught my attention when I watched him lean down and whisper into the man's ear.

"I see. It seems we have much to discuss beyond the traitor-ous and infiltrating activities," he said. Who was this guy? Was he now the head of the council in place of the Maeshiren?

"Traitorous and infiltrating? Do you really want to start this?" Gavin said, challenging this man's authority.

"It has come to my attention, Gavin, you have committed the highest act of treason by murdering members of the High Council's guard," he stated with a righteous glare. Collective gasps and whispers rose amongst those seated at the table.

"You call them murders. I call it self-defense," Gavin stated.

"In whose defense? Were you not once a member of this guard that you so cold-heartedly slain? Does that no longer mean anything to you? Are you as every bit the savage traitor we have always known you to be?" he declared, speaking louder with each question he threw at Gavin.

"You want to talk about traitors? Look in the mirror, Servi-us! It wasn't I who helped Braeden take out the Maeshiren's and make Daten run into hiding to protect his lineage," Gavin shout-ed. He fumed with every bit of rage; his eyes tinted with red.

"Blasphemy! Don't disgrace this high chamber with your lies and hypocrisy. Was it not YOU who fled with Daten, only to come back without him? *He* was the rightful ruler of this High Council. How do we know he wasn't slain by your murderous hand?" Servius stated, quick to throw back accusations.

"Come now. Let's not throw out accusations and heresy in this chamber," another man of the high council intervened to Servius's left. "You both can have your heated debate later after we have dealt with the matters at hand."

"This murderer *is* the matter at hand. I say we make haste in dealing with this traitor, then we can move on with the motions of the rest," Servius declared.

"Hardly. The current murders of today we will deal with,

but we have much to discuss. Such as, who are these three who stand before us dressed in peculiar attire? It is clear they are not from here and could be an even bigger threat than Gavin's antics," the second high council member said. "You three, who are you? State your names."

"Do you mind telling us who you are first?" Garrett spoke. I turned to him as if he were as thick headed as the glass walls surrounding us. Couldn't he see we were standing trial?

"As a matter of fact, I do. It is not I who is standing trial for the crimes committed, but you," the man stated.

"What crimes? We have committed no crimes. Why are we guilty before being proven innocent? Is there no law and order here?" Garrett shot back.

"Since you are not from here, we cannot expect you to know the laws of this land. We will excuse you on this, however - is it not customary to answer a question where you are from?" the man replied.

"Only if one wants to answer," Ryder responded.

"And who are you, young man?" a woman to the far right spoke. Her blond hair matching the color of her angelic alabaster skin.

"My name is Ryder. I'm the son of Deacon and Marie Walker," he answered. Murmuring rose among the council as they discussed this new revelation amongst themselves while taking surreptitious glances at us.

"And this would make you two his siblings, I presume?" Servius asked, as he pointed his finger back and forth at Garrett and me.

"What of it?" Garrett asked.

"If I may, the three who stand before you are direct descendants of Daten Walker and children of Marie Walker. They are of royal Maeshiren blood, come to retake their rightful place and restore order back to our lands," Kartcher explained.

"This is *most* interesting," a woman to the far left exclaimed. The council murmured in agreement.

Talk amongst the members erupted once again as one or two voices carried over the noise.

"Is the prophecy to be fulfilled?" one man asked.

"Could this be the start of the beginning to the end?" another added.

"How do we know they are who they say they are?" asked a woman sitting closest to the head of the table.

"Silence! I will not have this chamber in disorder!" Servius chided. "Katernius, I see you have been standing there without a word. It is much unlike you," he turned his gaze to Kate with a sly smile.

"What is there to be said that hasn't been said already?" she questioned.

"Much dear child, much," Servius closed his eyes and shook his head in disconcertment.

"Please. Then enlighten us, father," Kate said, challenging Servius as a petulant teenager would an annoying parent. My mouth dropped at the revelation of Servius being Kate's father. *How could that pompous prick be Kate's father?* They looked nothing alike.

"It pains me to see you on the wrong side of the line, Katernius," Servius said with mock sadness.

"It's Kate. And I highly doubt that. The way I see it, I'm situated perfectly on the right side. I can't say much for you." She glared at her father with as much hate and rage as I had seen in Gavin's eyes when he stood in front of Emily. The enmity ran deep, it seemed.

"Do explain yourself, Katernius. Whatever do you mean about being on the right side? Can you prove these three are who they say they are?" asked the angelic woman to the far right, whose ivory coat gleamed when she moved in the light, giving her a heavenly aura.

"As if my words would hold any merit in this chamber, Madame Celestia, but yes. I can," she said, vowing for my brothers and me.

"And how do you propose to prove not only who they are, but their innocence?" Servius intervened.

"Why would I have to prove their innocence? What are they being convicted of?" Kate challenged.

"Of treason, of course. As far as we know, they are from the opposition sent to overthrow the sovereignty we hold so dear here in this High Council. We know they passed through a gate no one is allowed to pass through. This leads us to believe they are working with dark forces that be," he stated.

"Wow. You're truly reaching for straws," Gavin stated. "And what evidence do you have to back up your claim?"

"Other than the fact that you six stand here before us in this chamber says much!" Servius declared.

"All it says is that you're reaching and are threatened by the unknown because of what it will do to your seat on the high council," Gavin stated.

And there it was. Out in the open.

This direct challenge of corruption in the High Council didn't sit well with any of its members, making Servius turn an unhealthy shade of red. The man sitting next to Servius held back a smirk at Servius's rising anger.

"How DARE you come into this chamber and insult those who have been of service to this city and the protection of its people," Servius declared.

"If by serving yourself is to the protection and service of this city's people, Servius, then you're doing a remarkable job,"

Gavin stated.

Adrenaline trembled through my limbs. The high charge of this High Council had me on edge, wondering if challenging them would be to our end. The animosity between Servius and Gavin was heated and palpable.

Though I knew little about the council, or the history between Gavin, Kate, and Kartcher with the High Council, it was apparent Servius could not be trusted. I kept seeing a picture of a snake in his stead.

"Let's all calm down. Servius. Gavin," said the man sitting next to Servius, as he stood to put a hand on his shoulder. Servius pushed his hand away in a show of anger at being quieted. He looked much younger compared to Servius, with a kind face and dark features.

"Let's start over. My name is Relbek. I am the head of this council in place for the Maeshiren. This council here has been appointed by your grandfather Daten to rule until he, or a direct Maeshiren descendant, has come to take his place.

Now, here the fact lies, not only do we have one possible direct descendent, but three. This comes as quite a shock. As you can understand, we on the High Council are wary when an outsider claims to be of Maeshiren decent," he said, seeking cordial relations rather than the 'shit show' that had transpired when we first entered.

"Now, how about you each tell us who you are and how you came to be here?" Relbek asked.

Ryder turned to Garrett and me, unsure of who should go first. I glanced over at Gavin and Kate, but they were giving nothing away. Should we allow the chips to fall where they may?

"My name is Garrett. I'm the oldest, with Ryder being the second oldest and Aurora being the youngest. Our oldest brother, Tanner, has since passed away. We didn't even know this world existed until a few days ago," he replied.

"And how did you come to find this world?" Relbek questioned. Garrett looked to Kartcher, who nodded his head towards him.

"Kartcher and Kate brought us here once we found out Aurora went missing," he answered.

"Interesting. Do tell us young Aurora how it is you came to be in our world," he turned his gaze to me. Twelve pairs of eyes stared me down, awaiting my answer, which was unnerving. Public speaking wasn't my forte.

What do I say? How should I start? Should I say anything about my mother's pendant? Something about divulging this information didn't sit right.

"Aurora," Relbek pushed for answers.

"I went walking in the forest by our home. A small creature beckoned me to follow, and so I did. It led me to two talking trees and a gate, which unlocked and allowed me passage," I recited. Even to my own ears, it sounded false.

"She's lying," Servius boomed. How could I prove my innocence when I could barely believe what had transpired? I glanced at Gavin, his mouth downturned at this admission. *Did I say something wrong?*

"No. She isn't," the woman on the far left spoke, defending my story. Servius crossed his arms away from her in a huff.

Among the three women who sat before us, she was by far the most beautiful. Her dark, mahogany hair cascaded in loose ringlets over her shoulders, contrasting splendidly with her embellished mint colored gown.

"I am Madame Marbella. While I do know you are not lying, dear Aurora, your story seems to be missing a few holes," she stated.

"Such as?" Garrett asked.

"Well, for one, how were you granted access without the key?"

Here laid the crux to my problem. My mother's words echoed clearly to tell no one about the pendant. As it was, I already told all of those who stood with me. However, to not tell them would present an even greater problem I wouldn't know how to talk my way out of.

"When I stood before the sentinel trees, they asked me questions and grilled me to no end. They must have seen something within me because they had me touch the gate and before I knew it, it opened and I entered into this world," I said, hoping she wouldn't see through my half-truths.

"Hm. I see," Madame Marbella said, bringing her hand to her chin as she narrowed her eyes at me. I stood there, feeling every bit exposed, preparing to be called out as a liar and a scoundrel.

"What I don't understand is how you were able to unlock it without a key. To be granted access, you *must* have this in your possession," she stated once again.

"While this may be true for a majority of us, Madame Marbella, if I may, is it not safe to say that a safeguard had been put into place for those who are of a direct lineage? Do they not possess the power of incantation over these gates as they are the rightful rulers to this kingdom?" Kartcher asked, bringing more information to the table.

"That is possible," she agreed, though not fully convinced.

"And if that is the case, few will have known about this safeguard. Not even those on the high council," he stated.

"Are you saying safeguards have been put into place without the high council's knowledge of this weakness? Rubbish!" Servius stated.

"Possibly. While the high council knows most, it does not

know everything that had been discussed within the Maeshiren council," he retorted.

"How do you substantiate this claim, Kartcher?" Servius challenged.

"How do you substantiate your claim to these three rightful rulers being traitors and intruders? You can't. If the Maeshiren had put safeguards in place, the only ones who would know about them would be the Maeshiren's. Unfortunately, any knowledge of this has since passed with Daten," Kartcher said.

"Can you prove this?" a tall, slender man with a long skinny neck asked.

"No. It is one possibility I would like to be considered. Aurora knew nothing about this world or how to gain entrance when she stumbled upon that gate. She would not have known how to unlock it or that she would even need a key to do so. With this knowledge, it is the only explanation that makes the most sense," Kartcher said.

Murmurs and head nods once again rose in the High Council's chamber. They agreed with Kartcher, who appeared to be in complete peace over their deliberations. His stance remained relaxed as his hands were clasped together in front of his cloak.

"We cannot just take them at their word that they are Maeshiren and hand the council over to them blindly. They *must* prove who they are," Servius stated, slamming his fist on the table. I didn't like this Servius, he exuded ulterior motives.

"Yes. This is true," Relbek agreed. "While I must admit your stories are wildly outlandish, Madame Marbella sees no falsehoods in your story. This leads me to believe you are all telling the truth. However, there must be some substantial evidence to show you are who you truly say you are."

"What do we have to do?" Garrett asked, ready to prove it.

"We must deliberate further. We do not take light of what

we are about to request of you. This is a serious matter and thus, must have serious discussion. If you will please wait in the ante-chamber for our verdict on this matter," Relbek said, extending his arm towards a door to his left.

"Of course," Kartcher spoke in agreement for the group as he bowed his head. We shuffled out until Servius stopped us.

"Wait! We are not finished here. What about the murderous atrocities Gavin has committed?" he seethed. All eyes turned to Gavin as he faced a glare at Servius. His eyes tightened as he stared Servius down.

"Oh yes. Neven, can you give a brief account of what happened when you were apprehending them?" Relbek asked, turning to Neven.

"Yes Consul. While Einar had tracked down Gavin, Aurora, and Kate with his men, my men and I apprehended Kartcher, Garrett, and Ryder with minor incident. It is my understanding Einar's men had received the brunt of the fight from Gavin, who refused to bring Aurora in at the High Council's orders," he stated.

"I see. Is this true Gavin? Did you refuse to bring Aurora in?" Relbek asked.

"I didn't see the need to bring her into the hands of this mess," he said.

"Even though you knew it was a direct decree from the High Council?" he asked. Gavin shrugged.

Relbek closed his eyes, sighing through his nose. "Einar, can you give a brief account of your encounter with Gavin?"

"Yes Consul. When we first arrived at the scene, only Gavin and Aurora were present. Gavin stood defending Aurora from our approach. When he refused to come willingly, I sent my men to apprehend him. Instead of conceding, he fought my men viciously, all but tearing them apart before our very eyes," Einar stated.

"And how did you end up apprehending them?" Relbek asked.

"Katernius approached and talked sense into him. They came willingly after that," he said.

"Ha! Leaving a few details out, are we? Like how one of your men attacked Aurora. Or how you came already threatening without proof of the decree," Gavin scoffed.

"Do tell us your side of the story, Gavin," Madame Marbella encouraged.

"Einar and his men showed up without the official decree in hand. Instead, they came at us in the predawn hours, trying to strong-arm us into following this unofficial demand.

My sole job, my one duty per Daten, is to protect the Maeshiren bloodline. Per Marie, it's my sole responsibility to protect Aurora from all dangers. Each of us were assigned one sibling Maeshiren member each. As you very well know, this duty is to the death of those who seek to cause harm to any of them.

Your High Council guard and assassins came without just cause and so I did not see it fit to subjugate them to these demands," he stated with authority. The severity of which he took his duty over us was sobering. While I understood they were part of Daten's guard, it was a new revelation they had each been assigned to us by our mother.

The depth of their commitment to us, and to the Maeshiren bloodline, gave me a new perspective on Gavin, Kate and Kartcher. Though the respect I had for them deepened, I still felt put out about learning this information in the most inopportune ways. Why, in light of a crowd, was I just learning about this? Why had this not been mentioned when we were discussing this at Gavin's? Why didn't Gavin divulge this when we were at the lake?

"Einar, is this true? You did not present an official decree?" Relbek asked.

"Yes Consul. It is true," Einar admitted, though sheepish. He knew he had messed up.

"Does anyone have anything else to add?" he asked, both of the High Council and us.

"Yes Consul. I do," Neven spoke. "As we prepared to apprehend them a second time to ready them for the wagon, Aurora let out a power I have never witnessed before. Through a piercing scream, percussive forces blew back my men, some so powerful that two of our guards were impaled to the surrounding trees," he stated. "Sir, this is both worrisome and unknown as we had to rethink our approach."

I couldn't help but shrink back behind Gavin as the high council turned to me in astonishment. How would this new revelation sway their decisions? It seemed having *unknowns* was a threat to them. Hearing the apprehension in Neven's voice was sure going to leave an impression.

"Well, it seems you are all full of shocking surprises. This is a very interesting turn of events. Neven, we will take what you have said into consideration. Now, please, if you all will hasten to the antechamber and wait to be called upon for our verdicts and *official* decrees," Relbek requested.

"Hmpf," Gavin huffed, rolling his eyes as he walked towards the exit. His shoulders were stiff with agitation.

I watched the group sitting at the table as I followed in his path. Some were staring, shaking their head in disapproval. Others were already chatting amongst themselves. Servius, however, watched our departure with cold, angry motives in his eyes. Though I did my best to take hold of myself during the deliberation, I couldn't help but tighten my eyes at his stare. With our eyes locked into place with each other, the communication we

exchanged pitted us on opposite sides.
 It was clear as day who my enemy was.
 The Council.

Chapter Seventeen

Official Verdicts and Decrees

***

"To know, yet to think that one does not know, is best; Not to know, yet to think that one knows, will lead to difficulty." – Lao Tzu

***

We stepped into a room much smaller than the grand High Council chamber, yet to call this room anything but grand was an insult. Tall ivory pillars were situated around the room, each with gold filagree laced towards the clear, towering glass ceiling. The beauty of the encroaching night sky was on display.

"Well, now what?" Garrett huffed, as he plopped down on one of the many stone benches in the room.

"Now we wait," Kartcher answered.

"And what are we going to do if we don't like their *'verdicts and decrees'*?" he asked, mocking their tones.

"I don't know," Kartcher replied, clasping his hands behind his back. He turned from Garrett towards the colorful night sky.

"I say we fight," Ryder said, taking a seat next to Garrett.

I rolled my eyes. "Oh? And how do you suppose we do that?"

"Easy. We are all capable fighters. We bust out of here and give these pompous pricks the middle finger," he replied.

"Alright! Good plan, my brother!" Garrett laughed as he high-fived Ryder.

"You both are idiots," I said, shaking my head. Behind me, Gavin snorted and Kartcher shook his head as I was.

"Idiot's is right. *That* is a death sentence," Kate chimed in. "We will get through this. With the High Council knowing you're all *possible* Maeshiren, it's unlikely they will put you to death or imprisonment."

"How can you be so sure?" Ryder asked.

"Because stupid, what we went in there and proclaimed is what this whole world has been waiting on! Others have come and tried to claim it before, but it always had disastrous consequences. The difference here is they were lying and could never prove their true origins of being Maeshiren," she responded.

"Disastrous how?" I asked.

Kate turned towards me with her mouth set in a grim line. "They made examples out of them. I wasn't here to witness what happened. I was already on the other side of the gate, but it wasn't pretty from what I understand."

"So how is there hope for any of us, then? According to them, we can't prove it," I said, throwing my hands up in exasperation.

"You may be right, but what those others never had, besides the truth, is us to back up their claims. Remember, we *were* part of Daten's guard," she said.

"We still are," Kartcher amended.

"How does that help? As far as they're concerned, you all

are traitors and Gavin is a murdering savage," Garrett pointed out, his hand emphasizing this point.

"Watch it, boy," Gavin warned, his back leaning up against one of the marbled pillars with his arms crossed.

"Hey! Their words. Not mine," Garrett stated, throwing his hands up as a sign of mock surrender. Gavin added nothing more, giving him a tight-eyed glare before looking away.

I settled my gaze on Gavin before breaking away. Any head-way we had made earlier was effectively cut off. He stood as de-tached as ever, which made the yearning for the sweet embrace I had experienced from him hurt that much more. He wasn't just back in his quiet, angry shell. The distance he put between every-one and himself was mostly being directed at me.

I'm the one who conceded to Neven and brought us here.

I'm the one who defied Gavin's orders.

He hadn't laid eyes on me since we left his home in the se-clusion of the forest, let alone said a word. He was only doing his duty of being my appointed bodyguard. Well, that was just fine. As much as my body remembered the warmth of his embrace at the lake, I could be as equally distant and cold. Hell, I had enough experience cutting people off and keeping them at arm's distance too. I knew the game well.

More than one pair of eyes fell onto my retreating back as I sauntered towards a statue of a kneeling knight resting his hands on the hilt of his sword in front of him. With head bowed in a sign of sorrow, it had been staged in front of a large window with wide sweeping views of the city.

What caught my interest was not just the statue itself, but also the position it had been placed in. It wasn't looking out over the city, and it wasn't faced towards the room we were in. In-stead, it laid situated towards the towering waterfall.

"That is Reinard. He was one of the wisest Maeshiren to

ever rule this land," Kate said behind me. I turned to see her apprehensive stance before offering a tight smile. She must have seen the question in my eyes because she continued as she stepped forward.

"During the time of Reinard, there were rumors of unparalleled evil in distant lands, but never any of which this kingdom had ever experienced. He ruled for over a thousand years before that rumored evil came to our shores," she said.

"A thousand years?" I asked, astonished.

"Yes," she replied.

"What happened to him?"

"As the story goes, when the rumored evil came to our great city, we were ready. He made sure of that. Many battles were fought, but their attacks were relentless. The city itself had almost been obliterated, but he stood with an unwavering bravery and remained a steadfast ruler. With every battle, he learned how the enemy fought. With that, he changed tactics and changed them quickly. Eventually, through his wise battle tactics, he ran the enemy off, but not before being fatally hit from behind," she said.

"From behind?" I asked. "That doesn't make sense. Weren't they running *from* him?"

"They were. It wasn't from one of them. It was from one of our own. A traitor in the midst." Her downcast eyes matched the tone of her somber voice. I gasped at such a tragedy.

"Did they catch him?" I asked.

"Of course. He was dealt with from what I understand. Reinard didn't have an expedient death. A deep gash in his neck festered, and no healer could help him. It was excruciating and lasted for days. Knowing of his impending demise, he brought your grandfather in and crowned him the next ruler," she said, staring at me.

"My grandfather?" I asked, dumfounded. Somehow, this story of times past didn't seem related to me.

"Yes. Reinard is your great grandfather, Daten's father. He is your family, and this is your lineage," she stated with pride, raising her hand towards the statue. I stared at her in a stupor, letting her words sink in. I turned away from her and back towards the statue of Reinard, her words echoing in my mind.

My great grandfather, a wise and battle-hardened ruler - the brave ruler of this very kingdom that had been left in the hands of a corrupt council.

I gazed out through the window framing the very city my great grandfather stood to protect. Pride in what he fought for and died to protect swelled within my chest. The reverence and power of that lineage flowed through my veins. The shocking reality of who I am came crashing in with a sea of understanding.

I *am* of a royal bloodline. The statue before me depicts the very strength of this. This is my kingdom, *our* kingdom, and though it feels a mighty stranger in this moment, I know it won't be for long.

It was right we came here. It was right we take it back and set things straight.

Though Kate and Gavin may have lied to me, they did it for our protection. It didn't mean they cared any less, or they aren't who I know them to be. It just means I have a lot to learn about being royalty. They were going to be the closest people I could trust to tell me. My mother's sentiment from her letter echoed in my mind – *'Trust no one.'* How could I not, though? At some point, I had to put my trust into someone.

Since I came here and learned of all the lies, I became angry with my parents and Tanner for keeping the rest of us in the dark. That anger gripped me no longer. Instead, understanding took its place with sadness still residing in my heart. I felt the deep love they had for us - a deep love strong enough to endure what they knew to keep us safe and happy.

I choked back a tear before steadying my voice, "Why does he seem so sad?"

"It isn't of sorrow for why his head is bowed. It's of respect. There is a lot you don't know, but I promise I will tell you," Kate said, grasping my shoulder with a gentle pull towards her.

"I'm so sorry we had to keep you in the dark about all of this. You must believe me, it was only to protect you all. To protect you! So many times, I wanted to tell you, but I couldn't," she said, her sorrow boring into my own. This was her form of apology, something completely uncharacteristic of her. I hesitated to allow her to continue apologizing, but she didn't know the shift that had taken place within me. I understood, and I forgave her already.

"I'll be honest. I was hurt and pissed when I first learned about all of this. We were supposed to be sisters," I started.

"We *are* sisters!" she exclaimed.

"I don't disagree with that," I said, giving her a small smile. "But when I learned you knew about all of this the whole time. You must understand the level of betrayal I felt on your end. You of all people know me the best and, in that moment, I felt like I didn't know you at all," I said.

Kate wiped away a tear escaping from her eye. "I'm sorry," she whispered, dropping her shame towards our feet.

"You didn't let me finish," I said, watching her sorrowful gaze lift back up at me. "I know why you did it. I understand and I forgive you. I may not know everything, and there is obviously a lot more I need to learn about you, but I do know you're still the same Kate I know and love deeply. That hasn't changed. You're just more badass than I knew you were," I said, smirking.

"And don't you forget it!" she smiled back, pulling me into a tight hug. "I'm so sorry. I promise, there isn't much more about me you don't already know."

"I doubt that, but that's okay. I know who you are. It's cool you have this whole other side to you, like an alter ego," I chuckled.

She released her hug and rolled her eyes. "Whatever." There's the Kate I knew.

The loud opening of the doors, and the clanking of the armored guard's approach, pulled us back to the present.

"The High Council will see you now," the guard stated.

Garrett jumped up, giving a salute as he walked past. Kate and I both rolled our eyes at each other. He was such a child.

We all filed in line in front of the High Council as we were once before. Gavin stood next to me once again. Though I had the shift of understanding change within me, it sure felt like he was paid to be standing here guarding me.

"This council stands in unanimous agreement. You are to prove your claim to the Maeshiren lineage," Relbek stated.

"And how are we to do that?" Garrett scoffed.

"Silence! Only speak when you are commanded," Servius barked. Garrett moved to speak out, but Kartcher silenced him with a hand on his shoulder. Instead, he took to silent grumbling.

"We deliberated over several ways you could do this, but the ultimate way is by fulfilling the prophecy," Relbek continued as he stood. "As I am sure you do not know of the prophecy, let me explain. Many years ago, when the Maeshiren ruled this land, there was undoubted peace. A symbol of that peace was the eternal flame that burned on for millenniums. It never went out."

Relbek moved around the High Council's table with two guards following in his path. As he approached us, he stopped in front of the towering window, staring towards the waterfall.

"When the last Maeshiren left these lands, that flame was

extinguished," he said, pointing towards the peak of the water-fall. To the very right stood a formation too high and obscure to be seen distinctly.

"Before Daten had left, he formed this council, appointing me at the head and Servius at my flank. When that fire went out, we were all in a panic. It wasn't more than a few years later the prophecy was born."

"Which is?" Ryder asked.

"When a Maeshiren of direct decent appeared, the flame would be reborn. As you can see, it is still extinguished," he said, turning towards us. His tall, lengthy figure became more accentuated at this proximity. Eyes that relayed that of trust, but also hesitancy, stared at us all.

"While I don't believe you are lying about your stories, the evidence is clear," he said, raising his hand back towards the formation.

"So that's it then? Because of some stupid flame that hasn't been *magically* lit by our appearance, that is enough to condemn us?" I spat, furious. Being subjugated to this council, knowing this was *our* rightful place to rule by bloodline and lineage, angered me. Who were *they* to question *us*?

"Please. Peace. I did not say we were condemning you. Not yet," he said with calm authority.

"What do you mean, *not yet*?" Ryder asked.

"Just because the fire has not been lit does not mean you are not who you say you are. We are under no impression it would be that easy," he stated, as he made his way back towards his chair.

"What do we have to do?" Garrett asked.

"Kartcher here will lead you to the way. He knows of the path that will lead you to the truth and the proof we seek. If the eternal flame is relit, then we know you are the true rulers of this kingdom," he smiled, nodding at Kartcher. I turned, gawking, as

Kartcher nodded his head towards Relbek without a word.

"What do you mean, lead us to a path? What path?" I asked, finding it hard to tear my eyes away from Kartcher.

"The badlands. There have been those who have come before you, claiming the very same thing you have claimed. We sent them on their quest to prove to us their true lineage. Granted, they didn't have these three standing with them," he gestured towards Gavin, Kate, and Kartcher. "They never made it back."

Kate's words echoed in my head — *'they were made examples of'*. Something wasn't adding up, but I filed that for later.

"*When* we prove we are the *rightful* rulers of this Kingdom, what then?" I challenged.

"Let's take this one step at a time, shall we?" Relbek answered, dismissing my question. Annoyed at his lack of answer, I looked to Gavin, who stared with murderous intent at Servius.

Servius answered with a taunting smile, their silent exchange saying so much without saying a word.

What was with that creepy smirk he always gave? I didn't like the way he kept zeroing in on Gavin either, as if he wanted him to lash out. I almost let my mouth lead when Kate spoke up instead. "You expect us to go to the badlands? You're asking us to walk into certain death!"

"I am sorry, Katernius. It is the only way," Madame Marbella stated.

"Doubtful," Kate turned her gaze to Madame Marbella. "And how are they supposed to prove their true lineage by going there?"

"I guess we will have to wait and see," Servius smiled.

"And what is your part in this?" Kate seethed.

"Why Katernius, whatever do you mean?" he asked.

"You know damn well what I mean. And it's Kate!" she spat.

"I'm sorry, child. I am afraid I do not," he said, dropping his smirk into mock confusion.

"Please. Let us not allow this session to deteriorate into the mayhem it was earlier," Relbek stated, bringing order back to the chamber. "Kartcher, will you be willing to lead them through the badlands?"

"I will do it," Kartcher replied as if it were his duty.

"And the rest of you, will you go to prove your lineage? Or shall we place judgment upon you here and now?" Servius asked. His motive for having us go to these *'badlands'* didn't sit well with me. He wanted us there for a reason.

"What choice do we have?" Ryder asked Gavin. Instead of answering Ryder's question, he turned to me.

The coldness was still there. The distance hung in the air between us. Regardless, his eyes were searching mine for something. Whatever it was; he seemed to have found it. He closed his eyes, releasing a breath through his nose, before he turned back towards the council to address Relbek.

"Do we leave now, or do we have time to prepare?" Gavin asked.

"Why, we couldn't very well have you leave under the cover of darkness. We will have you receive a good night's rest before your journey," Relbek said, ever the diplomat.

"Good. Lead us to our chambers so we can rest then," Gavin said.

"You act as if you are not on trial yourself, Gavin," Servius sneered.

"For the unjustified murders you claim I committed, Servius? When it was clearly self-defense?" he shot back.

"That isn't for you to decide. Regardless, we are withholding judgment upon you. It is conditional, however. If they cannot prove who they say they are, or if you come back without any of them, your life is forfeit and you will answer for your crimes," Servius said, giddy at exercising his superiority over Gavin.

"I will answer only for crimes in which I committed, which I've not committed any crimes that the High Council's guards haven't committed themselves," Gavin stated.

"Blasphemy! We should hang you here and now for your tongue!" Servius echoed in the chamber walls.

Gavin laughed, "You can try."

"How *dare* you!" Servius became enraged, setting my hair on end. My blood pumped faster through my veins. The amicable ending we were near fast deteriorated into a fight waiting to happen.

"Order! Order in this chamber this instant!" Relbek boomed. It was the first time I had seen him raise his voice since we first entered. "You both will stop with this aggravating nonsense. Servius, you are a member of this High Council and I expect for you to behave as such. And Gavin, you are not only standing trial but are to show your respect to this High Council as the directed rulers under Maeshiren orders. I expect you to behave as such."

Gavin looked tempted to retort, but thought better of it.

"Now, your official verdict is this. The High Council finds you all conditionally innocent. For your decree - the lighting of the eternal flame and fulfilling of the prophecy must prove your innocence. If you all shall return without this lit, your lives are forfeit for treason and impersonation of the Maeshiren lineage.

In special terms for Gavin, this High Council finds you conditionally innocent as well for the grievous crimes of murdering the High Council guards. Your decree? Should you come back without having the eternal flame lit, or choose to come back without these three in your midst, your life is forfeit as well. Does everyone on this esteemed council agree?"

"Yes. This High Council Agrees," all said in a cacophony of

agreement.

"It has been spoken then. Guards, please see them to their chambers for the evening," Relbek said, dismissing us. He turned out of the chamber, as did the rest of the High Council members. It was Servius who remained behind.

"Katernius. If you will, a word please?" he called out.

Kate stopped in her tracks, the disgust clear on her face. "Whatever for?"

"Humor me. It has been ages since I have seen my only daughter," he exclaimed with a tone that didn't match his words.

Paused in deliberation, she broke away from us, halting a few feet from her father.

"You wanted to speak? Speak," she stated, making no move to keep their discussion private.

"Please Katernius, don't be like this," he said.

We were being ushered out of the room, but I kept dragging my feet, watching Kate address Servius. It didn't feel right leaving her alone with him. Gavin zoned in on them with the same hesitancy.

"Move," the guard behind us bellowed.

"No. Not until *all* of us are together," Gavin said, challenging him. He reached out and pulled me behind him, away from the guard. My brothers and Kartcher, who had shuffled out before us, peered in through the doors with wary eyes as they shuffled back into the room. Would these nerve-wracking events never end?

Gavin stood rigid and immovable against the guard's order. The fierce stare down showed he meant business and would not be pushed around. I glanced over to an agitated Kate, the level of their conversation taking a more private tone. Feeling our stares, she glanced over to see the impending fight taking place.

"If you'll excuse me, I have more important things to worry

about," Kate said as she turned on her heel. "And what is going on here? I hope you aren't harassing us without just cause." Kate stood next to Gavin, increasing the defensive message to the guard.

"Let's go," Gavin snapped, not taking his eyes off the threat. The guard raised his hand as a gesture for him to lead the way. Kate wrapped her arm around my shoulders as we walked in step away from the following guard.

"What was that all about?" Ryder asked when we caught up to them.

"Nothing," Gavin said in clipped annoyance.

"Didn't look like nothing," he said back. Gavin continued ignoring him.

"It was nothing, Ryder. I'll tell you later," I said, trying to keep him from prying. He wasn't pleased at being left in the dark. With everyone's nerves frayed, and Gavin in no mood to be forthcoming, I didn't want his questioning to add to the tensions.

The armed guards led us back into the main hall we had first entered and through one of the doors leading to another long hall. Two of the three guards stopped at the entrance of the hall, taking a protective stance on either side. The third guard continued to escort us further.

Decorated with flickering multihued flames lighting the length of the hall, our feet echoed off the walls. A long, golden runner ran the length of the corridor to a dead end, where six white oak doors were stationed. Each door had been decorated with vining iron leaves and twining flowers. I began to see a pattern.

As the guard stepped to the first door, I watched with fascination as the iron vines lit up and moved of their own accord at the wave of his hand, opening the door into the first room.

"Whoa! How did you do that?" Garrett asked. Though I

had experienced this once before; it still amazed me. The guard made no move to respond, continuing to walk to each door, unlocking them in the same manner.

Once finished, he turned to us. "There is a room for each of you. I trust you can sort out who stays where yourselves. This hall has been deemed strictly off limits and will be heavily guarded from its entrance."

"Subtle. Very subtle," Kate said, shaking her head. The guard gave her an intense glare before walking away.

Nobody moved. Kate looked annoyed while Gavin stood tired and apprehensive. Kartcher hid under his hood so there was no telling what his expression held.

"Do you think it's a good idea we split up?" Garrett asked, worry marring his face.

"Yeah, I don't like this," Ryder agreed.

"We will all be fine. Pick a room and go to sleep. We will need it for the journey ahead," Kartcher cut in, turning to take one room closest to the hall's entrance.

"And what is your part in all of this?" Kate asked, staring at Kartcher's back.

"Kate, there will be plenty of opportunity for me to discuss this later. We are wasting precious time to rest which we will not recover. So please, let us continue this discussion tomorrow," he said over his shoulder as he walked into the room and shut the door. That was the longest winded shut up if I had ever heard one.

"What's his problem?" Garrett asked.

"Who cares, it's none of our concern. Let's get to sleep," Kate said, taking the room next to Kartcher's.

"You two head to the end rooms across from each other. I'll take the other front room. Aurora, you can take this one," Gavin said, gesturing towards the middle room on the left.

I understood it for what it was. He was keeping my brothers and I protected. He would hear if anyone slipped by his room in the dead of night. He trusted no one. Without argument, we all did as he asked.

"Good night, guys. I don't say it enough, but with all this craziness, who knows what tomorrow holds? Love you guys," Ryder said, looking to Garrett and me.

"Love you too," I said, before turning in to the most ostentatious room.

True to this castles fashion, white pristine floors led to a wall of glass windows. The glow of the colorful night sky cast an ethereal glow on the town below, accentuating the clusters of buildings and the ridges of the cliff face the castle was built into.

A pretentious chaise lounge beckoned me to sit next to a spacious fireplace, but I wasn't in the mood. The light of the multicolored flame danced in the darkened room, glinting against the golden four-post bed, engulfing much of the space.

And here I stood, in the center of it all, feeling the weight of the world crashing onto my shoulders. I let out a heavy, exhausted sigh. *How did we get here?* It was so surreal. All of it. I pinched my forearm, just to make sure I was awake.

Though exhausted, I didn't want to lie down. I didn't want to sleep. There was so much I was in danger of reliving if I were to close my eyes. I wasn't just afraid of reliving my past; I was also afraid of reliving my fears.

What happens now? What if something happens to my brothers? I couldn't live with myself if I lost them too. I banished the thought from my mind, though it lingered with stubborn zeal.

I crawled onto the unnecessarily large bed, not intending to sleep but with the intention of having somewhere to curl up and think. Hugging my knees into my chest, I once again found myself staring into a fire. What *was it* about this element that lured me like no other? Its dance. Its fury. Its chaotic power. Its ability to subdue my thoughts and hypnotize my brain.

Thinking back to earlier events, how different would all of this have played out had Gavin and I been there when Neven and the guard showed up? Would it have ended peacefully? Well, relatively peaceful?

We shouldn't even be here. It was because of my own carelessness from not listening to my brothers' worry, or my mother's warning, that we were in this mess. Goosebumps raced down my arms and shivered up my spine, knowing we were here because of me. For all I knew, our fates were sealed, and it was my fault.

It wasn't just the heavy heart Kartcher held, or the subdued anger I knew so well in Kate. It wasn't even the fear in the eyes of my brothers which put me over the edge. No, it was the apathy from Gavin, the quick and easy detachment from whatever had transpired between us that burrowed painfully into my heart. Tears pierced my eyes anew, despair gripping my throat, as I buried my head into my knees and sobbed. *What have I done?*

Guilt and panic washed through me in tumultuous waves. My body rocked with every heaving reminder of my failures that cost the safety of those closest to me. I'm the one who ran away from home. I'm the one who crossed over to this world. I'm the one who talked us into coming here.

After I disobeyed his stance, the disappointment that Gavin had stood perfectly behind closed eyes. The flash of anger, and the cold indifference he showed me afterwards, shivered me to the core. He probably hated me for stepping into what I didn't understand. *Was I right to have done this?* It may have felt like it at first, but now I wasn't so sure.

I may not understand everything happening right now, but I understood this. Though he had made it clear, he wasn't happy about the circumstances of our meeting, he was happy to be in my life. Those were the words he had said. However, by his actions, he made it abundantly clear that was no longer the case.

This admission constricted in my chest, making it harder to breathe as it clawed its way up my throat. I wasn't sure how someone I hardly knew could have such an impact on me, but I knew it did. I had finally given my heart a chance to crack open; to allow someone else in. I knew I would never be the same for it. For all I knew, he now took his duty to protect me with a heavy heart.

My eyes were on fire, but the tears kept coming in hot. I felt raw. Exposed. Castigated. Not even the witches could make me feel as low and worthless as I did now. Anything that happened moving forward was a direct reflection of my careless actions. What could I do to even make everything right at this point?

"Aurora?" I heard my name whispered.

I froze. I thought I was alone. Though that should bother me, it didn't. What bothered me was the raw emotion of that voice dripping with every bit of what I felt.

I sniffled, wiping my eyes with the palms of my hands, as I fell into eyes that became my undoing.

Chapter Eighteen

Going Deeper

"The best kind of lovers are the ones who arrive without a proper invitation." – R.M. Drake

***

The fire's glow cast shadows across his face, highlighting the deep sorrow in his gaze. My heart, refusing to obey, fluttered against my chest. Neither of us broke the silence, allowing ourselves to taste the boundaries of our afflictions.

"What are you doing here?" I sniffled, wiping my damp eyes. My voice stayed even despite my internal quiver.

He didn't answer, though a silent confliction crossed his face. Releasing me from our intimate connection, he brought his attention overhead to the world outside the floor to ceiling windows.

"I don't know how else to put this - the truth, I guess," he said.

He paused in quiet contemplation. I couldn't look away.

Even if it weren't for the troubled expression in his darkened eyes, or the furrow of his brows, the thickness in his voice would be enough to relay how much his next words affected him.

"Aurora, I can sense your anguish. You have no idea what it's doing to me."

My breath faltered, causing his eyes to snap back to mine. In the internal struggle of his despair, I could see this truth in his dejected expression. Did he hear my cries, though stifled as they were? I expected the castle walls to be much thicker than paper.

I lowered my eyes, no longer able to meet him face to face. So much guilt sat on my chest. What more could I do to hurt those closest to me? Instead, I focused on my fingers picking at the muted patterns of the comforter. "I don't think I understand."

"Do you mind if I sit?" he asked, gesturing to the bed next to me. I shook my head but made no move to answer with words. I glanced up as he sat within arm's length; the small gap feeling as if it were a million miles between us. Even so, my cheeks warmed at knowing he was here at all.

"It's such a beautiful night, isn't it?" he asked, focusing on the window behind me. I turned my attention to the evening sky, watching the shifting hues of the dancing Borealis display its magnificence on the rooftops below. It was beautiful; even if his reason for saying so was to delay the hard, inevitable discussion due to take place.

Feeling the force of his attention on me, I turned back to his pained expression. "Aurora, I can sense other peoples, other beings, state of emotion. I know when someone is angry or sad. I can sense when they're in gripping pain. Call it a character flaw in my genetic makeup if you will," he stated, smirking without humor.

I gave him a blank stare in return. The implications of this admission stunned me. Everything I've felt, he felt *too?* The pain of losing my parents and Tanner. It wasn't just his pain he shouldered, but *mine also?*

And now, before he showed up, was he feeling the downward spiral of my self-deprecation? Is that why he was here? Could he feel my growing interest in him as well? My lord, is *nothing* off limits here? Even my own feelings couldn't be my own!

He sat in silence, observing - and no doubt feeling, the rollercoaster of emotions as I processed this.

With understanding and patience plastered on his face, I couldn't help but resign to being wary. How could I keep anything from him if he could figure out what I thought based on how I felt?

This was going to be complicated. Embarrassment flushed my cheeks, as he probably knew of my growing infatuation with him. I buried my face in my hands at the absurdity I found myself in. *Lord, kill me now.*

"Please, don't," he said, as he gently pulled my hands away from my face. "Don't hide from me." Chills coursed through my body at his touch. His hands, though rough, were warm and inviting as he moved them into mine, clasping them together with his.

My heart thrummed with every soft stroke of his thumb across my skin, making it even more difficult to control my emotions.

On the one hand, I wanted to revel in his touch, to allow myself to bathe in it. On the other, I wanted to suppress these emotions as deep down as I could, knowing they were on display. I couldn't be more mortified.

"Earlier, you were so distant," I choked out, as my heart constricted at the fresh memory.

The rhythmic stroking of his thumb faltered, dismay souring his mood. With saying so little, he said so much. I hit a nerve. The warmth from his hands began rolling off him in chilling waves. Feeling the sudden change within him startled me, keeping me frozen in place.

"I apologize. The way I acted earlier was abominable. Am I angry? Inexplicably so. You have no idea what you have done. By agreeing to come here, you have handed yourself to the council on a silver platter," he said, confirming what I already knew to be true.

All of this *is* my fault. Gavin had been distancing himself from me because of this. I couldn't blame him. I just brought danger upon everyone. Knowing what I know now of the council, I can see exactly what he meant.

It would be so easy for the council to do away with us. A simple 'random' attack along our journey to these badlands, a mugging gone wrong – no one would be the wiser. Despair rose within me once again. *How* could I have let this happen? Been so *stupid?*

I dropped my head, squeezing my eyes shut, as the tears dripped unbidden. "I'm so sorry." How could he *not* hate me for this? I hated myself for it.

"Hey, I wasn't finished," he said, lifting my chin to his remorseful smile. He wiped away the tears streaming down my face, only to be replaced by fresh ones once again. "I wasn't angry *with* you. Only at the crossroads fate has brought us to. I'm supposed to protect you, keep you safe, yet here I sit with you in one of the most dangerous places for you. I cannot even begin to express how powerless this makes me feel."

"That doesn't make sense. How could you not be angry with me? I'm the reason we are all here in the first place," I cried.

"No, Aurora. You're not. You just made it easier for them to bring you all here. One way or another, fate would have intervened and brought us here. I would have *preferred* to make them work for it," he said with a mischievous smirk highlighting his dimple.

"If you weren't angry with me, then why the cold shoulder all day?" I asked, wiping my cheeks free of the wetness.

"I cannot expect you to understand how this High Council works, but as you had seen for yourself today, there are those in power who can't be trusted. There are eyes and ears everywhere. Always remember that. If they were to see how close I am to you, you would become an even bigger target than you already are just because of *who* I am," he stated.

"And who are you?" I blurted.

He winced, as if I had slapped him in the face. He dropped his eyes towards the floor, his hesitancy making me wish I could go back and retract the words from my big mouth.

"I didn't mean to pry. You don't have to tell me," I said, chagrined. Though I wanted to know more about him, I didn't at the pain of his remembrance. I knew what it felt like to relive what you didn't want to relive.

"Tell me something, before I answer your question," he looked up through his thick, dark lashes. I gave him a nod.

"Do you believe in second chances?" he asked. What a weird thing to question. I couldn't deny him an answer, though. The anticipation in his expression belayed how much my answer might mean to him.

"Of course," I said, giving him a small, encouraging smile. How could I not? Lord knows I'm on my fifteenth second chance with all of them. I watched as the small hope he had been holding onto turned forlorn.

"Don't be quick to be so accepting. You might rethink your answer after I give you mine," he said with a grim smile.

"Why don't you let me be the judge of that," I said. He gave me a dubious look before sighing.

"I haven't always been on the right side; the *good* side. I've done a lot of bad things. Things I will always live to regret," he started. I didn't dare to speak. I only wanted to be a silent, understanding ear to his story.

"I was once Braeden's right-hand man. That doesn't mean much to you now. I can't expect you to know the significance of this, but you'll come to know this shortly," he said.

"Care to explain it?" I asked.

"He is directly responsible for the annihilation of the Maeshiren's and is the greatest threat to peace in this Kingdom," he said, watching me carefully. I gasped, hands covering my mouth.

"He is a bloodthirsty killer whose only pursuits in life are revenge and power."

"Why? What does he have against the Maeshiren's? Against the innocent of this kingdom?" I asked, my blood running cold. My thoughts turned to the filthy child in the alley shadows.

"It's simple. The Maeshiren stand for everything he is against. They're the one thing standing in the way of him taking full power and control over the entire region," he said. Kate's words echoed of my great grandfather Reinard and his battle of fending off the threats to this land.

"Is Braeden the *'rumored evil'* Kate talked about with Reinard earlier?" I asked. Gavin nodded as he watched the realization dawn on my face.

How long had this war been going on exactly? The gravity of the very real reality of this ancient feud hit me hard. My brothers and I were now shouldering the responsibility of this kingdom, and this ancient war, because of our lineage.

"That doesn't answer my question though. How does Braeden have any connection to you?" I asked. I didn't realize how close Gavin and I had gravitated towards each other until my question made him sit up and become withdrawn. Startled at his sudden movement, I sat back myself, looking at him with questions unanswered.

He dropped his eyes away from mine, shame turning in his

shoulders. Resolved, he looked back up at me and said, "I was Braeden's top assassin."

The room came to a deafening silence. The crackle of the fire no longer heard, only the pounding of my heart echoing in my ears as my breath failed to release from my chest. *NO. It couldn't be!*

I couldn't picture him being on the wrong side of the line; the line responsible for my people's demise. A proficient assassin, sure I could picture that, but seeing how close he was to Kate and Kartcher, seeing how much he cared about my brothers and me. No, I couldn't believe he was once the bad guy.

"I don't believe it," I said, knowing even as I said the words; what he stated was true. I turned away from him as I tried to wrap my mind around this turn of events. No doubt, he was reading my emotions as much as I was trying to filter through them. He sat without moving, watching, waiting for my final reaction.

He's dangerous. I knew this from the start. I could always sense a darker, more primal side to him. He had a past; I knew this too, which made being near him easier for me in some ways. It meant we both weren't perfect or expecting each other to be.

The way in which he annihilated those guards without a problem proved he was a proficient killer. The swift carnage of those occults showed this, too. While bothersome in its own right; it was how he smiled while doing it. As if he enjoyed the thrill of the kill. *And those red eyes!* I could never forget them if I wanted to. Did that point to the darker side of him? Did that point to him being bad?

Was he to be considered my enemy? My mother's words echoed to trust no one. *Was this the instance my mother warned me about?* I couldn't be sure.

Yet, I couldn't bring myself to care about all of that, either. He was here now, defending the Maeshiren's. Defending my brothers. Defending me. Daten must have seen something in him to bring him into his guard. Even befriending him. He may have been all bad at one point, but he wasn't anymore. From what I've witnessed, he has more good within him than bad.

I was realizing the softer, tenderer side of him as well. A realization I was beginning to understand was reserved specifically for me. The gentleness of his remembered touch wasn't allowing the deserved weight to be given to the seriousness of his admission.

The purity of his unforgotten words spoken earlier by the lakeside erased the meaning of the ones he spoke now. The trouble of what this spoken past did to his very soul became palpable and heavy.

My heart squeezed with such compassion as I looked back into his deep, stormy green eyes - his demeanor pleading for my understanding without him physically doing so. It was as if he were holding onto hope by a thread and I held the shears. With that vulnerability displayed before me, all my barriers came crashing down. My heart felt fuller, like it grew three sizes in this brief moment, and it was all reserved for this man sitting before me.

He continued to watch with a puzzled expression, waiting for a response that could mean his undoing. Could he not make sense of the many conflicting emotions running through me now? An epiphany grew more profound as I struggled with admitting this to myself; I think I might be falling for him.

Heat flashed through my body as my heart pounded at this realization. The reason his dark past meant nothing to me wasn't because I was negligent and blind. Maybe it was partly that. Mostly, it was because despite all that, I could truly see how much I meant to him. *Isn't that why he was here in the first place?*

Surely, my brothers were as distressed as I, but he wasn't in there comforting them. He was with me. His words at the lake held a much deeper meaning when he said *he always wanted to be in my life and now he gets to.* Was it possible he shared my feelings as well?

"Will you *please* say something?" he asked, staring intently into my eyes.

I didn't think it appropriate to come out with the fresh revelation I could hardly admit to myself. What could I say that wouldn't make it so blatantly obvious?

"I don't care," I said too quick.

"Excuse me?" he asked, incredulous.

"I said, I don't care," I stated, more forcefully.

"You don't care that I am single handedly one of the reasons for the demise of the Maeshiren? Or that I've taken many innocent lives for the sake of Braeden's agenda? Or that I'm a natural born killer whose one talent in life is to take life?" he asked, getting more and more heated with each question. The self-loathing he ran through in his head wasn't hard to miss, either.

"No. I don't," I said. I knew this to be a fact. That may have been his life before, even if he was still an assassin by nature and trade. He was on the right side of the line now. He was here with me. That's what mattered most.

"Why?" he asked.

"You asked me if I believed in second chances? What I told you is the truth – I do. I don't care about the life you led in the past. You're here now," I said, omitting the *with me* part. "Daten had seen something in you to bring you on as his top guard. You said so yourself. He was your best friend. That right there is enough for me not to care."

An odd expression flashed across his face before he rearranged his features into one of relief. One side of his lips turned upwards, followed by the other, until both sides met his jubilant eyes. It was the first genuine smile I had seen cross his face.

Before it registered with my brain, he pulled me across the small gap between us and into the cocoon of his tight embrace. I froze before wrapping my arms around his torso and resting my head on his chest. Heat warmed my cheeks at how comfortable it felt to be in his arms once again - how right. *It felt like home.*

We sat in communal silence, testing the sweet embrace we found ourselves in. A permanent smile spread across my face with each gentle squeeze I felt from him, as if he couldn't hold me close or tight enough. My chest swelled at the ecstasy of his continued embrace. If he didn't know of my growing infatuation before, the cat was out of the bag now.

The longer we held onto one another, the more the energy swirling between us transitioned beyond the innocence of our precarious situation. Heat pooled lower in my belly, every nerve ending operating on high alert, as my mind raced towards less innocent musings. A shiver ran down my back as he tightened his hold slightly before releasing me.

I shyly looked into his restrained, wild eyes. His chest heaved as mine did; the charged atmosphere between us continuing to be profound. It was intoxicating.

"I should let you sleep," he said, deep and hoarse, his gaze smoldering.

"I should *let* you let me sleep," I said, clearing my own hoarse throat. The longing for what I wanted hung in the air between us.

"But?" he trailed, smirking.

"But I don't want you to go yet," I admitted, smiling back at him and our playful banter. He chuckled at my response.

"I really should," he said with a serious expression, fighting his smile.

"If you must," I replied as I rolled my eyes, smiling. It had been so long since I felt this light. I couldn't remember a time when I had been able to smile and joke without a care in the world.

Our growing connection, our unbreakable contact, made something stir deeper within, and I couldn't help but smile brighter than I had before. How deep my love ran for this man remained to be seen, but I knew it was becoming unbreakable and multifaceted as time carried on.

He smirked, "I didn't say I *must*, only that I *should.*"

"Well, that settles it then," I replied.

"Settles what?" he asked, puzzled.

"You'll stay with me a little longer," I stated, as I reached for his hand. Goosebumps traveled the length of my arm at the energy of our touch; my breath catching as I tried focusing on what I was doing rather than on my nerves. He allowed me to pull him closer before I nudged him down onto the bed beside me.

He admired me with both wild abandon and longing; our playful banter turning stormier. It would be so easy to follow the natural progression of where this situation could lead. *Am I ready for this to go beyond the innocence of this moment?*

My breathing grew heavier the longer we allowed the suspense between us to continue. In the end, I let my shyness have its way as I shimmied down to his side, resting my head on his chest and running my hand across his hardened torso.

He didn't hesitate to wrap both of his arms around me, pulling me closer towards himself.

Brushing the hair away from my face, the soft stroke of his fingers against my cheek sent shivers to my toes. I leaned my face towards his hand, prolonging the contact with his skin against mine. Unexpectedly, he leaned his face down, gently pressing his lips against my hairline. My heart faltered before fluttering like a hummingbird's wings; my cheeks blazing with fire.

Rather than allow this to be awkward, I cherished it, hugging him closer – a smile once again plastered to my face.

Never has the depth of my feelings gone this deep for any-one. Not Tony, nor any of the other idiots I dated in school. This was something entirely more. Entirely different. Though it was still so new, still so innocent, it was more profound and encompassing. As if I was an island, and he were my ocean. The fullness of my heart was evidence of that.

A remembered quote from long ago, one of my old favor-ites from William James, sprang to mind:

We are like islands in the sea, separate on the surface but connected in the deep.

Those words gave substance to my inarticulate emotions.

"Thank you," I breathed.

"For what?" he whispered.

"For everything; for saving me. Twice," I said. "Well, *more* than twice really," I amended, thinking about how much he had helped me even before coming to this crazy world. I never gave him a proper thank you, and I knew now was as good as ever.

"You don't have to thank me for that. I'd do it a million times over if it meant you'd be here with me once again," he said, so effortlessly. Yet for me, it sent my mind and heart racing into a tailspin at the implications of his words.

Whatever was happening between us, there was no going back. There was still so much I didn't know; so much I was un-aware of. In the darkness that surrounded us, it was too easy to drop those inhibitions and allow this captivating spell to engulf us and spit us out on the other side, whatever that might mean for us later.

Even then, I had so many questions. This turn of events happened so fast. Never in a million years did I think I would be here, with him, like this.

Still, it did little to quench my thirst to learn more about him. Where was he from? How did he end up with Braeden?

How did he end up trading sides and coming into this role as guardian?

"Can I ask you something?" I turned my head to see his face better, unsure if he'd be willing to answer.

"Anything," he replied, opening his eyes with a contented smile, shifting his gaze down towards me.

With the way his eyes smoldered into mine, I lost the courage to ask my original question, instead asking, "How long is it going to take to travel to these badlands?"

"Oh, it depends on our mode of transportation, but no more than a few days' ride I'd say," he answered. I nodded my head in understanding; disappointed for asking only a passing thought.

"That wasn't the question you wanted to ask," he stated.

"Hm?" I said, playing dumb.

"What you wanted to ask, you didn't ask the question you wanted answered," he clarified.

"Observant," I stated simply. *Drat.* How was I ever going to get away with *anything?*

"How did you know?"

"Your tone changed. You were reluctant to ask me your question in the first place and the question you asked didn't match that reluctance. Besides, I could sense your mood souring after you asked it," he replied, textbook.

Wonderful. I had been ousted by my own body's physiology. "Very astute."

"Thank you," he said, smug. "So, are you going to ask me your original question?"

"No. I don't think I will," I said.

"Suit yourself," he replied, closing his eyes and making himself comfortable once again. A sly smile ghosted across his lips as if he wasn't affected at all by not knowing. I lay there feeling slighted at his indifference. Was it all for show or did he really not care?

"You *really* don't want to know?" I questioned, and not at all convinced against the contrary.

"Not if you don't want to tell me," he answered, his smile becoming more pronounced.

"You're just playing with me," I said, narrowing my eyes.

"No Aurora, I mean it," he said. Hearing the way my name rolled from his lips did strange things to my already overworked heart.

"I realize I haven't offered you much in terms of privacy, what with my duties and character flaws and all. I won't hound you for things you're not ready to bring out into the open," he said, his eyes still closed; smile gone. His understanding and sincerity dissolved whatever stubborn apprehension I held onto.

"I'm more afraid of causing you any more anguish at remembering your past," I said, testing the waters to see where this line of questioning would bring him.

"I suppose it's only natural we learn more about each other," he sighed. "To be honest, the hard part of my admissions is over. The rest is a distant past I've already made peace with."

Though he said he made peace with his past, the pensiveness in his words told me otherwise.

"But is it something you would be willing to talk about?" I asked.

"With you, yes."

"Thank you," I said, giving him a small smile.

"What do you want to know?" he asked.

"How did you end up working for Braeden?"

"It was long ago, though the details have become hazy after all this time. I will always remember the day I fell into Braeden's hands," he said, his demeanor growing dark.

"For as long as I could remember, my parents shuffled us from place to place, never staying at any given town for long. They were always looking over their shoulders, careful about how far I strayed and who I spoke to. I was only a boy, no more than thirteen by your world's standards," he said, pausing to collect his thoughts.

"We had been residing in Aberdeenshire, Scotland. It was the first time I had seen my parents breathe easier. It was also the longest we had stayed at any given place. My mother was a healer, much like yourself. She said because she was born with such gifts, it was her duty to heal those she could help. My father supported her in this mission, often helping her with whatever she needed. This was always the answer they gave me when I pried into our way of life."

"Why do you think they could relax there?" I asked, enthralled.

"I've often wondered that myself. They had formed a community of like-minded individuals – healers, alchemists, and shamans. Maybe they felt safer there because of this. Instead, it became their undoing.

"It was 1597. Calamity had been spreading across the whole of Europe for the latter part of the century, eventually coming to infect Scotland. City after city burned many innocent people in the name of witchcraft. If you were found connected with any supernatural healing, or suspected of such, it was to be to your death.

These were distant stories, though, in lands far from us. Too far for it to affect us. That is, until a man by the name of Alexander Rutherford came one day. They called him the prosecutor of witches and warlocks with hair white as snow and eyes sharp as the devils. I will never forget the hard set to his jaw as he laid his eyes on my mother; his loathing rage burning deep," he seethed, radiating with heat.

"My mother was tried as a witch, my father a sympathizer. His proceedings were swift, my fathers. He was given The Maiden. For my mother, she had a very different outcome. I watched as she perished in flames," he said, his throat tightening. "I'll never forget. She never took her eyes off me, pleading with me. For what? I'll never be sure."

Into pieces, at the bottom of my chest, was where my shattered heart laid for both the thirteen-year-old boy who experienced his parents' death in such a gruesome way, and for this man who still held onto their deaths. A tear escaped, running down my cheek. I brushed it away.

With every fiber of my being, I wanted to take away his pain. I wanted to wash his memory clean of such a horrible past, much as I had wished so many days ago would happen to me in my parents' bedroom.

"That is when I began working for Braeden. Alexander Rutherford was only a stage name – a front. Why he would ever need such a thing, I also do not know. I was pardoned under the guise that I had no knowledge of my parent's *evil* workings.

I wasn't employed into Braeden's army willingly. I was enslaved. He didn't make it easy for me, either. He broke me and broke me until I molded to his will. The only saving grace I ever had is that one day, I would find a way to avenge my parents," he said.

"So, how did you end up in Daten's guard?"

"My parents were good people. They raised me well. They taught me the ways of good and evil, though I had disregarded much of their teachings after Braeden abducted me. There was always a piece of their teachings that never left.

During a heated battle between Braeden's army and the Maeshiren Kingdom, a few of our men were converging on a warrior woman. She didn't stand a chance against the hoard that fell upon her, but she stood her ground. It went against my better judgement to turn a blind eye, so I stood with her, enemy and ally, against the greater threat. It was only after we dealt with the threat, had I learned who I had saved; the Maeshiren princess and sister of Daten – Johannes.

Of course, Braeden's ever-watchful eye had witnessed what had transpired. He came barreling down the line, prepared to met out his justice. I stood, ready for his retribution. That day, I didn't just save one Maeshiren royal, but two.

Daten rushed to protect his sister, nearly crossing paths with Braeden at the same time. I intervened – not something Braeden expected. That is the day Braeden almost lost his head at the point of Daten's sword. That is the day I had become a traitor to Braeden's kingdom and an ally to the Maeshiren's."

His mouth set into a grim line. How much this cost for him to remember, I will never know. Though he said he made peace with his past, the fury behind his words told me different. I understood it and couldn't help but feel the ghost of it as well.

"I'm sorry," I whispered. What else could I say?

"Don't be. It was long ago. As I have said, I made peace with my past," he said.

Though I wanted to say I didn't believe he had, I left it alone. The fact he could even speak about it showed how far he had come in his healing process. It gave me some measure that, even though he was still battling with his past in some way, I could heal to that degree as well.

"How often did you watch over me?" I asked. "Growing up, I mean. You said you watched over my brothers and me, but Kate and Kartcher were with you as well, weren't they?" It was a question I had mused over often since learning about his *guard duties.*

"When you were younger, Marie assigned Kate guardian-ship over you. I already had my hands full as the primary guard for your parents and Tanner. Of course, your parents did an amazing job at keeping you all together, which made it easier on all of us for the most part," he paused, whether in remembrance or to collect his thoughts, I couldn't be sure.

"From a distance, I watched over you and your brothers. As you now know, I can sense another's emotions. You were always so blissful and content. Especially when you and Tanner were together," he smiled at some distant memory. "It was easy to be drawn to your infectious nature. The world around us is always dark and full of peril. To even glimpse pure happiness is like a breath of fresh air."

His voice dropped. "When word spread about the tyrannical steps the High Council had taken, Marie wanted to reclaim her birthright to the throne. She would not be swayed," he said.

"Yes. I never understood how she could abandon us like that. Ryder and Garrett had a pretty difficult time with it. My father and Tanner were always more reserved. I guess now I know why," I responded.

"That comes with knowing. Per Daten, your mother was always a priority. She is who I was entrusted to protect. We came here, working to secure her place back on the throne, but as you can imagine, were met with a hostile resistance – much as you all were today."

"How could they deny her birthright?" I asked.

"Power hungry. Greed. You name it. They find ways that suit their agenda," he said.

I hated this *High Council* as much as I hated the man named Braeden, who caused such pain and torment to this man in my arms.

"When we came back, you were no longer a child but a

beautiful woman. Your happiness at seeing your mother despite her long absence was infectious. I couldn't help but think you were extending that to me as well. Though I didn't have a right to think that way, I couldn't help what I felt," he sighed, before turning to his side to face me. The sorrow etched in his face foreshadowed a darker turn to his story.

"But then your parents died and Tanner along with them," he said, his voice lowering further with the heaviness I felt. "I watched as you became a shadow of yourself; hollow. No longer did I experience the happiness emanating from you, only deep sadness that became all-consuming, even to this day. You did your best to replace the sadness with numbness. I could see it in you because I do that myself," he said, pausing to wipe away a tear falling from my eye.

"It's then that I began watching over you more frequently. Your mother instructed me, should anything ever happen to her; you were to be my next priority. Even without that directive, I would have watched over you more anyway, wanting nothing more than to bring that happiness back into your life. To this day, I'm still at a loss of how to do so," he admitted in a whisper. If our faces weren't so close, I might have missed what he breathed.

My heart constricted as the tears stained my cheeks. The details from an intimate outside perspective painted the unfortunate reality of my inner turmoil all too well. The somber retelling of my story, his story, *our story*, was a shared pain that cut deep. The physical pain of this settled within the pit of my stomach, overwhelming the little sense of control I had over my strained emotions. With the introspection of his honesty, I broke down in his arms.

"I'm so sorry Aurora," he said, cradling me to his chest. "I'm sorry I keep letting you down."

I hated myself for breaking down in front of him. I hated

that my problems, and my pain, would be how we connected. What made it worse was knowing he could feel my pain just the same. Not only through first-hand experience, but what I lived in this moment.

Each time I tried to regain control of my emotions; a fresh bout of tears would release more forcefully. It was all much too much. The agony I pictured of him witnessing his parents perish melded into my own pain and suffering. Guilt at knowing he could feel all these uncontrolled emotions within me only surfaced more tears. It wasn't fair to him. He had already been through too much as it was.

"I'm. Sorry," I tried to say in between sobs, but came out as more of a stuttering mess.

"Shh. It's okay," he said, smoothing his hand over my hair as I buried my face into his chest. Though I hated showing my pain, it also felt right to have Gavin be the one to hold me and bring me back together.

In a roundabout way, he was bringing me back to myself. Never had I faced my problems head on as much as I've done in his presence. Maybe it's because he was close to the situation and knows every facet of my past. I don't know, but being here in his arms, being able to freely speak these things into the open, said so much more about him and the trust I found myself placing in him.

Minutes passed as the waterworks slowed. Though my eyes were no longer gushing rivers, the shuttering of my chest as I worked to catch my breath was still audible. I couldn't say this cured me of never-ending pain, but coming out on the other side of this affliction gave me a small sense of renewal and lightness that felt foreign.

Unsure of what to make of it, and untrusting for it to last, I allowed my mind to expand within its confines and experience what it truly felt like to move past the anguish which has tormented me for years.

"Are you okay?" Gavin asked, his voice rumbling through the ear resting against his chest.

"No. And yes," I sighed, answering truthfully.

"Care to explain that?"

How could I put into words what I was experiencing? It was such a mix of emotions. I wondered what he was making of it.

"I can't explain it right," I started. "On the one hand, everything I've experienced and learned up to this point has hurt deeply, on top of the pain of loss I've experienced for so long. I don't know if I will ever be able to move past it.

Then, on the other end, there is this new sense of fleeting tranquility; I don't even know if it's tangible or worthy of trusting in. I don't know what to do or how to feel," I said.

"Mmhm, I can sense that," he said.

"I figured you could. I'm so confused. Will I ever stop hurting like this?" I asked, in a still small voice, curious for his introspection.

"The polarity of the two emotions, turmoil and peace, is constantly fighting for control. It's learning the delicate balance of the two, a *yin-and-yang* if you will, that will allow you to find some semblance of solid grounding.

I believe that whichever one you choose to feed will be the dominant one in this battle," he stated but added, "Though I don't believe the pain you feel will ever cease entirely. I do believe it *can* be managed, so you can start living in the present instead of the past."

"Tell me how to do that," I pleaded. His conclusion made so much sense. I just didn't know how to go about living life like he painted. Being able to be happy and at peace, living in the present, albeit still feeling the pain of loss. It was such a foreign concept to me, but not one I was against.

"Unfortunately, Aurora, that is something you'll have to figure out on your own," he said, leaving no further explanation.

"Wonderful."

"I'll tell you what though," he said, his tone suddenly lighter.

"What?" I asked, picking my head up off his chest to look at him, not realizing how close our faces were when I did.

"I'll be here to help you along the way. Whatever you need," he vowed. The promise in his words warmed my cheeks, a small smile spread across my face at his assurance. I couldn't help but feel so protected and understood by his declaration.

Locked into his smoldering eyes, I had a sudden urge to close the distance between our lips and relay the exuberance I felt swirl within. A ball of nerves rested in my core as I battled between being bold or playing it safe; instead, I refrained, unsure of how he would respond to such boldness. I closed my eyes, cutting off visual contact with him so I could settle down.

"Thank you," I said a beat late, with eyes still closed. I was grateful for his presence in my life. I never wanted him to question that.

"Of course," he chuckled. My eyes snapped open, seeing mirth replace the severity of our earlier conversation.

"Can I get in on the joke?" I asked, eyeing him.

"There's no joke Aurora," he replied, yawning. "I just find it odd how things work out the way they do." His eyes rested back on mine, though sleepy as they were. I couldn't deny his admission or the unspoken exhaustion taking hold. We had been going for so long with such stressful situations, it was a wonder we weren't passed out yet.

"I suppose you're right," I said.

"Of course I am. I'm always right," he yawned again, his heavy lids closing. I watched his features relax, a small smile present on his lips. Outwardly, he was always intense and ill-tempered; the peaceful expression resting on his face now was one I wished to witness more often.

As much as he said he wanted to make me happy once again, I wished that in return for him. I knew in my heart I would do anything for him. He had always been there for me, even when I wasn't aware. I wanted to be there for him. Without thinking, I leaned over, closing the gap between us, and gave him a gentle kiss on his cheek.

"Thank you," he mumbled through a sideways smile, as he sighed in his sleep-induced state. I startled, not realizing he hadn't fully dozed off yet. *Was he conscious enough to remember that tomorrow?*

My cheeks flared at being caught, though his response was reassuring. The rhythmic breathing of his deeper state of sleep eased my embarrassment. I would let myself worry about the consequences of what I did when the time came. Tomorrow's problems could be tomorrow's problems.

Despite being hyper aware of Gavin's hand resting on my hip, and the way in which I clung to his arm, I was oddly at peace. It was as if it were a natural thing happening between him and I. *Could this become a new normal for us?* Rather than allow my mind to race into tangents, which would surely keep me awake, I welcomed the lull of his peaceful breaths swaying me to promises of a dreamless sleep.

Chapter Nineteen

Dog Fight

***

"WHAT in the *hell* do you think you two are doing?" Kate's voice boomed, startling me awake.

I could barely lift my head over the confinement of Gavin's body entangled with mine, our legs provocatively intertwined with one another. Heat blazed across my face at Kate's furious glare standing over us.

I glanced at Gavin wearing a mischievous smirk staring at Kate, making no move to unravel our precarious situation. The door behind her creaked with Kartcher and my brothers peering at us through the doorway.

"Good morning to you too, Kate," Gavin said in his slight accent, his voice hoarse from sleep. He turned his head to me and smiled, "Oh, hello," as if he didn't realize I was lying next to him.

"Care to explain this?" Kate admonished, one hand resting on her hip as she used the other to circle over us.

Gavin turned to Kate, clearing his throat as if he were unsure. "We fell asleep?" He glanced over at me with a grin and winked. I tried to hide the smile from spreading across my face but failed miserably.

"I don't know what is going on between you two, but we need to go," Kate said, giving us both a hard stare.

"Yes ma'am," Gavin saluted, though he made no attempt to move.

"Now! Get up!" she yelled, clapping at us. "And you! You and I are going to have a talk!" she said, staring daggers at me.

"What? What did I do?" I said, defensive.

"Don't worry about that now. We need to be going. Aurora, I have clothes there for you to change into," she said sharply, as she turned on her heel and ushered the other three out, slamming the heavy door behind her.

"Well, that was interesting," Gavin said under his breath. "Good morning sunshine," he beamed at me.

I let out a nervous laugh, "Good morning."

"Ready to go before Fuhrer Katernius comes back to rip us another asshole?" he teased.

"I suppose. I do need to brush my teeth," I chuckled, covering my mouth with my hand.

"C'mon. I'll show you where you can wash away your dragon breath," he said, tugging at my hand as he untangled his legs from mine. He gave me a quizzical look when I pulled my hand from his to stretch, my legs still stiff from sleep.

"Better?" he smirked. I smiled and nodded.

"Here. Through those doors is the washroom," he said, pointing to the corner of the room where two double doors were stationed.

"Oh, don't forget these." He grabbed the clothes Kate laid out, along with my toothbrush and toothpaste she brought from home, placing them in my arms.

"Thanks," I said, before rushing through the doors.

The washroom was as grand as the castle itself. With a wall of mirrors to the left, and a clawfoot ebony bath centered in the room, there was more space in here than necessity dictated. I paused in awe of where I stood.

"Are you almost ready?" Gavin called from the other side of the doors.

"Uh… um… almost!" I yelled back, rushing through the pile in my hands. What in the world did Kate give me?

I yanked my legs through the black, form-fitting pants fit for a jockey, a ribbed line on each leg extended from hip to ankle, giving a slim, sexy appeal.

A long-sleeved white tunic, and a black sleeveless leather vest embroidered with floral lacing, were jumbled together in an obsidian hooded cloak.

"What the hell is taking you guys so long?" I heard Kate complain.

"Calm down Katernius. We can afford a few more minutes," Gavin chided.

"Don't tell me to calm down, Gavin. We are up shit's creek more than either of us realizes," Kate said, lowering her voice to a whisper just loud enough for me to hear. "What do you think you're doing?"

"It isn't what it looks like, okay?" Gavin defended.

"Really? Because I don't know how else you could explain *that*?"

I realized I had been holding my breath, pausing in absolute stillness, so I could be sure to hear everything they were saying.

Did Kate and Gavin have something going on between them? Is Kate jealous? If that were the case, why did Gavin say all those things to me?

"I don't have to explain anything, to be honest. Neither does Aurora. I would appreciate you keeping your nose out of our business and give us a few more minutes," Gavin said, his stern tone putting an 'end-of-story' edge to his voice.

"It may have slipped your thick skull, but don't forget *where* we are and *who* is watching. You're treading down a dangerous path for all involved," Kate warned.

"Duly noted."

The sound of the door clicking shut indicated Kate had left the room. I rushed, throwing on the rest of the clothes, pulling the tunic over my head and tying the knots around the neckline, which did nothing to hide the crests of my breasts.

The leather vest clung to my curves with two strips of leather embroidered on either side, giving the vest structure. The lines were pleasing to the eye as they extended from the outside shoulders, tapering in over my breast and down towards my belly button.

"Ugh, fucking buttons," I cursed under my breath as I fumbled with the ivory clasps centered up the vest. I cinched the mahogany belt attached to the vest around my torso, feeling more and more as if I were dressing for a Halloween party.

I shoved my feet into my converse before adding the last bit of this ridiculous ensemble together. The dark twist on the little red riding hood cape enveloped my petite frame. Securing the hood in place at my clavicle, I lifted the hood from my head and faced the wall of mirrors. I looked like a cross between a medieval Harley rider and a Comicon character.

I rushed to the washbasin, pouring the water into the bowl so I could brush my teeth. I raked my fingers through my hair, giving up on making it decent, before throwing it up in a pony-tail.

"Very nice," Gavin admired when I walked out of the room. I gave him a dubious look.

"No. Really. It… has a certain appeal," he smirked, taking a step back as if to admire the freak show.

"Okay, enough joking at my expense. Please and thanks," I said. He smirked. "Really though. What the hell is Kate *thinking*, having me wear this?"

"She is thinking of keeping you safe. You'll be less conspicuous this way on the road," he said.

"In *this?*" I shrieked.

"Aurora, you blend in more wearing this. Jeans and plaid shirts aren't in fashion here, if you know what I mean?"

"I get that, but why does it have to be so tight? These clothes fit like a second skin," I complained.

"Welcome to the attire of the average female traveler. Are you ready?" he asked.

"As ready as I'll ever be," I sighed, looking into his smiling eyes.

"Let's go," he said, holding his hand out for me. Before he opened the door, he turned, pulling me into a tight embrace. His breath tickled against my ear, sending chills rushing through my body. In the light of day, it didn't feel as easy to give into these desires I held for him.

"Remember what I said," he whispered. "There are eyes everywhere. I'm not giving you the cold shoulder when we are in public. I am keeping you safe from being an even bigger target."

He pulled back, keeping his hands on my shoulders, as he kept me at arm's length. He expected my understanding.

"I remember. I can't say I understand when I'm already a target as it is, but I trust you," I said, staring into his eyes, relaying to him the truth in my words.

The smile spreading across his face had the power to knock me off my feet. It was elation, adoration, and peace, all highlighting the handsome dimples on his face. He brushed his tender hand against my jawline as his bright eyes settled on my lips.

"Thank you," he said, inching closer, glancing between my eyes and slowly back to my lips. Every nerve ending zinged as he began closing the gap between us. My heart raced as he moved in ever so close. I controlled my shallow breaths, reminding myself to breathe.

He searched my eyes, seeming to ask if I was okay with taking it to this next point. I wanted to scream, *'what are you waiting for?'* but could only stand there like a stupid deer in headlights. Every inch of me beckoned to meet him halfway, to give the questioning look in his eyes an answer. Instead, fear of what this next move would do to us held me firmly in place.

"Today would be nice," Kate hollered, pounding away on the other side of the door. I pulled back, standing straight, not realizing how much my body gravitated towards his. He let out a sigh before rolling his eyes and dropping my hands.

Shaking his head, he opened the door, "We're coming! Cool your tits, Katernius."

"Gavin. Just. Don't," she said, pointing her finger in his face.

"Okay! Okay!" he said, holding his hands up in surrender.

"And you. Put these on," she barked, holding a pair of black knee-high boots in the air. "Converse don't go with your outfit." I was jarred, going from almost kissing Gavin to Kate's embitterment.

"What the hell Kate? What did you have me put on?" I asked, raising an eyebrow at her.

"Traveler attire. It's the lowest class I could go without making you look homely. We still need to get into places after all," she spat.

"Excuse you?" I stared at her. Her crappy attitude was getting on my last nerves.

"What she means is you will blend in, as these two do," Kartcher said, glancing at Ryder and Garrett. They, too, wore ridiculous attire, both with matching cloaks. Their clothes, however, were baggier than mine.

"Put these on," Kate said again, shoving the boots into my hands. I kicked off my converse and laced my feet into each absurd boot, petulant as a teenager. Gavin picked up my sneakers and put them in my bag.

"Not that bag. Here," Kate said, throwing it at Gavin. He caught it midair, giving her a death stare. Seems I wasn't the only one sick of her attitude. "That bag stays here. Whatever you need in it, transfer it to that one."

"And you'll want these as well Aurora," she said, tossing a pair of gloves to me. "They'll help keep the chill off your hands when we are riding." She turned, going over plans with Kartcher.

If Kate and Gavin had nothing going on between them, then why was she so angry? *Was she interested in Gavin? Did he know she may be interested in him?* Oh, I hope that wasn't the case. I couldn't dare hope to compete with her; she was my best friend after all. And besides, there are way too many previous events between them, time shared, I would never know about. A sinking feeling settled into my gut.

Gavin shifted his gaze down to me, sensing my sudden mood shift, but didn't move to comment on it. He gave me a tight, reassuring smile, which did nothing to quell my current worries. I glanced to my brothers, who were surprisingly silent, given the earlier ordeal they found us in.

Ryder gave me a tight-lipped smile with eyebrows raised. Garrett didn't bother to look at me at all, staring straight ahead.

Just perfect.

"Let's go," Kate ordered, as she started making her way down the gaudy hallway.

We all followed suit in silence. At the entrance hall, six guards in ivory suits stood ready for us, true to form.

"Follow me," said a large guard with a clipped tone. He turned on his heel and headed towards the castle doors.

"Quite the conversationalist," Gavin said, leaning in and rolling his eyes. I tried stifling a giggle with my hand, my heart clenching at the playfulness that didn't fade in the morning light.

Kate made a loud show of clearing her throat with the 'don't mess with me, I'm not in the mood' signature Kate look, before she turned her attention forward.

As they ushered us out of the castle and down the very steps we walked up yesterday, we were met with seven, eight-legged horses, much like the ones that brought us here by the wagon. Their coats glistened in the morning sun, highlighting their veiled wings, however, the presence of antlers and bony protrusions lining the backs of their neck were absent.

"Why are there seven Drygdals?" Gavin deadpanned.

"Avnor is going with you, to ensure you all keep to the end of your bargain," the large guard informed us.

Next to one of the Drygdals stood a lynx of a man, his furry, pointed ears twitching as he rested one hand against the chest piece of his ivory armor.

"We don't need him," Gavin stated, annoyed.

"The High Council ordered it," the guard stated.

"That wasn't part of the bargain," Kate said, her voice hard as steel.

"Doesn't matter. Whether or not you agree with it, Avnor *is* going with you," he stated. "Here are seven of our finest Drygdals to ensure you swift travel. Not a moment is to be spared, as

I fear time is of the essence. This High Council does not like to be left waiting."

Gavin mumbled under his breath but made no further audible comment. We moved forward to approach the Drygdals, which easily towered over any horse we'd ever owned. At once, they all lowered to their knees, making it easier for us to climb on.

I glanced at Gavin, seeing him struggle between helping me up and walking to his own horse. He chose the latter, and though my heart fell, I knew why he did it. He didn't want to make a show of ourselves. It seems we had already done enough of that.

Each guard walked up to us with a pack in hand as we mounted. Kate and Kartcher grabbed their packs, slinging them over their heads, and settled them at their backs. I watched as their seats reached out, molding their packs into place. Would I ever not be freaked out about all this mysticism?

"What's this?" I asked with eyes wide.

"Provisions," Kartcher said next to me on his horse. "We each carry our own weight in food and other necessities." I nodded in understanding. Of course.

I grabbed the heavy pack and flung it over my head as they did, securing it behind. An unexpected tingling sensation reverberated through the saddle as it molded to my pack. I didn't have long to ponder on the peculiarity as Gavin shouted, "Hang on!"

All seven of the leggy horses worked to stand up. I let out a squeal as my stomach dropped at how swiftly they rose to their feet. My arms grasped onto my Drygdals neck as it jostled me forward and then rocked me back. My heart thumped hard in my chest as I made the mistake of seeing how far I sat above the ground. This wouldn't be the best time to let them know I was afraid of heights, would it?

Sensing my panic, Gavin rode his horse next to mine, kicking up dust when it halted. "You okay?"

I glanced at him, giving him a shaky nod. He laughed at my obvious lie. "I know these saddles are unlike anything you've ever experienced. They built these for speed. You see the two handles facing out like single antlers?" he asked, pointing at the ones in front of me. I nodded.

"Hold on to them like this," he said, as he positioned his body forward towards the handles.

"Yeah, that's it," he lilted when I mimicked his position. In my peripheral, I could see Kate and Kartcher giving Garrett and Ryder the same spiel.

"With your feet, make sure they're in the foot holsters here much like riding back home," he stated, pointing to his own to show me what he meant. "But when you put them in, push them all the way forward. You'll feel the cradles binding to your feet," he amended.

"Okay," I replied, unsure. Sliding both feet forward to the front of the cradles, they quivered as the bindings fused together with the bottom of my boots, making it hard for me to pull my foot out of the strap.

"Whoa!" I exclaimed, the feeling of being trapped unsettling. *What if I needed a quick dismount?*

"It's okay. Don't be alarmed. It's to keep them from falling out, trust me," Gavin reassured. "And whatever you do, hold on for dear life," he chuckled.

"Wait what?"

"Kartcher, you lead since you know the way best," Gavin called out, ignoring my alarm. Kartcher glanced over, giving us a nod, before turning back to Ryder.

"Are you good?" Kartcher asked Ryder.

"Yep. Ten-four," he responded.

"Great. Garrett, you all good?"

"This is child's play!" he laughed.

"We'll see about that," Kartcher laughed. He trotted his Drygdal forward before stopping with a complete one-eighty to face us. Dust kicked up behind him, carrying with the breeze.

"There are three simple rules you must know while riding a Drygdal. First, they fuse with your energy. You can give them silent commands and they will listen.

Second, remember these commands! *Curre* means to run, *desisto* means to stop. Drygdals know no other command while riding, so get comfortable with the speed of their gait.

Third, though you may be bonded to your Drygdals by foot, hold on for dear life. The speed at first will be jarring," he said, ending his instruction. I glanced back to Ryder and Garrett, confident in their skill, though Ryder looked apprehensive.

"Let's ride!" Kate commanded.

"I'll be right next to you," Gavin said, giving me a tight smile. I took a deep breath, my knuckles white over the bone at my tight grip. I watched in horror, and utter amazement, as both Kate and Kartcher's Drygdals sped off at lightning speed. Ryder and Garrett followed, their screaming voices soon fading with their absence.

"Are you ready?" Gavin asked.

"In all honesty? No," I admitted.

"Well, it's a good time to get ready," he said, as he slapped my horse's hindquarter and yelled *Curre!* Both of our horses launched with me screaming at the sudden jolt of my Drygdal rocketing forward. I panicked as my sweaty palms slid against the grip of the handles.

It felt like I sat on the outside of a jet plane, holding onto the wing. The wind slapped against my face; the city surrounding us passing by in a blur as the townsfolk yelled obscenities at our rude departure. I choked back bile from the motion sickness that threatened to push me over the edge. In no time, we were through the city and caught up with the rest of the gang, galloping along a countryside trail.

An hour had passed with me suppressing the impending disaster that was my stomach before I could adjust to the pace of these Drygdals. What I failed to notice earlier was how smooth their gait was, even with so many legs. They were like the Cadillac of horses.

The mane of the beast beneath me shimmered in waves as the wind flowed through its ivory hair. The white iridescence of its body took on an ethereal glow, changing to the most beautiful pastel colors. Up close, the feathers of their concealed wings shuddered brilliantly. Being able to focus on the Drygdal beneath me took the edge off what I had been so afraid of.

"How are you doing?" Gavin yelled as he rode next to me, breathless.

"Better," I said, equally breathless. Though they were a smooth ride, going at these top speeds with high winds thrashing about made it hard to breathe.

"Hang in there. We have a ways to go before we stop for the night," Gavin said, trying to talk above the wind whooshing past my ears.

"Okay!" I said, raising my voice.

It seemed as if we had only been riding for a short while, but the sun was setting past the horizon, casting deep shadows in the treed area we were coming into. While the trail had been mostly wide, with lush green fields on either side, I could see the road ahead narrowing. A canopy of giant, colorful trees shaded the road ahead, making it seem as if we were running headlong into the dead of night.

The hairs on the back of my neck stood on end as we pushed past the shadow's horizon. The burst of energy I experienced when I had first entered this world made itself known once more. A sudden foreboding crept into my psyche.

"Prepare to stop," Gavin yelled, pointing with his chin towards a fast-approaching building. My eyes grew wide as I froze in place - I didn't know how to stop! Kartcher didn't cover that other than to say *desisto!*

As I thought the word, the Drygdals' eight legs came to a screeching halt, its massive wings expanding to slow its stride, throwing me halfway over as I held onto its head for dear life. Panting, I stared at the ground that almost became a resting pad for my face.

Ahead of me, I heard both Garrett and Ryder screaming as their horses came to a halt. I lifted my head in time to see them both get thrown over their Drygdals' head, with Ryder landing on his face like I almost did, and Garrett rolling on his side with an oomph.

A giggle bubbled to the surface before I let out a howling laughter. The absolute absurdity of it all had me in complete fits as my body shook with hysterics.

Not paying attention to the fact I still held onto my Drygdal's head for dear life, he reared up before flipping me over and depositing me on my backside. It stared down at me with nostrils flared.

"Was that necessary?" I all but yelled, my brows drawing in at the creature standing above me. As if to answer, he lowered his head and snorted through his nose, covering my face with snot. I laid there in stunned silence. Mortified wasn't even the proper word as the entire gang laughed at my demise. I wiped my hand down my face, collecting the wet slime and shaking it off onto the ground next to me.

"Oh. I forget to tell you, Drygdals can have a bit of a temper," Kartcher said, laughing behind his cloak.

I sat up as Kate walked over to lend me a hand. "And they don't like when someone yells at them," she said, hoisting me up from our locked hands.

"Dually noted," I replied to both Kartcher and Kate, slighted. I wiped the remainder of the snot off my face in disgust.

After tying our Drygdal's at the water troughs, we made our way to the entrance of the *Far Yew Inn and Saloon.* This place was falling apart, with one little flickering lamp lighting the entrance of the double swinging doors.

A commotion stirred inside before a short, blue-speckled creature was thrown out through the double doors, swinging them wildly back and forth at his departure. Behind it, a grotesque bald brute with the roundest belly protruding from beneath his shirt came walking out.

"If yew knows what's good for yew, yew'll stay out!" he hollered in a heavy accent. He turned to see all of us staring back at him before grunting and heading back inside. The cerulean creature, with folded ears, glanced back in a drunken stupor before stumbling down the road.

"Tough Crowd," Garrett said.

"Yeah. No kidding. What was that?" I asked.

"That was a Marmalane. Tricksters and drunks, the lot of 'em," Kate said, without elaborating further. *Well, that answered that question. Not.* She strode forward through the swinging doors with Ryder in tow.

"I'm sorry, a what?" I asked again, stumped.

"Don't worry about it. They're harmless," Gavin said, as he bumped my shoulder, encouraging me forward with the rest of them.

"We shouldn't be stopping. This is against orders. We must continue proceeding to the badlands," Avnor spoke for the first time since we left. I forgot he was even with us.

342

"Hey Avnor. Do me a favor," Gavin said, glancing back at him.

"What's that?" he asked, defensive.

"Fuck off," Gavin replied, as he turned back around, hooking his arm around my shoulders and striding forward to the swinging doors. I glanced back to see a shocked but angered expression on Avnor's face. Clearly, he wasn't top of the totem pole in this group.

The inn was as dark and dingy inside as it was on the outside, yet it was packed wall-to-wall with creatures of all different kinds. There were those who were close to human, dressed in furs and leathers. Some had markings or deformities on their faces, making them stand out amongst the rest.

I noted how some groups of similar kind huddled together in packs, like the short leprechauns with lengthy noses and rounded pointy ears. They sat in animated conversations, stroking their long graying beards while smoking their pipes.

Or the froggy group with bugged eyes and tall ears. Three of them sat back on their haunches, beer mugs strung around their necks, harmonizing an upbeat Gaelic drinking song as they played their instruments.

Gavin walked us through throngs of people to a back table in the corner, where a squirrelly man with long whiskers sat, drinking a beer with his companions.

"Move, you're in my seat," Gavin said, glaring at the group. Instead of arguing, they hastened to move as fast as possible. Without a second thought, Kate sat on the stool opposite the bench as Gavin motioned for me to sit. My brothers and I exchanged glances before they shrugged and moved to follow.

"What was that about?" I asked, eyeing Gavin as he sat on the outside edge of me. Instead of answering, he pointed up to a cockeyed sign nailed to the wall, which read:

Gavin's table. Do not sit here.

I gawked back at him. "You have your own table? Why am I not surprised?" I said, shaking my head as I chuckled in disbelief. He answered with a smirk and a sideways glance.

A busty waitress with the body of a well-endowed woman, but the face of a bunny, distracted his attention.

"Fancy seeing you here, Gavin," she said. "Where have you been, sugar? It's been ages!" She moved over to his side, wrapping her arm around his shoulders, coming close to touching me in the process.

"Been around Shareif. Taking care of a few things," he smiled up at her. I couldn't help the twinge of jealousy that snuck up at their familiarity. Was this someone he dated in the past?

"Well, we've all missed you. Don't be gone so long next time. What can I get you?" she cooed, smiling at him with her sultry eyes, hinting at something other than a cold beverage. My blood ran cold as jealousy reared her ugly head.

"We'd *all* like a round of the Storm Honey Ale, *thank* you!" Kate said, irate, as she glared at the bimbo bunny. Shareif pulled her reluctant arm from around Gavin's shoulders, letting her fingers linger a bit longer before releasing her hold.

"Hello Katernius. Fancy seeing you here as well," she said, her bubbly tone turning sour as she addressed Kate.

"Hm. Charmed. Now if you'll get back to doing your damn job so we can get back to enjoying ourselves, that'd be great," Kate barked.

Shareif turned red in the face before spinning on her heels and storming off, a smile spreading across Kate's at her response. Kate glanced at me and winked before focusing on my brothers.

I turned to Gavin with the surge of jealousy still boiling beneath the surface. The corners of his mouth turned down as he captured the severity of my expression.

"What?" he asked, surprised.

"So, you and bimbo bunny, huh?" I asked, raising my eyebrow and trying for nonchalant but fooled no one.

"What about her?" he asked, raising his eyebrow to mimic me.

"I just wondered how long you two dated for is all," I said, still feinting nonchalance.

"We never dated," he chuckled.

"Oh please, you don't have to lie to me," I said, rolling my eyes. "It's not like it's my business in the first place," I said, trying to take the sting of the pain away.

"Aurora, I've never even so much as looked her way. She's very friendly with the patrons. See for yourself," he said, pointing to Shareif sitting on another patron's lap, her fingers stroking his hair.

Though I wanted to hold on to my jealous pride, I knew I was being ridiculous. Whoever he did or didn't date wasn't my business. Even if we ever ended up dating – *Dating? Wow Aurora, you're in deep, aren't you?* Regardless, I didn't have any claim to him, so why did my jealousy rage? Was it the way she appeared so forward with him that caught me off guard?

"I'm sorry. That wasn't my place to even say anything," I said.

"It's okay. You're adorable when you're jealous," he snickered. My face flushed, but I couldn't deny it.

"Besides," he added, wrapping his arm around my shoulders and whispered into my ear, "I'm not into bimbo bunnies." The inviting heat from his breath caressed my neck and sent shivers down my spine.

"Good," I said, trying to contain my smile at his admission but failed miserably. A different waitress brought us each a round, the golden drinks sloshing back and forth in their misshapen canisters before she all but dropped them on the table.

"Hey guys!" the redhead smiled at Kate and Gavin.

"Hey Carmella," they both said over the noise of the bar.

"First round is on the house," she said, before turning and rushing to service the next order. At least *she* had the decency to not ogle Gavin.

"Well, well, isn't that nice!" Garrett said, eyeing Carmella as she rushed away, her bushy orange tail flicking this way and that.

"To awkward places that still have beer! Cheers!" Ryder said, lifting his mug into the air so we could clank ours with his. I brought the cold, golden ale to my lips and took a deep drink, not realizing how parched I had become. When I pulled the mug away, my eyebrows shot towards the ceiling. It was delicious! A perfect blending of honey and hops with a citrusy, smooth finish.

"What do you think?" Kate asked, glancing back and forth between us all.

"It's delicious!" I said, licking the foamy remnants from my lips.

"Yeah, what is it?" Ryder asked.

"A typical drink you'd find in this region. A house favorite," she said, smiling. I watched as she picked up her large mug and chugged the amber liquid to the last drop.

"Another round!" she hollered, slamming her mug on the table. I now knew why she was such a drinking champ; she had been well seasoned for too many years.

"Were you always letting me win or am I that good?" I eyed her with suspicion.

"Whatever do you mean?" She smiled innocently.

"You bitch! You always let me win?" I screeched.

"NO! No. You're good. Good enough to hang with me," she laughed, assuring me. I didn't know if I should take that as a compliment or an insult.

"Gavin, go grab us another round," she shouted over the noise.

"What's wrong with your legs?" he asked, narrowing his eyes.

"Oh, just go do it, would you?" she said, both telling and pleading with him to do so.

"Fine," he huffed, making his way to the bar. Those who knew him moved out of his way without a fight, making his way easy.

Garrett and Ryder were in deep conversation with one another; their beers more than half empty. I too was only halfway through mine and already feeling my teeth grow numb. This was some potent ale.

I startled as Kate bumped into me, throwing her arm over my shoulders.

"You and Gavin, huh?" she yelled in my ear.

"It isn't what you think," I said, turning towards her.

"I don't care about that so much," she said as I cut her off.

"You don't?" I exclaimed, skeptical.

"Not in the least. It surprised me when I came in to wake you, sure," she said.

"Kate, you were pissed," I said, giving her a deadpanned stare.

"Yeah? And? I was pissed because I thought you two were holding out on me this entire time. Don't think I haven't noticed what has been going on between you two," she said, narrowing her eyes. "I find you at the lake together – alone. I find you in bed together – alone. Don't think I can't feel the thick sexual tension between you two. It's so obvious you can cut it with a knife," she laughed.

"WHAT! Oh my gosh Kate, No. It's nothing like that," I

said, embarrassed because it was true.

"Sure, it isn't. You don't have to lie to me, Rory. To be honest, I've been waiting for the day you two would meet. I wasn't expecting you both to hit it off so suddenly," she explained.

"Wait what? You really aren't mad? I mean, you don't feel anything for Gavin, do you?" I asked. It was the one question that shook me to my core. I didn't want our friendship to be hanging in the balance because of it.

Her face scrunched. "Oh, Heavens no! Good Lord, woman! No offense, but I have better taste than that."

"Hey! Take that back," I said, smacking her shoulder.

"No," she laughed. "But he isn't a bad guy, Aurora. You could do far worse, honestly. Well actually, you have," she said, holding her chin in contemplation.

"Ouch," I said, stung by her insult, "Don't hold back."

"I mean, hello, Tony wasn't exactly the best choice ever. And do you remember Chandler from high school? Ugh!" she said, further cementing her original claim.

"I truly wish the best for you both though, I do," she said, giving me her blessings with a wide smile.

"Gee. Thanks. It's not needed, though; we aren't a couple, Kate. At best, we are becoming close friends. At worse, he's just my bodyguard. It doesn't go much deeper than that," I said, petulant because I found myself wishing it would. Even saying those words out loud didn't sound right.

"I *know* you know better than to believe that crap," she said, giving me a dubious look.

"What about earlier? In the room? I overhead you talking to him. You said what he's doing is dangerous," I said, unable to let this point go.

"Aurora, let me tell you something. While you may have a target on your head because of who you are, Gavin has many enemies because of what he's done. If they even suspect he feels for you anymore than duty allows, you'll be seen as his one true weakness. As of now, according to common knowledge, he has none," she said, the weight of her words striking fear into my heart for Gavin.

I didn't want to be seen as his weakness. I didn't want to put him in even more danger if I could help it. And if we were walking such a fine line, why were we even playing with fire?

"Who are his enemies?" I asked. I wanted to know who to watch for, who to keep my eyes on.

"I couldn't even count them for you Aurora," she answered, shaking her head with glossy, saddened eyes. "I will tell you this. When they find out you're his weakness, they will come for you. You specifically."

"Why?"

"How else do you take revenge against the one person responsible for the destruction of your livelihood? Or in the case of other more powerful enemies, for becoming a turncoat? You go after the one thing that could cripple them."

"Kate, you're in my spot," Gavin said, his voice grave as he set the mugs in the middle of the table.

"That's my cue," she said, smiling brightly, as if we weren't having this heavy discussion. She jumped up and sauntered over to Kartcher, sitting at the end of the bar.

Gavin's eyes were tight as he watched Kate retreating. "What was that all about?"

"Nothing," I said, giving him a tightlipped smile. He didn't believe me, but he didn't push me for details either. Instead, he handed me a fresh mug.

"I'm not even finished with this one yet!"

"Well, it's about time you catch up, frat house victor," he replied, bumping into my arm with a playful smirk. That night felt like ages ago, rather than last week – it was so hard to find a grip on reality here. I shook my head to clear it of its inner musings and flirtatiously bumped his arm back.

Garrett polished off his mug as he stood up, grabbing for a fresh one.

"I'm going to go see if ol' blondie wants to dance," he said, before walking over to Kate. I watched her laugh and shake her head no, but eventually giving in to his pushy antics. They joined the few dancing in front of the live entertainment, twirling and kicking about.

"Wanna dance?" Gavin asked with a twinkle in his eye.

"You dance?" I asked, unable to hide my skeptical grin.

"I've been known to throw it down from time to time," he smiled, holding out his hand.

The words Kate spoke earlier were in the back of my mind. *How would this keep others from seeing us as something more?* However, getting lost in his happiness was something I would likely not experience again. I couldn't afford to pass it up.

"Sure, why not," I said, rolling my eyes as he clasped his hand with mine.

"Hey! Wait! You can't just leave me here by myself," Ryder exclaimed.

"Don't be a loser. Go find a dance partner," Gavin chuckled.

"Oh, is that a challenge? Are you challenging me?" Ryder taunted.

"If it'll make your sorry ass get up, then yeah," he said.

Ryder nodded to himself with tight lips and a crease in his brow. Chugging back the last remnants of his ale, he grabbed a fresh glass Gavin had brought and stood up.

"Challenge accepted," he said as he scanned the dark room. His eyes zeroed in on the fox tailed Carmella from earlier, zooming about as she worked on refilling drink orders.

"Oh, I wouldn't...," Gavin said, trying to warn Ryder but trailed off when he bee-lined it for his conquest. He stopped her long enough to feel the sting of rejection as she gave him the cold shoulder. Watching Garrett's earlier success with Kate, he wouldn't relent. With two irate shakes of her tail, she dumped an unfinished beer on his head, and returned to busying herself with the patrons.

"I tried to warn him, Fairling's don't mingle outside of their social circle," he laughed, watching a dejected Ryder take a seat next to Kartcher at the bar.

"So how about that dance?" Gavin asked, turning to me.

"I was waiting for your lead," I smirked. His answering smile beamed at me as he led me by the hand. His rigid shoulders relaxed, a carefree nature I only had glimpses of, made him seem more youthful than ever.

Kate gave me the knowing side eye with a heavy smirk as we approached the makeshift dance floor. She was happy to be in on whatever was going on between Gavin and me, even though I didn't know where this was headed myself.

Gavin turned to me and bowed; one hand folded behind his back as he held the other out for me to take. I placed mine in his as he straightened up and smiled. Before I knew it, he twirled me around the dance floor, never taking his eyes off mine. I caught glimpses of Kate and Garrett dancing around us, Kate's ear to ear grin never dimming.

As the froggy trio shifted their upbeat song to a slow balled, Gavin brought me in close, sliding his hand across my lower back. The sensual touch of his warm hand, grazing the small patch of exposed skin under my coat, left me weightless in his arms.

"About earlier," he breathed into my ear, pulling back to make sure I could hear him. I gave him a puzzled look, not following his line of thought. *What about earlier?* There were so many instances.

"In the room this morning I mean," he clarified into my ear. "I apologize if I was too forward." Did he take my deer-in-headlights the wrong way? How could I tell him he was driving me insane? That I wanted what he offered just the same?

"It wasn't too forward," I said, pulling back to show him I meant it. Under his attentive gaze, a shy smile spread across my lips, leaving me emotionally vulnerable at his feet.

"No? I mean," he paused, as he tried to subdue his elation. "You would have every right to say yes." He pulled back to see my response. I shook my head before standing on my toes to reach his ear. He lowered his head to help my vertically challenged self.

"You're right. I probably do," I agreed. "There are still so many things I don't know about you. So many questions I still have. But I can say this: I've never felt about anyone the way I feel about you."

There. I said it. Alcohol helped, of course.

He pulled back; shock evident in his eyes before melting into adoration. The loving warmth he contained within enveloped me into a cocoon of bliss. Between us, our iron walls were being torn down. It didn't matter that we were standing still in the middle of the dance floor while the other patrons danced around us. We didn't care if we were in our own world while everyone else watched. We were entering into something pure and deep, something that couldn't be rushed but cherished before its ephemeral beauty dissipated with time.

He picked me up from my hips and hugged me into his chest, my arms wrapping around his shoulders as he spun us around. I squealed with a giggle at his unexpected glee. He set me back on my feet, lightheaded from the heated rush we found ourselves in.

"Who the hell let the Bentowin in here?" someone shouted, breaking into our perfect bubble. The noisy tavern became dead silent.

Across the room, two men stood over Kartcher and Ryder, sitting at the bar.

"You know your kind ain't welcome here," a heavy-set Viking of a man slurred, having difficulty holding himself upright.

"Yeah. Aren't your kind supposed to be reclusive?" his weasel-like counterpart, standing closest to Ryder, piped in.

"Who gave you permission to be in here?" the Viking man hollered, slamming his fist on the bar.

Kartcher sat in silence, staring down at his beer; the hood of his cloak concealing his eyes. Ryder turned a death stare to the lanky antagonizer standing next to him.

"What's that? Howling's catch your tongue?" the brute taunted, his braided beard resting in the ale he held.

Kartcher continued to stay silent, aggravating the heathen at his lack of response. He ripped off Kartcher's hood, exposing his reptilian face.

"Aren't you going to help him?" I asked, alarmed.

"Nah, he can handle himself," Gavin smirked. A menacing smile widened Kartcher's lips, as if in response to Gavin's confidence in his abilities.

"Why don't you boys sit down before you hurt yourselves," Kartcher taunted.

"Lookie here Tarven, we've got ourselves a talker," the heavy-set man said, turning to his skinnier companion, failing to notice Kartcher's tail slithering from beneath his cloak. The man turned back to Kartcher, coming within inches of his face. "Why don't you scram before I have to teach you a lesso—."

The brute found himself suspended in the air by Kartcher's tail, windpipes cut off from finishing his threats. Kartcher picked up his glass and sloshed back the last of his amber ale.

"I told you to sit down before you hurt yourselves," Kartcher said, whipping him across the room into an empty chair. Everyone's eyes watched as the wooden chair splintered under the man's weight.

The lanky Tarven lunged at Kartcher with a narrow blade he pulled from behind his back. As if it were choreographed, Kartcher kicked away from the bar, sliding his seat back, synchronizing his left arm with the trajectory of Tarven's body; the weasel's face kissing the bar's edge.

A pin dropped; the room erupted.

Fighting broke out in twos and threes. Stools were being broken over heads, and bottles were being thrown. I even watched as a crusty old sailor with an eye patch fought with himself in the corner.

"Screw this!" Garrett yelled, getting in on the excitement. Just as he entered the fray, a wild hook landed square on his jaw, making his head swing to the side.

My hands flew to my mouth, witnessing my brother get socked in the face.

Ryder jumped off his stool and tackled the guy who sucker punched Garrett to the floor, taking others down in the process. Garrett shook off the punch and began kicking the guy in the side before getting tackled to the ground himself by another unruly patron.

Kate came to stand by our side, her eyes scanning for anyone stupid enough to mess with us.

Gavin yanked me into his side as a bottle whooshed past my head, knocking one of the amphibious musicians out behind us. He turned his attention towards the source, seething. "I'll be right back," he said with a hard edge to his voice.

Kate held onto my arm to keep me close as I watched Gavin make his way across the room, shoving palms into noses, and heads into tables, as he headed straight for the Viking man who stared him down.

"You brought that filth in here," he hollered over the bedlam, challenging Gavin.

As Gavin advanced, the man threw a haymaker where Gavin stood. He pulled his head back with only an inch to spare, responding with an uppercut to the solar plex. A bone crushing snap reverberated through the tavern as Gavin made it a point to punch through the heathen, crumpling him forward to the floor.

With the threat down, he turned to make his way back towards Kate and me. The man lifted his chin, snatching Gavin's ankle and yanking him to the floor. The man staggered on hands and knees as he pummeled a fist towards Gavin's face.

I gasped, only slightly aware of Kate holding me back from running towards Gavin.

"Aurora. Stop. Gavin can handle himself," Kate said, tightening her grip on my arm.

I watched in horror as Gavin accepted the punch, not moving away in time as I expected him to.

The barbarian rested his fist on the floor next to Gavin's head, clumsy in his attempt to set himself up for another strike.

Gavin turned his face back to the savage, eyes glowing red with a smile. From this distance, though I couldn't be sure what, he said something which stunned the man. Before I knew it, he had the brute in a headlock with the man fighting to pull Gavin off him.

Kate shook her head back and forth at the childish display before us, rolling her eyes towards the ceiling. "Why do I even bother coming to these places?"

I turned to her in horror at what I was witnessing. I was sure

Gavin would have been knocked out by his opponent's heavy hand and she acted as if it were another day in the office. Everyone, everywhere, continued fighting except for one lone, older gentleman in the far corner of the bar, who sat oblivious to the commotion.

"You okay?" Gavin asked, standing before me. I shook my head, shaken, as I noted the bits of blood dripping down his cheeks and forehead.

"You're the one bleeding and you're asking if *I'm* okay? Shouldn't that be my line?" I asked, reaching up to wipe the blood from his cheek. He intercepted my hand, not allowing me near his face.

"C'mon, we need to get out of here," he said, intertwining his hand with mine. I welcomed it greedily, like a lifeline I didn't know I needed. In the background, I could hear Ryder and Garrett guffawing like a bunch of drunken fools as they traded punches with the remaining crowd.

I glanced back to the Viking Gavin fought, leaned against the wall - out cold - with a broken chair around his neck.

Littering the floor, bodies laid piled over others, some knocked unconscious while others writhed in pain. The lone bar patron in the corner still sat there, oblivious. The bartender dried glasses with a towel, unfazed, like this was a typical day.

"Let's go!" Gavin yelled at my brothers, who finished the last guy off between them. They both looked up, bloodied and bruised, but smiling like idiots at each other. Kartcher stepped over bodies towards us as he somehow managed to get carried over to the other side of the bar in the chaos. The heavyset bouncer laid out behind him.

Avnor stood by the door, as fresh as the moment we arrived.

"Where the hell were you?" Gavin barked, grabbing him by the neck.

"I thought I was to *fuck off*," he answered.

"Don't make me bury you," Gavin threatened.

"We can't stay here tonight," Kate said.

"I know. Let's get out of here and make camp," Gavin replied, releasing Avnor as we rushed out of the tavern, leaving behind the destruction that ensued. Garrett and Ryder continued laughing like drunken hyenas behind us, as we all jumped onto our Drygdal's and sped off into the night.

Chapter Twenty

On the Brink

The edge of a precipice is a very merciless school;
over there you either learn to be serious or you die foolishly!
– Mehmet Murat Ildan

***

Hours later, I lay on my back, watching the Borealis play across the starry sky. With camp made, and everyone settled in, I listened to stories being passed around the blue-lit campfire. Apparently, blue flames weren't enough to attract howling's, or so I was told; yet it put out the most heat - interestingly enough.

"Kartcher, so what happened back there? How did they sniff you out?" Ryder asked, eager to hear the missing holes in his understanding. I perched myself up with my elbows, as if seeing him with my eyes would help me to better hear what happened.

Kartcher's lips pressed into a grim line. "The first drunken buffoon bumped into me, apologizing haphazardly, might I add. I dipped my head in his direction, but I suppose it wasn't a well enough response. I suspect he looked closer at my hands as I reached for my beer. Even in his simple-minded stupor, he figured me out," he said.

"Not as stealthy as you thought you were," Gavin snickered.

Kartcher chuckled once at Gavin's dig before turning back to Ryder. "That was very noble of you to defend your brother."

"Eh, what can I say? Sometimes Garrett isn't as tough as he thinks he is," Ryder said, throwing his hands out as he shrugged and grinned.

"Oh, yeah?" Garrett said, giving Ryder a noogie as he pulled him into a headlock. Ryder punched wildly above him, trying to loosen Garrett's grip. We all laughed at their antics before settling into a comfortable silence. Except for Avnor, who made camp away from us.

A slight, cool breeze blew through camp, making me shiver despite the fire before us. I sat up, pulling my legs into my torso, trying to keep the body warmth in a tight cocoon.

"Here," Gavin said, handing me his blanket as he scooted closer.

"No Gavin, I couldn't. You'll have nothing to sleep with," I said, warming at his sweet gesture.

"Trust me. I don't need it as much as you do," he replied, wrapping the thick afghan-style blanket around my shoulders. Though I didn't want to leave him with nothing, I couldn't say no to his insistence.

"Thank you," I said, pulling the blanket below my eyes, taking secretive inhales of his intoxicating scent.

"What is going on between you two?" Garrett blurted, eyes narrowed, as he looked back and forth between us. My cheeks flamed red.

"What? Nothing!" I said, the high pitch in my voice doing nothing to dissuade him from his questioning.

"Don't bullshit me, Aurora. What were you two doing in bed together?" he asked, his accusing eyes tightening. I floundered under his impenetrable stare, mortified. What do I say? Would he even believe me?

"As if that's any of your concern," Gavin retorted. I swung my head to see him giving Garrett a hard stare.

"The hell it isn't! That's *my* sister," Garrett shouted, pointing to me but shooting daggers at Gavin. I wanted to bury myself and die in Gavin's blanket..

"That may be so, but she is an adult capable of making her own choices," Gavin stated.

"I. Don't. Care. It's my job to protect her from people like you," Garrett seethed, pointing his finger at Gavin.

"People like me? Care to elaborate on that one, boy?"

"Yeah, people like you. Dangerous. Secretive. Always walking around with a chip on your shoulder. Why is it that the people in *our* kingdom despise *you*?" he said, not holding back.

"Okay. I think we've all had a little too much to drink," Kate said, trying to diffuse the situation.

"No! Fuck that! I'm saying what should have been said sooner," Garrett slurred.

"And what's that?" Gavin laughed at him.

"You aren't right for Aurora. I don't care how tough you think you are," he said, as the camp grew silent. "So you can quit with the macho shit."

"Garrett, stop. You're being a jerk," I said at him.

"Shut up Aurora. Stay out of this," he dismissed me.

"Don't tell her to shut up," Gavin admonished, coming to my defense.

"Don't tell me what to do," Garrett spat, jumping to his feet.

"What do you think you're going to do, pipsqueak?" Gavin challenged.

Fire raged in Garrett's eyes as he stomped over to us. Gavin jumped up, meeting him head on, as Garrett reared back and threw a punch. In his drunken state, he telegraphed his intentions so blatantly giving Gavin more than enough time to react.

He grabbed hold of Garrett's fist, twisted his arm behind his back and pushed him forward, making Garrett tumble to the ground. Garrett laid there for only a second before jumping up, screaming, "You bastard!"

Garrett came at Gavin again, this time for a take down as he shot in at his torso. I stood up in time as Gavin stepped aside, letting Garrett catch nothing but air and dirt.

"You sure you want to keep doing this?" Gavin cackled as everyone stood up. Ryder became agitated Garrett was being toyed with.

Gavin turned and pointed at Ryder, "You stay there. Don't involve yourself."

At Gavin's threat, Kartcher placed a hand on Ryder's shoulder to hold him in place. Gavin nodded at Kartcher and turned back to Garrett, who picked himself off the ground once again. He swung around, eyes blazing, as he wobbled where he stood.

"I can do this all-night, boy. I can't say much for you," he said, giving Garrett an amused smirk. We only had a few drinks. *How strong were they?* Even I had to admit, I was pretty tossed myself.

"Stop calling me boy," Garrett hollered as he threw another belligerent punch, narrowly missing Gavin's jaw. Garrett started throwing blows while Gavin outmaneuvered him, swatting his hands away as if they were pesky gnats.

"Okay. Nighty night," Gavin said, deflecting one of Garrett's punches at the same time grabbing his shoulder, spinning him around and throwing him into a choke hold. Garrett thrashed before knocking out.

Gavin lowered him to the ground, grabbing a rope out of his bag, and hog-tied him to a tree.

"Do you really think the hogtying is necessary?" I asked, thinking it a bit excessive.

"Yes. We'll see if he's ready to behave when he wakes up," he chuckled, though we didn't have to wait long. Garrett started coming to.

"Wh-what the hell?" he said, thrashing about as he tried to release his hands and feet. "Guys, c'mon. This isn't funny. Release me!" he shouted as Kate and Kartcher laughed at Garrett's expense.

"You're on your own for that little display," Kate said through her laughter.

Garrett's eyes flashed to Gavin as he squatted down in front of him. "When you've calmed down and can have a real discussion with me, I'll untie you," he smirked, picking up a stick and poking him in the forehead. "Until then, lay there and shut up."

"Untie me, you mutha'!" Garrett yelled. An hour of various expletives later, he calmed down and passed out; like a child who cried themselves to sleep.

"Finally. I thought he'd never shut up," Kate said to no one in particular.

"No kidding!" Ryder chimed in. Though he had been prepared to help our brother at the start, he eventually started laughing with the rest of us, knowing how ridiculous he was being.

Seeing that Garrett would not be causing any more trouble, Gavin released his bindings, the deadweight of his arms dropping to the floor. It wasn't long after, his deep snoring began, causing the rest of us to grumble.

I laid back to resume gazing at the starry night sky; the murmuring around the campfire died to only the crackling and popping of the firewood. While everyone else settled in, I stayed wide awake. My mind raced with all the questions left unanswered, as well as new ones wiggling their way into my psyche.

I kept trying to wrap my mind around the surreal fact I was in a world other than my own. Yet, this world was also part of my history, my lineage. In many ways, this was now my world, too. With so many stark differences between here and the place I called home; I couldn't help but search for the similarities. Wherever I found some, it was still so drastically different, it could hardly be called a similarity.

Take, for instance, this campfire. It's blue! Sure, people gather around the fire at home all the time, but there was enough of a difference to remind me I'm not home. Then, on another point, they had cities and governments here which functioned much like the one's back home, albeit with a more magical medieval flare.

Which brings me to wonder, how did those on the High Council become so corrupt if Daten appointed them? *What are they after?* It had to be more than simply power. This was a question I feared learning the truth about.

Then with Kartcher, who was he? What did that brute call him back at the Tavern? *A Bentowin?* Why was he hated there? He was a gifted fighter; you'd have to be blind not to see that. His demeanor, however, spoke of civility and a moral high ground. There were so many holes in my knowing, I couldn't begin to speculate.

And with all those unanswered questions, I knew I was dancing around the real questions I wanted answered. A small smile spread across my face at remembering Gavin's arms around me on the dance floor. It was yet another side of him I had come to know. More playful, less concerned about the world around him.

Though Garrett acted like a drunken fool, he did bring a voice to my active concerns. *Why was Gavin living this secretive life?* With how open we had been with each other over the past seventy-two hours, I still felt like I only breached the surface with him.

Admittedly, he was dangerous. If the bloodshed and fighting I had already witnessed wasn't enough to convince me of this, I don't know what would. However, it was what Kate said earlier about his enemies, and me being his weakness, that bothered me. How am I to be his weakness? In what ways could I be used against him?

Even with this warning, and the threat of Gavin's enemies coming after me, I couldn't bring myself to admit he wasn't right for me, or that he wasn't good. This was where I believe my brother and I stood on opposing ends.

Or who knows, maybe Gavin wasn't right for me. In truth, I wasn't right for him; we all knew I was damaged goods. But what was blossoming between us felt pure - as natural as breathing.

Which begged the question, where were we heading in this strange limbo of 'more than friends but less than lovers'? Every touch from him, every glance, set my soul on fire. At times, I was incoherent around him. *If I'm his weakness, why did he feel like my strength?*

Frustrated with the roundabout back and forth in my head, I shifted to my side in hopes sleep would take me. Turning, I locked eyes with Gavin, his head resting on his pack. My breath caught from the sheer adoration expressed across his face. Heat began rising from my center to my cheeks, a smile blossoming with it.

"How are you doing?" he whispered, so as not to wake anyone else.

That's a great question. How *am* I doing? "Better than can be expected, I guess," I replied in a hushed whisper back. "How are you doing?"

"Roughly the same. Are you mad about earlier with Garrett?" he asked. I shook my head no. How could I be? Garrett was acting ridiculous. While I respected him for being my older brother and wanting to protect me, sometimes he could go overboard and step beyond his bounds.

"He's right, you know?" he said, his lips turning into a frown.

"About what?" I mouthed.

"Me not being right for you. I wouldn't even know where to start. All I know is, whatever this is between us, I don't want it to stop. I don't want to lose you," he confessed. My heart did a flip as I licked my suddenly dry lips, trying to form a coherent enough response.

"My brother is too biased to think objectively. Don't listen to him," I said, to reassure him I didn't believe the same as Garrett. "And I don't want whatever this is to stop either," I added, dropping my eyes from his, the shyness of my confession getting the better of me.

"So where does that leave us?" he asked, still smiling when I glanced back up at him.

"You tell me," I said, my lips quivering around my grin.

"I suppose time will tell," he answered, the playful smirk accentuating the dimple in his cheek.

"I suppose," I said, unable to stop my stupid grin from spreading.

"Good night, Aurora," he whispered, my name dripping from his lips doing nothing to quench the heat in my torso.

"Good night, Gavin."

I rolled over, breaking our connection for fear of never being able to catch any sleep. I'd stay up all night just to stare at his handsome face, resting so peacefully, as I had done the night before.

As tempting as it was to sneak-a-peek, I forced myself to stay turned away. Before too long, I could no longer fight the heaviness of my eyelids, submitting to their request to close.

"Stop right there," Garrett shouted, waking me from a dead sleep. Panic shot through my chest when I sat up and could see no one. A dense and heavy fog, illuminated by the morning sun, rolled in while we were asleep, cutting me off from the others.

"Garrett?" I called out. Who was he shouting at? Where was he?

The sound of crunching twigs underfoot echoed against the trees, distorted even more by the fog. A high keening whistle blew past my ear, blowing back my hair, as a stinging-hot trickle rolled down my cheek. I reached my hand to touch my face, pulling it away to the sight of blood on my fingertips.

"Gavin!" I shrieked, terror disorienting and paralyzing me where I sat. I didn't want to make the wrong move. I couldn't see. I also didn't want to be a sitting duck. What do I do? *Why wasn't Gavin answering me?*

I crawled out from under Gavin's blanket and towards the dead embers of the campfire. Why couldn't I hear anyone? Were they still asleep? Or perish the thought, *were they dead?* My breath came out fast and hard. *Please don't be so!*

On trembling legs, I stood. An out-of-body experience heightening my senses.

"On your right," that strange, familiar voice whispered in my mind.

My head swung to the right, alarmed at a cloaked figure materializing out of thin air. The glint of his bloody knife added to the menace in his eyes as they shone with thirst for a successful hunt.

I backpedaled as he advanced, hoping in vain to create some distance between us. For every step I took, he took three.

Terror turned my legs into lead, tripping me to the ground.

His eyes turned bright with expectation as he towered over me, raising his blade overhead. I clenched my eyes shut, waiting for him to administer the final blow.

A high whoosh, followed by a dull thump, sounded in front of me. In the absence of expected pain, I peeked one eye open to see an arrow pierced through the assailant's chest from behind. He continued to stand with arms hanging at his sides; his lifeless face pointed down. *Did he die standing?*

I scrambled to my feet; he made no attempt to move as I tiptoed around him, waiting for any signs of a trap. None would come. My chest heaved with shallow breaths, realizing how close I had met my end.

"Garrett! Ryder?" I cry-whispered as loud as I dared to. I received no response other than the silence of the fog and the random crunching of twigs echoing all around. *"Run!"* the voice yelled inside my head.

Run? Where to? I didn't stop to ponder on that any further. I took off in the direction that felt right, hoping to God I didn't choose wrong.

I was running scared – panting; the wind whipping me in the face as I dodge trees and colossal ferns hidden in the pea soup fog. Whatever was hunting me, I prayed I wouldn't run into them either.

The ground beneath me ceased to exist as I catapulted myself off a boulder, unable to see the drop before me as I flailed in midair, crash landing into a solid bed of ferns. The air forced out of my lungs from the sudden impact as I landed on my back.

I laid there, tangled in the fern's branches, shocked at my

sheer luck in this luckless morning as I tried to regain my breath. I didn't know if I wanted to laugh or cry, but I was fraying. A giggle escaped my lips.

The loud crunching of leaves pulled me back into reality - I was being hunted by a stealthy enemy. I thrashed my arms and legs about, trying to untangle myself from the ferns. With as much noise as I made, I probably telegraphed my location to every enemy within this vicinity.

Breaking loose, I dashed in the direction I originally headed – away from the crunching leaves.

A pair of firm hands grabbed me from behind, clasping over my mouth as I let out a shriek.

"Shhh," their hot breath whispered into my ear. I twisted back as much as I dared, Gavin's face coming into view. Relief flooded through me in that terrorizing moment. He released me as I turned, throwing my arms around his neck.

"Gavin!" I whispered through hot tears. His strong arms embraced me for but a second before releasing me. His eyes glowed with a deep, murderous red. He paid no attention to me; he scoured the surrounding area, his eyes never ceasing to rove back and forth over the veiled landscape.

His head shot to the left at the rustling of leaves. He pulled curved swords from beneath his cloak, standing tall and ready for whoever he zoned in on. The fog began to gradually lift, revealing two masked figures seeming to disappear and materialize at random in different locations. I couldn't keep up with their movements.

With nerves frayed, I didn't realize I clutched onto Gavin's cloak until he tensed. I released him as he dashed forward, breaking off the progression of one of our enemies.

With the sword of his right hand, Gavin slashed him from navel to sternum before spinning around with the sword in his left hand, connecting with the assailant's upper back.

Blood dripped down his face from the slaughter, adding to the menacing glow of his crimson eyes. He stood silent once more, tensing to hear where the other invader went.

The fog began dissipating further with the rising sun, giving us a better visual advantage.

Rustling in the nearby fern caught my attention as the second assassin jumped out in front of me. With wide eyes, I turned to Gavin, whose face morphed into a violent rage. Fear clawed at my throat at this assassin's proximity to me compared to Gavin. Too close.

Time slowed. My soul separated from my body as I turned away from Gavin and back to my attacker. In the heartbeat it took for me to internalize my impending demise for a second time this morning, I oddly made peace with it. Maybe the earlier close encounter primed me for this one. In the grand scheme of things, who am I to change the hands of fate? It seems the moment I stepped into this godforsaken world; everything has been trying to kill me.

If time was a rubber band, slowly being pulled tight to give me a moment to process this, it ran out of stretch. The seconds stepped on the throttle to catch up to the present.

The attacker dug his feet into the ground with each stride, kicking up dirt.

Gavin threw his sword at the attacker a microsecond too late.

The dagger in the attacker's hand came in hot towards my torso.

I staggered back by pure instinct when, instead of completing the motion, he arched unnaturally backwards before face planted into the earth beside me.

On the other side of him stood Kate, a silver bow stretched

out in front of her. The determination and panting relief in her face told me she had almost been too late herself.

Gavin stood over the attacker before glancing up at Kate. "Nice shooting," he said, before looking back down.

"Thanks," she deadpanned, as she ambled towards us. I stood motionless, unable to pull my mind from the replay of the sharp dagger preparing to rip into my innards.

"Are you okay?" Kate asked, putting a hand on my shoulder as she dipped her face to investigate mine. I gave her a nod, though I was anything but. She dropped her hand and took a deep breath, "that was too close."

A silent chuckle escaped, though my chest still constricted with anxiety. "I'd say."

Gavin used his foot to push the attacker onto his back, the point of the golden tip glistening crimson in the light peeking through the trees.

"Who are they?" I breathed.

Gavin bent down, ripping the gray mask off the assailant, revealing a woman with patterns of white etched across her face. "The Syndicate," he answered.

"What?" I gasped.

"Why would they be coming after us?" Kate asked, alarmed.

"They were hired," Gavin seethed.

"By who?" Kate asked.

"Who do you think? I'm sure none other than your worthless father," he spat.

"What makes you think this is his doing?" I asked, my blood running cold.

"He's the only one with enough motivation to pull something like this off," he replied.

"Yeah, but couldn't it have been someone from the tavern wanting us dead also?" I persisted. I didn't want the situation I envisioned coming to fruition with us being attacked at 'random' and no one being the wiser.

Gavin answered with a shake of his head, his eyes full of remorse at my lack of knowledge about how this world works. "The Syndicate are only for hire by royalty, or the filthy rich. No one in that bar had the means to pay ten assassins to murder us," he said.

"Ten assassins?" I shrieked, as my heart dropped. "How do you know there were ten?"

"I killed three, Kartcher two, Kate four, and that useless twit, Avnor one. I don't sense anyone else lurking undercover," he explained.

"Some assassins they were," Kate said with a straight face.

"No, they're good. We are lucky we pulled through this unscathed," Gavin said.

"My brothers! Where are they?" My heart dropped in fear.

"We're right here. We're okay," Garrett answered, as he and Ryder appeared through two large ferns following Kartcher.

"Ryder! Garrett!" I cried, throwing my arms around them both. Tears streamed down my face at the relief of seeing them both alive and unharmed. "What happened to you both? I called out for you back at camp, but you didn't answer me," I sobbed, staring at Garrett.

"We didn't hear you. I swear Aurora! Garrett woke me up with his shouting, but I heard nothing after that," Ryder quickly explained.

"My God, Aurora, you're hurt," he said, leaving his hand suspended in the air as he reached to touch my cheek. I brushed the wound, feeling the dripping blood drying. I had forgotten all about my first near death experience.

"It's okay, Ryder. I'm okay," I reassured him.

He stared at me for one tearful second before squeezing

me into a hug. "Really, Ry! I'm. Oh. Kay. Can't. Breathe," I said, patting him on the back as my air supply struggled.

"Sorry," he released me, wrapping his arm over my shoulders instead.

"Did you know there were ten assassins?" I asked him.

"Ten?" he asked, astonished.

"It seems to me the fog was some sort of illusion magic, meant to disorient and dull the senses. Did you see how fast it dissipated as the assassins diminished?" Kartcher mused, his hand stroking over his chin.

"I did notice the fog breaking apart unnaturally fast," Garrett replied. "But I didn't know if that was just a mechanism for how this world operates. Nothing seems to be natural in this world," he added.

"If you are all done prattling on about phantom fog and theories, I suggest we be on our way," Avnor said, his armor clanking as he walked up on us, wrapping the deep gash in his forearm.

"Ah, Avnor. Ever the useless one coming here to tell us how to live our lives," Gavin greeted him with arms wide open in a staged gesture.

"This will not bode well for you when I give my report to the High Council, Gavin. You must leave for the badlands this instant or—," Avnor threatened.

"Or else what? Your threats mean nothing, you spineless scoundrel. You're only here because you're being a good lap dog and following corrupt orders. Tell me you weren't aware of the hit put out on us today," Gavin demanded, scrutinizing his body language.

"I am aware of no such thing," Avnor defended himself.

"Sure you weren't. That's why you were nowhere to be found when the attack took place. The only reason you took one of these lowlifes out is because they came after you," Gavin said, kicking the assassin at his feet. "Maybe you should think, for one moment with that pathetic pea brain of yours, that you were included in this assassination order. Collateral damage."

Avnor stood stunned, his eyes flashing with fear. Without saying a word, he told us all what we needed to know. My stomach churned at this revelation.

"I'll let you chew on that one for a while," Gavin said, lowering his face toward Avnor as he shouldered past him. Garrett shook his head as he passed him in tow.

It sickened me how there were those who would follow orders of the High Council, knowing they were merely puppets in their schemes, positioned only to do their corrupt bidding.

Back at camp, the body of my attacker laid hunched on her side, gravity finally pulling her towards the earth. Twice I had come close to meeting my end today. Twice I stood helpless, hoping someone would save me, or accepting my fate if they didn't.

"I thought they were men," I said to no one, shaking my head as I stared at her.

"You'll find the societal norms of the world you grew up in does not apply here. Women can be just as lethal as the men," Kate said next to me, staring at the lifeless body.

"Was this one of your four?" I asked, remembering the arrow through her chest.

"Yep. When you called out, I couldn't come to you. I'm sorry. I had to move quick. It wasn't easy finding them in that fog."

"How were you able to find them? The fog was disorienting," I asked.

"It wasn't without difficulty, I assure you. I had to rely on my extra senses to guide me."

"What extra senses?"

"If you stood still long enough, you could pick up on their vibrations. They're quick on their feet, so you have to move fast or else you've lost the trail," she shared, giving me a nod before gathering her bedroll.

I stared back down at the body that could very well have been mine, thanking Kate's impeccable timing.

In this world, I became a frightened infant without a hope of defending myself. Secret society assassins, magical beings, and the penchant for *every man for himself* didn't exactly bode well for me. Throw in the fact I'm only days old to the ways of this world with a bullseye on my family, the odds were stacked against me.

I spun on my heel to gather my things. I may be helpless, but what was I going to do about it? As I packed my Drygdal's saddle with my belongings, Gavin's light touch grazed my elbow, sending shivers up my spine.

"Are you alright?" he asked, his gaze holding such raw emotion. He raised his other hand to cup my injured cheek, his brows pulling in when I flinched at his touch.

"Yeah. I'm good," I replied with a small smile, unable to give him any further assurances. I'm sure he knew I lied, but I wasn't at liberty to tell him my nerves were frayed and on the brink of snapping. I couldn't share with him I had accepted my death twice today; how useless and powerless it made me feel to be at the mercy of waiting for help or accepting my fate.

How could airing such grievances possibly help anyone? I wouldn't be able to stand the pity on his face, as I had seen countless times with Kate and my brothers', should I divulge this truth to him.

He released his grip from my elbow, letting his hand flop towards his leg, as he nodded in understanding. During these intimate encounters we kept finding ourselves in is where he knew how to handle me best. He wouldn't pressure me for more information. He would let me internalize this all on my own, as I've done for years, while he stood by on the sidelines waiting for me to come to him.

I watched his retreating back, his shoulders slumped forward in defeat, feeling as if my heart would shatter more. If only he knew how much he stitched the fragments of my broken heart back together, his name embroidered on the scar tissue. How could I not fall in love with this man who only sought my best interest? In what ways could I prove to him, I needed him more than he could ever need me?

Chapter Twenty-one

Kartcher

<hr>

"I have been a seeker and I still am, but I stopped asking the books and the stars. I started listening to the teaching of my Soul. — Rumi

***

After a few hours' ride, the canopy of towering trees and imposing ferns gave way to expansive hillsides and deep valleys. Brilliant periwinkle grass waved in the wind like a sea of wheat, covering the ground as far as the eye could see. In the distance, snowcapped mountains towered on the horizon, adding to the chill in the air.

"That! there!" Kartcher shouted, pointing to a town growing at our fast approach. "That's where we are heading." Those words were sweet music to my ears. The ache in my legs was screaming, as was my bruised derriere, from the high charged ride of the Drygdal beneath me.

An obsidian stone plaque, with *Bellfall* scratched across the surface, welcomed us into this entrenched town; a foreshadowing of what we could expect upon entering. The Drygdals came to a screeching halt outside of the town's stables - luckily without any embarrassing incidences.

Ambling up to the stone gates, two guards in dilapidated chain-mail stood on either side of the entrance. Kartcher hardly paused as he flashed his badge to one of the guards, allowing us access.

Just who is Kartcher?

The buildings were small, two-story cottages, made of the same tenebrous stone as I'd seen earlier, each a carbon copy to the next. The bustling main street had vendors by the hundreds, peddling their wares and food.

Clothes were suspended on laundry lines from window to window of the second story buildings. I watched as two stout women across from each other tugged on the clothesline, screaming profanities over who had the next turn to use the line.

"Where are we?" Ryder asked, taking in the commotion above.

"Bellfall," Kartcher mumbled.

"The stench of our Kingdom," Avnor quipped.

"For once, I can't argue with you there," Gavin agreed.

The members of this society were as versatile and rugged as the ones in the tavern. A scantily clad woman, standing proud as she negotiated at an arms table, had the hands and feet of a lioness; her dark leopard markings peeking from beneath her half-clothed torso before extending down to her legs.

A tall, chiseled brute with a turned-up nose and distinguishable curved horns conversed with a shorter, prong-horned man with the lower body of a goat. There were women with wings and talking cats that stood on two legs.

It was a sight to behold, even more so because none of them ogled us like we were the outsiders that we were. Creatures from all walks of life entered this strange town that it didn't faze them in the slightest.

Kartcher stopped at a vendor's table with the oddest character of them all. Though he looked to be every bit a regular man - the oversized vermilion duster and multihued scarf being the most distinct thing he wore, he was anything but.

He stood in total concentration, holding a flame in his right hand while reading a book suspended in midair, mixing a flowing concoction that twirled about with embers of orange and purple with his left. As he sensed our presence, he snuffed out the fire and halted mixing his concoction. I watched the book fold close and place itself on the table before him.

"Ah! A Bentowin! It has been many a moon since I have seen your kind come down from the mountain. What do I owe the pleasure of your visit?" he asked, a sly smile playing up his deep mulberry eyes.

"I'm in search of something unique. From what I understand, you are just the man who can help me," Kartcher said.

"Well, you have come to the right place! Ruømra's unique enchantments and more," he said, animated. "How can I be of service to you?" With a big smile, he opened his hands wide, revealing a collection of illuminated weapons, tinctures, and scrolls before him on the table, which weren't there before.

"Hm," Kartcher said, his hand to his chin. "Unfortunately, it is nothing you have displayed here already," he glanced back and forth before leaning in. "I'm looking for something a little more - cagey."

"I see. Follow me this way," Ruømra said, his earlier theatrics becoming austere as he scanned his surroundings. When he turned, the wares he peddled vanished. The table split in two as he beckoned us to follow him into the cottage.

We entered a simple room; what you'd expect of a studio apartment. I wondered why he had us follow him in here until he folded one corner of the rug over, unveiling a hidden staircase.

Garrett and I exchanged glances, unsure of what we were about to walk into, but Kartcher seemed confident enough – so we followed his lead.

As we filed in, the rug flipped back over, encasing us in darkness, hiding Ruømra's hidden under-dwelling once again. At the end of the stairwell, a soft light cast under a closed door.

A momentary blindness swept over my vision as the door flew open to reveal the other side. Once my eyes adjusted, I could never have anticipated what had been waiting for us.

"Whoa," Ryder breathed. The room itself was bright and open, unlike the town above. That wasn't what caught my attention.

Books were flying in and out of their bookshelves, back and forth through the air of their own accord. Beakers and science sets of all sorts bubbled with different elixirs, some deep crimson like that of coagulated blood, others with an effervescent sparkle that created its own light. Even those too were operating without a physical hand.

Enchanted tables, foreign equipment, and the suspension of a galaxy swirling overhead only added to the allure of this room.

"Ruømra! What are you doing bringing strangers in here for?" a hoarse, accented voice hollered. Across the room, a petite woman with a bun of ashen hair had her back hunched to us, her hands flailing about as books and beakers sped back and forth to them.

"They said they are searching for something only we could provide. Something… what's the word? Ah, yes, cagey!" Ruømra exclaimed, snapping his fingers.

The woman halted her busy work and spun around, her speculative eyes bulging behind thick glasses. Though her expression was hardened, with deep lines etched from eyes to cheeks, her thin lips morphed into a toothless smile. "Kartcher! My old friend!"

"Selpats, it's been ages!" Kartcher said, matching her enthusiasm.

"It sure has. How long has it been? Four? Five hundred years?" she asked.

"Nine hundred and forty-eight, to be exact," he corrected, chuckling. My brothers and I exchanged widened stares.

Selpats laughed, pointing at him as she turned to put the suspended books away. "Ah, I knew you'd remember. Ever the timekeeper."

"I trust business has been well?" he asked, continuing the small talk.

"Not well enough. Not since the Maeshiren lost to that necrotic curse!" she exclaimed, her brows turning down in anger as she punched her fist into her other hand. A deep welling of guilt sank into the pit of my stomach. Somewhere down the line, I was seeing firsthand how we as Maeshiren failed our kingdom.

"That is why I am here, Selpats. I need an enchantment scroll only you can give – the Phoenix Quaerit Pugnare," Kartcher said, his tone darkening as he spoke of the scroll he sought after.

Selpats gasped, taking a step back, with her fists balled at her sides. "Oh Kartcher, you know I am forever in your debt, but whatever would you need that dreadful enchantment for?" Chills ran down my arms at her reaction. The only word I understood was the Phoenix. What significance it had; I couldn't be sure.

Gavin stepped to my side, putting his hand on my shoulder in comfort, as Kartcher waved his hand at my brothers and me. "These are the Maeshiren children, direct descendants of Daten, who have come to take their rightful place at the throne," he said.

Selpats turned to us with shock in her eyes, her mouth ajar, as she stepped closer for a better look. With her short stature, she stepped first to Garrett, then to Ryder, reaching up to grab their faces with one hand as she studied them from side to side. Then she turned to me, my five-foot four frame making me feel like a giant.

She scrutinized me as she had done with my brothers, except this time she brought her cold, dry hands to my cheek, pulling my face to her level. She stared into the depths of my eyes, whispering barely intelligible words, as the inner workings of her mind clicked into gear. Whatever she had seen, her eyes lit up and her breath caught.

"I will do it," she said, taking a step back, the reluctance of what she agreed to etched on her face.

"Thank you Selpats. I knew I could count on you," Kartcher said, relieved. I wasn't aware of how tense he had been before, but he visibly relaxed at her agreement.

"It will take some time. You all might as well fill your bellies and rest your souls. You have a long road ahead of you," she said, as she waved her hand in a sweeping motion to the right. The wall encased in bookshelves folded back and moved to the side, revealing a large room with multiple beds waiting for us.

"Ruømra, fetch them food and drink, then hurry back here so we can get started," she ordered.

"Yes, Selpats," Ruømra obliged, bowing before running up the stairs we came from.

"Thank you for the hospitality," I said. I wanted her to know how much we appreciated her helping us.

"Ehhhh," she drawled, dismissing us with a wave of her hand as she turned away to ready the scroll at one of the enchantment tables. I watched in amazement as we made our way to the bedchamber. Her animated hands sliced through the air as the supplies she needed flew from all around the room at her direction.

"C'mon Aurora," Kate said, pulling me out of my trance.

"Oh. Right," I replied, reluctant to follow the others.

It wasn't long after we settled in that Ruømra brought us a selection of various foods, buffet style. Multiple dishes followed him on thin air as his hands were occupied with a bowl of thick brown liquid.

"I brought you all nothing but the best that Bellfall has to offer. Dry-roasted marsh sheep, steamed fluffy muskrat, Midindu bread, and crown savory surprise! I even hunted down some Whimsical Delight - a hard drink to come by around here. I hope you are all hungry!" he exclaimed, setting everything down on a table in the middle of the room. My stomach churned at some of the offerings.

"Thank you, Ruømra. We appreciate the hospitality," Kartcher said, bowing his head.

"The pleasure is all mine. If you'll excuse me, I must assist Selpats," he said, backing out of the room before shutting the bookcase wall back in on us.

"Well, let's dig in," Kate said, her nose scrunched as she made her way to the table.

"What's that?" I asked, pointing to the brown gravy Ruømra had been holding.

"That would be the crown savory surprise," Gavin said behind me, his voice queasy.

"Do I even want to know why it's called that?" I asked, my face scrunching at their apparent unease at the options.

"Not if you want to eat," he said, exchanging a wide-eyed glance with me. Just then, my stomach growled in protest; it was hungry. I dared to try a bit of everything, only placing small portions of each item on my plate.

The only edible item I could stand was the Midindu bread; slightly sweet and melted in my mouth like cotton candy. Everything else was questionable.

Though I knew I should eat, as this may be the last hot civilized meal we would have in some time, I couldn't bring myself to finish the food.

"Bleh!" Ryder said as he spit out his drink. "What the hell is that?"

"That's the Whimsical Delight. A true delicacy in this region," Kartcher explained, laughing.

"True delicacy, my ass. It tastes like bitter gym socks," he said in disgust. I eyed the sparkling, bubbly drink in my chalice and thought twice about trying it.

"You gonna eat that?" Garrett asked, eyeing my plate.

"No. You want it?" I asked with skepticism.

"Sure!" he said, snatching my plate from me. I watched with mortification as he shoveled the unappetizing food into his mouth.

"You like this stuff?" I asked, surprised and slightly disgusted.

"Not one bit, but I'm starving," he said, taking another monster bite of the dry-roasted marsh sheep. I glanced over at everyone else finishing up their plates - except for Kate. She looked at Garrett with disgust, too.

"So how do you know Selpats, Kartcher?" I asked, the need for wanting to know more about him overshadowing any reservation I may have had about prying.

"Oh, Selpats and I go way back," he smiled. "When I left my duty at the Valdöllen gates, I did so to fulfill a more important duty - to be a part of the protection guard of Reinard," he said, dipping his muskrat in the crown savory surprise. My eyebrows shot up at this admission. It spoke to how old Kartcher really was.

"Back then, Selpats was the top enchantress for Reinard. She fitted his armor with protection enchantments, among many other things. Due to the nature of our work, we were often in close contact during that time," he finished explaining.

"Wait, you knew Reinard?" I asked, astonished. "What was he like?" I was eager to learn about the type of man my great grandfather had been.

Kartcher had a ghost of a smile as his eyes took on a distant aura. "He was a powerful warrior but also a man of great peace. He didn't seek the glories of war, always putting his kingdom's people before his own needs. He was a worthy king to follow and fight alongside."

The way he venerated Reinard made me both happy and sad. Reinard sounded like one who was respected and was to be respected; it was a great comfort to know he was a good man.

On the other side of it, though, it made me miss a man I would never have the chance to meet. If he were here now, this war – and this world, for that matter - would probably be at peace. It did nothing to settle my nerves about us taking the throne back in his place. It appeared we had some big shoes to fill.

I glanced up at Gavin, sensing his gaze from across the room. He gave me a tight, comforting smile – his eyes swimming in compassion. Could he feel the duality of my emotions?

"Why did Selpats call you a *timekeeper* earlier?" Kate asked.

"Us Bentowins have excellent recall. For as many thousands of years we live, we can tell you exact times and events we have lived through," he said nonchalantly. "Selpats and I joke that I am like a living time capsule and so, she nicknamed me timekeeper."

"That's it?" Kate asked, clearly not impressed. "I hoped for something much juicier than that."

"Sorry to disappoint you Kate," Kartcher gently chuckled.

"Earlier, you said you left your duty to serve Reinard. What did you do before that?" Garrett asked.

"Where we are about to go is where my origins begin. I

haven't been there for over a millennium," he shook his head, crestfallen. "What you will learn about this kingdom is it's fragmented into factions of secret societies – some meant for protection, others with their own agendas in mind. My society is a secretive one with the incredible charge of protecting the gates of Valdöllen," he explained.

"Valdöllen?" I questioned.

"Yes, the place where we will ask my people to allow us to gain access. We take our charge very serious, and so we will no doubt be met with some hostility. It is imperative you do not engage them. Not only will it be a most certain death for every one of us, but it will guarantee access being denied if we miraculously manage to not get killed," Kartcher warned us.

The atmosphere in the room grew heavy, the realization of what we signed up for dawning on many of us for the first time. "What is beyond the gates of Valdöllen?" I asked.

"The answers you seek," he answered.

"And what are those?" Garrett asked.

"That is for you three to find out when you arrive there. I am not at liberty to divulge such secrets, for there are ears and eyes everywhere we turn," he said.

"What made you leave such a highly regarded position, then?" Avnor asked, breaking his silence.

"Reinard came to us requesting entrance into Valdöllen. When he found our favor, his request was granted. It wasn't long before he came back, sharing with us the formal decree for one of us to serve as his close protective guard.

As I have said, we take our charge seriously and close to heart - so all stayed quiet. I felt the higher calling to serve and so I came forth, for both Reinard and to relieve my fellow Bentowins of such a decision," Kartcher stated with pride. Though he had taken that call with a heavy heart, he also seemed to have made peace with that choice.

"If the Bentowins know you and your great deeds, why is it we need this enchanted scroll from Selpats?" I asked, confused. Though his past is something to behold, his earlier warning didn't rest well on my heavy heart.

"The Phoenix Quaerit Pugnare," he sighed. "That scroll isn't for them, it is for you — to present it as an offering once we can get past the Valdöllen gates."

"An offering? For what?" I asked.

"I'm fairly certain you will find out once we are there. First things first, we must make it through the badlands and then find favor with my people," he said. I didn't like how he danced around answering our questions out right. Why let us walk into this blind?

"What is the deal with the badlands? What can we expect?" Gavin asked. The calculated, militant expression he wore showed he didn't like the shifting variables any more than I did.

"Valdöllen is situated on the other side of the badlands for a reason. They are treacherous and few make it out alive. They are meant to deter those who would otherwise seek to cause problems for us. This town, Bellfall, is the closest most will ever get to the Valdöllen gates, as this is the last stop before heading into the badlands," Kartcher said, every ear captivated by his every word.

I scanned across the sea of faces of those I loved and cared for. A part of me didn't want to continue down this path. Not for my sake, but for the sake of not risking the potential loss of anyone I loved. I knew it was wrong. I felt this way only for selfish reasons, but I couldn't help the way I felt, could I?

"So that's it then? We subject ourselves to a high chance of death over a stupid council who seeks our demise? Why can't we go take the throne as is?" Garrett asked, angered.

"With you and what army?" Kate asked, rolling her eyes.

"As of this moment, you do not have the authority. You have a *possible* birthright that proves nothing. That isn't just to the High Council; it's also to many of this kingdom. They will not accept you without proper authority."

"And who is to give us proper authority?" Garrett spat back with just as much annoyance as Kate.

"Why do you think we are going through the hassle of all of this in the first place?" she asked, throwing up her hands.

Garrett stared at her, angered and dumfounded.

"To go claim you authority, dumbass!" Kate said, irate.

"That still doesn't answer my question, Katernius," Garrett barked out, irritation oozing from his core.

"Did you not hear what Kartcher said? We will all find out when we get there. Why do you always have to make things so difficult?" she grunted, as she threw her hands up once more.

"Excuse me for wanting more clarity instead of walking into this blind. I have more questions than answers," he said, annoyed.

"Welcome to the club," I agreed.

"Some things will have to be revealed in due time, Garrett. Patience is of utmost concern at this point," Kartcher replied, diffusing the situation. Garrett grumbled before crossing his arms in front of his chest and huffed – such a child.

We settled into an uncomfortable silence as tensions rose with the mounting stress. Despite the dread weighing down upon me, Ryder found a way to take the edge off.

"So Kartcher, why exactly didn't those villagers want you in their bar last night?" he asked.

Kartcher's chuckle broke the tension before his expression turned sheepish. "It seems Sülgrav has just as long a memory as us Bentowins," he grumbled under his breath before lifting his eyes abashed. "I may or may not have burnt down their entire village by mistake."

My eyes widened at the ridiculousness of him ever doing such a thing. "You what?" I choked.

"It was an accident. You see, I was clumsy back in the day. I had never been down from our reclusive mountain before and wasn't keen to the ways this Kingdom worked. Reinard and I stopped at the first inn that had been there. He wanted to have a celebratory Storm Honey Ale the region is known for. As I had never had a drop of the delightful elixir before, I had become disoriented and combative," he said, shaking his head in shame.

"How was I to know when I flung that man across the room, he would land on the table of lanterns?" he asked out to no one.

"It became a chain reaction. From table to table, each lantern exploded. Everyone trampled over each other trying to escape. With my shield, I tried to push the fire away from them, but in my disoriented state, I ended up bouncing the flaming tables into the wall of alcohol behind the bar." He buried his head in his hands at his confession.

"Thankfully, everyone made it out okay. The inn went up in a pyre. Back then, the village was much bigger and condensed. Buildings were closer, the fire jumped, and the water bringers weren't fast enough. The entire village went up in smoke. They all turned on me and blamed the Bentowins as a whole, as they had never seen us come out of our secretive society. They banished any Bentowin from ever entering their village again, though Reinard sent a relief squadron to help with the damages," he continued to mumble into his hands.

"It is the greatest mistake of my life. I was so afraid of Reinard being angry with me and sending me back. To my shock, he laughed his big, bellied laugh and said, 'whelp, looks like no more alcohol for you' as he slapped me on the back," Kartcher chuckled, lifting his head to us gawking at him.

He stared back at us, a blush coming to his reptilian cheeks.

"Wow, learn something new about you all the time, Kartcher. Tough break," Gavin laughed. "I wish you would have told us that *before* we walked in there."

"I didn't think they would have remembered. It had been so long ago. I haven't been there in ages," Kartcher admitted. "Besides, I was craving the Storm Honey Ale."

"Seems like you were wrong," Gavin said, still chuckling.

"So it seems," Kartcher replied, chuckling with him.

The sound of the bookshelves opening pulled our attentions away from the light banter. Ruømra stepped through the opening with the animated smile he always had plastered to his face. "Selpats is finished and would like to see you all." He turned on his heel, his shaggy blonde hair bouncing as he walked back into the laboratory.

"That was fast," Kate said, sticking out her bottom lip as her brows shot up in surprise.

We filed into the laboratory where Selpats stood at the edge of a long table. Lying amongst the surface were furs of many colors, weapons, elixirs and the scroll Kartcher had asked for.

"Kartcher, for the journey that lies before you, you must be well equipped," she started, walking over to the various furs.

"Where you are going will be mighty cold. You all are not dressed for such a climate," she said, "So I had Ruømra fetch me the finest furs this town offers. I have outfitted them with a protection enchantment. Don't rely on them, as they are there only to provide you with some elementary level of help. They are *not* armor!"

She first handed a dark gray fur to Kartcher, who didn't hesitate to put it on. It hung heavily over his shoulders, stopping before it reached the ground. "It is lovely Selpats. You have truly outdone yourself."

"You don't need to butter me up," Selpats laughed, blushing. She then handed us all our own furs.

I immediately pushed my arms through the deep auburn coat. The thick hood hid my eyes but didn't alter my vision. I glanced over at Gavin, pulling his coat closer to his face. A shallow gasp escaped my lips, the dark fur bringing out the deep green in his eyes. *How could I find him even sexier under a heavy fur coat?*

I dropped my gaze, blushing, the moment his eyes shifted to mine.

Kate's white hooded coat tapered in at the sides, while Ryder's brown and Garrett's yellow coats fit wide for their broad shoulders. I was amazed at how Selpats could figure the perfect sizes and cuts without fitting us.

"Katernius, I have fashioned you a new, upgraded bow and arrow," she said, handing a wide-eyed Kate a white and gold bow with arrows that swirled with silver patterns down their length.

"They're beautiful," Kate said, admiring her new weapon. It surprised me Kate didn't correct Selpats about her preferred name, but I had a feeling the beauty of the gift trumped that.

"You will be able to fire at longer ranges. Whether or not you miss your target, I have fashioned your arrows to always come back to you - like a boomerang. These are lethal and unlike anything you have experienced before," Selpats stared at her to relay the seriousness of her statement. Kate nodded in understanding.

"Maeshiren children, it is my understanding you are walking around unarmed. Not a smart thing to do in this kingdom. I have fashioned all three of you with new, enchanted swords. These are unique in that they will form only to your individual powers, which you no doubt all have," she said, handing each of us a silver sword with the blade down and two fingers holding the handle.

As I wrapped my hand around the grip, a surge of energy travelled through my arm and back down into the blade, illuminating the silver metal into a swirling array of colors. "Whoa," my eyes widened as I watched the blade go back to its earlier silvery form.

I moved the blade back and forth in the light, seeing a rising phoenix stamped into the center of the blade. *What did this Phoenix mean?* I turned to my brothers, who were as shocked as I was when they grabbed their blades.

"Whoa is right. Your swords are now bonded to you. The energy flowing through them will answer to only you. This means they will cut for only you. Should they be stolen, or otherwise lost from your possession, it will always find a way back to you. Maybe not as fast as Katernius's arrows, but eventually they will," she chuckled.

"Thank you," I breathed, still staring wide eyed at my blade before looking up at her.

"Don't mention it, kid," she dismissed, turning away from me, though I had seen her cheek turn up just a tad.

"Gavin, I know how partial you are to your curvies," she said.

"My curvies?" he questioned, giving her a dubious expression.

"Yes. The blades you are concealing underneath your cloak," she said, as if it were common knowledge.

Gavin's eyebrows shot up as his eyes went wide. "How did you know about those?"

"What do you take me for? A fool? I know many things, young man. Now lay them out here for me if you will," she gestured towards an enchanted table, scooting across the room towards us. I don't think I will ever be able to get used to inanimate objects moving of their own free will.

Gavin did as she asked, laying them side by side on the table. As he did, the table flashed a brilliant prism of light. Again, I watched in amazement as Selpats worked her incredible magic.

Her hands animated in the air as she brought forth the elixirs on the table and a scroll from one of her cabinets. She laid the scroll over the blades; the paper stretched out, as she mumbled over each elixir being poured over the scroll – the table flashing with each addition to the weapons.

Once she finished, she removed the scroll, revealing the blades that were nothing like their former selves. They had transformed from dull, scratched metal to a high polished black agate color. In multiple lines, along the center of the blades, were matching crimson markings in a foreign language.

"Your old blades were almost broken. When was the last time you replaced them?" she chided, not giving him a chance to answer. "That's beside the point. You will see the blades match your red eyes when you go berserk. These will not slow you down. You will find they are lighter, faster, and will help you focus the fire within into these blades." Gavin stared at her as if she had two heads. Who was this woman who knew everyone so well?

"And Kartcher, here is the Phoenix Quaerit Pugnare you requested. I trust it is in excellent hands with you," she nodded with a severe stare as she handed it over to him.

Kartcher snatched it and had it under his coat so fast, I wasn't sure I had seen it happen. "I will guard it with my life."

"Good," she said, pleased. "And Avnor, don't think I have forgotten about you, the scoundrel of the guard." Avnor stood towards the back of our group, ever silent unless he tried to order us to submit to his will. He perked up at his name being called.

"Come forward," she said with watchful eyes as he complied. She placed a seal on his breastplate. "This is also a protection seal for you. It will be strong as it reinforces the fibers of your armors precious metal. No sword will pierce through. Make sure you cover your neck, though," she said. As she turned away, grief marred her face. I remembered Kate's story of Reinard's death. I wondered if this had kept Selpats from continuing her work with the guard.

"I believe you are all as well-equipped as you can be," she said, turning around with her hands on her hips. A smug expression of a job well done plastered on her face.

"I don't know how I can ever thank you enough," Kate said in awe of her, squeezing her bow and arrows to her chest.

"Yes. Same here. Thank you so very much," Ryder said, holding his sword out in front of him. When he turned it just right for the light, I had seen an owl etched onto the blade where I had a phoenix, holding the weights of justice in its claws. *What did they represent?*

"Selpats, you have gone above and beyond what I came here to ask of you. How much do we owe you? How can we repay you?" Kartcher asked, pleading with her to allow him to reimburse her.

"Ehhhh," she scoffed. "It feels good to be of service to the Maeshiren once more. You can repay me by paying back that wretched Braeden with dirt and worms." Her expression turned severe.

That name, the one Gavin told me about, was the *necrotic curse* she spoke of earlier? Deep inside, I felt the sense of duty to serve and make this right. It was our duty as Maeshiren to keep the peace. It was now our duty to end this great injustice.

"You have our word," Gavin said, the strength of his promise ending with a tone of finality.

"You all should find rest; I will not keep you any longer. You have a long road ahead of you," Selpats said.

"Actually, we will be taking our leave now. Time is of the essence," Kartcher stated with reluctance. This was news to me; we hadn't discussed it.

"I understand. In that case, these are also for you," Selpats said, reaching down on the floor to hand us our packs. "I refreshed them with sustenance you will find appetizing."

My face flushed, as she must have known how much we didn't care for the food Ruømra brought us earlier. Sure enough, my pack was full of food I had never seen before. I could only pray for my future self they would taste good.

"Thank you Selpats! It has been nourishing to my soul to see you after so long," Kartcher said, smiling at her.

"As it has mine," she smiled back, lost in his eyes. I felt like we were intruding on something between them, which made it uncomfortable. Gavin cleared his throat rather obviously, breaking their connection.

"Right. Well, we must be on our way," Kartcher said, bowing to Selpats and Ruømra.

"Don't be a stranger," Selpats laughed as we made our way to the exit.

"I won't," Kartcher said with a promising smile over his shoulder.

"C'mon lover boy," Gavin said, hooking his arm around his neck before pushing him forward up the stairs. Loud snickers from us all had Kartcher blushing as we made our way up the stairs.

Chapter Twenty-two

The Gates of Valdöllen

"The things that are most valuable are often the ones you don't even know exist." – Xavier, The Gatekeeper

***

I suppose I should tell you now that we will be moving forward on foot," Kartcher said once we stepped out of the cottage.

"What?" my brothers and I shouted in unison.

"The badlands are no place for Drygdal's. I have paid the stable hands here to take care of them for as long as we will be gone for," he explained.

"Wonderful," Garrett whined, rolling his eyes as he threw his head back.

"No sense in crying about it. Let's get moving," Kate said, patting him on the backside.

The sun kissed the horizon by the time we were out of the town's limits. For the first time, I found myself missing the Drygdal's fast travel. Replacing the sun were the now familiar two moons, shining bright in the sky as they cast a celestial glow that lit the way.

"How long until we are there?" Ryder asked, focusing on his sword's details.

"Roughly two hours. We will make camp at the base, so we are well rested," Kartcher replied.

"You keep walking and staring at that thing, you're going to fall and skewer yourself," Kate chided. Ryder glanced at her like she was a school-marm.

"Does this marking here mean anything?" I asked, pointing to the phoenix on my blade.

"They are indicative of your powers and nature. When our weapons fuse with our abilities, symbols are etched into them by default. For instance, if you'll look here on my bow. An Ice Hawk is etched on the handle," Kate said, pointing to the symbol that held such detail in the beauty of its deep lines.

It held its wings out high and wide, each feather coming to a sharp icy point. In its talons were two arrows crossing each other in the front. Behind the intricate etching lay a multifaceted prism with mismatched edges, giving it a three-dimensional layer.

"How does that represent you?" I asked.

"I'm a long-range attacker, as are hawks until they're forced into close range combat. I'm light on my feet and can attack from above. That's my nature," she explained.

"And your power?" Garrett asked.

"I'm an elemental. I can manipulate water, but my strength is ice," she said, proud of her capabilities.

"So that explains why you can be such a frigid bitch," Garrett laughed. Kate didn't find his little comment amusing until she encased his feet in ice, making him fall forward. The plants around him deadened from the water leached from them.

"Want to say that again?" she laughed as she walked by him.

Garrett seethed.

"Cool your tits. She's toying with you," Gavin chuckled, as his hands melted the ice to set Garrett free. I gaped at him as what Selpats said sank in, '*you will be able to focus the fire from within into these blades*'. Gavin glanced from underneath his long lashes, his sheepish charm sending my heart into a fury.

"So, what's your symbol?" I asked, inwardly cringing at the flirtatious tone in my voice. I ignored the others' scrutinizing stares. He stood up from his crouch, not taking his sultry eyes from mine, as he pulled one of his blades out from underneath his cloak.

"A fire raven," he said, his voice low and thick, gauging my reaction based on this sudden revelation. I dropped my eyes to a crimson raven at the top center of the blade, engulfed in flames. My fingers twitched to touch the hardened metal, but I willed my hand to stay in place, balling it into a fist.

"It's beautiful," I whispered, looking up at him, still staring at me, the tightening of his eyes growing softer.

"Well, does anyone want to know what mine is?" Garrett asked, breaking our connection.

"No," Gavin replied, turning to give Garrett an annoyed eye roll before walking past him. Garrett stared at me with mouth agape and hurt in his eyes.

"Sure Garrett, why don't you show me?" I said, bumping into him as I strolled by his side.

"Thank you, Aurora. At least *someone* appreciates me around here," he hollered up at everyone else.

"Oh, shut up and show me your sword," I said, smiling. He held it out so I could get a good look. In the same position as mine, a wolf with four bushy tails sat on its haunches, its head held high with an air of regality.

"I wonder what it means," I said, curious.

"Beats me. It's pretty awesome though," he said, as he took

a slash in the air. "It's light too!"

"Don't let yourselves be separated from the group," Kartcher scolded. We didn't realize we were trailing behind them a ways. We jogged to catch up.

"We are getting close to the badlands. The closer we are, the more dangerous it becomes. Stay close," Kartcher scolded. We both nodded with our heads down, feeling reprimanded.

Up ahead, the hills inclined, a dull arctic light illuminated from behind their ridges in the darkness of night.

"We will make camp here," Kartcher said, pointing to a field off the trail. There were no trees or tall ferns for assassins to ambush us, which was comforting.

"Don't let your guard down. Enemies lurk everywhere," Kartcher warned.

"Safe feeling gone," I huffed as I dropped my bag.

"What's wrong?" Kate asked, puzzled.

"Can't we ever catch a break? Do we always have to watch our backs everywhere we go?" I asked, exasperated.

"Welcome to the joys of being royalty. Highly suspected ones at that," Kate replied, sour and remorseful, as she dropped her own bag in the same manner.

"Don't worry, after a while, you'll get used to it," she said, irate.

"I don't want to get used to it," I pouted.

"You don't have a choice. As long as you're alive, there will always be those who oppose you, who'll be jealous of you, and who will want you dead by their own hands. Comes with the territory," she said as she rolled out her flat. "The only thing to do is get strong, stay strong, and outwit your enemies. It's a deadly game."

Overhearing our conversation, Ryder gave me a somber smile. With how fast everything had happened, I never spoke to my brothers about any of this. I wonder how they were taking everything.

Settling in, I reached into my pack - starved. I reluctantly pulled out a box with the words *Moonridge pie* written across the top. Inside, a slice of dessert with reflective turquoise frosting revealed itself sitting perfectly upright, undisturbed by our trek here. Secured under the center of the lid, a golden fork fit for royalty. Selpats thought of everything.

The golden utensil sank into the soft, decadent frosting, exposing the deep cherry hue of the moist interior. With hesitancy from the remembered *delicacies* of Bellfall, I warily brought a piece to my mouth. *"Please let this be as good as it looks,"* I pleaded to myself.

I closed my eyes as I wrapped my lips around this mysterious delight. Sweet ecstasy enveloped my taste buds as the delicious complexity burst forth inside my mouth. Exquisite as a perfectly baked chocolate cake with pecans and strawberries, swirled with a hint of caramel and sea salt. The reflective frosting light and airy, like that of slightly heavier whipped cream. I cherished every morsel like I had died and gone to heaven. *Thank you Selpats!*

Opening my eyes in search of another bite, Gavin sat on his flat next to mine – his eyes shining bright with excitement. Heat rushed through to my center at the seductive allure of his gaze. His lips curled up with the charming smile I loved so much, as his gaze turned sheepish at being caught witnessing my moment of pure bliss. "Is that any good?"

"As if you couldn't tell," I said with a flirtatious grin, looking at him from under my lashes. He choked at my forwardness, grinning wide.

"Touché," he said, turning back to his food; both of our cheeks flushed with the charged energy between us. I glanced up at the others, but no one paid any attention to our little moment.

Relief rushed through me as I thanked God for *that* little break.

"Everyone, get some rest. I need you to be sharp and alert. Tomorrow, we enter the pits of hell," Kartcher said, foreboding.

"Because that'll let everyone sleep well," Kate said. I could hear her eyes rolling inside her head.

"Well… I… Um… Oh never mind," Kartcher said, giving up as he realized his mistake.

I settled in the best I could; every inch of my body was sore and heavy from the long journey we had endured over the past few days. If my swollen, bloodshot eyes were any indication of this, sleep was creeping around the corner.

A bitter chill crept into my bones, leaving me shivering in a tight ball in the corner of a dark, damp chamber. The smell of mildew strong; I couldn't see much beyond the light of one small torch hanging off the wall towards the room's center. Somewhere, water dripped into a puddle, echoing off the chamber's walls.

Where am I? It's as if I had blacked out for the entire event leading to this point.

"Hello?" my hoarse voice echoed across the room with teeth chattering. Still, I was met with more silence. Some way, somehow, someone had put me in here.

Reaching my hand to grab onto the wall, I wrenched it back, the slick wetness catching me by surprise. I fast realized why the stench of mildew was sharp; it covered the wall next to me.

Helping myself to stand, I made my way towards the only source of heat in the room. The torch had been positioned low enough that if I stood on my toes, I could possibly reach it. I stretched from tiptoe to fingertip, extending my body as long as it would go; my fingers inches from purchasing the icy steel handle.

In a last-ditch effort, I jumped, grabbing the handle and wrenched it down, almost dropping it in the process. Thankfully, I held onto it, pulling it towards my chest. I closed my eyes in euphoric relief as my body enveloped around the fire as much as it dared.

My eyes adjusted to the flickering light bouncing across the room as I opened them, bringing to focus a large pile of something I couldn't quite make out. With a trembling step forward, I reluctantly held my heat source out in front of me as I inspected closer.

Terror seized my chest as I staggered back. The pile comprised of bodies, some bloated, others in a further state of decomposition. The smell of rotting flesh assaulted my nose the moment I recognized what it was, my hand covering my mouth to both keep the smell out and the rising bile in.

I clenched my eyes shut, willing it to go away. When I reopened them, the pile had not vanished. Instead, their faces became more prominent. A sob bubbled to the surface before I screamed out in terror. The bodies before me were that of my family. Not just my parents and Tanner, but Garrett's and Ryder's as well.

At the top of the pile, Kate and Kartcher lay lifeless beneath Gavin's outstretched body, his head hanging back with eyes rolled into his head. I screamed louder than before, dropping the only source of light I held, enveloping the room into total darkness.

"Aurora! Aurora, wake up!" Gavin yelled, shaking me awake. His eyes bore down on me in a panic. I sat straight up, narrowly head-butting him in the face, as sweat poured down my temples. My eyes were wild as everyone I loved sat up from their flats, staring at me. Shaking, I gulped trying to quench the arid desert in my throat.

They were alive.

It was just a nightmare.

I let out a shaky breath, my eyes streaming with tears. Gavin engulfed me into his protective arms, trying to soothe away the demons from my sleep. It had been so real. I couldn't even tell I was dreaming.

"Shh, it was a dream. It wasn't real," he cooed, as I sobbed into his chest, his hand brushing my hair down my back. My fists clenched his shirt, pulling him in that much closer. I wanted to stay in his arms forever, just so I would never have to experience that again. Just so I knew he was alive.

"You okay, Aurora?" Ryder asked from beside me as Gavin released his hold. I wiped the tears away from my face, nodding in response, though the reality of that nightmare was still fresh.

"You want to talk about it?" he asked, concerned.

I shook my head no. "That's okay Ry. It was just a nightmare." I lifted my head to the others, still giving me a wary look.

"As we step closer to the gates of Valdöllen, we are susceptible to outside forces due to the higher vibrations in the atmosphere. This is especially true for those who have a higher sensitivity to those vibratory channels. Dreams and nightmares are not an exception to this," Kartcher explained.

He continued, "You must guard your thoughts, your fears, and even your dreams. If you don't, it will become sustenance for the wraiths."

"What's a wraith?" I asked through my tears.

"Specters attracted to negative thoughts and emotions. They hungrily seek to devour fear and can smell it with the bloody sharpness of a shark. Do not let your guard down, they are relentless, and will hunt you," Kartcher replied.

"Okay, well, with that bit of *great* news, I'm sure you have eased everybody's fears and anxiety," Kate chimed in.

"Better to be informed than dead," Kartcher replied.

I glanced at Gavin's pained expression, his brows drawn in with his hand partially stretched out like he was preparing to run away with me, and from the source of my nightmares. Instead, he dropped his hand.

"You were terrified," he stated, as he peered into my eyes. I stayed silent, nodding my head.

"But you don't want to talk about it," he deadpanned.

"No," I croaked. He closed his eyes with a heavy sigh before nodding.

"It's first light. We should head out," Kartcher said softly.

"Okay," Gavin said as he stood, his mouth set into a grim line that belayed his unease. As always, he didn't push, and he didn't pry. Instead, he began rolling up his bed, his shoulders set in the rigidity of his stress.

At that, we cleared camp with no one saying a word.

A heavy, low-lying mist bordered the entrance into the badlands. Bare, ghastly trees with expansive branches dotted the frozen tundra to the ascending sawtooth mountains. Not a sound could be heard, save for the thrashing of the glacial wind. Everything in this deadened forest seemed to be devoid of all life.

"Isn't there another way?" Avnor asked, hesitancy dripping in his tone.

"The only way to is through, I'm afraid," Kartcher said, facing the badlands entrance.

"If you're afraid, you can always run back to your *masters*," Gavin taunted with a side eye towards Avnor.

"Who says I'm afraid? It just seems perilous for the Maeshiren children, is all."

"Right," Gavin said, rolling his eyes.

"As we enter, please keep in mind, guard your thoughts and stay sober minded. It is easy to allow yourself to be tricked in the mist. If a wraith comes for you, strike down your fear. Think of only the path before you, not the dangers surrounding you," Kartcher said.

"And how are we to do that?" Garrett asked.

"Easy. If you see them, pay them no mind. They will not harm you or hunt you if you show no fear. That is what they feed on most," he said.

"And what do they feed on least?" Ryder asked.

"Apathy."

"Wonderful," Ryder said.

"Gavin," Kartcher called out.

"Yeah?"

"Keep a lid on your anger. They feed on that as much as fear," he said over his shoulder.

"Duly noted," he replied, indifferent.

"Oh, and one more thing before we go," Kartcher said, turning back to us. "There are traps set throughout the trail. Watch where you step."

"This just keeps on getting better," Kate sighed.

"Let's go," Kartcher said, leading the pack.

Entering the mist felt like walking into an ominous, headless horseman scenario. We could only see enough of the trail and what lay just beyond it. Anything past that, the mist thickened, turning the trees into shapeless shadows.

"Anyone else creeped out?" Ryder asked.

"Control your mind, Ryder," Kartcher admonished.

"I'm trying," he said, taking in a deep breath.

Slow movement ahead caught my attention as an obscure shadow moved through the shrouded trees, its lifeless form floating closer. Skeletal hands, peeking from beneath its tattered diatonic rags, became pronounced.

Holding my breath, I focused every thought on releasing it slowly. I dropped my gaze to the ground, knowing if I were to see any more of the wraith, I wouldn't be able to control my emotions. I could not think, nor could I pray. I could only will myself to act as devoid as the form floating by us. Without incident, I peeked back, watching as the wraith became one with the mist.

"Whew. That was close," Avnor said.

"We are not out of the woods yet," Kartcher said with tight lips.

As the path ascended the mountain, so did my nerves.

A wooden pike stood at attention to the side of the trail — a frozen corpse suspended through his chest high into the air. These must be the traps Kartcher spoke of.

No one made a noise to comment, though everyone glanced at the corpse's terror-stricken face. His eyes were frozen open with the panic he had endured before he took his final breath. His lower mandible hung loose, half ripped from his face, hanging in place by the frozen flesh still attached. I turned away, feeling the welling of fear for the safety of those with me.

Gavin's hand rested at the small of my back, startling me enough to jump. His wordless expression told me to calm down. *He's here. No matter what happened, we will get through this.* I nodded my head, turning my attention forward. I couldn't allow myself to feel anything, even for Gavin.

The arctic wind became fierce the higher we ascended. Once again, I found myself thanking Selpats for the gifts she bestowed upon us. Though I could still feel the sting of the chill trying to seep into my bones, the thick fur kept it at bay.

Materializing out of the mist, a large concentration of lifeless wraiths patrolled, swaying back and forth as they grazed the ground they floated above. Seeing one was alarming enough. Seeing a group of eight was damn near frightening.

We continued to push forward, as we had done earlier, focused on making it past them alive. These were much closer to us than the last, their frosty aura brushing against our mortal flesh. The mental focus became excruciating with the overwhelming urge to run, but I stayed my ground.

A single wraith gravitated out of formation from the rest, turning its hooded head to one side, then the next, as it drifted closer to us. With a slight lift of its head, it sniffed at the air behind me.

"Avnor, control yourself," Gavin said, tight-lipped through clenched teeth.

"I'm trying," he responded.

With a cautious glance over my shoulder, I watched as the wraith singled him out, sniffing at the base of his neck and running its hollowed nose along his cheek. Never did the wraith let up as we were walking, floating at the same speed as we dared to trek. Avnor let out a murmur.

The wraith wrenched back as it fully lifted its head. Its hollowed eyes burned bright as it shrilled into the sky, calling for the attention of the others drifting by it.

"Run!" Kartcher yelled.

Panic coursed through me as adrenaline commandeered my brain. My feet couldn't dig deep enough as they propelled me forward. I glanced back at all eight wraiths hot on our trail, screeching along the way. They were calling the attention of any wraiths within the vicinity. Soon, more entered the fray.

"Keep going," Kartcher hollered over his shoulder, the lactic acid torching my legs with each stride.

The ground rumbled as a pike pierced up through the ground, missing Garrett by a hair.

Terror gripped my chest at the near fatal miss. My adrenaline spiked higher.

"Watch where you step!" Kartcher yelled out, spinning at the last second around another pike shooting up in front of him.

"What was that?" Gavin yelled back, smirking.

I glanced behind us once more, the eight wraiths had grown to thirteen. "Shit," I breathed.

The stress on Avnor's face dripped with sweat. His movements became stiffer as he began slowing down.

"Avnor, keep going! You can't slow down!" I screamed at him; his terror-stricken eyes zoned in on me.

Gavin yanked my arm towards himself as a pike shot up where I had been running, my arm smacking against its splintered edge. I cried out in both surprise and pain, as slivered wood intertwined into the thin flesh of my forearm.

"Keep going. Stop looking back," Gavin admonished, releasing me. I didn't reply.

"Get to that canyon," Kartcher yelled back at us, pointing to a break in the mountainside. I began feeling the effects of being hunted, my legs becoming heavier now that we had a destination in sight.

The screaming of the thirteen wraiths grew stronger as the number of impaled, lifeless bodies littering the area became abundant.

Close to the opening of the canyon, I turned to see the wraiths within reach of Avnor's slowing figure.

"Avnor hurry!" I screamed.

A pike discharged from the ground, catching him in the torso and piercing through his back. I froze in horror as the thirteen wraiths descended on him, ripping the grey essence of his soul from his body while leaving his flesh intact.

Like a pack of hyena's ripping flesh from bone, they ripped

his soul apart, piece by torturous piece. Never did Avnor have a chance of making a sound. Instead, I screamed in terror for him, distraught at such a demise.

The wraiths, already finished with their soul-snack, turned to their next meal – me. They rushed forward with hungry eyes, eager to satiate their hunger. I couldn't move, I could only stare.

Gavin and Garrett grabbed me from behind, pulling me past the entrance of the canyon, as Kartcher hurled a prismatic force shield to block the canyon's entrance.

We watched on the other side as the wraiths stopped in their tracks, no longer sensing our presence. They went back to the lifeless forms they once were, swaying back and forth above the ground, scouring the forest for their next unfortunate meal.

Tears streamed down my face as I stood staring at the now lifeless Avnor; the terror in his eyes a permanent impression etched into my brain. This wasn't right. If it hadn't been for the High Council, Avnor would never have been serving such a corrupt leadership that had him meet such an end.

Or, if I were to take the blame upon myself - if the Maeshiren had never been defeated, this would have never happened. Somewhere along the lines, we failed. Avnor impaled before me stands as a representative for that failure.

I sniffled, roughly wiping the tears away from my eyes, and turned towards the others.

"Avnor may have been a lot of things, but this," I said, turning towards him with a hand extended out. "He didn't deserve this."

"He deserved whatever came for him," Gavin said.

"How could you say that?" I glared at him.

"He was a High Council dog, Aurora. He wouldn't have thought twice to stab you in the back, were he ordered to do so," he said.

"That may be so, but it's the fault of the Maeshiren being defeated which caused him to serve such a corrupt council in the first place," I seethed, not backing down from my stance.

"The fall of the Maeshiren has nothing to do with the immoral character and actions of the corrupt and corruptible," he said.

"You didn't see the terror in his face," I replied.

"Yes, I did. As I have countless others who have realized they were moments from their demise. It doesn't matter if you're corrupted or innocent, it's the same across all lines," he said.

"What's your point?" I seethed, crossing my arms, ignoring the sting in my forearm.

"My point is this is not your fault, nor is it the Maeshiren's. Avnor chose this path. He knew the risks involved and still made the choices that suited him. He didn't have to follow the council's orders, as he did back when The Syndicate attacked. Your sadness is misplaced," he said, heated with each phrase.

"If the Maeshiren were still ruling, this would have never happened," I said through clenched teeth.

"Perhaps," he conceded, his expression fierce.

"I hate to break your love quarrel, but we have a quest to finish," Kate said, standing next to us both with hands on her hips.

"Fine," I said, turning away from Gavin as I dropped my arms to my side. We could argue the finer points of this all day long and still never get anywhere. I understood his distaste for Avnor, but not his cold indifference to his death. Maybe after taking so many lives, seeing the horrific death of someone else no longer phased him. It did me, and I didn't like it.

I walked ahead with my brothers, too heated to think straight and too disturbed to care. I didn't know where we were heading, but I could only assume it was one way – deeper into the canyon.

Nobody spoke. The only sound between us was the crunching of snow under our feet and the wind whistling through the canyon.

The throbbing splinters buried deep in my arm had my attention, blood oozing from the wounds. They needed to come out. Wincing, I focused on digging the splinters out intact, my fingers bloodied. I cringed at the tugging and pinching of such sensitive skin that I almost gave up and left them there. However, I knew once they were out, I could heal the wounds. At least it gave me something to do while we walked through this blind.

The further we trekked, the more pronounced the ache became in my legs, continuing to remind me of our harrowing experience and Avnor's haunting, terrified stare. I was maxing out, my fuel tank running dry. The adrenaline rush left me feeling heavy and exhausted.

"Can we take a break? My legs are killing me," Ryder spoke my internal thoughts.

"For a few moments. This isn't a safe place to stop," Kartcher said, scanning our surroundings.

"Is any place safe to stop?" Garrett asked, throwing up his hands to the sky. "What. Is that?"

I turned to where he stared but could only see snow drifting over the edge. "What are you talking about? There's nothing there."

"No Aurora, I swear, there was something there. It was hunched down watching us," he said.

"What did you see, exactly?" Kartcher asked with hesitation. I slid my gaze to Kartcher, apprehension dawning in his reptilian eyes.

"I can't be too sure. It was there for only a split second, but it was covered in fur, hunched on two legs, watching us," he said.

"We need to keep moving," Kartcher said warily.

"Kartcher, what is it?" Gavin asked.

"Lycanthrope."

"You mean, like werewolves?" Kate asked.

"Precisely," Kartcher said.

"Why didn't you tell us there were werewolves here?" Ryder wailed.

"I wasn't planning on going this way. Let's keep moving," he said, scanning above.

"Is it a full moon here, then?" Garrett asked.

"These are not the werewolves of your folklore back home," Kartcher explained while we walked vigilantly through the canyon. "These are men who were subjected to the dark arts of the occults. Many a millennium ago, there were various wars waged to secure power over Estrea. Any way a faction could gain the upper hand – they would stop at nothing.

This came at the peril of many men being experimented on by the occults. They were trying to create ferocious beasts out of them; those they could control but who would be feared and ruthless in battle.

Unfortunately, these dark art experiments went incredibly sideways. These beasts they created were uncontrollable. No amount of magic could contain their behaviors, and so they abandoned their experiments and banished their failures to the badlands."

Hyperawareness raised the hair on my arms, feeling the eyes of monsters watching our every move. It was unnerving to know they knew our exact position, while theirs remained concealed.

"Okay, so any pointers you want to throw our way on this one?" Garrett asked, peeved.

"Whatever you do, don't let them bite you," he said, as rocks and snow echoed down the cliff face of the canyon.

Adrenaline pumped in my eardrums as I scanned the surrounding area. The high ting of metal on metal caught my attention as Kate pulled her bow and arrow to the side; her eyes roaming the landscape as she readied herself to fire at will.

I remembered she said if we focused, we could feel the vibrations of those around us. I tried to pull myself inward, seeking some internal connection to the vibrations of this world. I found nothing except the feeling of stupidity in my attempt.

Gavin's red eyes narrowed in on an unseen threat ahead as he reached for the blades beneath his layers. The agate metal rang out as he slid them against one another, announcing his readiness to attack.

Kartcher paused in place, halting our forward progression.

Around the bend, three dark-haired beasts trudged towards us on canine heels. The menace in their yellow eyes narrowed in on our group. They moved on pure instinct, nothing holding them back in their lust for blood.

Dread clenched my throat when they hunched down and charged.

Kate brought up her bow, launching an arrow at one of the beasts. He stepped to the side, away from the arrow's trajectory, unfazed. She scrambled for another as the beast jumped for her.

Gavin rushed towards Kate, knocking the beast away from her. They crashed and rolled on the ground, before turning on each other.

Kartcher pushed out his prismatic shield, launching one werewolf back into the air. It hit the ground with a thud before jumping back to its feet and charging Kartcher once more.

Garrett unsheathed his sword in time as the third werewolf knocked him to the ground, gnashing its sharp teeth towards him. He struggled to keep his sword between them as it came within inches of chomping his face.

I sprinted towards him, unsheathing my sword, but Ryder

was much quicker than I. The beast howled in pain as Ryder plunged his silver blade into its torso. It jumped away from Ryder and off Garrett, zoning in on Ryder as it favored its wounded side.

Ryder took a firm stance, ready for its attack as I helped Garrett scramble to his feet.

In the distance, two more werewolves sped towards our melee as Gavin finished beheading the werewolf he tackled.

The piercing howl of the beast in front of us brought my attention away from Gavin's carnage as it charged at Ryder. With sword in hand, Ryder readied himself for the coming attack, tripping as he stepped back.

The beast capitalized on this slip, jumping towards its prey. I screamed out for Ryder as I willed my body to move in time to his aid.

With a sudden flare, an obsidian-crowned owl, with eyes of fiery orange, picked the werewolf up by its head and slammed it into the canyon side. It ripped the beast apart with its talons; the pieces floating back to the surface. With wings spread wide, it flew high into the sky before diving straight into Ryder's blade, vanishing.

Ryder stared at Garrett wide eyed, none of us believing what we had seen.

The two approaching werewolves were now upon us, jumping into our skirmish.

Kartcher stood preoccupied with two, keeping one at bay with his shield while slashing at the other with his sharp claws. With a swing of his tail, he curled it around one beasts' ankle and flung it towards Gavin.

"Here ya go," Kartcher smiled.

It was quick, landing on its feet as it howled in Gavin's face. At this, his blades flared crimson. A dark shadow swirled around

Gavin's form, a wicked smile on his face as he snarled back at the creature.

Gavin and the werewolf met each other head on as the beast swiped at Gavin's head. Gavin caught his giant paws mid-air, dropping his swords, laughing as he wrestled with the horrendous monster.

"Is this all you've got?" he yelled out. The werewolf answered with a snap towards his face.

Kate's arrow pierced through the beasts' brain, splattering blood across Gavin's turned cheek, as it came full circle into her outstretched hand.

The werewolf crumpled to the floor in front of Gavin, lifeless at his feet. Gavin gave it a nudge, crestfallen, "Damn it, Kate. Why did you have to go do a thing like that?"

"Have fun on your own time. We have bigger problems," she said, reloading her bow. Above us, five more werewolves were descending the cliff face.

I readied my sword, prepared to use it when Gavin stood in front of me, staring at the coming threat. "You keep holding it like that, the only thing you're going to kill is yourself," he said.

"Excuse me if I've never held a sword before, *expert*," I bit back.

Kate moved quick, running as she shot two arrows at once, piercing the face of one werewolf but missing the other entirely. The werewolf she missed attacked, snapping in the air as she jumped over it. Twisting mid-flight, she aimed her arrow into the beast's throat, successfully meeting her mark. It crashed face first, somersaulting over its head.

Two down, five to go.

Kartcher still faced off with one, when two more entered his fight. He kicked off one, using the momentum to slam his knee in the face of the other. The third ran around his shield, swiping its claws into the air. Kartcher moved with the swipes, keeping the sharp points from grazing his skin.

The second werewolf ambushed him from behind, swiping at his torso as he ducked away at the right moment. Instead, the werewolf swiped four deep gashes across the chest of the other, causing it to stumble back. Rather than continue to go after Kartcher, they fought amongst themselves. Kartcher took the opportunity to focus on the third.

Garrett and Ryder stood shoulder-to-shoulder with swords pointing at the approaching beast in front of them.

"Hey little brother, wanna call that owl back?" Garrett yelled out.

"As if I could."

"You did it before," he said.

"But I don't know *how*," Ryder screeched.

"I think now would be a good time you figured it the *fuck out*," Garrett hollered as the werewolf charged them.

The clanking of claws on metal echoed off the canyon walls as Garrett's sword met with the beast's left swipe. The heavy weight of its left paw threw him off balance as it came around to catch Garrett with its right. My heart sank as I watched the trajectory of its claws meet with Garrett's head.

"NO!" I screamed, all reasoning leaving my body. I charged with sword in hand, prepared to take its head off. I slashed at the beast only to meet air. In a blink of an eye, it vanished.

Hot breath at the nape of my neck turned my blood ice cold, a deep menacing growl indicating where it disappeared to. I spun around, using momentum to swing my sword, hoping to put some distance between us, but instead met armor.

"Damn. Easy Aurora," Garrett chided, as he pushed forward on the beast.

"What the hell?" I said, faltering at his voice.

Garrett stood toe-to-toe with the monster in full black and royal blue armor. The pronounced shoulder plates added to his size as he matched the werewolf step for step – his movements swift as Kartcher's.

Ryder ran up beside me, shocked as I at Garrett's sudden appearance. "Looks like I wasn't the only one who needed to figure it the fuck out."

Gavin appeared behind the beast while Garrett kept its attention forward, severing its spine down its length. The animated beast ceased fighting as the light faded from its eyes. I clutched my chest as my heart tried to break free.

Garrett glanced down at his armor, in awe of it vanishing at the absence of an imminent threat.

"How did you *do* that?" I asked.

"I don't know. The moment that thing swiped at my head, I was covered in armor," he replied, shock coloring his face.

"I really think we need to figure out what we are capable of. And *soon*," I said, staring at Garrett before turning to Ryder.

"Yeah, I agree," Ryder said.

The deafening quiet became a sweet melody to my ears, knowing we made it through this battle. I turned to find Kate checking on Kartcher healing his wounds, walking away from a werewolf encased in ice.

"Is everyone alright?" Kartcher asked, lifting his eyes from healing his arm wound. "No bites?"

"I'm good," Garrett said.

"Yeah, I think we all are," Ryder piped in. "You guys?" he asked Gavin and me. I turned to Gavin, who nodded at Ryder.

"Yeah, we're good," I smiled with relief.

"Then we must keep pushing forward. There are more where those came from," Kartcher said, as I surveyed the carnage before us. I don't know how much my nerves could take if we were to run into more of them.

"What would happen if one of them bit us?" Ryder asked, continuing our path.

"It depends. You could die, *if* your body rejected their venom. That is - if they didn't devour you first. Or you would become a savage beast like them," Kartcher exhaled.

"Something tells me you've witnessed this firsthand," I said.

"No. Just the teachings passed down from those prior," he said with a heavy heart, not elaborating further on the topic. Though I felt there was more to this story, I didn't pry.

Rounding the icy corner, the canyon opened to a towering, rugged mountain blanketed in dense snow. Flurries floated down from the arctic blue clouds, adding to the thick layer covering the wide bridge between us and the mountain's entrance.

The same trees in the wraith's forest greeted us on the outside of the canyon's walls; large cages hanging from their bare branches. Frozen, hollowed corpses lay trapped behind their bars, scattered across the mountainside.

"Well, that's inviting," Kate said.

"We're here," Kartcher exhaled both in reverence and in warning, folding his hands as he bowed his head in prayer.

Whoever, or whatever, it was we were about to meet, the ominous entry didn't incite any confidence for our encounter. Instead, I said a silent prayer for us, and for those who never made it out. To make it through wraiths, fatal traps, and werewolves, only to finish out your last days caged in the bitter cold, was heartbreaking. The sheer numbers of those who had met such a fate before me were staggering.

Fierce howling echoed within the canyon, signaling approaching werewolves. I spun around to Kartcher standing in deep prayer, not moving an inch at the sound.

"Sorry to cut your prayer time short, Kartcher, but we have

to go," Gavin said to an unresponsive Kartcher. The howling grew closer, the clanking of their claws on glacial ice becoming prominent.

"Kartcher," he said again. No response.

The panting of their hot breath in the cool air became pronounced.

"Kartcher!" Gavin yelled, grabbing his arm and pulling him forward. Kartcher jarred from his meditation, dazed as if he didn't recognize where he was.

"We have to go!" Gavin yelled. The werewolves rounded the corner.

"Heavens! Run!" Kartcher blinked, as we sprinted towards the bridge. Our feet dragged and sank into the heaping snow, slowing our progress against the gaining beasts.

Halfway across the bridge, a werewolf jumped at Gavin as he twisted his body, catapulting it over the bridges steep drop off.

"Keep it moving!" Gavin yelled as we continued to scramble to the cave's entrance. Gavin, Kate, and Kartcher fell back into formation, shielding me and my brothers from the threat.

Kate turned, shooting an arrow at one werewolf. He dodged her attack with a sidestep, snarling as he snapped the air at her.

"Through those doors," Kartcher hollered to us. At the cave's entrance, two stone slabs were cracked just enough to squeeze sideways. Garrett made it to the entrance first, refusing to go in until Ryder and I were safely inside.

"Hurry! Get in," Garrett screamed at us.

Ryder rushed to slide his body through the opening, shifting his feet as fast as he could.

I glanced back at the others; Kate's shit-eating grin plastered on her face, her arrow returning to her through the backside of the werewolf's skull.

"Gotcha!" she said.

"Aurora, get your ass moving," Garrett demanded, the remaining werewolf nipping at Gavin's heels.

"No, you go first," I said, watching Gavin, waiting to ensure his safety.

"Damn it, Aurora. Don't make this difficult," he shouted.

"I'm not," I shouted back, refusing to take my eyes off Gavin.

Garrett glanced between me and Gavin, "He will be fine."

Kartcher turned the moment he reached us, placing his shield between Gavin and a frustrated werewolf. It was enough of an edge for Gavin to break away and sprint towards us. The werewolf was trying to find a way around his shield.

Knowing I was the one holding us up, I sidestepped into the cramped opening, my chest and back pressed against the opposing sides. If I could hardly fit, how could the rest of them?

Garrett crushed his body in after me, grunting with each move.

Growling and thrashing echoed between the cave's open walls as the werewolf fought to get through to us. I hoped it wasn't smart enough to follow. I scrambled to reach the other side just to be sure.

"Geez, that was painful," I said, clutching my chest. My lungs expanded at full capacity, feeling the relief of a full breath.

"You could say that again," Garrett said beside me, crouched with his hands on his knees.

"The werewolf?" I asked, panicked as I searched for Gavin.

"Is no more," he said from behind Kartcher. He stepped aside, coming into the light of the cracked opening, alleviating my fears. I smiled in relief, taking another deep breath.

"You guys, get a look at that," Ryder said.

Engulfed in darkness, a single illuminated path lay before us.

On either side, large cauldrons in the shape of swirling lotuses held brilliant blue flames lighting the way.

"What is this place?" Ryder asked.

"The path to the Gates of Valdöllen," Kartcher said behind us.

"What are those markings?" Kate asked, pointing to the inlaid etchings covering the walkway.

"Warnings," Kartcher said.

"Warnings?" Gavin asked.

"Yes. It is to give those who were fortunate enough to make it through the badlands a chance to turn back. What awaits for those who choose to proceed is far worse," he said.

"Can you elaborate further?" Garrett asked.

"No. We must continue," Kartcher said, walking through us to lead the way. Ryder glanced between me and Garrett before following, uncertainty settling on his face.

Gavin's rigid body next to mine alarmed me, the tightness in his eyes unsettling as he watched Kartcher march forward. He slid a side eye towards me, sending ominous shivers through my core at the worry etched in his expression.

"Are you okay?" I asked, the cave picking up my hushed voice.

"We are about to find out," he whispered, raising a hand for me to take the lead.

I did as he asked, falling in step behind the rest. The shuffling of our feet echoed in the darkened cave; the light from the flames blinding me to what lay on the other side.

"Gavin, settle your hand," Kartcher murmured. I glanced over to see him sheathing his sword, keeping his hand on the pommel.

"What are they?" Gavin asked, scanning the darkness beyond the fire.

"Bentowins," he said. I strained my eyes to see what they were talking about but could see nothing.

The path opened to an octagon shaped room encased in a city of ice columns. Reflected light cast a cerulean glow from the various lit flames. If it weren't for the fact of knowing Bentowins lived here, I would think this cave city had been abandoned.

The flaming cauldrons fanned into a wide circle in the room's interior, framing the etched warnings on the ice chipped floor. We came to stand in the center of the circle as a united front, waiting to meet our fate. Kartcher bowed his head.

Every nerve ending vibrated to life, as my fingertips zinged with a numb charge. I became acutely aware of the energy pulsating around me, a foreboding premonition alerting me to our coming judgement.

"No one is here," Garrett said.

Kartcher lifted his eyes. "Oh, they're here. And they see you." He bowed his head once more as I scanned the room, wide eyed and wary.

Without warning, the flames extinguished. Other senses heightened as my eyesight dulled, the adrenaline in my ears pumping to a beat.

I jumped when Gavin's hand engulfed mine, bringing me closer to himself. The tension in his arm relayed the message of what I wasn't comprehending in my blindness.

A cool touch rested against the side of my neck as the flames flickered back on, revealing icy blades at each of our throats.

Chapter Twenty-three

The Bentowins

"While all deception requires secrecy, all secrecy is not meant to deceive." — Sissela Bok

***

On cue, hundreds of Bentowins in a sea of white and grey stood around us, hoods concealing their heads with hands folded in front of them. Kartcher kept his head down, in reflection of those who stood before us, though his tail confined Gavin's hands reaching for his swords.

Those who held their blades to our throats stood still as statues, waiting for our next move. I held my breath, afraid if I breathed wrong, I'd lose my head. Above us, lizard men leered down from every open crevice and platform carved into the icy pillars.

The similarities to Kartcher were striking, from their cloaks to the way they held their stance — poised, with a refinement not seen in this world or mine. The powerful difference was that

Kartcher was more animated. A life of living amongst the world, rather than being with the reclusive gate guards of Valdöllen, no doubt.

Movement caught my eye as three figures moved forward in salmon-colored cloaks, the mass of Bentowins breaking formation to allow them passage. They appeared as if they floated towards us with the way they moved, the length of their attire concealing their feet. They stopped before us in a triangular formation.

"State your affair," the gruff Bentowin in the front said. My nerves coiled tight as adrenaline surged. Gavin gave my hand a gentle squeeze.

Kartcher brought his hands up before him, balling his right hand into a fist, pressing it into the outstretched palm of his left. A humbling gesture.

From the peripheral, Kate slowly mimicked him, seeming unsure of her actions. From this action alone, it stirred some of the Bentowins in the back to take notice. Their heads lifted, uncovering their eyes, revealing the superiority they knew they could reign over us.

I peeked at Gavin; his eyes were tight as he took in the secret guard before us. He was probably tabulating and calculating strategies – moves and countermoves – to get us out safely. I traded glances from Gavin to my brothers. Garrett stood stark still, his eyes darting from left to right, giving away the unease simmering beneath the surface.

Ryder wore his worry on his sleeve as he watched Kate follow in Kartcher's footsteps. The etched lines between his brows were a sign of his contemplation on how to proceed. His gears clicked into motion as he lowered his eyes, pressing his fist into his palm.

Garrett's brows rose high before he conceded, following in

his footsteps. I scanned over the crowd; more Bentowin heads rose in acknowledgement of our regard to respect and honor their presence.

I shifted my gaze back towards Gavin, already staring down at me. The exchange swirling between us left me without a shred of doubt that we were on the same page. I knew he didn't enjoy conceding; he wasn't the type. After seeing the way they responded to the rest, we needed to do what we could to move past the Valdöllen gates.

We both turned, making the hand gestures at the same time. I lowered my eyes to the floor as the blade to my throat bowed with me. Three sets of scaly feet, with four toes and a dewclaw, stepped into my line of sight.

"Rise and state your business," an accented voice, with the power of authority, spoke out once again. I lifted my eyes to see the others coming out of their respective stances.

The hoods of the salmon-colored robes were pushed back, exposing the reptilian faces before us. Their eyes held a cold hostility at our intrusion. Up close, the differences between them were striking.

The charcoal gray Bentowin on the left, with piercing blue eyes that contrasted with his darker complexion, held a more elongated face than the rest, giving him a fuller mouth.

"We came here on critical business," Kartcher stated to the forest green Bentowin in the middle. His white tribal-like markings cascaded from his brow bones to the back of his head, disappearing beneath his cloak.

"We have orders from the high council of Höllengrad to prove authority of these three," Kartcher said, raising his hand towards my brothers and me.

"And why should we be inconvenienced with Höllengrad's orders?" the viridescent Bentowin asked on the right, his violet eyes the fiercest of the three.

"Because Terbius, these are the Maeshiren children – direct decedents of Daten, the ruler over all of Elderon, the sworn protector of the Niveh gates, and the last Maeshiren to have kept order in this land," Kartcher's voice rang with such authority and conviction. He matched the superiority of the three Bentowins before us. "They have come to prove their authoritative right to rule and restore balance once again to this world."

"Few have come before you, seeking the same as you. What proof do you have for us to believe your story?" the heavily accented middle Bentowin asked.

"My word as a fellow Bentowin, once belonging to this secret society, for one Cirílicó," Kartcher began.

"Yes. A fellow Bentowin who is no longer a part of this society, but has since been corrupted by the very world you seek to save," the darker Bentowin barked.

"Dèroon, that may be so, but it is I who took the oath and sacrifice of Reinard to spare my brothers and sisters from making the hard decision themselves. I may have seen the world and its darkness; I have also seen its light and have not strayed from the teachings of the Bentowin way," he defended.

"Make no mistake, Kartcher, your sacrifice and great deed are not going unnoticed. It is our reverence for your past sacrifice which gives us pause now," Terbius stated, his brows turning in on his light green face.

"I am grateful," Kartcher replied.

"Regardless, you know our laws. You must have concrete evidence of your claim, or else I am afraid your journey is for not," Cirílicó stated with glaring saffron eyes.

Kartcher's lips formed into a grim line, unhappy with the stubbornness of his ex-compatriots. His reluctant eyes slid to mine for the briefest of moments, conceding to a defeat I wasn't privy to.

"One of the Maeshiren children is in possession of a key to the Niveh gates, passed down from their mother, which had been passed down from Daten," Kartcher explained. Surprise registered on their faces as three sets of eyes scanned over each of us.

My breath caught at Kartcher's admission to my mother's pendant. No one was supposed to know, not even them. *How could he?* My face flushed hot with betrayal.

"That is something," Dèroon nodded, his cold eyes searching us over. The other two nodded in agreement.

"Let us see this key so we can inspect its authenticity," the scrutinizing yellow eyes of Cirílicó scanned over us once more.

"Aurora, if you will," Kartcher said expectant, hand outstretched for me to proceed. I gave him a cold, hard stare, refusing based on principle. I slowly shook my head no, as he minutely nodded yes.

"It's okay Aurora. This is where the key originated from," he explained, trying to calm my flaring anger, as if *that* was supposed to make everything right.

Kate glared over Kartcher's shoulder at me. "Just do it Aurora," she said through clenched teeth.

Was I being irrational about this? Is this the only way?

With a heavy sigh, I lifted the pendant by the chain from beneath my shirt, refusing to remove it fully. I remembered how it fused to my body when the occults tried to take it. If I was wearing it, no one could take it from me.

Exposing what my mother told me to hide, all three Bentowins came to stand in front of me to further inspect this *key*. They inspected it from side to side, their eyes searching for something I wasn't sure of.

"Flip it over," Terbius commanded, his striking violet eyes

offset by the sea foam green of his complexion.

I did as he asked, watching their expressions closely.

As if someone flipped a switch, their expressions became a mixture of shock and suspicion. They glanced from the pendant to me, and back to the pendant. I followed their interest to see what had them flabbergasted.

Inside of the intricately carved pendent, a holographic phoenix shimmered opalescent with its wings spread wide, much like the one on my sword. I turned the pendent this way and that, watching as the three-dimensional wings became animated with the movement.

How could I have not noticed this before? What did this Phoenix signify? And what is it in relation to me?

"Surely, I tell you brothers, these three before you are the rightful heirs to the throne," Kartcher pushed on.

"We can vouch for the authenticity of this highly sought-after relic," Dèroon stated. Cirílicó and Terbius nodded their heads in agreement.

"However, this does not prove they are the Maeshiren children," Terbius stated.

"Do you realize what you have in your possession, young Aurora?" Cirílicó asked, eyeing me with speculation.

Placed in the spotlight, the room stared at my awaited answer. "Yes. I have the key to the Niveh gates. A family heirloom passed from generations which holds the power between Elderon and Earth."

The room grew quiet as I impatiently waited to hear if I passed their scrutiny.

"Regurgitated nonsense heard from earlier, and more than likely coached," Cirílicó stated, "What we want to know is if you know its secrets. If it has revealed to you its namesake?"

It's secrets? Namesake? How could an inanimate object even

hold such things in existence to reveal to me in the first place?

"We take your silence as a no," Cirílicó said, his hardened eyes flashing to Kartcher. "You dare bring imposters to these gates? You dare threaten the security of Valdöllen? The world has turned you against the Bentowin ways, brother."

"No! Cirílicó please. You have it all wrong, brother," Kartcher said, turning out his hands hospitably. The cool blade pushed tighter against my skin.

"Close your eyes," a voice whispered in my mind. Close my eyes? *At a time like this?*

"How so? How can you tell those of us assembled here you did not give this key to Aurora and mentor her words?" Terbius asked.

"Close your eyes," the voice repeated. I tightened my lips, glancing up at Gavin, giving me a strange look. Against my better judgement, I closed my eyes; a secondary sight bringing awareness to my surroundings.

"Knowing our ways, how would my deceiving you serve us?" Kartcher reasoned.

"Shut out the world around you. Listen to your heart center," the voice said.

"It is *because* you know our ways, you could attempt to do such a thing," Dèroon stated.

"How?" I asked back in my mind, feeling foolish for even entertaining my deranged inner ramblings.

"Stay focused on my voice," it answered back, as if this were a completely normal exchange. Complying, I allowed it to guide me to whatever revelation it sought for me to discover.

"Follow my voice to your heart. Take a deep breath," it said. I inhaled deep, exhaling with a steady breath.

"Focus in on your heart. Breathe in and out from its center."

The erratic beating within its bony chamber slowed. The

outside voices no longer carrying the sharpness they once had.

"Good. Let your thoughts and feelings come and go without judgement. Listen to what your heart has to say," the voice encouraged. I could feel myself crossing over from one area of my mind to another, transitioning me between space and time.

I stood before my scarlet heart, demanding my full attention to its vital teachings. It beckoned me to watch, as layer upon emotional layer peeled away like a Rolodex; each layer a direct emotional chord reverberating through me tenfold.

The layer of stubbornness I guarded my hardened heart with crumbled away brick by brick, exposing the delicate copings I held within. Tears stained my cheeks with the raw, resurfaced pain of exposing these suppressed, hidden emotions.

Denial of unacknowledged grief shattered to the pain of loss, agony doubling me over in its vice grip of suffering. In the years leading to this turmoil, I had made peace with my grief, building these layers to cope. Why would I have to suffer through this now?

"What do you want from me?" I wailed out to my heart, willing for the torture to cease. I lifted my tormented eyes to see the next layer peeling away. With the lifeless layers of my pathetic coping mechanisms strewn across my feet, the torment I had endured washed away.

Revealed beneath the layer of pain was a seething inferno. Rage flashed through my center, all rationality escaping my control.

"I said, what the fuck do you want from me? Why are you bringing me through this shit?" I screamed up at my heart, resenting the decision to allow my broken mental state to bring me through this bullshit. My fists shook with the rage coursing through my veins. With jaws clenched, I let a frustrated growl escape my lips.

As if my heart took mercy on my soul, the fire within extinguished as the layer of gripping anger burst into a flurry of charred ash. Exhaustion seeped into my bones at being pulled through the mental ringer in such a short expanse of time.

Behind the dissipating ash, my heart pumped anew.

Hope glimmered in and out of its chambers. Love encompassed its walls. Happiness exuded with each beat. A well spring of renewal washed over me, bringing me back to life.

Like a proud badge of honor, my heart wore the markings of the phoenix that have plagued me since finding my mother's letter.

"My namesake is Solara," it beat with pride. *"I am you. We are one."*

"What does that even mean, Solara?"

"I am your secret. I am your higher self."

"Please Solara. Please help me!" I pleaded. There were so many questions unanswered, but my pleas for help fell on deaf ears. Though it beat before me, it no longer continued answering me.

"Lock them in the prison cages," Terbius bellowed, jolting me to the present. The Bentowins holding us hostage jostled us away from the judgement circle.

"Solara!" I yelled out in the commotion, not allowing myself to be moved. The pushback stopped, Terbius, Cirílicó, and Dèroon snapping their eyes to me.

"What did you say?" Cirílicó asked.

"The key. Its secrets. Its namesake is Solara," I breathed, my chest heaving. They turned to each other in quiet deliberation.

"How did you learn of this?" Dèroon asked.

"She told me," I said. I felt Gavin's shocked gaze burning against my face.

"Come forward," Terbius said, waving away the Bentowin guards. I stepped forward, staring into Terbius' violet eyes.

"If you will, turn the pendent over," he asked. I turned the pendent over, revealing the holographic phoenix inside once again.

"Solara te revelare," he spoke. I watched the phoenix flash in acknowledgement, flapping its wings forward. He glanced back to me, his eyes glimmering with reverence. "You are the phoenix."

He stepped back, turning to his Bentowin brothers. "She is the phoenix. Prepare brothers. We are to allow them to pass."

"You are sure of this?" Cirílicó asked.

"As sure as I am of our duty to guard Valdöllen," he stated.

"Before we allow them passage, what of the demon in their midst?" Dèroon asked. I glanced at Gavin, flicking an icy stare in their direction.

"We cannot allow such darkness to infiltrate the light," Cirílicó stated. Heat bubbled deep within, speaking of Gavin as if he were filth; a lower citizen than the rest of us because of what he was born into.

"How dar—," I began to say.

"Gavin is the epitome of darkness turned to light," Kartcher spoke over me. "He has served the Maeshiren for many moons. I must speak to his accolades and take full responsibility for him as the Maeshiren overseer."

"That is all well and good brother Kartcher, however, he has been inflicted by the occultist curse," he said. Kartcher flipped around, fear coloring his reptilian face as he glanced over Gavin. Alarmed at his demeanor, I turned to Gavin with an unknown fear.

"Where have you been bitten?" Kartcher demanded.

My world came to a stop. *Gavin had been bitten?* The occultists curse. Kartcher's story of the occults failed experiments – the werewolves. Gavin's wordless nod when asked if anyone had been bitten; *he concealed it?*

Sadness and shame colored Gavin's eyes as he locked them with mine. He pulled his arm from beneath his fur coat, rolling up his sleeve. There, festering into his flesh, was the unmistakable bite mark on his forearm.

"When?" I croaked, holding back my tears.

"In the canyon," he half whispered. A single tear slid down my cheek.

"Why didn't you say anything?" I asked.

"There was nothing to say," he responded.

"Do something!" I raised my voice, turning to Kartcher.

"There is nothing I can do," he said. "It is a curse only an occult could lift, if you could find one who would be willing."

"I don't believe you. There has to be something," I said, turning to the other Bentowins.

"We cannot allow him passage. He can stay behind while the rest of you move forward," Terbius stated.

No! I will *not* accept that. If he can't go, neither will I.

"I refuse to leave him," I said through clenched teeth.

"Aurora. Listen, it's okay," Gavin said.

"No Gavin. I will not leave you," I turned to him, both afraid and angry at the hands of fate.

"Then you leave us no choice but to ask you to leave," Cirílicó said.

"Don't throw this away for me," Gavin pleaded with me.

"There has to be another way," I said, tears clouding my vision.

"There is no other way," he replied.

"Gavin," I choked, "Don't say that." I shook my head back and forth as my face crumpled. He pulled me into his arms, willing for me to stop making a scene in front of the Bentowin society, but I didn't care. They could all be damned.

Kartcher's story from earlier repeated in my mind, only now

regarding Gavin. He would either be killed by the venom, or he would become a mindless beast like them. We were running out of time. I needed to find a cure for him, and fast.

Could whoever be on the other side of the Valdöllen gates cure him? Could I trade them something to save his life? I had to go. I had to leave him behind. If I were to save him, I had to leave him.

I stepped away; my tear-stricken face resolved. He gave me a saddened smirk, not realizing I already made my own moves and countermoves inside my head.

"I'll be back," I whispered, relaying my promise to him through my stare. He gave me a tightlipped smile.

"I will go," I said, turning to the head Bentowins. "I will go *now*." I didn't give them an opportunity to stall my meeting with fate.

"Come with us," Cirílicó said, as the three of them turned away.

Following, I glanced over my shoulder at Gavin standing alone – forlorn. My heart ached to have him near me. There was an uncomfortable void in leaving him, at feeling like this was the last I would see of him.

The Bentowins led us to a mirrored wall encased in ice, its circular border etched with fine markings similar to the path that led us here.

Terbius and Dèroon stood on either side of the circle with Cirílicó standing at the head. They spoke out in various tongues as they lifted their arms, swirling them down and around towards their left, repeating the movement over and over.

The mirrored wall swirled as the ice liquified, spiraling into a whirlpool of fresh water. As the water rushed faster and faster, three more Bentowins came to take their place, keeping the water liquified.

"Kartcher will lead you through the Valdöllen gates," Terbius said.

Kartcher nodded, turning to the rest of us. "Follow my lead. Stay close. Two can go in at a time," he said, as he and Kate stepped towards the portal. Kate's eyes were bright with excitement as she turned to Kartcher.

"Ready?" he asked.

"Ready as I'll ever be," she said. With that, they stepped forward, the swirling liquid caressing their frames before they vanished.

Garrett and Ryder were up next, stepping up to the water's edge.

"See ya on the other side, brother," Garrett laughed, as if they were crossing over to their death.

"Very funny," Ryder rolled his eyes as they both stepped forward.

Standing before the roaring current, I hesitated in this strange limbo of severing my connection with Gavin and entering my future, even if it was only momentary.

Glancing behind me, I searched for him, but he was no longer here. My heart sank. He must have turned away, knowing this was the end of the line between us.

No, I wouldn't allow it. I'm *going* to save him.

I spun to face the loud sloshing of the undulating portal; my resolve strengthened.

A vibratory current reached out its tentacles, beckoning me to step forward. The heightened energy I felt at the gate when I crossed into this strange world was present and forceful. My heart accelerated at the remembered rush, but my mind stayed at peace, knowing it had been through something like this before.

Behind me, the Bentowins were stirring into an uproar. *Was I taking too long?*

Turning to see what the commotion was about, Gavin shoved me into the portal, his arms engulfing me as we fell through to the other side.

Chapter Twenty-four

Valdöllen

"Fall away from the past, enter into the future; for what once was is no more and what will be is yet to come." – Brittany Bowman

***

We landed on hard packed ground; Gavin's arms wrapped around me like a cage, shielding me from our fall as he slid on his back.

"Are you okay?" his breath caressed my ear.

I lifted my head from the nook of his neck, our noses mere inches from touching. The concern and adoration in his emerald gaze held me hostage. My heart warmed as a smile spread free of its own accord, carrying with it a blush that swept across my cheeks. "I am now."

His answering smile would have knocked me off my feet if it weren't for the fact I was already wrapped in his arms. He tightened his hold, pulling me in closer as I laid my head onto his shoulder, pure happiness beating between us.

I didn't have to move forward without him. He was here with me; we could conquer anything.

"How did you sneak past the Bentowins?" I asked.

"I have my ways," he said. I could hear his smirk without looking at him, see the dimple in his cheek I loved so much. He released me from his hold, the image of his smirk replaced by reality. My mind didn't even do him justice.

"Would you like to tell me *what the hell* is going on here?" Kate asked. Gavin shifted his gaze back, looking at Kate upside down, as I lifted my head towards her. All four were staring at us in shock. I pushed off Gavin's chest as he let out an *'Oomph'*, brushing myself off when I rose to my feet.

"What? Nothing!" I said, feinting innocence. *Why was she always hovering during our intimate moments?*

"I wasn't talking about *between* you two idiots," she said, rolling her eyes at me. "I'm talking about that idiot right there." She pointed at Gavin, scowling. "What did you do, Gavin?" she asked, her tone biting.

"I did nothing I wasn't planning on doing the moment they told me I couldn't cross over," he said, as he picked himself off the ground, brushing off his pants.

"Do you not have any regard for anyone's safety at all?" she exclaimed.

"Sure, I do. You were already crossed over. What were they going to do, come in here and kill us on *sacred ground?*" he mocked her.

"You can be a real shit sometimes, you know that?" she said, stomping off in the opposite direction.

"Sheesh, you would think she would at least be happy we are all together," he said, shaking his head.

"Well, I'm happy you're here," I said, internally kicking myself for beaming up at him like a schoolgirl.

He smiled back as he hooked his arm around my shoulders. "Thanks."

"How's your wound?" I asked, concerned at how fast it was spreading.

"Manageable," he replied, leaving it at that.

"Way to give it to those old stiffs Gavin," Garrett said, play punching him in his shoulder. Gavin chuckled.

"Glad you're here," Kartcher said, surprising me. I was sure he would be angry with Gavin for skirting around the Bentowin's judgement.

"Me too," he replied, glancing down at me. My cheeks reddened as I looked away.

The scenery before us jarred me. We stood in a luscious green forest surrounded by tall stone pillars, like those you'd find in ancient Roman architecture. No longer were we standing under the diffused light of the ice cave, but under brilliant sunlight filtering through the trees in an ethereal glow. Fireflies visible in the daylight danced bright against the low-lying shrubs while the melodious song of birds rang throughout the trees.

Beyond the pillars stood nothing but darkness - the trees and light not spilling even an inch outside of them. What a strange, heavenly place! What exactly was Valdöllen?

Scurrying noises above made our heads snap up as a booming voice echoed loud over the sky. Above the confines of the pillars were figures shrouded by the shadows. I squinted as I tried to focus on what stood beyond the edge of darkness. Deep, rolling growls echoed all around, striking terror in my soul.

Flaring nostrils set into broad snouts crept into the light, revealing a row of sharp fangs protruding over their lower lips. On every pillar, the light exposed dragons of every color and size coming forth, resting on their haunches — their haunting eyes zeroing in on us as if we were hardly a snack.

"So, this is what you Bentowins have been hiding?" Gavin whispered to Kartcher, not taking his eyes from the winged beasts.

"Every society has a secret they protect," he said.

At the head of the pillars stood a platform nearly the size of the garden. It didn't take long to imagine the size of the beast occupying it, as the penetrating prismatic eyes of the dragon in question came forward, scanning those of us below. Bony protrusions adorned the center of its face, cascading to the tip of its tail. It lifted its pearlescent head to the sun, bristling as the light warmed its body, closing its eyes in pure bliss.

Gradually, it lifted its lids, zoning in on us once again. Its wings expanded wide as it stepped from the pillar, landing with a soft, graceful thud onto the plush meadow below.

My heart beat frantic, paralyzing me where I stood. Gavin's hand steadied on my shoulder, bringing me behind him as his wide eyes zoned in on the coming threat.

The dragons above bristled as the one stalking forward curled its lips, revealing rows of razor-sharp teeth. A tremor ran through my body.

"I admire you for your protective nature, Gavin of Estrea, but what is it *you* think you can do against the likes of *me*?" the dragon's deep voice purred with humor.

"Whatever I have to," Gavin growled, his jaw muscles flexing.

The dragon closed its eyes and snorted in laughter, as if Gavin's threats meant nothing to him. How did this monster know Gavin's name?

"Do you know who I am?" the dragon stopped its forward advance in front of Gavin, lifting its head high above him in superiority.

"I'm afraid I don't." Gavin's hands balled into fists as he

stood his ground, his barely contained hostility bubbling beneath the surface.

"I am Voedene, seer over this realm. I am the one who gives authority and can take it away," his voice rang supreme. "You came here seeking my authority, but why should I give it to you? Who amongst you is worthy of such a privilege?" His eyes scanned over each of us while we remained silent.

"I can tell you not one of you is," he boomed. "So why have you come here to waste my time?"

The flash of his anger reverberated through me with a penetrable force, taking my breath away. I was nothing but a mere mortal in his presence.

"Ahem. If you will your excellence. We have come to fulfill the prophecy of the Maeshiren," Kartcher explained. "We have been sent here on orders from Höllengrad to claim authority for these three here – direct descendants of Daten, the son of Reinard who you had once given authority to a millennium ago."

"Kartcher, the noble Bentowin who made great sacrifices for his people and the Kingdom of Elderon. What do you know of the prophecy?"

"Just what we were taught throughout the ages; should the crowned Maeshiren lose their place on high, a direct descendent of unknown regard will come to reclaim their rightful place, restoring order once more," he recited.

"That is correct. However, a few crucial elements are missing which have been lost over the ages, even to your own kind," Voedene stated, lifting one clawed finger for emphasis.

"Which is?" Gavin asked impatiently. Voedene slid his eyes to Gavin before addressing Kartcher further.

"They sacrifice much for the sake of many. Two worlds they hold, the power of peace, the path of strife, destruction is imminent. A thin line is walked between revenge and remedy. Should they lose that battle, they will also lose the war."

His ominous words hung in the air like a thick cloud of smoke, heavy and burdening. Though I couldn't fully grasp the big picture of his words, it was clear as Maeshiren decedents — we were to prepare for war.

"I don't understand. I thought the fulfillment of the Maeshiren's return would cement the prophecy and restore order. How could we not have known the rest of this prophecy?" Kate's voice quivered.

Voedene's eyes slid to hers before lowering his head to her level. "You could not have expected a prophecy to be so easily fulfilled. Could you Katernius of house Vasuvius?"

Her mouth set into a grim line as he continued, "For a Maeshiren to retake their throne, it is certain they will be met with hostility. The failures of the Maeshiren run deep, as does the enmity to the name."

"That is well known," Kartcher agreed. My brothers and I turned to him, astonished.

"You think that would have been told to us before we agreed to this venture?" Garrett said in shocked disbelief.

"It was already set in motion," Kartcher said, staring straight ahead.

"This is true," Voedene nodded in agreement. "From the time of your birth, it was fated you would stand before me here."

"Do we not get a choice, then? What if we decide to go back and not answer to this choiceless *fate*?" I asked. The way our hands were bound by a fate not of our own choosing was saying we were powerless, like a pawn on a chest board, a piece only as useful as the role it plays.

"That is certainly one choice you have, Aurora of Brookings, daughter of Marie," he turned a menacing eye towards me as the sunlit meadow darkened. "Though you may want to reconsider such a dire path."

Pulled from the stillness of where I stood, I was thrown into an image of chaos.

As if I were a spectator hovering above, I watched as my brothers and I crossed through the Niveh gates, hurrying for home. We were caught in a bloody battle chasing us back into earth as the gates failed to close. Our two worlds collided. Death and suffering felt at every corner as both went up in a pyre. Spearheading the carnage was a tall figure with long white hair and hatred in his eyes, surrounded by bloodthirsty demons.

Jarred back to the present, the light of the meadow returned to its former splendor. I trembled in the wake of such a terror, turning to Ryder panting next to me. His eyes were wild with fright.

"What was that?" he choked.

"The consequences of your choice should you choose to ignore this calling, Ryder of Brookings – son of Marie," Voedene stated. "Every choice has a consequence, an effect of repercussions. The choices you make today do not just affect you, but those all around you. Not just those you know, but those you will never have the chance to meet. If you do not answer to it, then fate will wipe you off the face of both worlds, allowing a new fate to take its place."

"Is there no hope, then?" Garrett gasped, disheartened.

"Fear of the darkness is to succumb to its nature, Garrett of Brookings, son of Marie, the last of the Maeshiren wolves," Voedene replied.

"What did you call me?" Garrett whispered in shock.

"The *last* Maeshiren wolf. You have a powerful connection with the spirit warriors who are ingrained deep into your lineage. It will be up to you to establish that connection and draw strength from it. I can tell you no more," Voedene said, cutting off any further questioning from Garrett, though a multitude of questions were set upon his face.

"There are three of you standing before me who are of direct Maeshiren descent, but only one of you is worthy to see this prophecy through," Voedene said, raising his head high above us as he glared down.

"I thought you said not one of us is worthy of that authority?" I questioned. Why was it resting on our shoulders to set things right, even if we are Maeshiren, if we weren't worthy of such a calling?

"Dare you question my authority, Aurora of Brookings? You pathetic bunch, as you stand before me, not one of you is worthy of such, but with my blessings I will make you worthy!" he angered. The stoical dragons above bristled.

"I will do it. I will stand as representative for this family," Garrett bravely stepped forward, eyeing the beasts above with his fists shivering at his sides.

Why was he doing this? Did he feel, as the eldest sibling alive, that he should be the one to shoulder the burden of this calamity? I feared for him and what this could mean.

"I admire your courage Garrett, but it is not you who will lead this prophecy," Voedene said.

"What? Why?" Garrett asked, astonished. He was prepared to shoulder the heaviest of burdens and was shut down as if unfit for the job.

"Because it isn't the wolf that leads this world to its inevitable conclusion, but it is the wolf that defends and protects the Maeshiren authority. It is an important position to be in," Voedene explained.

Garrett's shoulders slumped forward, dropping his gaze to the ground. With a sharp turn of his head, he glanced between Ryder and me in fear.

Ryder stepped forward; his somber eyes fixed to the ground

before him. Lifting his gaze to Voedene, he said, "then that would leave me to answer to this fate."

"Ryder, the last of the Maeshiren Magistrate Owls, you are also not the one to bring forth the prophecy of this world. Silent and observant as you are, your clairvoyance gives you an insight into the heart of truth. You have the great charge of keeping a balance and subduing what threatens that balance. You as well must establish that connection from within to further develop your mind's eye," Voedene said, taking Ryder by surprise.

"What am I supposed to do with *that?*" Ryder asked, confused.

"All will be revealed to you in due time. You will know the hour when you gain a consciousness," Voedene replied, leaving Ryder with a puzzled expression, before bringing his full focus onto me.

"And now that leaves you, young Aurora, first Phoenix of the Maeshiren. As I can imagine, you are beginning to internalize what this means," he said, his eyes hovering in line with mine as his irises churned in a prismatic storm.

Time stood still. His words echoing of the Phoenix loud and clear. The scroll of the Phoenix Quaerit Pugnare, the Phoenix etched onto my sword; the Phoenix contained within my mother's pendent, the one my heart proudly wore. *Am I the one who is supposed to rise to such an occasion?*

"What does that even mean?" I whispered.

"If the Phoenix will rise to its destiny, the prophecy has the chance to be fulfilled," Voedene revered.

"I… don't understand. Why me?" I asked in a low voice, fidgeting with my fur coat. I knew what he said. The signs were all there. What I didn't understand was why I was the one everyone had to count on. *Wasn't I a total failure? Two shakes from a mental breakdown?* I didn't know the first thing about being what this world, or mine, needed.

"Why not you?" he asked, turning his head to the side as to better understand where I was coming from.

"I have nothing to offer. I'm more lost in this world than in my own," I said, truthfully.

"While that may be true, it no longer has to be. You have the guidance of the Maeshiren owl, protection of the Maeshiren wolf, and the accompaniment of three strong warriors who know this kingdom and its standards better than most," Voedene nodded his head as he spoke of each of us. "Don't let fear and doubt cloud your place in this world."

"What did you mean by the first Phoenix of the Maeshiren?" I asked. Garrett and Ryder were the last of their kind within this new and foreign family lineage. Why was I the first?

"Never before has there been a Phoenix among the Maeshiren. Not only is the direct descendent of the Maeshiren to come and fulfill the prophecy; they were to also embody a set of powers and nature that fell in line with the prophecy," he said. "You fulfill every marker."

"And that is…?" I trailed off.

"Hold on. Let's just slow down here a minute. Do you expect us to allow our little sister to be placed into harm's way all for the sake of a fate we knew nothing about until a few days ago?" Garrett asked, stepping to my side.

"Expectations and reality are a funny thing, Garrett of Brookings. You cannot protect her forever," he said.

"Like hell I can't."

"Spoken as a true Maeshiren wolf. Your stubbornness can be both a blessing and a curse to you. Did I not say you are the protector of the Maeshiren? Would it not then be up to you to decide who and what it is you will protect?" Voedene asked, before sliding his variegated eyes to mine.

"Aurora Marie Walker of Brookings. Are you willing to step into your role as the first Phoenix of the Maeshiren, the one who has been presented to answer the call of the prophecy?" he asked, extending his proud, lengthy neck up high, glaring at me from above.

Garrett turned to me with eyes unblinking, his body trembling next to mine. It was the first time I had ever seen him terrified in all my life.

Ryder's chin quivered, holding back the words he wanted to say. His eyes blinked rapidly at the wetness pooling in his lower lids.

Kate stood next to an ever-unreadable Kartcher, impenetrably still as she internalized the meaning of what Voedene asked.

I slid my gaze to Gavin, the pain in his eyes piercing through me like a million arrows. Anger and fear flashed back and forth across his face, as defeat encompassed all he was processing.

And Voedene stood still, waiting patiently for my response.

If I didn't say yes, the alternative was disastrous. Two worlds would perish, and so would we. That didn't mean it wouldn't if I said yes; that future was unknown. In the end, was having one option even an option at all?

"You make it hard to say no," I sighed, dropping my gaze to Voedene's clawed feet. I gulped in an attempt to wet my parched mouth.

"So be it," Voedene said, "come forward."

I did as he asked, sliding a shaky step towards his monstrous frame. My head craned back; the rugged details of his hardened scaly exterior glimmered in the sun's radiant light. I glanced over my shoulder, Gavin's wide eyes locking with mine. The anxiety taking hold of him morphed into fear as he shouted, "NO!" His outstretched hand raced towards where I stood.

Before he could reach me, pale wings folded around me,

shutting his way. My heart skipped a beat.

I spun back to Voedene, surprised by his face mere inches from mine. Engulfed in darkness, the brilliance of his eyes cast a kaleidoscope of celestial nebulas in the confinement of his wings. I could hear no one. I could see no one. Not my brothers or Gavin, not Kate or Kartcher, not even the dragons that leered down at us from above. I was totally, and utterly, alone with Voedene.

"Settle your fearful heart, Aurora. You have no reason to be afraid. For the safety of the others, this must be a path you walk alone. Within you resides the Phoenix. You are the Phoenix, and that will soon be realized," he said.

"How will that be realized?" I stammered, afraid of where this line of questioning would take me. Remembered pain from my various encounters in this world flashed through my mind.

"You are the catalyst that will bring destruction and rebirth to this world. It is your destiny to bring this world back to itself, to restore balance.

However, I can see two paths before you – fulfill your destiny and bring this world back into a state of peace before the time of Reinard; or follow in the footsteps of revenge and allow this world to be taken over by the forces seeking to annihilate it. Your choices will ultimately lead it to its final conclusion," he said.

"How do I do that? How do I keep from the path of revenge?" I cried out.

"Stay neutral. Do not allow yourself to be caught up in the pains of this world. Regardless of the path you choose, destruction is imminent. There is no other way around it," he sighed.

"As for the path you choose, that is entirely up to you. If you do not stray from your destiny, you will know what to do when the time comes. If you choose to seek revenge after the injustices and corruption you shall witness, you may very well destroy what you are destined to save. Ultimately, it rests upon your shoulders. This is what it means to have the authority of Valdöllen."

"You're saying I'm to play judge, jury, and executioner?" I asked, both afraid and disgusted it would rest entirely on me.

"In so many words, yes. The power I am about to unleash within you, and the knowledge I will bestow upon you, will give you more insight as to why that is than what your limited mind can comprehend in this moment," he said.

"What power is that?"

"Aurora, you are an elemental healer, as was your great aunt Johannes," he stated. "She was an elemental who had limitations in ways you do not."

"Limited how?" I asked, both intrigued and wary.

"She could only access two elements rather than all four — air and earth. Since birth, you have had this strong innate power imbedded within. Even on earth, where abilities are much weaker, you still exhibited signs of it when you healed yourself," he stated, as if this were common knowledge.

"Your powers, once unshackled, will be unleashed at a far greater capacity than you have ever felt. It is imperative you learn to control this at once. If you do not, you will destroy yourself and anyone within your reach. Each element — Fire, Water, Earth, and Air — works independent and interdependent of each other. You must master all four elements before the rebirth of the Phoenix can be realized," he warned.

"As if this all wasn't terrifying enough, now you're preparing to turn me into an effective weapon hellbent to destroy?" I shrieked.

"You are only an effective weapon if you learn to control it. If not, you are just a dangerous bomb - ticking.

Within this treacherous scroll is a protection seal," he said, bringing forth the Phoenix Quaerit Pugnare, the very one Kartcher held. How did he get it from him?

"Protection seal?" I questioned, eyeing the scroll. "Why would I need such a thing?"

The way Kartcher and Selpats regarded it, you would think they were holding an unpinned grenade.

"Your abilities are directly connected to the Phoenix within you. As of now, they are subdued, as is your Phoenix. When I awaken your powers, so too will the Phoenix begin to rise. In doing so, should you not have this protection seal, you will perish. Your Phoenix will not. It will be untethered and unstoppable."

"What is it that makes this scroll dangerous?" I asked.

"A Phoenix's nature is rebirth. Before the rebirth, its only objective is to destroy. Left to its own devices, it will not distinguish between right and wrong, corrupt and innocent. It will not play favorites; it will annihilate all. The Phoenix must have a master to guide it from misdirection.

This scroll will sever your ties with the Phoenix, leaving it unmastered. It is a necessary evil to allow you to master your abilities without being influenced by its penchant for destruction. It will bind your Phoenix in an ironclad cage until you reach the height of rebirth.

Your Phoenix will sense this change within you. It will goad you to release it and fight. When it does, you must be ready to re-cement your bond with it. Break the seal early, all will be lost, and you will perish," he explained.

"How do I break the seal?" I asked, not wanting to do it by accident.

"Remember these words - *praevaricator caveam*," he said.

"What does it mean?"

"Break the cage."

With that, he raised his clawed hand, releasing the scroll into the air between us. It glimmered a brilliant red as it unfurled; cursive letters in a foreign language swirled off the parchment in rufescent light.

"What does this mean for you? Should I fail?" I asked.

"We are appointed seers, not just of this world. The utter annihilation of it will spark a chain reaction throughout the galaxies, upsetting the balance and harmony we keep," he said.

The enchanted cursive orbiting the scroll flew towards me, encircling me in its cardinal glow. I lifted my arms as it spun around my torso, ripping apart the fur coat Selpats had gifted me. Winding tighter, closer and closer, my exposed skin melded to the seal, taking in the surreal energy flowing from within its vortex.

I lifted my gaze to the dragon, his reptilian skin shimmering bright, his eyes peering into my soul.

Ever so slowly, he reached forward with his clawed hand, hovering one talon between the center of my eyes and one over my heart.

The moment he made contact, all my physical capabilities became null and void. No longer was I Aurora. No longer was I in this strange world, or mine. My thoughts, my feelings, my wants and needs no longer carried any meaning. I was being ripped apart, rolled into a ball, and remolded.

Image after image passed through my vision in a blur. All at once, I could see nothing and everything. I couldn't focus on one image for long. I could only see glimpses of what appeared to be Reinard preparing for battle, wars breaking out across the land, battle after battle raging near the Niveh gates. All too fast, I couldn't fully perceive what each image meant.

The corruption happening even now - Servius stalking down a dark alley that looked nothing like Höllengrad, unsightly creatures made of nightmares roaming, the same man with hatred in his eyes I had seen from Voedene's earlier vision giving orders in a distant fortress.

Gavin - his face full of terror and crumpled into crippling pain. A woman at a stake burning alive, cold calculated eyes of a hidden face staring into those flames. An underground world full of people suffering – half starved and dying; the filthy child I had seen in the shadows of Höllengrad. Kate and Tanner talking over a table next to a fireplace.

All the disturbing images came to a halt, immersing me into darkness. To my right, a sliver of light shone bright, expanding as the dragon opened its wings to reveal the universe.

We were suspended amongst millions of stars, galaxies, and nebulas. Muted silence, save for a gentle hum buzzing in and out of rhythm, settled with the twinkling of the stars.

"Where are we?" I asked with wonder.

"We are in the central hub of the universe — a vast inter-connection of planetary orbits and galaxies. I have brought you here for two reasons. The first is for you to understand the importance of your destiny. To fulfill your destiny, you will give up much for many," Voedene explained.

"What will I be giving up?"

"Life as you know it. You will exchange naïve ambitions for the knowledge of pain and suffering. The path you will now lead is one that will test your limits beyond measure," he said, his voice grave.

Life as I know it? The only thing I could imagine needing to give up were my brothers and Kate; to give up Gavin. My heart clenched at the thought. Voedene said they would be with me, though, helping me, protecting me. So, if not them, then what?

I turned back to the numerous galaxies below, each having a single pirouetting planet brighter than the rest. Between each brightly lit planet, a shimmering silvery line connected them together. Save for two, which were connected together but isolated from the rest.

"Why are those planets isolated?" I pointed at the two galaxies teeming with life.

"Since the infancy of its creation, these two galaxies have been a problem for the entire universe. The planet you see in this galaxy here," he pointed to the right, "is Veradin, the current orbit you are destined to save. To the left is Earth, the planet which will be saved by your actions in Veradin."

"Why were they a problem?"

"Veradin became infected by darkness, a fast disease which breeds evil. As it took over Veradin, it followed its path to Earth, working to infect it as well. Before this sickness could infect the rest of the universe, we sealed it off in its path — no longer to be a part of the interconnection of this universe. As you can see, this universe is no longer in balance. Your destiny seeks to restore that balance."

"Where did this evil disease come from?"

"Just as Veradin has a balance to maintain, so does the universe. This darkness is from those within Valdöllen who thought they were above this balance. They sought to take over, rule without checks and balances. They started first in Veradin before swiftly moving into earth."

"How did they become so powerful?" I asked, realizing the multitude of layers this war had taken.

"Little by little, chipping away at the center that makes us whole. We in Valdöllen did not anticipate those in our own realm to be responsible for such a demise until it was too late. They chirped in the ears of those around them, rallied and gathered all those who would lend them that ear. Over time, their ways of thinking became normal amongst a crowd, infecting those who believed their lies," Voedene said, both saddened and angered.

"It grew out of control. Before too long, we had realized we were dealing with a universal pandemic. Those who were the fire starters were dealt with, but not before the damage had been permanent," he said.

"Why can't you eradicate it yourself? Why use me?"

"It certainly is within our power to, but that would mean total annihilation and a permanent imbalance to the universe. It is our obligation to give these worlds a chance to turn away from this sickness and seek to bring harmony back to themselves. We once sent a representative, someone who could have helped bring them back to peace, but they refused him. This is where the prophecy was born, and the appointment of the Maeshiren began."

I now understood the part of the prophecy where it said *two planets they hold.* If I failed, the consequences rippled to far greater than those in my circle. It held the consequences of life or death for two planets I'm a part of.

"What do you expect of me? To eradicate evil?" I asked, in disbelief at such a feat.

"Not eradicate. Subdue. You are part human, part Maeshiren, which means you are connected to your humanity in a way no one in Veradin is. You will soon understand the duality of such a creation. The second reason I brought you here is to break down the barriers stopping you from reaching your full potential," he further explained.

"How?" I stared at him, full of questions.

"By fusing your humanity with your powers. There must be full separation before you can emerge as the siren call to your destiny," he said, flapping his wings.

The glow of a raging Borealis surrounded us, encasing my senses with a pulsating energy of its multihued dance. The low hum of its pulse beat in and out of my body, like standing next to the speakers at a rave concert. I didn't know where I started, and it began.

A fierce whirlwind rushed me from behind, blowing my hair forward, as heat radiated against the front of my body. A fiery bird flapped its wings before me, narrowing its face towards mine. *Was this the embodiment of the Phoenix?*

Without provocation, it screeched its head back before dive bombing for my chest. It pierced into my heart, pumping hot liquid through its chambers until there wasn't a flame left in sight. An intense inferno radiated from my heart center, seeping into the outlier veins before scorching its way through my lymphatic system.

The intensity with which I was scalding became unbearable. No longer was I in control of my body; my arms and legs locked out in a torturous version of Da Vinci's Vitruvian man. I was shackled to this pain and imprisoned to this fate, screaming for mercy.

A flooding relief of water chased after the burning inferno, quenching my desiccated veins. There was no longer a trace of heat, only the remembered pain of being burned alive. This life-giving water felt rich and invigorating, rebirthing what perished in the eternal flame.

As my soul felt heavy and drenched, breaching the capacity of what it could hold, a transitionary wind flowed through my body, drying out the deluge that poured forth. As fast as the wind came, was as fast as it ceased. No longer did I burn, no longer did I drown, no longer was I porous and exposed.

I found myself lying in green grass beside a gentle river; the sun shining bright in the afternoon sky. I could feel the gentle tremors beneath me as the birds of the air sang in harmony. The earth below was alive and teaming with energy, communicating with the energy in my palms.

For the first time since entering this strange world, I understood my place and purpose here. If I were being honest, I finally understood my place in life, period. The reason behind why I could heal myself, why my mother had been afraid of my powers being exposed.

Through all the necessary evils, I understood Voedene in all his infinite wisdom, guiding me to the truth. The images of Reinard, the battles, the evil lurking through this world; I understood completely.

I'm now a part of something much greater than myself. I'm to stand as representative for the Maeshiren's, to finish what we started. *Would that be enough to save this world? Was I strong enough to sacrifice everything to see this through for the greater good?* God, I could only hope.

The ground beneath me rumbled, awakening to the energy surging through my trembling palms.

I could not stop it. I could not control it.

The earth rose in jagged peaks, creating steep valleys all around, before falling away beneath me – plunging me deep under the darkest waters.

I twisted and somersaulted, scrambling to find my way to the top. I opened and closed my eyes, futilely trying to see something other than darkness.

A fiery glow reflected above, undulating with the movement of the water's surface. *Thank the heavens, I found the way up.*

I kicked my feet, eager to reach the top, but the dark depths held me hostage, unrelenting in my attempt to be freed. I used what little air reserves I had left to disengage my captor, leaving my body heavier in its grasp.

In the depths of this darkness, I could sense it beckoning for me to stay; manifesting into the depression I spent years trying to escape from, only to be held underwater by its iron grip.

No longer did I want to relinquish my life to it. No longer did I want to be held underwater, never getting the chance to breathe again.

I lifted my eyes to the fiery surface, scrambling once more to reach it as I chanted to myself, *"C'mon Aurora. Just a little longer. Hold on just a little more."* Though unsure of what awaited me when I emerged, I was sure of what I fought my way from.

I fought with the darkness, kicking it away from me as I reached my hand for the surface. I grazed just beneath it, but I couldn't break free. Panic tightened its grip around my throat as I realized I was being dragged back, away from the salvation that would breathe life back into my burning lungs.

I cried out, releasing what breath I had left in a flurry of bubbles as a hand plunged beneath the surface, Gavin's face reflected above the water's edge. He clasped his hand around my forearm, a lifeline I so desperately needed, and pulled me away from my deepest perdition.

Chapter Twenty-five
Plot Twist

"The world is full of monsters with friendly faces and angels full of scars." – Unknown

***

Gavin pulled me into the safety of his arms; my fingers clenched to his ebony cloak as I gasped with sweet relief. I buried my face into his chest, the last picture of him reaching for me cemented into my mind. *I never wanted to let him go.*

The warmth of his cheek pressed against my temple gave way to his lips caressing the soft skin, sending chills fluttering to my lower belly.

"I thought I lost you," he whispered, tightening his embrace as he dropped his cheek back against mine.

"Didn't anyone tell you?" I croaked, "I'm the phoenix. I can't be offed that easily."

His body shook with a chuckle, the air around us lightening

with his mood.

"Thank the heavens for that," he said, taking a step back without releasing our connection, his hand clasped in mine. The dimples in his cheeks appeared with the relief spread across his face. His deep emerald eyes shone bright with an overwhelming sense of love and adoration, firing straight into my soul.

For the first time in years, I had something more to fight for. No longer was I submerged underwater. Gavin became my life-saver, the only one who could physically and emotionally grasp hold of my hand and pull me out of my darkness.

The corners of my lips turned up as I stood in this surreal sense of finding peace, of finding where I belonged. While I knew little about this world or my place in it, I knew I belonged with Gavin. That was good enough for me.

With trembling fingers, I dropped my eyes from his as I brushed the soft skin of his inner wrist. My heart quivered as he shivered in answer to my touch. I stepped forward to close the gap between us, committing to memory the heady and carnal way the leather of his cloak mixed with the fresh earthen scent of the field we were standing in.

I lifted my gaze from beneath my lashes, my body overcome with a mind of its own, as my eyes slipped to his lips, my chin tilting up just a hair. Where this bravery came from, I haven't a clue, but something primal deep inside needed more of him.

His breath hitched, and his brows furrowed, as if he were focusing on my unspoken wants. I trailed my eyes back to his, burning bright in response. Every nerve ending hyper aware of his very being, I wanted nothing more than for him to pull me flush to his body.

As if he could read my thoughts, his free hand came down to rest on the outside of my hip, his fingers pressing in ever so gently. I shivered with the delicate brush of his fingers against my skin, as he readjusted his hand above my waistband.

His eyes smoldered with our connection. My body naturally bowed towards his silent call to come closer.

He pulled me in, satisfying my need for his body against mine, closing what little gap stood between us.

His excited eyes searched mine, taking in our charged chemistry. My breath faltered as he brought his hand to my cheek, his gentle touch sending shivers down my spine. Without a word, he answered the call I craved, as he lowered his soft lips to mine, ending the excruciating torture of anticipation.

No longer could I call myself my own. The love and adoration growing between us awakened into something more, something deeper. The weightless ecstasy coursing through my being morphed into a carnal need for him, and him alone.

I wrapped my arms around his neck, deepening the kiss. As if it wasn't enough, he slid his hands to the small of my back, drawing me in even closer. We could have been surrounded by a field on fire, and I wouldn't have had a clue.

There were no fields. There were no worlds to save. There was he and I - just us.

Our lips parted as he rested his forehead against mine. Emerging on the other side of bliss, I became a foreign version of myself. I welcomed this version with open arms, as long as it meant I could be here with him.

"That was some first kiss," he breathed, grinning.

"I'd say," I pulled back to see the excitement in his eyes matching mine.

He brushed a few wayward strands from my face before resting his palm against my neck. An unmistakable joy, a deep peace, settled over him. The tightness around his eyes softened. The stress in his shoulders relaxed. Pure radiance brightened his face.

He gazed upon me like a man in love and I realized in an

instant; it was my new favorite look – probably ever. I would do anything to see him look at me like that over and over again.

Gavin's bite mark flashed through my mind, reminding me what I had forgotten to ask Voedene. Cursing my idiocy, I snatched his arm up, taking him by surprise, as I pushed his sleeve to his elbow. There wasn't a trace of the lycanthropes bite mark, only healthy skin as there should be. I glanced at him, puzzled.

"When I was teleported here, it was healed," he answered my wordless question. Relief swelled inside my chest as I let out a cleansing sigh.

Being caught up in my euphoric disposition, I wasn't ready for his mood to shift to a darker path. "I thought I'd lost you," he said again, as he lowered his eyes.

"But you didn't." I brought my hand to his cheek, imploring him to lift his gaze to mine. I wanted to chase away the memory darkening his face. He glanced at me with a troubled pain before turning away.

"I was teleported to this field; I didn't even have a second to figure out where I was when the heavens echoed with a crack. It was then I could sense you entered this field with me, but I couldn't find a trail to your essence. I searched in a panic, sensing you fighting for your life. Then…" he took in a deep, shaky breath.

The sorrow in his eyes dropped me from my euphoric pedestal. "I felt you weakening. That was when I found you, falling away from the water's surface, your life fading from your eyes." He closed his lids, a tear escaping beneath his long lashes.

I never realized how close I had come to losing it all. To never feeling the caress of Gavin's hand on my cheek, or the love flowing from his lips when he kissed me. Never feeling this sense of rightness, like I belonged in his arms, or standing strong next to his side.

The fresh memory of being dragged down into the dark depths of the lake flashed through my mind. Coupled with the fresh realization I would be laying at the bottom of it, if it weren't for Gavin, made me flinch.

"What? What is it?" Gavin asked, sensing the change within.

"Much like you, I'm unsure of how I ended up in that lake. I remember floating in the universe amongst the stars as Voedene unleashed my powers. Without another word, I was underwater, fighting for my life against some unseen forces pulling me under."

"Amongst the stars? How did he unlock your powers?" he asked, disturbed by each admission.

"Were you not taken into the universe above the galaxies?" I asked, as he slowly shook his head no. "He brought me into the universe. I had come face to face with the Phoenix, who is a part of me. It's then I had my powers unlocked. He said I'm an elemental healer like my great aunt Johannes."

Gavin's eyes grew wide at this admission.

"What?" I asked, wary.

"It's nothing," he shook his head, gaining composure over his face once more.

"If it's nothing, why did you look surprised?" I squinted as I watched him close. I knew what I had said had some significance for him.

"It's a rare gift is all," he dismissed with an answering smile. "We need to figure out where we are and find the others." I knew his changing the subject was a way to deflect from me digging further. I catalogued it for later, realizing for the first time - we were alone.

"Where are the others?" I scanned the field, seeing nothing but landmarks and swaying of the blue wheatgrass.

"I don't know, but this isn't good," he said, alarmed, as his shoulders turned rigid.

"What isn't good?" I asked, sensing his unease.

"Those damn dragons dropped us off in a combat zone," he said. Anger flashed across his face as he scoured the countryside before us.

"They what?" I yelped, moving closer to Gavin.

"We are on the dividing line between the Northern Kingdom of Elderon and the Southern Kingdom of Estrea. This area is a hotbed for attacks breaking out as Braeden moves to seize power in this region."

An iciness shot through me, knowing we were near enemy territory, and even closer to Braeden.

"We have to go. *Now*," he said.

The Gavin I knew was back; his eyes intense and calculating. I could see his mind working as he tried to figure the best strategy without getting caught in the crosshairs.

"Let's go back to Bellfall. If I know Kartcher, he'll go there to wait for us," he said.

"How do you know?"

"Our Drygdals are there. It's the only logical meeting place in proximity to this region. Put your hood on and move swiftly. We need to move from here fast." Though he looked in control of himself, I could hear the underlying panic in his voice. It sobered me to the real danger we were in.

As I lifted my hood, he paused, his rigid posture zoning in across the field. Standing in regimented formation, no less than twenty-five soldiers in black were fixated on our location. Leading the pack behind enemy lines was Emily, wearing a mischievous grin, a sword in hand as she taunted Gavin with a wink.

I turned to Gavin, his jaw flexing, as he deliberated over how to proceed. Emily and her men were stationed between

Bellfall and us, her greedy eyes full of dark joy. My hands shook with adrenaline.

Emily turned her head, giving orders over her shoulders as they advanced. Anxiety showered me in dread.

"Run!" Gavin yelled, grabbing my hand as he directed us to the tree line in the distance.

Emily's voice carried over to us as she screamed out orders to her men. I glanced over my shoulder, seeing them break formation. The group with Emily stayed in hot pursuit while the second group worked their way around us. Gavin's grunt brought my focus back to the front. A small contingent materialized through the trees.

We were surrounded; a bead of sweat dripped down my temple.

What could we do but stand and fight, or be captured? Gavin had never let my hand go; I could feel his muscles twitching with the coming threat.

"Whatever happens next, do not stray from me. We will be stronger if we stick together," he commanded.

"Are we going to fight?" I asked, my voice high and tight.

"We have no other option," he growled.

I turned my attention towards Emily's approach with wide eyes. My breath hitched. Should I pull out my sword? Would that send the wrong message? *Did it even matter at this point?*

I'll wait and see how this plays out. Resting my hand on the sword's hilt gave me some semblance of control. I had the power; it was time I learned how to use it.

"Well now, look what the gods dragged in," Emily sneered as she and her men stopped a few yards from us.

Gavin stayed quiet and rigid, not giving in to her taunt.

My heart fluttered as I stayed hyper vigilant to our threat, cognizant of the heightening of my senses.

With clarity, I could sense the ground rippling messages to

me from all around. The slight twitch of a soldier's hand on his sword to my right, the shuffling of a foot inching closer from the left, the forward pressure of the armies' feet poised to strike at the go ahead – it was like seeing through a whole new set of eyes.

"What's wrong Gavin, cat got your tongue?" Emily asked, a short bark leaving her.

"No Emilian, I just choose not to converse with the devil herself," Gavin bit back.

"Oh, ouch. That *really* hurt," she said, narrowing her eyes. "You were always such a bore." She slid her vicious glare to mine, smiling wide.

"Still running with wrong crowd, I see, Aurora," she goaded. "Too bad your little *boyfriend* couldn't be here to join us." Her devilish smirk boiled my blood.

"What did you do with Tony?" I yelled, murdering her with my eyes.

"Do you mean, what *didn't* I do with him?" she snickered.

"How dare you," I stepped forward with a fury; I was going to rip her head off. Gavin clasped his hand on my shoulder, reminding me to stay with him.

"Come on, little kitten, show those claws," she laughed.

"Enough!" Gavin bellowed, his eyes turning red. "We know what happens next, so let's get on with it." He grew tired of her small talk, as did I.

I remembered when he said Emily liked to toy with her prey; he wasn't giving her the satisfaction. With the army mounted and us surrounded, there was no other option but to fight.

"As you wish," she said, lifting her hand to signal the army to attack. I pulled out my sword and readied my stance. This was it. The defining moment Voedene had prepared me for.

"Stand back-to-back. We can protect each other better that way," Gavin said to me. I spun around to see the enemy's fast approach. There were too many. *How were we going to escape this alive?*

The clanking of their heavy armor became deafening as the cacophony came closer. With a clash, the forces were upon us. I brought my sword up in time to block the downward thrust of one soldier. The power he brought down upon me made my arms tremble as I tried to push him off.

Blue, glowing blood splattered across my face as Gavin's sword came over the top of my head, cutting deep into the enemy's throat. He was protecting me at the expense of exposing himself.

"Focus on yourself. I've got this," I yelled. I didn't want him to get hurt or killed because of me, even if protecting me was his job.

It wasn't long after that enemy dropped; another rushed into his place. They were converging from all sides.

The dying vibrations of the blood across my cheek flashed me back to the night at the ranch. The same sensation, the same appearance of the blood – it was the same from that night. Had it been one of these beasts who lurked outside that night? And *who* killed it? *Was it Gavin?*

Heat from my palm surged into my sword, emblazing the Phoenix emblem into an inferno – guiding me to follow its will. I slashed my sword at my enemy's approach, admiring how the blade melted his iron breastplate like cutting through butter, penetrating his fleshy torso.

I cried out as he came crashing down, his blade nicking the outside of my arm from the trajectory of his swing.

"Aurora!" Gavin yelled, coming around the side. In a blur, he slashed through four soldiers, his searing blades melting into their armor; the heads of two rolled to the side as their bodies crashed to the floor.

"Are you okay?" he glanced at me.

"I'm fine," I said as he pulled me towards him, his sword

meeting with the downward thrust of another. He released me, focusing on outmaneuvering his enemy, who was as light on his feet as Gavin. I couldn't take my eyes off him, despite being surrounded.

With my extra 'sights', I catalogued every guard's movement across the field – where they stood, how fast they approached, which ones were heavier on their feet than the others. A heavy pressure rippled behind me - the pivoting of a foot, the twisting of a torso, the heavy blade reaching over a shoulder as it coiled for power and momentum.

I ducked as the contraction of his body sprang loose, the wind from his blade kissing my hair. I flipped my blade along the backside of my arm, thrusting up into the exposed underside of his armor, digging in deep. His innards spilled as I tore my blade from his cavity.

The fleeing feet from my center location alerted me to the wide birth the surrounding enemies were giving me. A flaming arrow whizzed past my face, sinking into the earth before exploding. I flew in the air, knocked back, as the heat from the blast seared through to my skin.

A high-pitched ring enveloped my ears, throwing my equilibrium from its stable bearings. I closed my eyes, the wound in my leg throbbing with my pulsing adrenaline. I covered it with my hand, crying out at the searing pressure.

Despite the pain, I needed to move. I was a sitting duck. I opened my eyes, glancing around me as I prepared for more coming threats. Stabbing my sword into the earth to pull myself up, I hobbled on my uninjured leg.

In vain, I tried healing my leg using the knowledge Kartcher gave me, but I didn't have enough time. A heavy-set brute the size of an SUV stomped towards me in hot pursuit. His pounding feet, coupled with those who were still left standing on the battlefield, felt like five sumos jumping on a trampoline. It was disorienting. *Or was that due to my equilibrium?* I couldn't be sure.

His heavy swing startled me, as a flash of what that blade would do to me should it connect entered my mind. I dodged it in time, weaving at the right moment. He was powerful, but his heavy frame made him slow. He came back around, swinging his blade back over me as I rolled out of the way. If I could stay outside his reach, I may be able to dodge him long enough to figure out his angle.

In my peripheral, a flaming arrow whistled through the air towards Gavin, landing near his foot. Gavin sidestepped out of the way before the arrow exploded, his body concealed in shadows. "*He's safe,*" I sighed. Did his shadows protect him?

I followed the trajectory of the arrow to a long-range attacker smirking next to Emily, his eyes trained on Gavin. I couldn't allow him the opportunity to hurt him.

The attacker next to me dug in his feet, swinging his blade down towards my shoulder. I brought my blade up, but his downward pressure threw me off balance, pushing me back. His forward momentum was too strong against my weak stance as he plunged his sword deep into the earth.

Struggling to pull his sword from the ground in a 'sword in the stone' kind of way, I used this to my advantage, dropping to my knees as I slammed my hands into the hard earth. The unrestrained force I used shook the ground beneath us, creating tremors big enough to knock him to the ground.

I scrambled to my feet, wide eyed at my hands, remembering what had happened when I laid next to the stream in relative peace. *Was I the one who caused the earth to fall beneath me then, too?*

Scanning the battlefield for Gavin; he had fallen to the other side. We were separated. Something he was explicit about not happening. Together we rise, divided we fall. Everywhere

I turned, enemies were coming at us both, overwhelming our abilities.

My attacker stood, still disoriented. Seeing an opening, I rushed to take advantage, lifting my sword to strike, when a flaming arrow stopped me in my tracks. I threw myself back, away from the concussive force of the explosion, before it could reach me.

I turned to the grinning archer. He commanded my attention away from the threat in front of me for a second too long. The brute regained his sense of balance. His sword came down as I defended myself the best way I could. There was no offensive strike, only defensive blocks. He overpowered me with each attack, knocking me closer and closer to Emily's side of the line. Every time I tried to move around him, an arrow would push me back to where they wanted me to go.

I was being herded.

In the distance, I heard Gavin calling out my name. I couldn't focus on him.

The enemy struck me down with a hard blow, knocking me to one knee. I kept my sword up to block as he kept thrusting over and over into my blade, digging me into the hard-packed earth. My arms shook with each impact, my hands bloodied from the edges of my blade cutting in, but I refused to give up. If Gavin still fought, so would I.

A blast of cold air, and the absence of my enemies' attack, had me searching to see what changed. In the distance, Kate — along with the rest — were running to our aid. Even from her distance, she encased my attacker in ice. Hope swelled in my chest before it faltered, as a guard fighting Gavin took advantage of his attention being elsewhere, plunging his sword deep into his side.

My world stopped; a chill settled through me as I screamed

out in agony. *Not him.*

Gavin folded over, clenching his side before slicing the guard where the armor exposed his underbelly, taking a staggered stance as he fought the next attack.

The icy chill gave way to fevered rage. I slammed my hands on the ground to steady the overwhelming surge ripping through my veins. The earth trembled as my body shook with anger, channeling the rage into something grounding. Fissures spread out around me, the epicenter of fury, taking those who were standing too close by surprise.

The blade in my right hand burned bright with the violent rage I felt inside. I caught the guard running towards me unaware, meeting the upward thrust of my blade from groin to throat. Still, the fury gripped me.

I turned to the archer, who toyed with me like a puppet. I could see nothing but violent rage as I zoned in on him.

Rational thoughts? *What were those?* The only rationality I could see was destroying those who sought to destroy me and my own. This power I held inside became intoxicating; I never felt stronger.

I stalked forward, foreseeing myself ripping this archer's throat out with my bare hands. Murderous intent was the only thing steadying the violence ripping through me.

The flames from his arrow nicked at my skin as it whirled past me, but I channeled that pain into my blade. The way he kept missing me with those arrows told me he was either a horrible archer - which was unlikely, or their orders were to keep me alive. In the grand scheme of things, it didn't matter. He wouldn't live long to find out how this battle ended.

He kept backing away the closer I approached, fumbling with the arrow in his bow. Well, that wouldn't do. I slammed my palms into the earth, focusing my rage on him. The earth trembled, falling away as it opened wide. The archer couldn't move fast enough, the fissure swallowing him whole into the depths before closing back in on itself.

My rage smiled like a savage. I stood up, disoriented, as the anger that gave me strength waned. Time slowed as I scanned across the battlefield – Kate, Kartcher, and my brothers finally made it to the battle, giving Gavin much-needed reinforcements.

With all his might, Gavin fought to get to where I stood wavering, panic locked into his face as he kept turning to look at me between attackers.

The taste of iron and salt infiltrated my tastebuds. I brought my hand to my nose.

Slick wetness slid across my upper lip as I pulled away my bloodied hand. I dropped my arm. The world spun faster as a heaviness took over.

"Well, aren't you a sight for sore eyes?" Emily piqued. I rolled my head to where she stood.

"Whatever you just did, I'd say it took its toll on you," she jeered.

"Get away from her!" Gavin's voice echoed across the battlefield. I tried to turn to him, but Emily squeezed my jaw between her hands.

"You're *mine* now," she said, leering at me. A hard blow to the back of the head slammed my face into the hard packed earth, knocking the wind out of my sails. Against my command, my eyes blurred and closed of their own accord, slipping me into a dark oblivion.

"I want to survive this world that keeps trying to destroy me." — *Leigh Bardugo, Ninth House*

***

A frigid wind howled into the night, whipping my damp hair across my face. Hardened metal knocked against my ribcage, alerting me to the monster carrying me over his shoulder. *Where am I?*

The creaking of opening gates drew my attention as we crossed over a dark stone bridge set over a deep valley. I struggled against the monster's hold, trying to find some relief from the upward thrusts of his armored shoulder.

"Settle down," he said with a gruff voice, jostling me harder to make his point, shoving the armor deeper into my torso. Bile rose in my throat from the blow.

"She'll no longer be our problem soon," I heard Emily dismiss.

It all flooded back to me — the battle, the disorientation, Emily standing before me. More vividly, I remember the sword plunging deep into Gavin's side; the fear misplaced on his always controlled face. Nausea hit all over again.

Everything I could see; I viewed in reverse. I couldn't see what was coming, only what we had already passed. So, when the muffled high pitch of multiple violins reached my ears, followed by the deep baritone of the cello, I was taken aback. The beautiful sophistication of classical music was at odds with the darkness surrounding the icy grounds.

"State your business," I heard a man's deep voice say.

"As if it's any of your concern," Emily said, not giving pause in her stride.

Two guards gaped at us as we passed through the opening doors and to the source of the portentous euphony. A woman's voice rang out in a beautiful soprano, echoing a language strangely familiar to the words Kartcher had spoken to me during my healing.

Haunting shadows danced around the formidable stone chamber from the iron chandeliers hanging from its high arched ceilings. Crimson tapestries, extending from ceiling to floor between flaming wall sconces, added to the glow of the Cimmerian shade.

At our approach, the music died. Gathered in lavish, sultry attire, hundreds of beings halted in their dance to glare at our intrusion.

Without warning, I was flipped backwards through the air, the monster dumping me onto the hard stone floor. I curled in at the pain of landing on my back; the wind whooshing out of my lungs.

Did he have to treat me like a sack of potatoes?

Knowing the scrutiny I was under, I pulled myself together.

"Don't show weakness in the face of your enemies, Aurora," I whispered to myself.

I lifted my gaze to a pair of piercing blue eyes staring at me over a long, slender nose. I derived no warmth from his face, only the cold, calculating approach of a man who scorned all who walked amongst him.

A golden glint from the buttons of his raven waistcoat caught my eye as he stood from his iron throne. The deep crimson of his scarf contrasted with his long, snowy hair, framing the grim, downward turn of his full lips. The length of his obsidian overcoat brushed along the floor as he domineered over my crouching state.

"Why are you bringing me trash on the eve of my celebration, Emilian?" he asked, bellowing loud for all to hear.

I turned to Emily as she kneeled with one knee, her eyes downcast as she addressed him, "Apologies your excellence but I thought you would—"

"I do not want to hear your excuses. None of them are good enough. Take this to the chambers," he said, scrunching his nose and waving his hand as if to brush away the stench of my presence.

"Yes, your excellence," she said, conceding to his demand. The subdued side of Emily caught me off guard. She was always so coy and vixenish.

She turned to the brute who brought me in, giving him a nod as her hateful eyes rested on mine. As if I were a feather, he tossed me over his shoulder once again; the impact causing me to wince as I bit my lower lip to keep from crying out.

The fair-haired authoritarian rolled his eyes away from our retreating figures, turning to the ballroom full of sophisticated party goers. "Proceed," he said, waving his hand for the quartet to continue.

A woman with wild, apricot hair sang out with her soprano voice once more, belting a high octave as the man nestled back onto his throne, folding in his hands.

The guard shouldered me through a labyrinthine of high, narrow walls descending lower into the castle's belly; the chill in the air turning frigid.

My heart sank at knowing I was being locked away. I didn't have a hope of escaping or being rescued from this wretched place. I couldn't allow this to happen. This couldn't be my fate. Panic crawled up my throat as I thrashed against the monster's back. "Put me down!"

He didn't.

Instead, he jostled me to shut up.

I couldn't.

It may be too little too late, but I couldn't let them lock me away.

"Let me down," I screamed. The walls cracked around us with the force of my wail. The missed step in his gait belayed his surprise at my ferocity.

"Sure thing," he said, throwing me into the dark cell before slamming the door shut.

"NO," I yelled, jumping towards the heavy wooden door. I pounded it with my fists as hard as I could. "Let me out!"

It was no use. I was trapped.

I slid to the floor with my back against the door. I was royally screwed. *What do I do now?*

It didn't take long for the deep chill to begin settling into my bones, shivering me to the core. I glanced around the dark, musky cell, my eyes laying on the single torch flickering against the chamber's wall. Déjà vu hit me hard in the face; this room was just like the nightmare I had.

Peering across the room where the stacked bodies of my

loved ones had been laying in my dream; I was met with nothing but darkness.

"Oh Gavin. Please help me," I whispered, bringing my legs into my chest, too petrified to follow the nightmarish path of my horrendous nightmare.

A polar breeze whistled through the cracks of the cell, making me second guess my decision about not grabbing for the only source of heat. I blew into my hands, praying the heat from my breath would help, but even that came out a few degrees too cold.

At this rate, I would shiver and die before Gavin could find me in the bowels of this dungeon.

I couldn't succumb to the elements here; too many people depended on me. Gavin's face, full of fear, was something I wanted to chase away. He rescued me from drowning in more ways than one. Now I wanted to make sure I could do the same for him.

In that, I had to fight.

There was also my destiny I had to fulfill. I couldn't allow the destruction of two worlds to happen because I gave up.

No, I could no longer go back to that weak, pathetic girl that I was. In my time with this world, I had been beaten, tortured, captured, and turned into a magical weapon. My family was being threatened at every turn.

More than anything, I wanted to create the world Voedene had painted where my family could find happiness and peace once again. My eyes are open wide. No longer could my naivety allow me to turn a blind eye.

A shiver rolled through my shoulders, bringing me back to my reality. This capture would not take me down. I had to take Kate's advice. I had to become stronger and learn how to play this deadly game. I had to kill off the old Aurora and rebirth someone new.

I rubbed my hands together in a fury, hoping for heat, but gaining more than I bargained for. The heat generating between my hands burst into a flame that squelched in an instant. I yipped in surprise, unhurt.

Staring at my hands, my lips turned up in a slow smile, realizing again how powerful I could become. Eager for warmth, and to see the extent of my powers, I rubbed my hands together once more. The flame wouldn't materialize.

How did I do that?

Frustrated, I rubbed them harder, but still did nothing. I became so wrapped up in the task; I didn't register the sound in the dark corner of the chamber at first.

Sandals dragging on grainy rock echoed from across the room. I froze in place, staring into the darkness. Adrenaline pumped in my ears; keenly aware of no longer being alone.

A lethargic figure slid against the crumbling wall into the torch's light. The deep set of his eyes, framed by a sea of matted hair, focused on me. He searched me over with an air of familiarity, a glisten watering his lower lids. I couldn't find the words to speak.

A ghost of a smile turned up in his overgrown beard. "Aurora, I've been waiting so long for you."

About The Author

Brittany Bowman is an Orange County, Ca. native who thrives in an active and creative environment. When she isn't sitting around, dreaming up different lands in faraway places, you can find her lounging with her 3 canine furbabies, surfing with her husband, getting lost in the pages of a good book, hitting the gym, or being a self-professed foodie. Her motto in life is - Sushi is life, Hawaiian food is good for the soul, and tacos are an everyday staple.

Website: www.BrittanyLB.com
Instagram: @AuthorBrittanyLB
Facebook: @AuthorBrittanyLB
Youtube: @ArcticFoxPress